Hummingbird's Squash

Created by
The Native Diabetes Wellness Program

Based on the original Eagle Books characters by
Georgia Perez

Written by
Terry Lofton

Illustrated by
Patrick Rolo

The Eagle Books

In the original *Eagle Book series*, a young boy, Rain that Dances, discovers an unhappy eagle. Mr. Eagle is tearful because many of the people in the community are developing a disease called type 2 diabetes. Rain that Dances invites his friends Thunder Cloud, Little Hummingbird, and Simon, to hear what the eagle has to say about staying healthy. The great bird assures the children that people can help to prevent type 2 diabetes by eating nourishing foods, being active, and following the traditions of their ancestors.

Coyote and the Turtle's Dream

In the original *Eagle Books stories*, Rain and his friends were about six years old. However, in this new story, *Coyote and the Turtle's Dream*, they are entering the seventh grade. Once again, the eagle gives a warning to Rain, but this time it is about the disappearance of water on their reservation. Never forgetting the health messages taught to them by the eagle, the kids embark on a mystery/adventure to solve a riddle about ancient fossils that will restore the water's flow.

Hummingbird's Squash

In *Hummingbird's Squash*, our young heroes continue their adventures under the watchful eye of Sky Heart, the eagle. In this story, Hummingbird pursues an ambitious plan to grow healthy foods that will help the community prevent type 2 diabetes. Little does she know that Coyote is leading her, Rain, Boomer, Simon, and her new "sister" Arianna, on a path of knowledge that reveals what it means to embrace all of one's relatives and honor the wisdom of ancestors.

Hummingbird's Squash

Created by
The Native Diabetes
Wellness Program

Written by
Terry Lofton

Illustrated by
Patrick Rolo

Based on the original
Eagle Books characters by
Georgia Perez

Hummingbird's Squash

Created by the Native Diabetes Wellness Program

Written by Terry Lofton

Illustrated by Patrick Rolo

Graphic Design by Linda Beatty, Westat Graphics

Based on the original Eagle Books characters by Georgia Perez

DEPARTMENT OF HEALTH AND HUMAN SERVICES

Centers for Disease Control and Prevention
Division of Diabetes Translation
Native Diabetes Wellness Program

This book is dedicated to Buford Rolin, Chairman of the Poarch Band of Creek Indians, for his lifetime of achievement as an advocate for the health of Native peoples and his tireless work in the prevention of type 2 diabetes.

For more information about CDC's Native Diabetes Wellness Program and Eagle Books educational materials, please go to www.cdc.gov/diabetes/projects/diabetes-wellness.htm. Additional information about diabetes and diabetes prevention can be found at the National Diabetes Education Program's website, http://ndep.nih.gov/. Under "Find Publications for Me," select the drop down box for "Age" and find "Teens and Children." Posted are tips for teens with diabetes, and tips for how kids can lower their risk for developing type 2 diabetes.

About Diabetes

Diabetes is a disease in which blood glucose levels are above normal. Most of the food we eat is turned into glucose, or sugar, for our bodies to use for energy. The pancreas, an organ that lies near the stomach, makes a hormone called insulin to help glucose get into the cells of our bodies. When you have diabetes, your body either doesn't make enough insulin or can't use its own insulin as well as it should. This causes sugar to build up in your blood.

Type 1 diabetes, which was previously called insulin-dependent diabetes mellitus (IDDM) or juvenile-onset diabetes, may account for about 5 percent of all diagnosed cases of diabetes. The causes of type 1 diabetes appear to be much different than those for type 2 diabetes, though the exact mechanisms for developing both diseases are unknown. The appearance of type 1 diabetes is suspected to follow exposure to an "environmental trigger," such as an unidentified virus, stimulating an immune attack against the beta cells of the pancreas (that produce insulin) in some genetically predisposed people. Researchers are making progress in identifying the exact genetics and "triggers" that predispose some individuals to develop type 1 diabetes, but prevention remains elusive.

Type 2 diabetes, which was previously called non-insulin-dependent diabetes mellitus (NIDDM) or adult-onset diabetes, may account for about 90 percent to 95 percent of all diagnosed cases of diabetes. A number of studies have shown that regular physical activity can significantly reduce the risk of developing type 2 diabetes. The Diabetes Prevention Program (DPP), a major federally funded study of 3,234 people at high risk for diabetes, showed that people can delay and possibly prevent the disease by losing a small amount of weight (5 to 7% of total body weight) through 30 minutes of physical activity 5 days a week and healthier eating.

For more information, visit the Centers for Disease Control and Prevention's Diabetes Public Health Resource at http://www.cdc.gov/diabetes/consumer/index.htm

Preface

In 2005, the U.S. Centers for Disease Control and Prevention's (CDC's) Native Diabetes Wellness Program introduced children in American Indian/Alaska Native communities to the *Eagle Books*. In these stories, written by Georgia Perez, an eagle brings important messages about the prevention of type 2 diabetes to a young Indian boy and his friends. The eagle teaches that Native knowledge provides the wisdom and power that helps friends and families stay healthy. By eating the foods their ancestors did and being physically active, children learn that much can be done to prevent type 2 diabetes.

Because the *Eagle Books* were so popular with elementary school children, we decided to develop books that would appeal to middle schoolers as well. In the first youth novel, *Coyote and the Turtle's Dream*, Sky Heart (the eagle), Thistle (the rabbit), and Coyote lead Rain that Dances (Rain), Thunder Cloud (Boomer), Little Hummingbird (Bird), and Simon to deeper understandings about the health and well-being of their community. They learn that it is the people's cultural values and their relationships to each other and their environment that are the sources of a healthy life in balance. They also learn from their new friend, Arianna, who has type 1 diabetes, that balance in nutrition and physical activity is essential for her health, too.

In this new book, *Hummingbird's Squash*, we once again find our heroes working to improve the health of families on the Medicine Cave Indian Reservation. In this story, the focus is on Hummingbird as she pursues a "giant plan" to grow huge fruits and vegetables that will provide abundant food to everyone. A bit full of herself, she believes that her "giants" will make Native seeds and growing methods unnecessary. She is unaware, however, that Coyote is playing tricks that will teach her and her friends about the history and wisdom of the foods their ancestors grew. His schemes also bring them into conflict with a school bully who has other plans for their giant garden. However, with help from Sky Heart, Thistle, the teachers at Thunder Rock Middle School, and their favorite store owner Boo, they find ways to prevent bullying and restore harmony to their school. By the way, you might like to know that in this story, Coyote performs the biggest trick (it is 9 feet tall) and oldest trick (about 4.5 billion years old) that he ever played. One of them is so spectacular (and traditional), the trickster even makes Miss Swallow, the science teacher, lose her cool!

To help you imagine new characters and events in the book, Patrick Rolo returns as our illustrator. He brings Coyote's tricks to life, and draws a terrific basketball game—not to mention a flying hamburger bomb that is pretty funny. Patrick has also updated the map of the town of Thunder Rock—just so you will know where you are.

On behalf of the author, Terry Lofton, and all the people at the Native Diabetes Wellness Program, we hope that you enjoy *Hummingbird's Squash*. If there are some words or terms you don't understand, we have included a glossary at the back of the book. Don't let a word stump you, just look it up and keep reading!

Acknowledgments

The Native Diabetes Wellness Program (the Wellness Program) would like to thank the following people who have helped to develop *Hummingbird's Squash* and those who will play a role in the future dissemination and use of the *Eagle Books* youth novels.

We once again express our gratitude to the Tribal Leaders Diabetes Committee (TLDC) for their enduring support of the *Eagle Books* project. We want to personally thank Buford Rolin, Chairman of the Poarch Band of Creek Indians, Chair of the TLDC and Vice Chair of the National Indian Health Board (NIHB); Judy Goforth Parker, Chickasaw Nation Health System, former TLDC member; and H. Sally Smith, NIHB board member and Alaska Area Representative, former TLDC member. They saw, almost a decade ago, the potential for storytelling as a way to reach children with a message of hope: type 2 diabetes is not their inevitable future.

Many thanks also go to Indian Health Service, Division of Diabetes Treatment and Prevention, for their continued partnership and friendship. The Tribal Advisory Committee (TAC) for the Centers for Disease Control and Prevention (CDC) and the Agency for Toxic Substances Disease Registry (ASTDR) additionally provided much appreciated support.

The Wellness Program also says 'thank you' to Georgia Perez, the author of the original *Eagle Books*. Her work as a Community Health Representative for the Nambe Pueblo and her dream of an eagle who brings healing messages encouraged her to write *Through the Eyes of the Eagle, Knees Lifted High, Plate*

Full of Color, and *Tricky Treats.* Her characters still inspire us to write stories about good health and good friends.

Continuing in his role as the principal illustrator for the *Eagle Books* project, Patrick Rolo (Bad River Band of Ojibwe Indians) has once again performed his magic for *Hummingbird's Squash.* Patrick breathes life and excitement into the written characters with pencil and paint, motivating our graphics team to create products of the highest quality.

Reading and reviewing manuscripts is an important job. For their insightful reviews and detailed feedback, we express thanks to Dr. Lawrence Barker, Associate Director for Science, CDC's Division of Diabetes Translation; Melinda Frank (Navajo Nation), health scientist/epidemiologist with CDC's Division of Diabetes Translation, Native Diabetes Wellness Program; Lorelei DeCora, R.N. (Ho-Chunk), our valued consultant and promoter of *Eagle Books* Talking Circles; and Arianna and Shirley Baros (the real Arianna and her mother) for sharing their very personal perspectives on the type 1 diabetes messages in the book. Other appreciated readers are Dr. Sanford Garfield, National Institute of Diabetes and Digestive and Kidney Diseases, National Institutes of Health; Dr. Carolee Dodge-Francis (Oneida Nation of Wisconsin), Executive Director of the American Indian Research and Education Center, University of Nevada, Las Vegas; Randy Chatto (Ramah Band of Navajo), Coordinator of the ERNEH Project: Empowering Ramah Navajos to Eat Healthy Using Traditional Foods; and Rosalie Carter, mother of the late Dr. Janette Carter of the Indian Health Service, who encouraged Georgia Perez to write the original story, *Through the Eyes of the Eagle.*

The Wellness Program is grateful as well to the families and middle school readers who read early drafts of *Hummingbird's Squash*. They represent the Navajo Nation, the San Felipe Pueblo in New Mexico, the Santee Sioux Tribe of Nebraska, and the Winnebago (Ho-Chunk) Tribe of Nebraska.

Additionally, we want to say how much we welcomed the participation of Coach Darren Wilkins of Salem High School in Conyers, Georgia. He provided expert knowledge of basketball training techniques for boys of middle school age and advised us on basketball procedures and rules.

Looking to the future, the Wellness Program further recognizes those who are building on the foundation established by the TLDC. We value so much the investment that has been made by the Chickasaw Nation under the leadership of Governor Anoatubby and Judy Goforth Parker. They have enthusiastically supported development of "Eagle Adventure," a program based on the four books in the *Eagle Books* series. A USDA-funded program, "Eagle Adventure," was developed by Chickasaw Nation Nutrition Services in partnership with Oklahoma State University (OSU), under the direction of Stephany Parker, OSU Department of Nutritional Sciences. The program shows great promise as a significant means of *Eagle Books* sustainability. It has strong appeal to many tribes across the country and features a design that can accommodate books for older readers.

And lastly, we acknowledge our wonderful partners on the *Eagle Books* project: Westat, for implementing the writing and graphics production for *Hummingbird's Squash*, and Kauffman and Associates, Inc., the designers of our website and promotional strategies.

Praise for *Hummingbird's Squash*

"Reading *Hummingbird's Squash* was extremely meaningful to me. It portrays the importance of being a good relative—to one's family and friends, and even to those who have forgotten how to be good relatives. Good relationships between people, like the sacred relationships between humans, plant life, and Mother Earth, help to create good health—whether it is preventing diabetes or healing the spirits of those who bully and are bullied."

—**Lorelei DeCora**
Winnebago Tribe of Nebraska (Ho-Chunk)
Health Educator/Diabetes Talking Circles Facilitator
Former Alternate, Tribal Leaders Diabetes Committee

"A great inspiration for all young and old! The story is fun and exciting and captivates the imagination. I can absolutely relate to the messages told by the children and whoever reads this book will as well. It teaches not only the importance of the health and wellness of our body, mind and spirit, but also the health and wellness of the renewable resources within our environment."

—**Randy Chatto**
Ramah Navajo, Project Coordinator
Empowering Ramah Navajos to Eat Healthy Traditional Foods Project

"I read '*Hummingbird's Squash*' and was impressed with how good a story it is (independent of its purpose). The plot incorporates the life of the now older children in a world that is real and full of symbolism and imagination—all to teach the message of health. The children of the *Eagle Book* stories learn how their environment and culture is a source for understanding and how both, when lived as Native Peoples always did, lead to health and, as in the Diabetes Education in Tribal Schools K-12 curriculum, give the message—Health is Life in Balance."

—**Dr. Sanford Garfield**
National Institute of Diabetes and Digestive and Kidney Diseases
National Institutes of Health
Co-Director of the Diabetes Education in Tribal Schools
Health is Life in Balance, K-12 curriculum

Praise for *Hummingbird's Squash*

"Promise the readers a tale of magic and adventure. Deliver them one even better than you promised. And, while you are delivering it, teach some important lessons about life and health, and teach those lessons in such an entertaining way that the reader might not even notice they are being taught. In other words, give them one thing under the guise of another. Coyote (on at least his relatively benevolent days) would approve of *Hummingbird's Squash*."

—**Dr. Lawrence Barker**
Associate Director for Science
Division f Diabetes Translation
Centers for Disease Control and Prevention

"My daughter, Janette Carter, would be so thrilled to see what has become of the *Eagle Book* stories with the second middle school novel, *Hummingbird's Squash*. Janette's faith in stories to "reach, teach and heal" has proved its worth to inspire the continuation of storytelling as a significant part of type 2 diabetes prevention programs. How fortunate we are to have the team who continues this work. The book is really a good one!"

—**Mrs. Rosalie Carter, Albuquerque, New Mexico**[1]

"The story and character content segue from *Coyote and the Turtle's Dream* to *Hummingbird's Squash* is beautiful! The book constantly reinforces the message of hope and positive change, for our Native communities, families and within ourselves."

—**Dr. Carolee Dodge Francis**
Oneida Nation of Wisconsin
Executive Director
American Indian Research and Education Center
University of Nevada, Las Vegas

---

[1] Please see Acknowledgments. Mrs. Rosalie Carter is the mother of the late Dr. Janette Carter who inspired Georgia Perez to write *Through the Eyes of the Eagle*.

Contents

1. Elephant's Toothpaste 1
2. A Catalyst for Bullies 13
3. Soap Bombs and Burgers 21
4. Courtyard Conferences 33
5. Shake-Ups and Shake-Downs 41
6. Coyote Drumming 53
7. Too Much and Not Enough 69
8. A Giant Plan 75
9. Sheds and Gardens 81
10. Coyote's Diagnosis 91
11. The Poisoned Apple 97
12. Bullies R Us 105
13. Toads and Targets 115
14. Wins and Losses 123
15. Thinking Big 133
16. Fast-Grow Formulas 147
17. The Big Burp-Off 157
18. Guarding Gardens 167
19. Pulp and Seeds 175
20. Back the Way it Was 189
21. Green Ancestors 199
22. The Miraculous Tree 209
23. Lessons and Confessions 221
24. Rabbits in a Hat 231

25. Healthy Secrets 237

26. De-Bullification . . . . ·245

27. Drills and Thrills 253

28. Harvest Time . . . . ·263

29. Coyote's Garden 275

30. Moving Mountains 287

31. A Grand Entry 297

32. Pumpkin Arguments . . . . ·305

33. Holes and Soft Spots 315

34. All In It Together 331

35. The Offering . . . . ·339

36. Cast of Characters 355

37. Glossary 361

Chapter 1

"Ha! She can't resist. She can't. It's too tempting. She's going to do it!
Tell Thistle what you see, Eagle."

Elephant's Toothpaste

Lester nervously licked his lips and lowered the flaming splint into the mouth of the test tube. As expected, his efforts were rewarded with a loud "Poof!" Murmurs of "Hey, cool" floated across the classroom in appreciation. Smiling, Lester looked up, seeking the approval of Mr. Pence, the 7th grade science teacher.

"Thank you, Lester. So, what is the name of the gas that caused the 'pop' we heard?"

Lester's smile faded. He shrugged his shoulders and guessed. "Diesel?"

Amid the laughter, the teacher sighed and double-wrapped his muffler around his neck. Mr. Pence was always cold. For him the early days of October were arctic, not crisp. He walked over to the thermostat and checked it for the third time that morning. It always read 70 degrees. Mr. Pence had tried putting ice cubes on the bogus instrument in hopes of pushing the room temperature into a balmier range, but to no avail. Resisting the urge to pull the thermostat off the wall, he wiped his ever-icy nose with a tissue and turned his attention back to the class.

Mr. Pence nodded and smiled amiably, but suspicioned that Lester wasn't being funny. A kindly soul, the science teacher always enjoyed a joke from his students. "That was a good one, Lester. You can go back to your seat. Well, anybody want to identify the gas?"

Hummingbird shot up her hand. "Hydrogen! It's hydrogen. That's the gas that blew up the Hindenburg. It was this giant airship…like a big blimp! I saw a movie on TV about it."

Remembering last week's rubber tubing catastrophe, the science teacher thought, Yes, Miss Birdie, you do seem to like things that "go boom." Checking his lesson plan, Mr. Pence noted that his star science student's demonstration was next. "For our last activity today, we are going to generate oxygen from hydrogen peroxide. Hummingbird, come on up and show us how it's done." As Hummingbird came up to the lab bench, Mr. Pence whispered, "No antics, right? You promised you would be good."

Hummingbird whispered back, "I promise, Mr. Pence. No tricks."

"Okay, let's take a look at the chemical equation for this reaction. And define what a catalyst is. We will be using a catalyst in this experiment."

While Mr. Pence went to the board, Hummingbird began to remove the items she needed from her cardboard "goodie box:" liquid soap, green and red food color, and a bottle of 3% hydrogen peroxide from the drug store. She wished that RD, Boomer and Simon (her best friends—of the boy variety) were in the 3rd period science class. They would love this demo! She and Mr. Pence had practiced the experiment the day before. It was really cool, but she was a little disappointed that it wasn't more *exciting*.

On a low hill overlooking Thunder Rock Middle School, Coyote crouched, half-hidden behind a clump of bushes. He balanced a pair of field glasses on his snout with one paw while he scratched aggressively at a flea with the other. This displacement activity released only some of the excited tension that was building in his quivering haunches. Staring intently through a window into Mr. Pence's science class, the trickster began to hum and then sing-song breathlessly: "She's gonna do it, she's gonna do it…"

"So what are you so happy about?" The question came from an eastern cottontail rabbit that had quietly joined Coyote behind his bushy cover.

Coyote ignored her.

"Excuse me, but helloooow! Do you mind telling me why you wanted me to come here?"

Ignored again, the rabbit became impatient and hopped in front of Coyote to get his attention. When she saw his new optical equipment, the rabbit knew full well that someone on the Medicine Cave Indian Reservation was short a pair of binoculars. She asked the question anyway: "Where did you get those?"

Coyote still said nothing.

"Don't tell me. I know—you found them lying beside the road."

Annoyed, Coyote growled, "Shut up, Thistle! Can't you see I'm working?

"Hey, you asked me to this party. I didn't volunteer." Thistle shrugged and began to nibble while she waited for the arrival of Sky Heart, the eagle. Of all the "Animals of Stories," he was the one to which Coyote would give most respect. Perhaps he would reveal his intentions to the Great Messenger.

Presently, Thistle heard the eagle's flapping and raised her head to watch him land in a nearby opening in the underbrush. Once on the ground, he advanced with hops so precise that he did not even rustle the dead weeds. Just like Sky Heart, Thistle thought, he never makes a big show. When his majestic white head appeared above a stand of golden rod, she called out, "Sky Heart! Over here."

With good humor, the eagle replied patiently, "Yes, Thistle, I see you."

"So, do you know what this is about?"

"No, but it can't be good."

Coyote jerked the glasses' strap from around his head and held out the binoculars to Sky Heart. "It's about these. I asked to borrow your eyeballs—just *borrow* them for just a few minutes. But, no, you wouldn't share those precious peepers of yours. So I got something just as good." He raised the field glasses back to his eyes and continued his vigilant observation.

Sky Heart explained to Thistle. "He said he wanted to exchange eyeballs for a while. Thought I might enjoy seeing the world from his viewpoint."

Thistle harrumphed, "What would that be? The back end of another coyote?"

The eagle laughed. "What are you looking at, Trickster?"

"Look for yourself. You don't need binoculars."

Finishing up his explanation at the board, Mr. Pence retrieved a small bottle of liquid sodium iodide from a locked cabinet off limits to students. The sodium iodide was the catalyst—the all-important substance that could speed up or slow down a chemical reaction. He would allow Hummingbird to handle the weak solution of sodium iodide since it was relatively harmless. Deciding to have some fun, Mr. Pence asked, "So, how many of you brushed your teeth with people toothpaste this morning?" Hands shot up all over the classroom.

Sammie, one of Hummingbird's friends, protested, "Mr. Pence, this is science—not health class. Besides, what else would we brush our teeth with?"

"Sammie, I think you'll find that science and health can really be two peas in the same pod." As he expounded on the relationship between scientific research and good health behaviors, Mr. Pence set up a plastic safety screen at the front of the lab bench. This experiment was not considered dangerous because the 3% hydrogen peroxide was so weak (unlike 35% hydrogen peroxide which could severely burn the skin). But Mr. Pence always followed the rules—for safety sake and to protect the student's clothes from exposure to the bleaching or staining effects of various chemicals.

Smiling mysteriously, Mr. Pence continued. "All I'm suggesting, kids, is that there are other kinds of toothpaste. Today, we are going to make some very big toothpaste—like the kind that elephants use."

Several students protested, "Oh, come on, Mr. Pence, elephants don't brush their teeth! You don't mean *elephant's* toothpaste!"

"Yes, that is exactly what I mean—elephant's toothpaste." After he and Hummingbird had donned their safety goggles, aprons, and gloves, Mr. Pence stepped aside and said ceremoniously, "Hummingbird, please proceed."

Clearing her throat, Hummingbird described the procedure. "First, we add 20 milliliters (mls) of the hydrogen peroxide to the graduated cylinder. Next, we add 5 mls of liquid soap—a couple of good squirts. Then, we add food coloring." She dribbled several drops of red food coloring down the inside of one side of the glass cylinder and green food coloring down the other side. Hummingbird looked up and smiled sweetly at the class. Then she wiggled her eyebrows up and down as if to say, Hang on. This is going to be fun!

The class strained forward in their desks.

"Ha! She can't resist. She can't. It's too *tempting*. She's going to do it!" His eyes gleaming, Coyote flashed a look at Sky Heart. "Tell Thistle what you see, Eagle."

Sky Heart turned his head and focused his extraordinary vision through the classroom window. "I see Hummingbird standing in front of a classroom." Looking at her now, so grown up, the great bird smiled. He remembered this pretty Indian girl when she was a spunky little six-year-old. Yes, he thought, that was the summer when the "Animals of Stories" had talked to the Rain that Dances, Hummingbird, Boomer and Simon at the old tree stump. Talking to humans was something rarely done these days, but the message was too important to ignore. The people *had* to start eating healthier...and moving their bodies. He, Thistle, and Coyote had decided that the children were the answer—the answer to helping their families and friends prevent type 2 diabetes.

Coyote interrupted the eagle's thoughts. "Yes," the trickster chuckled, "Little Hummingbird is indeed who you see."

Alarmed that Coyote was up to something, Thistle asked, "What is she doing Sky Heart?"

"She's holding a bottle over a tall glass tube."

"Yes, heeeee-heeeee. Whahhh! Haaa! Here it comes...here it comes!!!

"Then last, but certainly not least, we add the catalyst that will speed up the release of oxygen from the hydrogen peroxide." Hummingbird held out her hand to Mr. Pence. As the bottle of catalyst transferred from teacher to student, Mr. Pence made a move that would set a string of events into motion that Hummingbird would remember for the rest of her life. What small innocent act, you ask, could be so momentous? He merely reached down to pick up a tissue he had dropped on the floor.

In the moment that Mr. Pence diverted his eyes from Hummingbird, she made a lightning-fast decision based on a belief (the demonstration should be more exciting) and an assumption (more excitement meant a faster chemical reaction). Her decision? *To add more catalyst.*

Instead of the recommended 2 mls, she poured half the contents of the bottle directly into the soap/hydrogen peroxide mixture. In a flash, not even a nano-second, a pink and green-striped soap *bomb* fueled by the oxygen from the hydrogen peroxide zoomed from the cylinder! At first it looked just like a gigantic squeeze of toothpaste, but as it blobbed out in ever bigger billows of bubbly foam, it took on the appearance of a shape-shifting, mutant, pinky-green mushroom. Like a fungus, it began to grow up and over the safety screen where it fell in bulbous lumps on the floor.

Hummingbird stumbled back from the still-blossoming eruption that obscured her view of the classroom and Mr. Pence. She could hear gasps, shrieks, and scraping desks as kids ran for the door or retreated to the back of the room, bunching up against the windows. Sammie yelled, "Bird! Get away from that thing!"

The chemical reaction spawned "toothpaste" for several more seconds. Then, it stopped as abruptly as it had begun. The foaming mound seemed to emit a hot exothermic sigh as its short life expired. The hydrogen peroxide was "dead." Each of its molecules (H_2O_2) had lost one atom of oxygen. All that was left over from the reaction was H_2O—plain old water—and the catalyst.

Quiet descended on the room. Hummingbird took several faltering steps backward and bumped into one of the now empty desks. Dumbly, she looked back and forth between her classmates and the humongous load of puffy goo that covered all of the lab bench, the surrounding floor, and Mr. Pence's desk.

Suddenly, the classroom door flung open! Miss Betty Swallow stood in the door frame, her eyes bright and alert for potential danger. Quickly scanning the classroom, she demanded, "What is going on in here?"

Lester pointed his finger at Hummingbird and bleated in the whiny voice of tattle-tales the world over: "She did it…"

———

Coyote flung himself into the air with glee. "She did it!" The field glasses went flying into a clump of bushes. "Yes, yes! She did it!! Oh Gahhh, that was funny! Wahh. Ha-ha!" He rolled on the ground, pounding it with his fist. "Hee-Hee…haaaa!" He laughed so hard he started to choke. Gagging, Coyote fell down flat on his face, his shoulders heaving. He raised his head for a gasp of air; then he laughed some more. "Ha ha ha. Haaaaaa!" Coughing out the last of his delight, he finally rolled on his back, panting.

Thistle looked to Sky Heart. "I couldn't see it. Was it that funny?"

Sky Heart's beak was open. Stunned, he looked down at Thistle, then back at the scene in the classroom. "Well, let's put it this way. It was very entertaining."

Thistle went searching for the field glasses. When she found them, she fit her eyes as best she could to the position of the eye pieces. She watched the classroom for a few seconds and asked, "Did she make that foamy stuff?"

Coyote answered dreamily, "Yes, isn't she wonderful?" Then he added with a sly grin, "Of course, I helped."

"Well, it looks like Miss Swallow just showed up," Thistle reported. "Maybe she'll put a stop to this nonsense."

"Awww…patooties," Coyote pouted, "little Miss Betty is going to spoil everything." Suddenly very annoyed, he barked, "Here, gimme those glasses!"

Handing over Coyote's new "eyeballs," the little rabbit narrowed her own eyes and cast a suspicious look at the trickster. Suddenly she realized why Coyote had invited them to join him. Hopping over to Sky Heart, she whispered, "Coyote's started a game, hasn't he?"

"Yes. A Hummingbird game. Looks like we are going to be busy."

"Right," Thistle sighed. "Watch over her, Sky Heart, and let me know what happens. I have to get back to my nest building now." Mustering the considerable muscle energy in her haunches, Thistle bounded into the brush and quickly disappeared.

Coyote lowered the field glasses. Feeling empowered by his trickery, he stood up on his hind legs and toddled toward the low branch where the eagle now perched. Grinning at Sky Heart, the trickster declared, "I hope you're in good shape, Eagle. This is going to be grand sport. And just in case you were worried, Miss Swallow *hasn't* spoiled it." "No indeed," he giggled, "this game has only just begun!"

Chapter 2

Suddenly, a hole began to drip open where the creature's mouth should be.
One of the boys hollered, "He looks like the Scream Monster!"

A Catalyst for Bullies

"Where is Mr. Pence?" No one spoke. Worried, Ms. Swallow called, "Mr. Pence!"

A peculiar sound came from the direction of the lab bench. Miss Swallow thought it sounded like a boot being pulled from a mud hole. All eyes turned to the front of the classroom where a greenish (minty fresh?) slurp of foam began to rise and take on the blurred outline of a humanoid form. The big bubble stretched out its arms as if pleading for help and began to blindly squish toward Hummingbird.

Hummingbird's hand flew to her mouth in shock. This is terrible, she thought, what have I done? Overcome by guilt, Hummingbird could only stammer, "Oh, Mr. Pence, I'm so sorry. Please...don't be mad..."

The bubble creature cocked its head to the side, seemingly confused by the apology. It turned slowly, like a ship setting new coordinates, and headed toward Miss Swallow. Leaving a striped pinkish slime trail, it trudged step by step toward the beautiful 8th grade science teacher. Suddenly, a hole began to drip open where the creature's mouth should be. One of the boys hollered, "He looks like the Scream Monster!"

Miss Swallow ran to Mr. Pence. "Oh my gosh, David, are you all right?" She pulled off her lab coat and began to brush great wads of foam from his head and shoulders.

From the mouth hole came the sound of laughter and protest, "No, no! Stop, Miss Swallow. I like it. It's wonderful! I'm warm! I'm *sooo* warm! It's the first time I've been warm in months!"

"Yes, of course, the chemical reaction gave off heat. But we need to get this mess off of you." Miss Swallow looked at the clock—the class period was almost over. The bell would ring in a few minutes. An expert at classroom management, Miss Swallow took charge. "Everybody, return to your seats and get your things together." Amid the erupting classroom chatter, she continued issuing orders that would restore normalcy to the situation. "Sammie, run get the janitor. You, George, get some towels from Coach Brown." To Mr. Pence she said, "Thank goodness, your next period is planning. Hold on. I'll be back in a few minutes." She was almost out the door when she turned and called out, "Hummingbird, please remain. I want to talk to you."

When the bell finally rang, the class surged out of the trailer. Hummingbird dejectedly sat down next to a window and watched her schoolmates run to the main building. They can't wait, she thought, to tell everybody in the whole school. She looked over at Mr. Pence who had removed his safety goggles and was untying the rubberized apron that had protected most of his lab coat and shirt. The bottom of his pants and shoes were another matter. Following Mr. Pence's example, Hummingbird took off her safety gear and laid it on the desk beside her. Looking sadly at the goggles and gloves, her thoughts became glum and confused: I'm in real trouble now. What was I thinking?

Floyd, the school custodian, knocked on the door. "Heard you had a problem."

Mr. Pence pointed toward the gloppy mess. "Over there, Floyd. Sorry about the extra work."

"That's okay, it's my job." Floyd wheeled in his bucket and mop, then hesitated. "It ain't poisonous, is it?"

Miss Swallow bustled into the classroom behind Floyd. She answered for Mr. Pence. "No, it's harmless, Floyd." As the custodian set to work, Miss Swallow handed Mr. Pence some towels and a clean track suit from Coach Brown. When he went to the trailer bathroom to change clothes, Miss Swallow took a seat beside the abashed young girl. Quietly she said, "Do you want to tell me about it, Hummingbird?"

"I'm sorry, Miss Swallow. I don't know what made me do it. I just wanted it to be more exciting, I guess. You know, go faster—be bigger? I didn't know this would happen."

"What exactly did you do?"

Casting her eyes downward, Hummingbird confessed, "I added more catalyst than I was supposed to."

Miss Swallow frowned and looked quizzically at Hummingbird. "Yes, but what *else* did you do?"

Her voice quavering, Hummingbird replied, "Nothing."

Mr. Pence emerged from the bathroom—his arms crossed tightly up against his body. He was already cold again. The fact that he was wearing a dry pair of athletic socks, but no shoes, probably added to his discomfort. The enormous crush he had on Miss Swallow didn't help either. Looking at her adoringly with his pale blue eyes, Mr. Pence said shyly, "Thanks so much for your help, Miss Swallow. That was a bit of a disaster." Then he turned to Hummingbird. Feeling betrayed, he said, "I'm very disappointed in you, Hummingbird. You've become so irresponsible! Last week you didn't follow directions and blew up two feet of rubber tubing. The week before that you turned a test tube into a missile." Turning to Miss Swallow, he added, "It shot across the room and landed in our aquarium!"

Tears began to form in Hummingbird's eyes. If Mr. Pence was a mean teacher, she could at least have mustered some resentment toward him. But he had always been kind and understanding—even when she pushed the envelope sometimes. Now, she had let him down.

"What I really don't understand is where you got the strong solution of hydrogen peroxide. Who got that for you?"

"Nobody. The 3% hydrogen peroxide was what I bought at the drug store, Mr. Pence. It was the same bottle I used when we practiced yesterday."

"That's impossible." Mr. Pence got up and went to the locked chemicals cabinet. He searched the shelves until he found the recently ordered 35% solution of hydrogen peroxide. It was still sealed. He stepped over some foam that Floyd had not mopped up yet, and picked up Hummingbird's bottle of hydrogen peroxide and read the label. "Three percent," he muttered.

Miss Swallow explained. "Hummingbird, there isn't enough oxygen in the 3% solution to create that big explosion." Turning around in her seat, Miss Swallow called out to Mr. Pence who was examining Hummingbird's "goodie box." "There is something else that is puzzling me."

Hummingbird thought, Oh, no. What have I done now?

After Mr. Pence rejoined them, Miss Swallow went on. "Hummingbird says that she added more of the sodium iodide than was called for…and that's all she did. She believed it would make the reaction go faster and make more foam."

Mr. Pence laughed and shook his head. "That just doesn't make sense."

Looking at both teachers, Hummingbird asked, "Well, isn't that what made the foam blast out…instead of just dribble?"

Miss Swallow said, "No, Hummingbird. There's not enough oxygen gas released from the 3% solution to make the foam shoot out of the cylinder that fast. What's more, the 2 mls of sodium iodide will immediately release almost all of the oxygen in the 3% hydrogen peroxide—so adding more catalyst won't produce more oxygen. Without more oxygen, there won't be more foam."

Brightening for a moment, Hummingbird asked hopefully, "So, I didn't really cause the explosion?"

"I don't know what you did," Mr. Pence answered. "What concerns me is that you *intended* to create a bigger effect. If not an explosion, then something like it." The science teacher uncharacteristically became very stern. "Until I understand what happened here today, your participation in lab activities will be restricted. I'll have to call your parents...and talk to the principal." He paused and then added, "This might even require a suspension from school."

Hummingbird's face crumpled. "Suspended?" she whispered. Suddenly realizing the consequences of her actions Hummingbird jumped up from the desk. "Oh, no, Miss Swallow, the science fair! I might not be able to participate..."

Miss Swallow was very solemn. "Perhaps not, Hummingbird.

A polite knocking at the door interrupted the teachers' consideration of Hummingbird's fate. The president of the science club peered inside the classroom. "Excuse me, Miss Swallow, but..."

"Oh, I forgot! Sorry, sorry, Chris. Please tell Miss Oliver I'll be right there. I promised to do a demo for the sixth graders."

The boy withdrew, but did not immediately obey Miss Swallow's request. Instead, he stood to the side of the door and continued to listen as he had been doing before his well-mannered intrusion. So, Hummingbird could be blocked from the science fair? He smiled to himself. Miss Smarty, it seems, may have taken herself out of the competition…Chris was pleased, very pleased, with this new development. Elated at Hummingbird's misfortune, he slipped quietly down the steps of the trailer and headed back to the main building. There was a decided bounce in his step as he pondered how to use the "toothpaste fiasco" to his advantage. As he amused himself with devious thoughts, his smile suddenly twisted into an ugly smirk. Chris Sorrel didn't like competition. He wanted the science fair's blue ribbon for himself.

Chapter 3

Suddenly, an incoming ball of tinfoil flashed between Arianna and Simon's heads.

Soap Bombs and Burgers

Hummingbird nervously clutched the note that Mr. Pence had written to explain her late arrival to her 3rd period class. She ran to the 7th grade wing, and then walked rapidly to her locker, avoiding the stares of the few students in the hallway. Releasing the combination lock, she jerked open the locker door and crammed in her science book. Fretting about the quiz she was missing, she tugged at the blue spine of her history book—too forcefully. The book and a pile of papers spewed from the locker and scattered on the floor.

"Seems like everything is exploding today."

Hummingbird jumped. "Oh, hi. I didn't see you, Chris." Nervously, the young girl focused her attention on the 13-year-old boy who had slipped up on her so silently. Like her girlfriends, Hummingbird liked to engage in giggling chitchat about the most popular boys at school. Chris Sorrel, captain of the 8th grade basketball team, was at the top of their list. Good-looking and tall for his age, the girls thought that he was conceited. But that didn't detract from his appeal, especially to Hummingbird, since Chris was also on the math team and president of the science club.

Hummingbird reached down to pick up her papers. Her voice tight, she said, "So, I guess you heard what Mr. Pence said."

"Uh-huh. I wonder how long it will take Mr. Pence to trust you again? I'm sure it won't be long. He's so stupid—he'll probably believe anything you tell him."

Not appreciating the comment about Mr. Pence, Hummingbird said, "I thought Miss Swallow asked you to deliver a message for her."

"Miss Swallow? She doesn't order me around. Nobody does."

Noticing that Hummingbird had stopped picking up her papers, Chris said, "Here let me help you with those." He walked across the hall and picked up a set of stapled sheets. He saw that it was a science test with a score of 100. Fixing Hummingbird with a bright stare, he crumpled the test in his hand and shoved it in his pocket. Smiling coldly, Chris shot his poison arrow. "Yeah, he's so dumb he'll probably believe what other people tell him about you, too."

Hummingbird froze. Not even breathing, she watched Chris turn and saunter down the hall. At the intersection with the 8th grade wing, he stopped in front of a glass partition to examine his reflection. Satisfied with his fashionable "bed head," he disappeared around the corner.

That morning, Hummingbird had come to school a bright, vivacious girl. Now the joy and the morning were gone. She glanced at the hall clock and saw that the bell would ring in a few minutes. Hummingbird returned the history book to her locker. She decided to take the late note to Mr. Braun, her history teacher, between classes. That way she would attract less attention. In the meantime, she would hide out in the girl's restroom.

Hummingbird walked quickly down the hall and gently pushed open the door to the girl's restroom. She peeped inside. No one was there. She slipped into the last stall and locked it. Leaning her head up against the door, the former star of Mr. Pence's class waited for the bell. She could feel herself sweating. Oh geez, she thought, what was that with Chris? Hummingbird knew that some kids didn't like him or his brothers, but what had she ever done to him? What was he going to say about her? Oh, come on, please ring! Out loud, she whispered, "I've got to talk to RD…"

Finally, the bell yielded to the clock and the halls came to life. The restroom door thumped open and the clamor of laughing, chattering voices immediately displaced the quiet. Stalls banged and faucets gushed as girls combed their hair, applied lip gloss, and traded the latest juicy tidbits. As Hummingbird expected, she was the tidbit. "Did you hear—she blew up Mr. Pence!" "I heard Miss Swallow had to save him!" "Yeah, she made a soap bomb!" "They say she put gun powder in the soap…" "Who said that?" "I don't know, but Wanda saw everything…" The rumors grew and flew until the 'elephant's toothpaste' had evolved into an explosion that could only be described as atomic. At last, the crowd dispersed and headed to the lunchroom. Hummingbird didn't move. She stood staring at the stall door, but not seeing it. Her only thought was an irrational one. Maybe I can stay in here until school is out.

Apparently, that would not be an option. A familiar and friendly young voice whispered, "Bird, you can come out now."

Hummingbird pulled the stall door open and peeked out. "Oh, Arianna! How did you know it was me? There's nobody else in here, is there?"

"I recognized your shoes, Silly." Looking around, Arianna said, "No, they're all gone."

"You heard all that? What am I going to say to people?"

"I'd be more worried about what you were going to tell your mom and dad." Since Arianna was temporarily living with Hummingbird's family until her parents relocated to the reservation area later in the fall, she was well aware of her friend's recent troubles in science class. "What really happened anyway?"

"Wait until we get to the lunchroom. Then I'll tell all you guys everything. Right now, I've got to take this note to Mr. Braun."

Hummingbird and Arianna headed for the history classroom. Mr. Braun was standing in the hall, locking his door.

Noticing the approaching girls, he said, "You almost missed me, ladies."

Hummingbird said, "Mr. Braun, sorry I didn't make your class. Um, here is a note from Mr. Pence." Mr. Braun took the note, but didn't read it. Smiling, he said, "I take it then that Mr. Pence has survived."

"Oh, yes. He wasn't injured or anything."

"That's good. So, you missed a quiz, young lady. You can make it up later. It won't take long. Well, I'm going to lunch. Would you like to accompany me?" Both girls nodded. Thus, under the wing of her history teacher, Hummingbird approached the full glare of her new notoriety as the "soap bomber." As they drew nearer to the florescent brightness of the lunchroom, Hummingbird felt as if she were being wheeled into surgery. She steeled herself for their entry. Suddenly, she heard her name being called.

"Bird!"

It was RD! With great relief, she watched Rain that Dances run to join them. Of all her friends, this slim, quiet boy with the faraway look in his eyes was the one who would most understand her feelings of disappointment and confusion. They had grown closer and closer ever since that long ago summer when the eagle had told Rain and his friends about the healthy ways of their ancestors. Now, the two of them spent hours talking about ways they could help their families and friends eat healthy traditional foods, play sports, and get active. Preventing type 2 diabetes was their dream. Her science fair project had been part of that dream. Now, she thought guiltily, because of her foolishness, the school might not see her project's important messages.

"Bird, I've been looking everywhere for you! Hi, Mr. Braun."

"Well, it looks like you are in good hands," the history teacher said. He gave Hummingbird a reassuring pat and joined Mrs. Corn who was on duty as lunchroom monitor. Mr. Braun whispered something to Mrs. Corn that raised her observation of student behavior to a higher level. There would be no catcalls or heckling of Hummingbird with Mrs. Corn on duty.

Rain looked hard at Hummingbird. "So, is it true? The 'elephant's toothpaste' went bad?"

"Yeah, real bad."

"Where have you been? Simon said you weren't in history class."

Arianna told on Hummingbird. "She was hiding in the girl's restroom."

"Well, she can't hide in there," Rain said, pointing to the cafeteria. "Come on, let's go."

With Rain "riding shotgun" on one side and Arianna on the other, Hummingbird marched down the middle of the lunchroom. She kept her eyes focused on one goal—the table where Simon and Boomer were sitting. As they passed each row of tables, whispers and giggles replaced the normal din of conversation.

Noticing the change in noise volume, Boomer looked up. He nudged Simon, and then started waving energetically. The easygoing boy with the megaphone voice and equally big sense of humor was a joyful sight to Hummingbird. Pulling his nose out of a book, Simon turned and waved, too. A "science freak" like Hummingbird, he was eager to ask her about the experiment gone wrong.

Running the gauntlet without incident, Hummingbird slid into the chair beside Simon—her back to the lunchroom crowd. She breathed a big sigh of relief. Rain plopped down beside Boomer and pulled out a copy of this month's *Mammoth Boy*, the boys' favorite comic. He delivered it to Boomer as promised. The boys exchanged a wordless "thumbs up." Taking the seat on the other side of Simon, Arianna asked, "What are you reading, Simon?" Rain and Boomer furtively watched Simon's reaction. They knew that he *really* liked Arianna.

Smiling, Simon said, "It's called *The Fall of the Dinosaur Empire*, about the big meteorite that hit earth and wiped out the dinosaurs. It has great pictures."

Laughing, Arianna replied, "I should have known it was about dinosaurs. You love those lizards…" It was well known that Simon was the ultimate "dino-geek."

Shyly, Simon said, "Yeah, and more than ever now."

Everyone at the table knew exactly what Simon meant. In the weeks since Rain and Simon had returned the missing bones of the Great Turtle, the boys had talked to their friends constantly about the ancient creatures they had seen in her cave at Shell Ridge. Simon would never get those images of the great marine reptiles out of his mind. And he didn't want to.

Holding open one of the illustrated pages of the dinosaur book so Boomer could see it, Simon made an offer: "I'll trade ya for that *Mammoth Boy* when you're finished, Boom."

"You bet. Those dinos look cool!" Noticing that Hummingbird wasn't eating, Boomer asked, "Where's your lunch?"

"In my locker. And I'm not going through the lunch line…"

"Here, you can have some of mine." Boomer cut his turkey sandwich in half and placed it on a napkin. Simon shoved over one of his cartons of low-fat milk, and Rain lobbed an orange across the table, hollering, "Catch!" Arianna opened a package of unsalted seeds and nuts (toasted) and a snack box of dried choke cherries. She offered them to Hummingbird. These snacks were some of the most popular traditional foods sold at Boo's Gas 'n Grocery. (Arianna said the treats were good for kids like her who had type 1 diabetes and everybody else, too.) For sure, Hummingbird wouldn't go hungry.

Comforted by the presence of her good friends, Hummingbird launched into the story she knew they wanted to hear. She spared no details (even the fact that she could get suspended), pausing only to take bites of sandwich and sips of milk. Arianna and the boys hung onto every word. Ending her story, Hummingbird surprised them with Miss Swallow's conclusion. "She said that extra catalyst couldn't have caused the explosion of foam."

Intrigued, Rain asked, "Then how did it explode?"

"I don't know. If anybody could figure it out, I thought maybe Simon would be able to…"

Boomer interrupted. "Wait, wait! If the catalyst didn't cause the explosion—that means you're innocent." Putting two and two together with his lawyer's genius for arguing "not guilty," Boomer cried, "They can't punish you for something you didn't do!"

"Yes they can. Mr. Pence said I was trying to make the experiment more exciting—without knowing what would happen. I had even promised him I wouldn't pull any tricks."

At the mention of the word "tricks," Rain frowned. "It just doesn't add up," he said quietly. Deep down, his subconscious mind began to dig into his experiences with all things tricky.

Simon pushed his glasses up on his nose and said, "Okay, Bird, let's go over it step by step. Where did you get the hydrogen perox...?"

Suddenly, an incoming ball of tinfoil flashed between Arianna and Simon's heads. The crumpled hamburger wrapper with the apple core payload hit Boomer right in the middle of his forehead. A runny goo of ketchup, mayonnaise, and meat grease ran down his nose and dripped onto his shirt.

A sudden burst of loud laughter erupted from the other side of the cafeteria. Boomer's eyes swiveled to a pack of kids who were "high fiving" Walter, an 8th grader. Known as Dumptruck, Boomer recognized him as a kid with a bigger reputation for being goofy than a real troublemaker. Like Dumptruck, his applauding fans, Tater Tot, Freddie, and Lester, were members of the Invisible Club—that bunch of kids in every school who hung out together because they were excluded from every other crowd. Tater Tot, a freckle-faced redhead who was a recent arrival on the rez, was actually visible because of his flame-colored hair, but so socially obscure that nobody even knew his real name.

Boomer stood up and yelled, "Hey, Dingfod!" (For some reason, Boomer had recently invented the word "dingfod" to describe anyone he thought was acting like a dope or a jerk). Boomer forked his fingers in front of his eyes and pointed at Dumptruck. "Big D," as some kids called him, got the message and the challenge that went with it. Unfortunately, Mrs. Corn did, too. She strode to Dumptruck's table and ordered him to follow her. She also signaled Boomer to come forward.

Wiping off the ketchup mess with a napkin, Boomer griped, "Aww, man. What did I do? Nothin'!"

"No sweat, Boom, you know how to talk to Mrs. Corn," Rain assured him.

"Yeah, but don't wipe off all the evidence," Simon advised.

Boomer sighed and got up from the table. As he was making his way toward the teacher, a ripple of snickers followed him. Hummingbird's eyes drifted in the direction of the mocking laughter—a table of popular 8th graders. Chris Sorrel was leaning back in his seat at the head of the table, presiding over his groupies. Yuk, Hummingbird thought, he is so stuck-up. She figured that Chris had put Dumptruck up to throwing the burger ball, but he was just too cool to even check out her reaction.

Still thinking about tricks, Rain was curious about why Bird had started doing funny stuff in Mr. Pence's class. "Hey, Bird, what were you trying to prove when you blew up that tubing last week?"

"Huh? What?" Hummingbird looked at her friend—then her eyes wandered back to Chris.

"Oh, nothing. We can talk later." What's Bird looking at? Rain wondered. He followed her gaze and saw she was looking at Chris Sorrel. They both watched him take a scrunched up bunch of papers out of his pocket and smooth them on his lunch tray. Satisfied to the paper's flatness, he leaned over to Mindy Two Horses and whispered something in her ear. Mindy nodded. She took the paper, folded it, and placed it in her purse. She immediately got up from the table and left the lunchroom. Chris carefully folded his hands on the table and raised his eyes to Hummingbird. His face had no expression. His eyes didn't blink.

A chill came over Hummingbird. She gasped, "Why is he doing this?" Her next thought was, I've got to get out of here! Snatching up her sweater, she accidentally overturned Simon's water bottle. The water streamed across the table and ran under *The Fall of the Dinosaur Empire*. Simon jerked up the book, yelling, "Hey! Watch it! This is a library book..."

Hummingbird choked out an unapologetic "Sorry" and ran for the courtyard exit. Startled, Arianna cried, "What's wrong with Bird?"

Rain looked back to where Chris had been sitting, but the big man and his troops were gone. "I don't know, Arianna, but we're going to find out."

Anxious about her best friend, Arianna hurriedly bunched up the napkins and wrappers that littered the table and plunked the wad in front of Simon. "Here, please throw this away, okay? And please wipe up that water, Simon." Then, she dashed after Hummingbird.

Rain grabbed his books and followed Arianna. At the door to the courtyard, he called over his shoulder, "Hey, Simon, get Boomer's stuff..."

Simon sat there staring after his friends. Protesting his involuntary status as a busboy, he grumbled loudly, "Oh, sure. Want me to mop the floor, too?"

Mr. Berry, the principal, was patrolling nearby when he heard Simon's question. He smiled and thought, that young man should be on our 'Keep the School Clean' committee. Leaning over his new candidate for promoting lunchtime sanitation, the principal said appreciatively, "Mopping won't be necessary, Simon, but thanks for offering."

Chapter 4

When it was Rain's turn, he stared at the photo so long that Sammie had to ask for the phone back.

Courtyard Conferences

Rain and Arianna stood in the middle of the courtyard—the open space at the center of the school. From this hub radiated the three wings that housed the sixth-, seventh-, and eighth-grade classrooms. Each day Mr. Berry gave the students free time after lunch. He believed that unrestricted chatter and blowing off steam was healthy for middle schoolers.

Arianna spotted Hummingbird sitting on a bench by herself near the sixth-grade wing. She wasn't doing much chattering.

Her two best friends meant to change that. They hurried over to find out what had scared her.

"So, what's going on with Chris Sorrel?" Rain asked.

"Who's Chris?" Arianna wanted to know. Being new to the reservation, she didn't know all the kids at Thunder Rock Middle School.

Unfortunately, the answers to both questions would have to be postponed. Being a girl with lots of friends, it was no surprise that other kids would want to talk to Hummingbird, too. Sammie, Star, and Little Deb (everyone called her that because her mom's name was Big Deb) were suddenly swarming around Bird like inquisitive bees. They were nosy, to be sure, but they were supportive, too.

"Are you okay?" Star asked. "That foam stuff didn't get on you, did it?"

"I told you it didn't get on her, Star. I was there!" Sammie said impatiently. To prove it, she reached for her back pack. She fished out her cell phone, bursting to show everyone a photo she took of the 'elephant's toothpaste.' Pushing the photo in front of Hummingbird's face, Sammie insisted that she appreciate the catastrophe. "Look, look at that, Bird! It just went *whoosh!*"

Reluctantly, Hummingbird glanced at the photo. "Yeah, that's what it looked like all right…"

Sammie passed around the phone. Until Arianna saw the size of the foam bomb, she didn't realize how big it really was. When it was Rain's turn, he stared at the photo so long that Sammie had to ask for the phone back. The girls couldn't stay long—they were on the yearbook staff and had to turn in assignments to Mr. Braun for this afternoon's meeting of *The Flash*. Star had drawn a new design of the yearbook logo—a Thunderbird with zigzag lightning coming from his beak. She thought it looked very "flashy."

Before they left, Little Deb tried to be reassuring. "Don't worry Bird, everything will turn out okay. Mr. Pence really likes you." A believer in the wonders of cosmetics, Deb dug out some blush from the bottom of her purse and gave Hummingbird's cheeks a couple of pink swipes. She smiled, "You needed a little color."

Sammie agreed, "Yeah, that looks better." Looking at the time on her cell phone, Sammie said, "Well, gotta run." Making a little joke, she added, "Don't worry about the picture, we won't put it in the yearbook!"

Suddenly, Rain said, "Hold up a second, Sammie, I want to give you my mom's email." He scribbled the address on a scrap of paper and handed it to her. "Um…send me the picture of the 'elephant's toothpaste,' okay?"

Waving "bye," Sammie said, "Okay. No problem."

Hummingbird gave Rain a funny look. He just shrugged. "We might as well keep a picture of the explosion. It is pretty amazing."

Eager to pick up where they left off, Arianna repeated her question. "So who is Chris Sorrel?"

Just then there was a commotion on the other side of the courtyard. A pickup truck had pulled into the delivery zone between the sixth-grade wing and the back of the school gym. Two young men got out of the cab and started unlashing a tarp that covered the bed of the truck. A small crowd began to gather—Boomer and Simon among them. Suddenly, Boomer's yelled across the courtyard, "Hey, RD! Come on over! Joe's got the new drum!"

Excited, Rain said, "I better check it out. Be back in a minute."

Trying to lift Bird's spirits, Arianna said, "Come on. Let's go see the drum, too." Bird got up without saying anything. As they walked slowly across the grass, Arianna made small talk. "Bird, do you like singing with the drum?"

"Oh, yeah. It's one of my favorite things." Hummingbird's mother, Darlene, had made sure of that. She was a well-known singer at pow-wows and had always encouraged her daughter to join the circle of "chorus girls" whose high voices complemented the lower register of the male drummers.

As the girls drew nearer they saw Joe Red Crane, a tall man in his 70's, get out the driver's side of the truck. All the kids loved Joe. He managed the school's heritage program which included Native language, drumming, dance, and Tribal history and culture. Joe taught the language and drumming lessons himself. He was glad to see the students' enthusiasm, but asked that everybody stand back so that the big drum (almost two and a half feet in diameter) could be unloaded. The community had invested some dollars in this beauty—a deep barreled instrument made of elk hide and cedar.

After the drum passed safely (but not without struggle) through the doors to the gymnasium's band room, Joe came back out to remind the crowd that 7th grade drum practice would be at 3:30 that afternoon. The kids began to peel away. Only five minutes of free time remained before 4th period. The boys spotted Hummingbird and Arianna near the only clump of trees that shaded the courtyard. Arianna called out, "Looks like you didn't get in trouble, Boom."

Arianna had no trouble hearing Boomer's answer. Even when he was trying to talk quietly, he sounded like a P.A. system. "No, Mrs. Corn just told me 'to control the volume of my voice.'" Boomer did a pretty good imitation of Mrs. Corn's high-pitched warble. "Dumptruck got detention though."

Hummingbird waited until the five friends had re-grouped. Then she revealed her suspicions. "Chris Sorrel put Dumptruck up to it." Boomer and Simon looked surprised. Rain did not.

"Okay, I'm going to ask again," Arianna sighed. "Who's Chris?"

Hummingbird finally answered. "He's an eighth grader. If you weren't new to the school, believe me, you'd know him. He's really smart and athletic. He's been the president of every club at least once, and he's the captain of the basketball team. It's like he's the king of everything."

"His father's on all these Tribal committees," Boomer said, "and his mother runs this mail-order business. My mom works for her at Christmas. She says Chris's mother is real nice."

"Well, his mom might be nice, but his brothers think they're the big bosses around here. Like the rest of us are a bunch of dweebs," Simon said resentfully.

When his family had moved back to the reservation the previous year, Simon had had a run-in with Chris's older stepbrothers, Jesse and Melvin. They had chased him out of the recreation center gym, threatening to beat him up if they saw him there again. The brothers boasted that the gym was their territory. They set the rules. Rule number one, according to Jesse's balled up fist, was that only real Thunder Rockers could hang out there.

Simon complained about the harassment to Clifford, his cousin, who was a junior at Thunder Rock High. He just shook his head and told Simon not to take it personally. A fan of old *Star Trek* reruns, Clifford joked that the brothers considered it their "prime directive" to make life miserable for everyone over the age of six. They got away with everything because the Sorrels were big wheels on the reservation. His message to Simon was to stay out of their way.

Boomer broke into Simon's disgruntled thoughts. "I *told* you, Simon, we're not dweebs—we're dingfods!"

"Yeah, right! And I'm the biggest dingfod!" Giving Rain a playful punch on the shoulder, Simon turned his grouchiness on his best pal. "Thanks, RD, for getting me put on the 'Keep the School Clean' committee."

"How did I do that?"

"Mr. Berry thought I was being so responsible. Cleaning up the mess you guys left."

Boomer started laughing. "Woo-hoo! Maybe you can work your way up to chairman of the 'Keep the School Clean' committee!"

"Ha, ha. So funny," Simon grumped.

"Sorry, Simon," Arianna apologized. "I guess that was kind of rude. Dumping that trash on you."

Simon melted. "Oh that's okay, Arianna. I didn't mean you. You can give me your garbage anytime." The kids would have burst out laughing had it not been for the goofy smile on Simon's face.

Boomer cleared his throat. For Simon's sake, he thought it best to change the subject. "So, what were we talking about? Oh, yeah, Chris. Why would he put Dumptruck up to throwing stuff at me? What have I done to him?"

"I think Dumptruck was aiming at me, not you," Hummingbird said. "Chris is trying to freak me out."

Boomer and Simon's "Huhs?" and "Whys?" drowned out Arianna's predictable question, "Who's Dumptruck? What kind of name is that?"

Hummingbird explained. "Chris overheard Mr. Pence get mad at me about messing with the 'elephant's toothpaste.' So, he comes up in the hall and says some stuff like he's going to spread rumors about me. Make Mr. Pence think I'm a creep or something."

Before Boomer could say it, Hummingbird said impatiently, "Yeah, I know, Boom, not creep—dingfod." Finishing her story, she said, "He even took my science test we got back yesterday like he hated me or something and wadded it up." Hummingbird imitated Chris balling up the paper in his fist.

"That still doesn't explain why he's after you," Simon said.

Looking at Hummingbird, Rain said warily, "The test—that must be what he gave to Mindy?" Rain had been unusually quiet since looking at the photo on Sammie's cell phone. He had not joined in the conversation very much until Bird reminded him of Chris's actions in the cafeteria.

"You saw that?" Hummingbird said, surprised.

"Yeah. I wonder what he's up to?"

"Whatever it is, I don't want to find out."

Chapter 5

The boys spotted Chris and his two playmates on the walkway in front of the gym. Simon muttered, "Oh-oh. It's Big Frog and the 'toad patrol.'"

Shake-Ups and Shake-Downs

As the kids were talking, Arianna spotted Mr. Pence walking across the courtyard. When he saw Hummingbird, the science teacher altered his route and headed toward the tree where the five friends had gathered. Arianna said, "There's Mr. Pence and he's coming over here."

"Oh, no," Hummingbird whispered, "Does he look friendly?"

Rain replied, "Not particularly. But he does look cold. He just tied a scarf around his neck."

Stopping short of the small group, Mr. Pence called out, "Hummingbird, could I see you for a moment?"

Hummingbird swallowed hard and looked nervously at her friends. They watched quietly as she approached the teacher. He handed some papers to her. Despite straining to hear what was being said, all they could pick up was murmuring. When Rain saw Hummingbird's shoulders slump, he thought, Uh-oh.

Mr. Pence abruptly turned and walked away. Hummingbird didn't move. She just stood there. The kids hurried to her side.

Arianna was the first to speak: "What did he say?"

She handed over a set of stapled papers to Rain. It was the test. "He said Mindy told him she found this in the garbage in the girl's restroom. Since the test had a 100 on it, she thought the person who 'lost' it would want it back."

Simon asked the question that he thought Mr. Pence would have asked: "Why didn't Mindy just give it to you?"

"Oh, my name was conveniently torn off, like she didn't know who it belonged to…"

"But Chris knew Mr. Pence wouldn't forget who made 100 on that test." Simon replied.

Hummingbird nodded. Then she took a deep breath and forced out her words in a frantic rush—as if she wanted to get rid of them as quickly as possible. "Mr. Pence said he was disappointed that I would throw away my tests. Because he thought I cared more about science than that. Then he said…" She stopped. A big tear slowly rolled down her face, smearing Little Deb's pink blush. "Then he said he was disappointed to find out that I would say really…really nasty things about people." The tears that had pooled on her lower eyelids suddenly spilled over into real misery.

Their voices tumbling over each other, the kids protested their disbelief. "What? Come on, No way! He didn't say that!"

Hummingbird wiped her eyes with the back of one hand. "Oh, yes, he did. Look on the back of the last page…"

Rain turned over the test. In large block capitals was written: MISS SWALLOW SAYS MR. PENCE IS A LOSER AND A DORK.

Sky Heart heard the bell ring and saw the middle schoolers scatter as they headed back to their classrooms. The eagle had keenly observed Hummingbird's dejected posture and the way that her friends gathered protectively around her. Clearly, she was upset. He had never seen this bright and beautiful girl cry before.

From his perch on the telephone pole, the eagle turned his attention from the school and made a brief scan of Thunder Rock, the largest community on the reservation. The town was quiet. Feeling a bit stiff, he stretched out his wings and flapped them several times. Sky Heart had been on duty all morning and felt the need to fly. Hummingbird wasn't his only concern on this day. His role was to give heart to anyone who sought the reassurance of his presence. He was a messenger of hope to all the people.

The eagle launched himself and quickly rose into a low cloud. As he circled upward, his mind focused on Hummingbird's tears. Yes, he thought, something was very wrong. He resolved to return to the school after his mid-day flyover.

The last bell of the day signaled that exhilarated sense of freedom that meant only one thing—it was Friday. Students grabbed their books for homework assignments and teachers stuffed ungraded tests in their briefcases and totes. But these responsibilities could wait until Sunday evening. Tomorrow was Saturday!

Rain and Boomer, however, didn't have to wait for their good time. Drum practice was scheduled for that afternoon. They had convinced Simon to go along—at least to watch and listen. Simon was shy about learning how to drum. He had been teased by his cousins (not Clifford—he was cool) when they saw him trying to do some pow-wow dancing. They called him a "city boy" who didn't know how to dance "ind'n." Simon had become very self-conscious after that, but the boys thought Joe could bring him out of his shell.

Needless to say, Hummingbird did not share her friends' enthusiasm for the weekend, drums, or anything else. She and Arianna usually attended after-school activities. But not today. Hummingbird just wanted her mother's comfort.

Circling above the school, Sky Heart saw Hummingbird and Arianna join the crowd of students that were scheduled for the first bus group. As soon as he saw them board their bus, Sky Heart arced away from the scene below and made a wider sweep of the school area. He wasn't surprised to see Coyote nestled comfortably on the hill above the classroom trailers. The eagle had to smile when he saw Coyote raise the binoculars to his eyes. He was wondering who the old scoundrel was watching now— when a slight disturbance in the bus loading zone attracted his attention.

Sky Heart lowered his altitude and re-directed his gaze to the group of waiting riders. He observed two boys herding a smaller child off by himself. Although he could not hear, the eagle could see what was going on.

Keeping an eye on the two teachers on bus duty, Dumptruck slyly maneuvered the sixth-grade boy behind the hedge that bordered the front of the school. Thrusting out his hand, Big D said, "Okay, whatcha got left?"

The boy reached in his pocket: "Just a quarter."

"Then, gimme it," Dumptruck said impatiently.

Tater Tot, who was on look-out, called out. Hurry up. Mrs. Biddy's walking this way.

Dumptruck gave his victim a kindly word of counsel: "Tell on us and you'll be real sorry." Then he pushed the back of the boy's head and let him go.

Tater Tot joined his partner in crime. "How much we get today?"

Dumptruck fished out some coins and one crumpled dollar bill from his pocket. "About six dollars."

"Too bad we don't get to keep any of it," Tater Tot grumbled.

"Is Chris watching?"

Tater glanced toward the school's big double doors. "Yeah, he can see Old Biddy's getting too close. Come on, let's go."

When the two boys vacated the cover provided by the hedge, Chris emerged from the school entrance. He walked toward the courtyard, knowing that Dumptruck and Tater Tot would follow. Suddenly, Chris side-stepped behind a fence that shielded a row of garbage cans. He didn't like to advertise his association with Dumptruck or Tater Tot—especially when he was making collections. "Okay, hand it over. How much is it?"

"Six dollars."

"Is that all? Last Friday it was fourteen."

"Yeah, but that was the field trip money from those girls."

Chris counted the money. He frowned and looked up with disgust at these idiots he intimidated into doing his dirty work. In Chris's view, guys like Dumptruck and Tater Tot were the bottom of the social and mental ladder he used to rank people. Angrily he snarled, "This is nothing, man. You better find somebody else to squeeze."

In truth, Chris was more afraid than angry. His stepbrothers would be expecting more than this measly handful of change. The few times he hadn't coughed up money from the middle school, they had made him very sorry. Chris turned his fear on the two boys. Smiling menacingly, he said, "Come up with more money or you'll be having a little talk with Melvin and Jesse."

Dumptruck and Tater Tot hastily agreed, and the three boys continued on their way to the courtyard in search of new prey. At the same time Rain and his pals were headed down the 7th grade wing to the courtyard exit. Rain and Boomer were speculating about the new song Joe was going to teach that afternoon. They had learned memorial songs, veteran's songs, and honor songs…Joe knew them all. A new song was always fun, but today was a special day. They would play the new drum for the first time. Even Simon was getting excited.

As they exited the building, the boys spotted Chris and his two playmates on the walkway in front of the gym. Simon muttered, "Uh-oh. It's Big Frog and the 'toad patrol.'"

At almost the same time, Chris caught sight of Rain. When he saw that Rain was with his friends, he switched his objective from a "shake-down" to "shake-up." He thought it would be a good opportunity to put a little pressure on Little Miss Birdie's buddies—especially Simon. Small for his age, Simon looked like a kid easy to push around. What's more, he was too smart for Chris's liking. Chris whispered to Dumptruck and Tater Tot, "Come on, let's show 'em whose boss around here."

Rain watched Chris strut toward them—backed up by his "muscle." He couldn't help but play out the frog joke: "Looks like they're hopping this way." Joining in the fun, Boomer popped off, "Don't touch 'em! You'll get warts!"

The boys fell out laughing. Or rather, Rain and Boomer laughed. Simon snorted. When he got really tickled, Simon inhaled his "ha-ha's" and they came out as oinky snorts. Simon's 'nose grunts' literally tore up Boomer. He started laughing so loud, other kids turned to see what was going on.

Despite Chris's big swagger, some of the puff went out of his chest. Why were they laughing? Anxious to buck up his tough guy image, he whispered to Dumptruck and Tater Tot, "Watch this." Chris planted his feet apart, blocked the walkway, and launched his first dig. "Oh, look, it's Veggie Man, the 'you'll get diabetes' dweeb and Thunder Thud! The Soap Bomber's friends! And the wimp, Simonosaurus!"

The boys stifled their giggles. Trying not to move his mouth, Rain said quietly, "Don't say anything."

Disappointed that his punch didn't land, Chris tried again. "Hey, Simonosaurus's new name is bigger than he is!" Like an audience that had been paid to applaud, Dumptruck and Tater provided the appropriate snickering and fist-bumps.

Rain folded his arms and looked bored. Simon polished his glasses. Boomer scratched his stomach and performed his own ventriloquist act. "We're psyching him out. He's starting to sweat."

Getting desperate, Chris threw out a champion insult guaranteed to offend any self-respecting dino-geek: "You know, Simon, you're so stupid, you got another brain in your tail to make your legs work!"

Appreciating the intelligence and humor of the insult, Simon whispered admiringly: "Too bad he's such a creep. That was funny!"

Running out of patience, Boomer whispered back, "Yeah, well, explain it later. Right now I'm going to drum practice." The boy with the big voice started rolling his shoulders, stretching his arms, and cracking his knuckles. Then he began to twirl his arms in circles. It was quite a show.

Dumptruck and Tater Tot took a step backwards, leaving Chris out front and alone. Tater was freaked out. "What's he warming up for?"

After a couple of deep knee bends, Boomer announced his intentions. "Oh, yeahhhh...I feel a song coming on!" Feeling no guilt since their adversaries had been fairly warned, Boomer let loose with the Tribe's flag song: "Our flag will stand forever. Under it the people will grow." True to his name, Boomer's singing was so deafening that Tater Tot broke ranks and ran off. Not being from the reservation, he didn't recognize the flag song. To his ears it was an air raid siren that screamed, 'Run!'

Suddenly the side door to the band room flung open. Joe Red Crane stuck out his head and called out, "Hey, fellas. You wanna sing—get in here!" Boomer halted his solo performance and yelled, "Coming, Joe!"

When adults got in the act, Dumptruck wanted no trouble. He stuck his hands in his pockets and shuffled off into the grass—leaving most of the walkway unobstructed. Chris didn't move.

Boomer and Simon ran past Chris, but Rain lingered. After the door closed behind his two friends, he stepped closer to Chris. Quietly but firmly, he said, "We know you wrote that stuff about Miss Swallow and Mr. Pence on Hummingbird's test, Chris."

Chris eyes flew open. He was surprised that his role in Hummingbird's harassment had been so easily detected. Not only had the Veggie Crowd laughed at him, they were way too sharp. Pointing a finger at Rain, Chris said in a barely controlled voice, "If I catch that little runt Simon by himself, he's gonna wish he never came back to this rez—or ever knew you guys...." Then he turned quickly and stormed down the walkway.

Rain was shocked. In just a few minutes, Chris had gone from silly insults to real threats. Rain had always thought of Chris as just that stuck-up guy who lorded it over other kids. Now he wasn't so sure. He seemed like he really wanted to hurt somebody—namely Hummingbird and Simon. But why?

As Rain hurried past Dumptruck, he gave the big 8th grader a searching look that said 'What's with you?' Big D turned away confused and not a little scared. He and Tater had backed out on Chris. He dreaded the consequences. Dumptruck knew he had to find Tater Tot before Chris did.

Rain watched Dumptruck scurry away in the direction that the redheaded boy had fled. When Boomer stuck his head out the door and yelled, "Come on, RD!" he eagerly ran to join his friends. Entering the brightly lit band room, he was struck by the contrast between Chris's dark anger and the happy voices of the boys standing around the new drum. Rain didn't notice Joe coming over to offer him a drum stick. Of course, being lost in his thoughts was not out of character for Rain.

Joe waved his free hand in front of Rain's eyes. "Hey, RD, are you with us?"

Startled, Rain re-focused his eyes on Joe's kindly wrinkled face. Without any explanation for the unusual question, Rain asked, "Joe, in our language, what is the word for 'bully?'"

Chapter 6

"Well, um...Bird got in trouble in Mr. Pence's class." Looking from Darlene to Chick, she added, "Again."

Coyote Drumming

Hummingbird ran up the dirt path to her house, followed closely by Arianna. Because her mother, Darlene, only worked half days at the hospital on Fridays, Hummingbird knew she would be in the kitchen with Aunt Chick. Her aunt always brought over fresh vegetables from her garden on Friday afternoons. When she burst through the back door, the sight of her mother's soft, round face, flushed from the heat of the stove, immediately brought on the sobs Hummingbird had held back all day. The distraught girl hesitated then called out "Mother..." in a tiny wail. Darlene immediately knew something was wrong. Her daughter only called her 'mother,' instead of 'mom,' when something was wrong. Darlene quickly abandoned the onion she was chopping and wiped her hands on a dish cloth. Alarmed, she asked, "Bird, what is it"

Hummingbird ran to her mother and buried her head in her shoulder. Darlene, an inch shorter than her growing child, held her close with her with her short, sturdy arms. Aunt Chick, who had been stirring a bubbling vegetable stew, brought her big wooden spoon to a sudden stop. She repeated her sister's question, only louder: "What is it!"

When Hummingbird continued to cry, Arianna answered. "Well, um...she got in trouble in Mr. Pence's class." Looking from Darlene to Chick, she added, "Again."

Darlene guided her daughter into the living room, leaving Arianna and Chick to finish preparing supper. They sat down on the old blue and white afghan that had covered their couch ever since Hummingbird could remember. "So, what happened, Sweetie?"

Between sniffs, Hummingbird haltingly told her mother about the events in Mr. Pence's class. To comfort herself, she nervously picked at a frayed corner of the afghan. When she finished, Darlene sighed and said, "I told Mr. Pence when he called last week that you would be more careful. Now this, Bird. If you're trying to impress other kids by pulling these..." Darlene searched for the right word. "Pranks...or whatever you call them...then you're chasing after something this family doesn't approve of. We thought you loved science because you wanted to find ways it could help the people—not because it gave you a chance to show off."

Somewhere deep inside, Darlene had struck a nerve. But the young girl wasn't prepared to go there. "Mother, I do want to help the people. I just honestly don't know why I did what I did. I know I was wrong. But I'm just so scared that everything I've done for the science fair is for nothing! If I'm suspended, maybe I can't participate. And…and everybody is talking about me. Chris Sorrell is even trying to make Mr. Pence think bad things about me!" Squeezing her eyes shut, Hummingbird wailed, "Oh, nooo, Mom, now Richard and Dale will tease me—forever! (Richard and Dale were Bird's older brothers who went to Thunder Rock High School.)

"Bird, stop that. Richie and Dale aren't the problem here. Now, look at me. What has Chris Sorrell got to do with this?"

When Hummingbird explained about Chris's bullying and the note written on her test, Darlene was puzzled. "I don't know why he would do that. Are you sure he wrote it?"

"Not exactly. But he took the test."

"I'll talk to Miss Swallow. Don't worry—she knows you better than that. She'll set it right with Mr. Pence."

"Please, mother, when Mr. Pence calls, don't say anything about it unless he does. It's just so…embarrassing. Everybody is always talking about how he is always making goo-goo eyes at…"

The ringing of the phone suddenly interrupted Hummingbird's repeating the most popular grist in the school rumor mill. Aunt Chick called out, "For you Darlene. It's Mr. Pence!"

Hummingbird couldn't listen. She got up and ran to the security of the bedroom she shared with Arianna. Banging the door behind her, she leaned against it, eyes tightly shut. Hummingbird trusted her mother to help her, but she dreaded what Mr. Pence would say. Slowly, Hummingbird opened her eyes. There on the table in front of the window was her science project—a careful mapping of the areas where the Tribe's bison herd grazed and the plants that grew there. She had been working on it off and on since last summer. Now it was almost finished. The poster she had made of the reservation was actually quite pretty. Differently colored areas showed the presence of native and non-native plants, mostly grasses. Miss Swallow had suggested the project because the Tribe wanted to expand their native prairie land. The science teacher said controlling invasive plants that degrade native prairie habitat was critical to promoting healthy food for the bison, as well as protecting food and cover for wildlife.

Hummingbird walked to the table and picked up some dried samples of non-native plants she had collected—European buckthorn, crown vetch, and loosestrife. She wrapped them in clear plastic film and laid them beside the sample of native grasses she had collected for her exhibit. The rustling sound awoke her old cat, Scooter, who had been sleeping on the windowsill. He jumped on the table and sat down, watching her labeling the plant samples. Not so strangely, this simple activity calmed her down. As she finished the last sample, she heard a small knock at the door: "Bird?"

"Yes, Mom…?"

The door opened. When her mother said nothing, Hummingbird turned around. Darlene's face said it all. "Bird, Mr. Pence discussed the situation with the principal. They decided on an in-house suspension for three days next week."

Hummingbird simply absorbed that news and moved on to what she really cared about. In a quiet voice, she asked, "What about the science fair, Mom? Am I suspended when the science fair is going on?"

"Yes, I'm afraid so. But Daddy and I will talk to Mr. Berry, Sweetie. Maybe we can get him to delay the suspension ..."

Hummingbird slowly sat down on the bed. "When is Daddy coming home?"

"Sunday night."

Hummingbird said, "The science fair starts Monday morning, Mom."

Sympathetically, Darlene said, "I'm sorry, Bird. I wasn't thinking."

Hummingbird picked up Scooter and sat on the bed. She started thinking about her father. Daddy will be so excited when he gets home. He'll want to tell us all about the food sovereignty conference and the stuff that kids on other reservations are doing...and then Mom will say, 'Do you want to know what Hummingbird did?'

Sighing, she stroked Scooter's soft cheeks—his favorite thing. The cat pushed his head aggressively against her hand and purred. Suddenly, she kissed her old friend on the head and put him down. "Sorry, Scooter, but I have to finish my exhibit."

Darlene smiled. One thing you could say about her daughter—she wasn't a quitter.

By the time the boys left drum practice, it was getting dark. They stood in front of the school waiting for Gerald, Rain's father, to pick them up. Tonight, Boomer and Simon would be eating supper with Rain's family. Simon often ate dinner at Rain's house when his dad, Henry, a long-haul trucker, was on the road, and his mom, Ellen, a nurse, worked the night-shift at the hospital. The appetites of two more 12-year-olds would put no strain on the cooking pot. Extra plates were already being set for his mother's cousins and their kids who were visiting from another town on the reservation. Rain's mom, Roberta, liked cooking for a crowd.

Keeping an eye out for his dad's car headlights, Rain started singing the new song Joe had taught them. Boomer chimed in, then nudged Simon to sing with them. Simon smiled shyly and shook his head. Boomer suddenly called a halt. "Okay, Simon, I guess I'll just have to sing for both of us."

Rain clapped his hands over his ears. Laughing, he pleaded, "No, Boom, don't!"

Simon hollered, "I'll sing—I'll sing!"

Fixing his eye on Simon, Boomer started the song. Rain joined on the second round, and as promised, Simon sang, but only the chorus. Boomer smiled, "Hey, that wasn't half bad, Simon."

"Man, I could never sing like you, Boomer. You're great."

"That's why he is the lead singer for our drum," Rain said. Changing the subject, Rain laughed, "Wow, Boom, when you started singing the flag song—I thought I'd die! Did you see how fast that Tater guy ran off?"

"Yeah, he really freaked!" Then getting serious, Boomer asked, "So, are we gonna talk to somebody about Chris?"

"Yeah, our parents I guess," Rain said. He actually realized more than his friends that Chris wasn't to be taken lightly. "We could tell my dad about it."

"Good idea." Simon agreed. "I guess I should have told my mom and dad about Chris's brothers running me out of the rec center."

Just then, Rain's father pulled into the school driveway. As soon as the car stopped, the boys jerked open the car doors and piled in, chucking their backpacks where there wasn't a stack of papers or a box of reports. Gerald, the economic developer for the Tribe, was notorious for bringing home office work.

Turning to the boys who had somehow squeezed themselves into the back seat, Gerald asked, "How was drum practice?"

"Dad, you wouldn't believe the new drum!"

"Yeah," Boomer said excitedly, "this drum is gonna make people wanna dance!"

Eager to be part of the conversation, Simon added, "I could feel the 'boom' fill up my whole chest. Just like it was my heart beating."

Boomer looked over at Simon. Yeah, he thought to himself, that's what Joe says—it's the heartbeat.

"Dad, Joe did a tobacco blessing for the drum and taught us a new song, too. He says we got to start rehearsing more—for the Harvest Pow-Wow. I thought we could go out to the shed and practice some after supper."

Gerald was glad to hear the boys' enthusiasm. "I wish I'd known somebody like Joe when I was your age. Sure would have saved me a lot of catching up. The school I went to didn't offer Native Heritage." Fiddling with the dial on the car radio, Gerald followed up with the usual parent question. "So, what else happened at school today?"

The boys exchanged glances. "Well," Rain replied, "lots of stuff. Let's see. Hummingbird blew up her science class."

Gerald glanced in the rearview mirror at the boys. "You're kidding. Was anybody hurt?"

"No, but it made Chris Sorrel start acting like a real weirdo."

"Yeah," Boomer said, "he got this guy to throw a wad of hamburger at me in the lunchroom."

Simon figured he should get in his two cents, too. "Um... and Chris was real nasty to Hummingbird. He took a test of hers and wrote some stuff on it like Miss Swallow doesn't like Mr. Pence."

"Even though everybody knows he's in love with her," Boomer explained earnestly.

Confused, Gerald asked, "You mean Chris Sorrel loves Bird?"

"No, no! I didn't mean that!" Boomer protested. "It's Mr. Pence who likes..."

Finally finding the sports program he was looking for, Gerald interrupted, "Well, if it gets any worse than spitballs and love letters, let me know." He turned up the sound and started listening intently to the latest NFL football analysis.

Simon whispered, "Boy, did we sound lame."

"Yeah, lame," Rain admitted. When he had asked Joe about the word 'bully,' he had said he should talk to his parents if he knew that bullying was going on. Now, Rain realized that adult ears could process information in different ways than expected, especially if you didn't have their full attention. Next time he and his friends talked to grown-ups about Chris they would have to be a lot clearer.

As Gerald pulled the car to the back of the house, the porch light flicked on. He had not even opened the car door before Danny and Del, Rain's 5 year old twin brothers, and Margie, his little sister, came pushing through the screen door. Behind them, the yellow warmth of the kitchen framed the silhouettes of family—their outlines softened by steam from the stove's simmering pots. As was his habit every night, Rain hugged Margie and ruffled the twin's hair. Then he made an immediate detour to check what was cooking.

Boomer and Simon headed to the small living room, its only light coming from the TV screen. Simon switched on a lamp and flopped on the floor beside Granma's big brown recliner. Boomer made himself comfortable on the couch.

Hearing the unusual sound of a laugh track from the TV, he said, "Hey, look, the weather's not on. I didn't think she watched Gilligan's Island."

All regular visitors to Rain's house knew that his great-grandmother was an avid watcher of the Weather Channel. Grandma said that as she'd got older she'd learned the difference between the things she could do something about—and the things she couldn't. She said that wisdom lay somewhere between the two. Granma liked to say that people couldn't control the weather—the biggest reality show on TV—but they could learn to recognize storm sign and to make themselves ready. She wasn't much for fatalism.

Rain came in and joined Simon on the floor. "Mom's supper looks great. We're having chicken & wild rice soup. It's got carrots, celery and onions in it. And Mom's made her baking powder biscuits."

Boomer's voice awakened Granma from one of her little snoozes. "Oh, it's you boys," she smiled. "I must have dozed off." She fished around in her chair for the TV remote. "Rain, where's that clicker gone? How'd that show get on?"

"Here it is, Granma. On the floor."

"Switch it over to the local weather, honey. I want to see what tomorrow looks like. I got a big day. Joe's coming by to take me to the Senior Center."

"What's going on over there, Granma?" Rain asked.

Before answering, Granma pulled her sweater around her tiny, thin shoulders. "Well, us old folks are planning our own booth at the pow-wow. We're meeting to come up with ideas for making some money for the center. Joe thinks we could raise money by selling stories. A dollar each. Kinda like folks used to sell kisses at fairs." The image of herself selling kisses tickled Granma so much she started laughing at her own joke.

As always, her good humor drew the boys in. Simon thought the storytelling was a great idea. Joining Rain on the floor, he said, "Say, I bet people would pay more than a dollar to hear Delbert's story about the coyote and the cave. Not everybody's heard it."

Granma reached over to tousle Simon's head. "Just about the whole world's heard about it now, Simon."

Simon cast his eyes down guiltily. "Yeah, you got kidnapped because of me, Granma Hettie. If I hadn't told everybody that the Great Turtle was in the cave where the coyote took you and your brother, Delbert... well, then Vernon Smeed wouldn't have thought you could show him where the cave was."

"Well, don't you feel bad, Simon. It all turned out for the best. That fossil poacher got caught and didn't make a cent off the old turtle. And you were a brave boy—helping Rain to put her bones back."

Sitting up in her chair, Granma looked around at each of the three twelve year olds. Smiling, she said, "You boys did the right thing. You're all my heroes."

"Granma, um, we need some advice," Rain said. "About that 'right thing' stuff. There's a guy at school that's trying to bully Hummingbird and he was messing with us today, too. Did you ever get bullied at school?"

"I remember kids getting bullied. But nobody bothered me much. Not when Delbert was around. We really stuck together. That's my advice. Stick together. Friends can look out for each other." Frowning, Granma asked, "Did you say somebody's picking on Hummingbird?"

"Yeah, Chris Sorrel played a bad trick on her," Simon replied.

"Oh, my, I hope she tells her parents or her teachers. Some tricks aren't funny." Looking at the boys over her glasses, she added, "I think we've had enough tricks for a while, especially the coyote kind."

Rain thought, Hmm, yeah, but has the coyote had enough of us? He walked over to the small table in the corner where Roberta had set up her home computer. He logged on.

Roberta brought in the boy's plates. Seeing Rain standing in front of her old PC, Roberta said, "Now, you guys eat before you start playing with the computer. Rain, get that pitcher of ice water by the sink, okay?"

"Okay, Mom." Rain brought in the water and put it on the card table. Then, he watched Roberta help Granma to the kitchen where the rest of the family was already seated. Once they were alone, he turned on the computer. "Hey guys, come over here. I want you to see something."

Walking over to Rain, Simon said, "Do you think Granma will tell your mom and dad about Chris?"

"Yeah. They'll ask me about it, for sure." Laughing, he said, "I'll get the facts straight next time."

"Come on, RD," Boomer broke in impatiently, "Can we eat and look at what you want to show us? I'm hungry."

"Me, too," Simon agreed. While Boomer and Simon picked up the card table and shifted it next to the computer, Rain logged into email. Not waiting for their host, the boys tucked in. After swallowing all of his soup in three slurps, Boomer threatened, "If you don't want yours, RD, I'm gonna eat it!"

Grabbing his plate, Rain hollered, "No way!" He shoveled in some chicken and rice and tapped the computer screen. "Take a look at this picture."

The boys got up and crowded in next to Rain. Squinting his eyes at the image on the screen, Boomer asked, "What's that pink cloud?"

With his mouth full, Simon garbled, "Hold it! Oh, wow!" He coughed and swallowed. "It's the 'elephant's toothpaste!'"

Boomer hollered, "Oh, geez, is that Mr. Pence? This is so bad! Who sent this?"

"Sammie. She showed it to me at lunch."

"Oh yeah," Simon said, nodding his head. "Bird is definitely going to get suspended. It's huge! How did she do that?"

"Do you see anything weird about the picture?"

"The whole thing is weird, man," Boomer said.

"Look at the window." Sammie had taken a shot that captured the view outside the back windows of the school room. Simon pointed his finger to a fuzzy shape that appeared beside a bush about forty yards from the classroom trailer. "What's that?"

Boomer stretched out his neck for a better view. "Call me a dingfod, but it kinda looks like...a coyote?"

"Can't be, Boom, the eyes are too big," Simon said.

Rain agreed. "I thought it was a coyote, too. But, yeah, the eyes are too big. Let's try this." He zoomed in on the shape and began enlarging the frame. The pixels broke up into a jig-saw puzzle, but the mystery was solved. Rain and Simon looked at each other—speechless.

But Boomer, whose tongue was never tied, cried, "Binoculars. He's got a pair of binoculars…!"

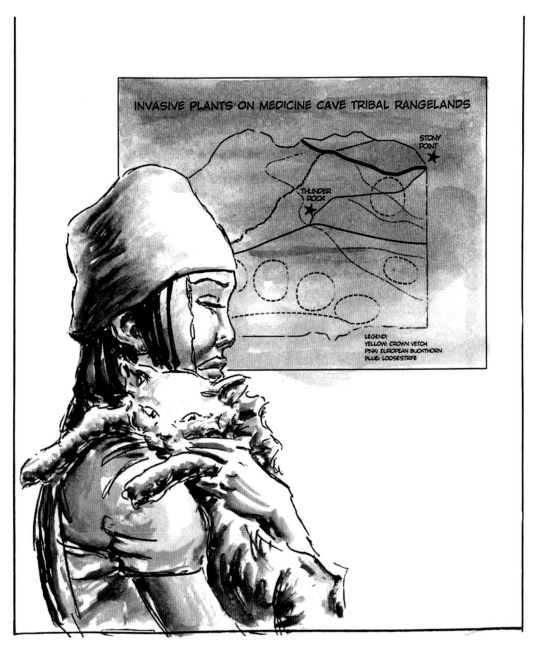

Sighing, she stroked Scooter's soft cheeks—his favorite thing. Suddenly, she kissed her old friend on the head and put him down. "Sorry, Scooter, but I have to finish my exhibit."

Chapter 7

Ramen noodles
Lunch meat
Box of macaroni & cheese mix
Grape soda
Canned sausages
Hot dogs
Chocolate Milk

Bird peeped into shopping carts and observed what was being bagged at the cash register. Several times she picked up discarded shopping lists and coupons.

Too Much and Not Enough

The next morning, Sky Heart watched the sun's rays pierce the dark blue sky, bringing a new day to the Medicine Cave Indian Reservation. From his perch high atop a tall pine, he saw the community, both human and animal, begin to awaken and stir. Thistle was among the early risers, having already done some voracious grazing before the sun came up. After all, she was eating for her unborn babies.

Sky Heart approved of the location she had chosen to build her nest. She was favoring an old brush pile overlooking a garden soon to be planted with winter vegetables. The pile of debris provided good cover and was surrounded by thick grasses. Noticing that she had finished her breakfast, the eagle glided downward to join her. "The eating is good here. May you produce many." he said, using an old formal greeting among the animals.

"Thank you, Sky Heart. Yes, it is a good place. That is Aunt Chick's garden down there. She's Hummingbird's aunt, you know." She paused for a moment to sample a bit of clover, but it was too mature and not to her liking. "So, tell me what happened yesterday at the school after I left."

Sky Heart described what he had seen in the school courtyard, paying special attention to Hummingbird's interaction with Mr. Pence. "There were a lot of emotions—sometimes laughing, but also fear and anger. I can see what they do, Thistle, but I need your ears to understand what is going on." He also expressed alarm about the disturbing behaviors he had witnessed after school: "Later, two boys took money from a small child, and then joined the boy, Chris, to start trouble with our young friends."

Thistle understood. "Just tell me where you want me to go. I will listen for us. It sounds like Coyote is working something big."

Hummingbird sat at the breakfast table—staring at the bowl of oatmeal. She had not slept well and kept rubbing her eyes. Although she was trying to be brave, the disappointed girl was not thinking positive thoughts. All she could think about was the gossip she had heard in the restroom—and the laughter in the cafeteria. Hummingbird had never been the butt of jokes before; nor had she ever been suspended.

Arianna noticed her friend's lack of appetite. She tried to think of something "perky" that would cheer her up. "Bird, I heard that Janie's mom is having one of those make-up parties at her house. We could go and get some of those little samples..."

Hummingbird picked a raisin out of the oatmeal with her spoon. She looked at the wrinkled brown fruit as if it were some kind of bug. Disgusted, she plunked the spoon in the cereal and pushed the bowl aside. "No, they probably wouldn't want the soap bomber to spoil the party."

Darlene, who had just come into the kitchen, overheard her daughter. "Well, I think that you girls should come to the store with me. Arianna, Rain's mom gave me some new recipes that are low carb. Check them out and see if it's stuff you would like. Then, what do you say we go over to Chick's and help her with her garden? I told her we might come over. It's a pretty day."

Arianna always liked to try out new recipes and was eager to go. The grocery store didn't have much appeal to Hummingbird, but she agreed to help her mother shop. Unenthusiastically, she pulled on her sweater and slumped to the car. The drive over to Medicine Cave Plaza wasn't far. Darlene always shopped at the tribally-owned retail center. She believed in a dollar being touched several times before it left the reservation.

By the time they arrived at the store, Arianna had thumbed through Roberta's recipes and had selected two which she gave to Darlene—a cherry tart with only 23 grams of carbohydrates and a chicken enchilada recipe with 26 grams. She was always thinking about carbohydrates. She paid attention to the simple ones like table sugar that enter the blood stream very quickly and raise blood glucose levels. She also was very aware of starches in foods like white bread that boost blood sugar levels almost as fast as table sugar. To keep an eye on her glucose levels, Arianna had to do several finger sticks a day. She had a little sticker that she used to prick her finger. After a drop of blood appeared she would put it on a special strip of paper and insert it into a blood glucose meter that fit in the palm of her hand. The meter had a small screen that displayed a number that told her how much glucose was in her blood. Arianna's blood sugar could vary-- from low to high. If it was high before lunch, she would eat a lower carb meal; if it was low when she got home from school, she would eat a higher carb snack. She had to work at keeping her body healthy all day long.

Arianna organized her shopping list carefully. She needed a variety of foods that would help to keep her blood sugar in proper balance. For snacks she loved crackers and part-skim milk cheese, all kinds of fruits (especially berries), and she was a big fan of celery and low-fat cream cheese.

While Arianna went in search of her favorite snacks, Hummingbird got a cart and followed her mother to the produce. They picked over the fruits and vegetables. Because the reservation was very rural, produce that wasn't in season or grown locally had to be trucked in. It was often expensive and not very fresh. Nevertheless, they found some decent bananas, oranges, and green peppers on sale.

Picking up a plastic bag of grapes, Hummingbird noticed a small boy staring into her shopping cart. She recognized him. It was Donny, one of the elementary school children who rode her bus. He looked up at her with a puzzled frown. "You've got a lot of stuff." Hummingbird looked back into the boy's big brown eyes. She just nodded and smiled. Feeling a bit guilty, she didn't know what to say.

"I like grapes," Donny said. Smiling, he reached into the fruit bin and picked up a large bag of grapes with both hands. He glanced over his shoulder at Hummingbird as he walked toward his mother, a harried young woman with a fussing toddler. She had no cart, only a hand basket that contained two loaves of day-old bread and some cartons of ramen noodles.

"Mom, can we get these?" the boy asked quietly.

"Put those back, Donny."

"But, Mom…"

"They cost too much. I've run out of food stamps. It's the end of the month."

"You got any WIC vouchers?"

She sighed, "Yes, but that's for formula. Nothing else."

The boy didn't beg. He replaced the fruit and tagged along with his mother to the baby food. Hummingbird abandoned her shopping and followed them. From a distance she watched to see if they would buy anything else. When Donny and his mother headed to the checkout, Hummingbird began to circulate throughout the store. She peeped into shopping carts and observed what was being bagged at the cash register. Several times she picked up discarded shopping lists and coupons.

Finally, Hummingbird sat down in an empty chair in front of the customer service desk. An idea—a big idea—was forming in her brain. Something wild—the ultimate "what if." Hummingbird was staring straight ahead when Darlene interrupted her churning thoughts. "Bird? We've been looking for you. Where did you go?"

"Mom, everybody's just eating starch, starch, starch... starch and sugar, starch and salt. Our families can't buy what they need! I've had it all wrong. I've got to find a way to speed it up. Not all this slow stuff!"

"Speed up what?"

"Growing vegetables! My science project is stupid. It'll take years for a healthy prairie to produce healthier meat for people! I've got to do something now!"

Exasperated, Darlene said, "Can we at least pay for the groceries first? Why don't you and Arianna wait for me outside?"

Hummingbird took Arianna by the hand. "Come on. You're going to have to help me with this. I can't do it by myself."

"Do what?"

"Grow *giant* vegetables. And grow them really fast!"

Chapter 8

Darlene saw the familiar look of determination that meant Bird's mind was made up. "Let's see what Chick says. Let's get what we need from the shed and head on over to her garden."

A Giant Plan

Darlene drove home to drop off the groceries before heading over to Aunt Chick's. She kept one eye on the road, while glancing repeatedly in the rearview mirror at the Hummingbird and the Arianna. The girls had their heads together, conferring quietly, but intensely. Words like "fertilizer," "compost," "irrigate" and "weeds" floated out of their conversation; and occasionally, Hummingbird made big round-shaped gestures with her arms. Darlene was sure that when they were ready, she would hear all about it. She didn't have to wait long.

After they had unloaded the car and put away the groceries, Darlene saw Hummingbird look at Arianna as if to say, 'okay, here goes.' "Mom, I...we...have a plan. Um, I'm going to keep right on with the science project. So, don't think I'm dropping that. But, I want to start a new project. My idea is to...ah... grow really big fruits and vegetables. If they're really big then they can feed everybody. There would be summer and winter vegetables—that way, we could have some all year round."

"Another project?" Darlene said doubtfully. "What kinds of vegetables?"

"I don't know yet. I promise I won't try to do it all by myself. I want to talk to Daddy about it. And Aunt Chick, too. I know that Rain, Boomer, and Simon will help."

"It will be my project, too, Aunt Darlene." Arianna said brightly.

Darlene was skeptical, but she didn't want to discourage Hummingbird's ambition to make her community a healthier place. She could see that the girls working together would be a good thing, too. There would be time for hard questions and reality checks later. "I'll talk to Daddy. I know he'll help. He's so proud of you. But, please, honey, don't think you girls have to solve all these food problems by yourselves. Daddy and the guys at the bison co-op have been really successful this year. And he's worked so hard on the Tribe's food sovereignty policy. That's all volunteer work and he's done it because of you, Bird." Glancing at her daughter, Darlene saw the familiar look of determination that meant Bird's mind was made up. "Well, we'll see what Chick says. Let's get what we need from the shed and head on over."

After loading the trunk with garden tools, Hummingbird enjoyed the short drive to Aunt Chick's. The road passed by green and yellow fields, edged by stands of red cedars and black locust trees. Hummingbird loved the eastern part of the reservation. Her family had ranched and done truck farming on this land for over a hundred years.

Bird spotted Aunt Chick sitting in the backyard when they drove up. She jumped out of the car, eager to recruit her aunt into the "giant plan." Leaving Arianna to wrestle with a shovel that had wedged in the trunk, Hummingbird grabbed a hoe and charged to the back of the house. Darlene followed, carrying a box of flower bulbs. Hummingbird was pleased to see her mother sit down in one of Chick's old metal lawn chairs. Good, she thought, we can talk before we get to work.

Thistle was snoozing in her nest when the chattering of human voices woke her. She had extremely sensitive hearing, although her ears drooped down instead of standing erect like a wild rabbit. This odd transformation had occurred many, many years ago when she had abandoned her homeland to follow the tribes to the west during the Great Removal. Since that time she had lived in many places and near many nations. Once a member of a powerful trickster family, she had abandoned their wily and joking ways. Now she was proud to live as an animal helper—mostly to children.

Yawning, Thistle sat up. She began "nose blinking," that funny wiggling of the nose that everyone imitates when they want to act like a rabbit. Her powerful sense of scent confirmed that people were visiting Aunt Chick. She squeezed from her nest enclosure and hopped on top of the brush pile. From that perch, she easily identified the visitors. Ah, she thought to herself, I can do some listening for Sky Heart.

Thistle bounced down the slope of the hill, following the patches of brushy cover. She halted when she reached a fence overgrown with wild privet that bordered Aunt Chick's backyard. Nestling in the camouflage, Thistle focused on the human's conversation.

———

Aunt Chick liked to be properly equipped before she started preparing one garden for its "winter sleep" and another for a winter crop. A great believer in electrical tape, glue, and never throwing anything away, she asked Hummingbird to repair some rusting spots on her old wheelbarrow. Pulling off a length of tape, Hummingbird launched her sales pitch. "Aunt Chick, what do you know about giant vegetables?"

"Nothing much, Bird. Just the giant pumpkins I've seen at the Harvest Pow-Wow. Those are some whoppers, aren't they?"

"Well, we're thinking of growing some. I thought you might let us use one of Grandpa's old garden plots—maybe the one with the red fence around it?"

"This isn't the time of the year to start growing a giant pumpkin, honey, or any kind of pumpkin. They're being harvested now."

"Oh, I know. I'm thinking of experimenting and getting ready for next year. So, um, the old shed might be perfect. You know, sprouting some seeds under a plant grow light; figuring out which seeds grow fastest. Then get a head start and set out some seedlings by April or May. Maybe Arianna and I could grow some winter vegetables, too."

"Grandpa ran an electrical line out to that shed years ago," Aunt Chick said. "He used it for a workshop one time. But the electric doesn't work anymore. It will get mighty cold in that shed without a heater."

"Boo could help us with the electricity," Bird said. "He's got tons of secondhand stuff in his garage. And RD, Boomer and Simon can till up the garden."

Aunt Chick looked at Darlene. "If she wants to work in the shed, it's fine by me. Those old cold frames next to the shed are in good shape. They keep the ground warm. Good enough for some mid-winter vegetables."

Bird jumped up. "Come on, Arianna, let's go over to RD's house and tell him about the 'giant plan!'"

"Hold on, girls," Darlene said, "there's work to be done here first."

Aunt Chick handed a rake to Hummingbird. "Come on, ladies. Let's do some cleaning."

Thistle popped open her eyes as the human voices began to fade. She peered through a crack in the fence and watched the women and two girls walking toward a recently harvested garden. Thistle knew that plot well. She recalled with relish the tasty treats that she had eaten there. Naturally, as a rabbit, she supported the idea of growing giant vegetables. However, she'd heard nothing that would explain the odd behavior Sky Heart had witnessed at the school the day before. Thistle was baffled. Sky Heart had said Hummingbird was upset. Upset? The girl was positively cheery! Thistle frowned. Have I missed something?

Chapter 9

Hummingbird ran on ahead and stood in front of the shed door, which hung on valiantly by a single hinge. She waited until the others joined her: "Well, guys, this is it."

Sheds and Gardens

After raking off the debris from Aunt Chick's vegetable patch, the girls took off. They followed the road for a short time, and then detoured along Salt Lick Creek until they came to the meadow near Rain's house. Arianna challenged Hummingbird to a race across the expanse of tall yellow grass. The girls ran— laughing too much for it to be a real race—until they crossed Old Schoolhouse Road and reached the gravel driveway of Rain's little blue house. They heard singing and drumming.

Running around to the backyard, the girls saw Rain and Boomer beating on an old wooden wire spool. Simon was lying on the ground listening. When Boomer saw them, he stopped and yelled, "How do you like our drum?"

Hummingbird was fast with the compliments. "You guys are sounding pretty good."

Pleased, Boomer said to Rain: "See I told you this old spool would work."

Jumping right in, Hummingbird said, "Um, guys, I know you're practicing right now. But I wanted to talk to you about this really great idea I had. I thought you might want to help." The boys looked at Bird like 'what now?' Glancing at Arianna for support, she said boldly, "I think we should experiment with growing giant vegetables."

"Who is we?" Rain wanted to know.

"All of us. Look, if we want to get people to eat more fruit and vegetables, then we've got to grow more of it. But not little stuff—I'm talking about big stuff. Giant fruits and vegetables. Then we could feed everybody. You know, it would be like a short cut?"

Rain was confused. "Isn't your science project about helping native grass grow better—so buffalo can graze on it and produce lean meat? That's about healthy food."

"Yes, of course, it is and it's important to Miss Swallow's Bison Project and the Bison Co-op. But it's so slow....It could take forever to re-create native prairies, RD!"

"How do you grow giant vegetables?" Simon asked. "Have you read up on it?"

Cheerily, Bird answered, "Not yet. I thought you could do that Simon!"

"Gee, thanks."

"Look," Bird continued, "Aunt Chick is giving us the shed. And the garden for next spring and summer."

Boomer, whose throat was dry from singing, sipped on a cup of water and said, "Well, it sounds kinda crazy, but…"

Rain interrupted. "What gave you the idea?"

"When I was looking in people's shopping carts at the grocery store. They're just eating junk! The good food costs too much." Bird stood up and crossed her arms. Fixing her friends with a firm stare, she declared, "And we are just sitting around doing nothing about it!"

Rain stared back and crossed his arms, too. "You wouldn't be trying to impress somebody, would you?"

Simon picked up on what Rain was saying. "Yeah, like Mr. Pence? Getting back on his good side after the big blow up."

Miffed, Hummingbird yelped, "What? I'm just doing like the eagle told us!"

Arianna gave Bird a funny look—a look that Simon didn't miss. He thought to himself, I bet she's wondering what Bird meant by that.

"This shouldn't be about how smart you are, Bird," Rain said quietly. "If we agree to this, it should be because we really believe in it…"

Bird was indignant. "Is that what you think I'm trying to do—show off?" Despite her protest, deep inside Bird was asking herself the same question. Is that what I am trying to do? Mom said almost the same thing…

"Yeah, it's perfect," Boomer laughed. "Mr. Pence would be a big dingfod for suspending the girl genius that grew the giant turnip!"

Irritated, Arianna asked, "Why are you picking on her?"

"It's okay, Arianna," Hummingbird sighed. "They're just keeping me honest." Thinking more deeply about her motives, she confessed, "Well, yeah, it is kinda like 'I'll show 'em' and 'won't they be sorry for suspending me.' It's not like I haven't thought of that. But…I really do want to do this. I felt so guilty at the store. We had stuff in our shopping cart and other people didn't."

Rain got up and laid his drum stick on the make-believe drum. "What do you say, guys? Are we with Arianna and Bird?"

"I am!" Boomer yelled. "I'm ready for something big around here—besides Chris Sorrel's mouth!"

"I guess I could substitute a few 'thunder vegetables' for 'thunder lizards,' Simon smiled. "But, just for a little while, of course."

"Then, take us to your shed!" Rain cried.

As the kids walked the short distance to Aunt Chick's, Simon pulled Rain back and whispered, "Should we tell Bird about the coyote and the binoculars?"

Rain glanced up ahead at Hummingbird. She was almost skipping she was so happy. "No, I think it would freak her out. Let's just be cool for a while."

Hummingbird turned around and yelled, "Hurry up, guys!" Rain and Boomer ran to catch up. Passing by Aunt Chick's house, Hummingbird pointed across a recently harvested field. "The shed's behind that red fence over there." The kids cut directly across the stubbly ground. Soon, they spotted the shed. It didn't appear that the fence had done a very good job of protecting it from the wind. The little building was a bit worse off than Hummingbird remembered it. Its unpainted wooden exterior was badly weathered, the roof sagged, and the two front windows were missing some panes.

Hummingbird ran on ahead and stood in front of the door, which hung on valiantly by a single hinge. She waited until the others joined her. "Well, guys, this is it."

"Looks kinda creepy," Boomer said. "What does it look like on the inside?" He tugged open the door and the kids entered, hopping over some tall weeds that clogged the doorway. Shafts of afternoon light slanted through the broken, dirty windows, dimly illuminating a small room. Leading the way in, Rain stepped gingerly around a clutter of rags and rotten cardboard boxes. Almost immediately, he bumped his head on an old cobweb-festooned light fixture that hung by a single cord from the ceiling. It swung crazily, spewing out a cloud of dust with each back and forth.

Pulling cobwebs out of his hair, Rain turned in a circle, quickly assessing the possibilities. "It's going to take some work."

Arianna nodded. "Yeah, the mice have been having a good time." Pointing at the droppings on the floor, she laughed, "There's your fertilizer, Bird."

Trying to be optimistic, Hummingbird smiled. "Yeah, all I have to do is sweep it up in a nice pile. Yuk! Well, at least, it's got lots of shelves. And there's a table."

Simon was carefully examining the walls and ceiling, looking for signs of water damage. "Doesn't look like there's many cracks and it's dry in here." Reaching up to check a shelf that was coming away from the wall, he suddenly brought down an avalanche of dust that enveloped him from head to toe. Fighting for air, Simon erupted into a coughing fit that sounded like a barking dog.

Boomer's face lit up. "Gee, Simon, when you laugh, you snort like a pig, and when you cough, you…"

Simon interrupted, "I know, I know," he laughed. "…bark like Scooby-Doo."

Rain grinned at Boomer. "Unless we want Simon to turn into a "were-dog," we better clean this place up."

"I need some air," Simon wheezed and hurried outside.

The kids followed him out into the clean afternoon sunshine. They fanned out, seeing what else the property had to offer. Happily, Rain found a water spigot that worked. (A godsend to Simon who cleared the dust from his throat with a cool drink). Arianna stumbled on a box of glass jars and old clay pots, and

Bird unearthed a half-buried roll of tough plastic sheeting. But they didn't find much else of use. However, moseying around to the back of the shed, Boomer made a major discovery. Looking to where the open ground rose toward a hill covered in small bushes and weeds, he spotted the wooden pole that had linked the shed to the utility pole on the road. "Yo, I found where the electricity line comes in!"

Unknown to Boomer the wooden pole lined up almost exactly with the location of Thistle's nest. He was actually staring directly at the rabbit, who was peering at him from a hole in her brush pile. With keen interest, she watched Boomer walk over to help Rain force open the garden gate. Then, as soon as the girls followed the boys to the garden, Thistle bounded down the hill—again. She found a convenient weed clump nearby and huddled there, listening intently.

The kids checked out the garden. Boomer started walking off one side of the fence, following a gravel path that separated the fence from the garden soil. Figuring that his foot was approximately 10 inches long, he calculated that it was a fifty feet on each side. Dismayed by the weeds and poor condition of the soil, Rain said, "Doesn't look like anything's grown here in a long time. Man, this needs some big-time tilling. My dad can bring over our tiller."

Arianna turned to Bird. "So what kinds of vegetables grow really big?"

"Um, I'm not sure. Cucumbers? Tomatoes?"

Boomer said, "The only giants I've ever seen are the big pumpkins at the pow-wow."

"I've seen those on TV. They're awesome! Are we gonna grow some of those?" Arianna asked.

Hummingbird smiled pleasantly. "Sure, why not.'

"Hey," Rain laughed, nudging Boomer, "you know who always wins the giant pumpkin growing contest at the Pow-Wow…"

Boomer let loose with his best "evil" cackle. "Heh-heh-heh. Sure. Chris Sorrel's family!"

"Oh, crud," Bird said, the smile dropping off her face. "I forgot about that."

Boomer was really tickled now. "If you win next year, Chris will really have it in for you. Then Dumptruck will have to throw rocks at me! I'll be a dingfod for sure then."

"Well, Chris will be laughing his head off when he finds out my suspension starts next week. I'm out of the science fair, guys."

Rain was stunned. "You didn't say it was next week!" He stared at her. She looked away and didn't meet his eye.

Rain and Simon hadn't entered the science fair this year. Simon had been more interested in building dinosaur models and Roberta had put her foot down, saying Rain didn't need any more responsibilities or activities—drum practice and basketball were enough. But Rain had helped Bird with her science project, mostly collecting plants. Hummingbird knew he cared about the project's success.

Feeling guilty, she said, "You know I'm keeping on with the science project."

"Well," Rain admitted, "the science fair isn't everything." He was disappointed that the school wouldn't see the project's messages about healthy environments and healthy people, but he didn't say anything. He didn't want Bird to feel too terrible. Then switching back to the subject of Chris, he said, "You all might as well know, Bird's not the only one Chris is trying to bully. He's after Simon, too."

Simon started to laugh. "Oh come on, RD. He was just saying stupid stuff last night. He wasn't serious."

"Yes, he was, too. After you left, he said you'd be sorry if he caught you by yourself."

"But why?"

Bird sighed. "Maybe it's because you're one of the Veggie Crowd...or the Soap Bomber's friend,"

"I know why. It's because I'm short—and he thinks he can push me around! I'm never going to grow!"

"I think he's jealous because you're smart—like Bird," Arianna said.

Rain thought, 'Veggie Crowd, jealous, smart, short, Bird's friend'—apparently there were lots of reasons why someone might become Chris's target. Resolving to buck up his friends' spirits, he repeated Granma's advice. He also added what Roberta and Gerald had told him after Granma had clued them in about the bullying. "Look, I think we should all stick together. Don't go running around by ourselves. Chris and his toadies won't bother us if we're tight. And if somebody tries to start something, just keep cool and don't get drawn into a fight." Involuntarily, he glanced at Arianna. Would "has type 1 diabetes" be on Chris's list of reasons to pick on a kid? Would she be next? Rain immediately cut off his thoughts. He just didn't want to go there. Little did he know that at that moment Chris was aiming at another target—but it wasn't Arianna.

Chapter 10

Mindy liked Chris's "bad boy" image. He was always full of surprises and never boring.
He had everybody snowed…

Coyote's Diagnosis

Coyote lay on his back in the grass not far from the gravel road that led to the Sorrel's house. Tired from his exertions, he snuggled into a comfy pile of straw and propped his head against a fence post. Thus positioned (with the handy pair of binoculars nearby), Coyote had a good view of the road and a nearby pasture. That morning he had woven into the pasture a complex network of over-lapping trails whose purpose only he understood. As he patiently waited for the one who would enter his web-like maze, he crooned a song a spider had taught him

Round, round—loop and twist (sticky-sticky)
Round, round—warp and weave (sticky-sticky)
Round, round—trap and trick (sticky-sticky)

Presently, a car drove up and stopped. A boy and girl got out from the backseat and waved to the teacher who had given them a lift. Coyote grinned. He picked up the binoculars and began to observe.

Chris set a fast pace to his house, leaving Mindy Two Horses on the road. She hurried to catch up with him. Puffing slightly, Mindy tried to make conversation. "That was nice of Mr. Braun to give us a ride." Chris didn't say anything, so she tried again. "Gee, Chris, none of the other guys at the carwash raised as much money for the newspaper as you did. You're sure to get editor." She glanced at him to see if he appreciated the flattery she'd been heaping on him all afternoon. Unfortunately, a preoccupied smile on his face told her that he wasn't listening. Mindy thought, Okay, time to be shameless. "Oh, Chris, I can't wait to see your science project! Thanks for showing it to me. I know you'll win first prize."

"What? Oh, yeah. I plan on it. You'll be impressed by my exhibit. I've got it set up in Mom's workroom."

Mindy smiled. Success! She liked Chris's "bad boy" image. He was always full of surprises and never boring. Nobody knew him like Mindy. He had everybody snowed—the teachers most of all. Chris was always so polite, but she knew they couldn't control him. His favorite saying was, "nobody tells me what to do." What Mindy really liked was that other kids did what he told them to. Nobody ever pushed him around—he did the pushing. She had to admit to herself that Chris could be mean, and he was so conceited that it *was* a little creepy. Well, maybe more than a little… but it was worth it. Mindy liked the sense of power she felt when she was around him.

"So, Mindy, we really jerked Hummingbird around last week," Chris said, laughing.

"Oh, yes! That was so funny!"

"You know, I think it's time we told everybody the truth about the Veggie Crowd."

"The truth?"

Chris and Mindy didn't know it, but they were approaching the part of the road where Coyote had laid down his first trail. In anticipation of what was to come, the trickster stood up. He began to watch more attentively.

"Yeah, the truth. RD made up the story about his Granma following a coyote to a cave full of bones. I was there when…" Suddenly, Chris couldn't finish his sentence. Even worse, his head abruptly started to vibrate like a tuning fork. Chris grasped his head in his hands, but he couldn't stop the rapid shuddering or the slow twisting of his head to the left. When his head stopped turning, his whole body rotated so that he was facing forward. Then, he began to march, robot-like, off the road.

Mindy watched Chris wading into the high grass. Mystified, she followed him. "Chris! Where are you going? I thought we were going to your house." When he didn't answer, Mindy got annoyed. "Chris…Chris!"

Turning his head stiffly toward her, his eyes wide with terror, Chris found his tongue: "I don't know where I'm going! I can't stop!" But just as he said he couldn't stop—he did stop. He stood rigidly at attention for several seconds—and then took off! He began running first in one direction and then the other—making a big zigzag across the pasture.

Once he reached the other side, Chris began to run in circles that got bigger and bigger until he bumped into the fence that enclosed the Sorrel's horse corral. Two young horses standing nearby spooked and dashed off to join an old mare drinking from a water trough. The old one raised her head and regarded the boy. Not liking what she saw, she led the youngsters to the other side of corral, where all three horses watched him warily.

Chris held onto the fence for a moment. Then, without warning, he flung himself into another charge—but backwards this time! Mindy stood with her mouth open, staring at this bizarre sight. Alarmed, she saw that he was now retracing his steps to where she was standing. As he drew nearer, she could hear Chris panting, "Loop! Warp! Trick! Sticky! Sticky!"

Before he got any closer, Mindy started to run, too. Coyote laughed as she dumped her backpack and doubled down on her speed. The last he saw of her, she was disappearing down the blacktop, headed in the direction of Thunder Rock. Turning his attention back to Chris, he saw that the boy was now standing in the middle of the gravel pathway where his journey had begun.

Dr. Coyote sat back down on his straw couch, intertwined his fingers behind his head, and considered the evidence. He replayed Chris's actions in his head—creating a mental map of the boy's performance. Then he analyzed it, starting at the end and working to the beginning like a true trickster.

First, he examined the backwards running. Coyote knew that a straight forward path lay within the trails he had laid down. That path led to respect, harmony, and sharing. It was immediately clear that was not the path Chris had taken. For most people, when they did something backwards they knew that it was the wrong way. Or as Coyote preferred to think of it, an unexpected way that would make people laugh or help them to think in a different manner. But for Chris, the backwards route reversed respect into disrespect, harmony into jealousy, and sharing into "always having to win." Ahh, yes, Coyote thought, 'warp and twist' is right.

Next, he looked at Chris's circling patterns. Even Coyote struggled a bit with the meaning of it. Usually a circle indicated something whole, open, and complete. But, after much flea scratching and pulling at his whiskers, Coyote saw that Chris's spirals were not truly circles, but the loops of snares that trapped the boy. Apparently, the snares had been woven and set by members of his own family—some consciously and others unconsciously.

Finally, he studied the zigzagging. It was obvious that it was a lightning bolt. So, Coyote thought, there is some possibility for change—an unexpected adjustment so to speak. Lightning, the trickster knew, had the power to shock Chris—to transform him from what he was now to what he could be. Coyote stared at the captain of the Thunderbird's basketball team. To himself, he said, "Hmmm, so lightning frees a Thunderbird." The father of clowns laughed. So many twists in this maze! So many surprises!

Remembering, he turned and looked toward Red Water Mountain. Raising the binoculars to his eyes, he smiled in delight as its crags and peaks drew close to him. Only he and Sky Heart knew that thunderbirds once nested there. Only the Trickster and the Great Messenger knew the real origins of Thunder Rock. But that was a very, very old story.

Chapter 11

FORUM: Student Behavior

September 27

Need some help—what would you do?
Posted by Popcorn32

I'm sure that most teachers in our district read in the newspaper about two boys at my school who supposedly broke up a fossil poaching operation on the Medicine Cave Indian Reservation. The story in the paper said that one of those boys got the fossil poachers arrested and saved his great-grandmother from them at the same time. Well, I am sorry to say that I don't believe their story and I have good reason.
I am the newspaper advisor at Thunder Rock Middle School. One of those boys wrote up an interview with his grandmother, saying that that when she and her brother were little kids they discovered an old cave that had dinosaur bones in it. We printed the interview in our school newspaper. You can imagine how shocked I was when one of his friends came to my class and

Chris's jealousy provided him all the justification he needed to punch "enter" and launch his cyber attack.

The Poisoned Apple

Coyote released Chris from his power. The boy awoke with no conscious knowledge of what had happened. He tried to pick up his sentence where he left off, but he was a little fuzzy. He strained to remember what he was talking about. Suddenly, the memory flooded in—the Veggie Crowd! Jubilantly, he smirked, "Oh, yeah! I was there when Boomer told Mrs. Corn they made up the whole story." Pausing to let this information sink in, he added: "Let's spread it around that RD is a fake." Anticipating her enthusiasm, Chris glanced to where Mindy should have been standing. But she wasn't there. Chris twirled around. Where did she go?

"Mindy!" He called out her name again, but there was no answer. Disappointment flickered over Chris's face. He thought that the girl liked him. Shoulders hunched, with hands in his pockets, Chris began to trudge up the road to his house. As he walked, he became angrier with each step. By the time he reached the back door, Chris was furious with Mindy for dissing him.

He flung open the door, stormed past his mother, and ran down to the basement workroom. Her reprimand, shouted from the top of the stairs, just made him angrier. So what if he'd almost run her down? So what if he didn't say 'Hello.' What did she care? All she thought about was her mail-order business.

Chris dumped his backpack and immediately went to check out his science project. The exhibit, now finished, was undisturbed. Not like last week when Melvin and Jesse had stolen three rubber balls that were part of his three-panel display. Althea, his mom, had made them return the balls, but his stepfather had said nothing. Chris twisted his mouth bitterly. *They* get away with everything.

Chris reached out and carefully adjusted the text posters. Everything was ready for tomorrow—the first day of the science fair. The posters described how he had produced the rubber balls from the sap of a small potted rubber tree and the juice of morning glory vines that grew on an old fence near his house. The rubber, he thought proudly, was just like the stuff the Olmecs had made 3,000 years ago! Chris stood back so he could also see the full effect of the Maya ball court and players shown in the center panel. He had placed the white balls so that they seemed to be emerging from the picture. It was so cool! He loved his exhibit!

Chris had labored over the project for this year's Native Science theme. He'd spent hours drawing the illustrations of the rubber making process. But he never let anyone see how hard he worked. It wasn't part of his image.

Smiling, he fantasized about how proud his family would be when he won the science fair. But the smile quickly faded, to be replaced by the tight-lipped expression he usually wore when at home. His stepdad didn't care about him, he thought. Nothing would ever be good enough. His mood turning hostile, Chris slid into a chair and popped open the laptop on the card table where he did his homework. Pulling a notebook from his pocket, he flipped to the page where he had jotted down Mrs. Corn's password to a local message board for teachers. Peeping over shoulders while delivering messages for the school office came in handy at times.

He logged onto the computer and went to a popular site called "Apple for the Teacher" that was managed by the local school board. Entering Mrs. Corn's school email address and the password Popcorn32, Chris began his masquerade. Clicking on a forum about 'student behavior,' he pretended to be Mrs. Corn describing how Boomer had told her that RD's interview with Granma was phony. Then he typed, "Maybe Rain's saving his great-grandmother from a fossil poacher was all made up, too!" Giggling, he added: "What should I do? I feel so guilty not reporting my doubts. Maybe some innocent people have been sent to jail! All advice is appreciated."

Chris remembered the smiling photos of RD and Simon with their families ("Local Boys Foil Fossil Poachers") in the reservation newspaper. His jealousy provided him all the justification he needed to punch "enter" and launch the cyber attack.

Mrs. Corn marched across the parking lot, a box of *The Thunderbird* held proudly in front of her. She sniffed appreciatively. The language arts teacher loved the inky smell of fresh newsprint. Bustling into the school office, she glanced at the clock and signed "7:45" under the Monday column in the attendance ledger. Next, she bestowed a school newspaper on Louise Shield, the secretary, and then began to shove copies into the teachers' mailboxes. Working her way down the alphabet, she bumped into Mr. Pence at the P's.

"Good morning, Mr. Pence. Would you like a copy of *The Thunderbird?* It's hot off the press!" Without waiting for a reply, she thrust the paper in his direction and moved on to the R's.

"Oh, thank you, Mrs. Corn." Wiping his nose with a tissue, he added, "Um...I just wanted to say that I understand your dilemma, but I'm sure there is an explanation. Rain and Simon seem like honest boys."

Mrs. Corn gave Mr. Pence a puzzled look. What is he going on about? Turning suddenly, she almost ran into Miss Otter. The 6th grade math teacher was looking at her sympathetically. "Oh yes, Mrs. Corn, I'm sure the Tribal police can confirm that the kidnapping really happened."

At the mention of the word, "kidnapping," the two student office aides pricked up their ears. When Mr. Berry opened his door and asked Mrs. Corn to step in, their ears stood up even higher. Something was going on! By 8:00 the office was filled with faculty. The few teachers who had visited "Apple for the Teacher" soon had the whole room buzzing. The loud whispering suddenly halted when a muffled shriek was heard behind the closed door of the principal's office. "What! What! I never, Mr. Berry!" In the silence that followed, the listeners strained to hear more of Mrs. Corn's indignant protest.

Without warning, Mr. Berry flung open the door and asked a student aide to notify Boomer's homeroom teacher that he should report to the office. He stared at the teachers and barked, "Well, don't we have some teaching to do today?" Looking everywhere but at the principal, the embarrassed crowd quickly dispersed. As teachers headed for their classrooms and office aides delivered their messages, a thick cloud of gossip began to form over the school. Had the fossil poaching ring been a hoax? Were Rain and Simon's families in on it?

Boomer hadn't been at school five minutes before he was sitting in the hot-seat across from Mr. Berry. As the principal listened, he retold Granma's story about a cave full of bones. Rain, Boomer explained, didn't know that the story would be printed in the school newspaper. He was afraid that the fossil poacher, Vernon Smeed, would read the story and go after his Granma. Boomer looked apologetically at Mrs. Corn. "The interview was true. But I figured that you'd give us a pass to round up all the papers if you thought it was bogus. I'm sorry."

"That's okay, Boomer. I didn't give it another thought after we found out about the fossil poacher." Turning to Mr. Berry, she said, "Boomer may have been a bit misguided, but his intentions were good.*"

Mr. Berry took off his glasses and rubbed his forehead. Leaning across his desk, he asked Mrs. Corn, "Who else was in the newspaper room besides Boomer that morning?"

"Some members of the newspaper staff," Mrs. Corn replied.

"Then, someone on your staff started this rumor."

Mrs. Corn looked shocked, but only nodded.

Mr. Berry said, "I'll make an announcement during homeroom tomorrow. I want this rumor stopped dead in its tracks. Mrs. Corn, I need a list of your newspaper staff."

---

*Note: As the reader can see, Coyote's tricks can cause mischief long after they have been played. Indeed, some tricks may have no expiration date at all.

Chris stood back so he could see the full effect of the Maya ball court and the players shown in the center panel. He had placed the white rubber balls so that they seemed to be emerging from the picture. It was so cool!

Chapter 12

"David, I just saw Chris Sorrel and two boys go over behind the air conditioner. Could you check them out?"

Bullies R Us

Chris rushed into the noisy gymnasium, lugging a box and a big flat folder that held his posters. Everybody was setting up their exhibits and he was late. He searched the rows of tables until he found the numbered space reserved for his entry. Skirting around other students carrying an assortment of plants, posters, and papier mâché models, Chris made his way to Exhibit #10. Hurriedly, he assembled his table-top display. He was positioning his samples of latex and the rubber balls when Sammie looked over from a neighboring exhibit.

"Wow, Chris. That's awesome."

Chris nodded. "Yeah."

Sammie had stepped behind Chris to see his posters better, when Star and Little Deb ran up. To be polite, they briefly admired Chris's exhibit, then excitedly drew Sammie aside. Big-eyed, Little Deb said, "Have you heard?"

"Heard what?"

"About all that stuff in the newspaper that said RD fought a fossil poacher and saved his Granma. It was a big lie. They're saying that it was really RD's father that was stealing the bones."

Chris's hands suddenly halted their busy activity.

"No way! You're kidding!"

"No really. Mrs. Corn said it's true!"

"Come on," said Sammie excitedly, "let's find Hummingbird! She'll know what's going on."

Whistling happily, Chris resumed arranging his exhibit. Yes, tomorrow would be the big day. The award ceremony was scheduled for first period. Chris closed his eyes, blissfully imagining his triumph. He smiled—for many reasons.

The girls headed for the drive at the front of the school. While they waited for Hummingbird's bus, Sammie dug as much information out of Star and Little Deb as she could. Most of it was nonsense from the "gossip virus" that was spreading like wildfire through the school.

When Hummingbird's bus finally pulled in, the girls ran to the curb. As the kids unloaded, they could hear the name "Arianna" and the word "pump" being repeated over and over amidst the usual chatter. Bird and Arianna were the last to get off the bus. Oddly, a muffled dinging sound seemed to be emanating from inside Arianna's pocket.

"What's that noise? A cell phone?" Star asked.

"No," Arianna said wearily as if she had already explained it a thousand times. "It's my insulin pump. I have type 1 diabetes. The alarm went off and I can't make it stop. It means I have a low battery."

Sammie said, "Oh, your insulin pump," like she knew what one was.

"Come on," Bird said to Arianna. "Let's go to the office and call Mom. She'll bring over a new battery." Looking at their welcoming committee, Bird asked, "Were you waiting for us?"

"Uh, yeah," said Sammie. "We'll go with you. We've got something to ask you."

The girls hurried to the office accompanied by the nonstop complaining of the pump alarm. Fortunately the office phone wasn't in use. Bird called her mother. Darlene said she would be at the school in a few minutes. Bird explained Arianna's situation to Miss Shield, and they took a seat in the waiting area. Reluctantly, Little Deb and Star said they had to get to homeroom, but Sammie didn't seem to be in a hurry. She leaned over and said something that Arianna couldn't hear. Hummingbird turned and looked at Sammie, her mouth open.

Just then, Rain and Simon walked into the office. Simon nudged Rain and pointed at the girls. Surprised, Rain whispered, "What are you guys doing here?" But before anybody could say anything, the secretary announced the boys' arrival. Rain shrugged his shoulders as he and Simon were herded into the principal's inner sanctum.

The soft 'ding-ding' of the pump filled the silence. Finally, Arianna asked quietly, "Are they in trouble?"

A bewildered look on her face, Hummingbird said, "Let Sammie tell it." Sammie started re-hashing every bit of rumor she had heard. Most of it was about Rain faking Granma Hettie's rescue from the fossil poacher.

Arianna quickly got fed up with all the baloney. "Just stop, Sammie! None of that is true. I was at the house. The fossil poacher tied up Aunt Sissy and took Granma Hettie. Margie, his little sister, saw everything."

Hummingbird was about to add her two cents when Chris Sorrel walked in. He gave the girls a dismissive look as he sauntered up to the counter. Plopping two extension cords on top of the "IN" box, he said to the student office aide, "Floyd said they don't need these in the gym. They got enough." Chris leaned against the counter, and coolly re-directed his attention to Arianna. "Why don't you answer that call?"

"It's not a ring tone, Chris," Sammie answered self-importantly. "It's the alarm on her insulin pump, if you'd like to know!"

Chris pretended to ignore her reply. Smiling, he said, "Sammie, did you tell them about my awesome science exhibit?"

Hummingbird's response was frosty. "We weren't talking about you, Chris."

The homeroom bell suddenly rang, terminating their conversation. "Sorry, I gotta get to class," he said, as if he were prematurely ending a friendly chat. He started to leave, then turned around and added spitefully, "I guess you better report to in-house suspension, Hummingbird, or you might get a detention for being late."

Sammie watched Chris wave "tootle-oo" as he disappeared into the moving crowd in the hallway. Looking at Hummingbird, she said, "I forgot you were suspended."

"Well, I haven't forgotten," Bird sighed.

One would have thought that the cyber attack was bullying enough for one day. But, the success of the "poisoned apple" he had sent to Mrs. Corn emboldened Chris. Between homeroom and the end of third period, he'd devised another scheme. He couldn't thank Sammie enough for the idea. Mustering his toad squad outside at lunchtime, Chris was, however, having a hard time getting across his plan.

"But why call her Miss Ding-Ding?" Dumptruck argued. "How about Miss Ding-Dong or Miss Dum-Dum? That's funnier."

"I'm not trying to make Arianna *laugh!* It's the sound her pump…Oh, forget it. It's about showing the Veggie Crowd they can't laugh at me—at us, I mean."

Tater Tot, only half listening, was busy probing the mystery meat in the sandwich his mom had packed for lunch. He looked up at Chris and frowned: "How does yelling Miss Ping-Ping make them not laugh at us?"

"Not ping! Ding! Ding!" Chris shouted. Exasperated, he switched targets. "So what's going on with Simon? He's walking around here like he owns the place."

"I stepped on his heels yesterday," Tater offered. "It must've hurt."

Dumptruck giggled, "Yeah, but when he turned around, you said, 'Excuse me.'"

"So what did *you* do that was so great?" Tater challenged.

"I thought up this great name for Simon 'cause he's so little." Dumptruck started giggling agin. "I called him "Gnat-Boy!"

Chris was impressed. "That's pretty good. What did he say?"

"Man, Simon's so funny. He told me to 'bug off!' Get it? Gnats are bugs?" Dumptruck cracked up. "Then, he said, 'Get out of my way, I'm having lunch with a spider!'"

"You fell for that?" Chris yelled. "You guys are totally worthless!"

"We can't do anything to Simon!" Tater protested. "He's always with somebody. He's never out of Boomer's shadow. All of those guys stick together like glue."

"And the teachers are telling kids to snitch if they see anybody picking on people," Dumptruck complained.

"Well, we'll just wait until there's no little snitches around! I'll meet you back here in fifteen minutes. Watch for Arianna."

Chris cut across the courtyard and slipped into a side entrance to the gym. Making sure that no one was around, he bounded up a short flight of stairs to a second tier of seats that looked down on the gymnasium. The upper level of the gym was deserted. Down below he saw a small group of teachers filing out the gym entrance. "They finished the judging!" he murmured to himself. Bending over, he scurried quickly to the side of the gym where he could see his exhibit. Peeping over the seats, he ran his eyes down Row 2, until he spotted Exhibit #10.

Chris sharply drew in his breath. There it was! The blue ribbon! He stared unblinking at the award. It was beautiful! A blue sun had replaced the yellow one that illuminated the Maya ball players. The new sun's ribbon rays fanned downwards proclaiming "First Prize" in gold letters.

Worried that he would be discovered, Chris did not linger to savor his victory. He made a fast getaway by the same route that he had entered the gym. His head full of triumph, Chris wanted desperately to share his success with someone. He thought of Mindy, but dismissed it. She was still avoiding him.

Pumped up by his win, he ran back to get Dumptruck and Tater Tot. Chris couldn't believe how everything was turning out the way he'd planned!

Miss Swallow was usually not in the cafeteria or the courtyard during first lunch. But today, her class was in another classroom watching a film. So, she was available to fill in for an absent teacher. She was walking slowly across the grass, keeping a casual eye on the milling students, when she spotted Chris pushing two other boys behind the library air conditioning unit. She wondered what he was up to. The boys didn't appear to be part of his usual "crowd."

She strolled over to Mr. Pence who was also on lunch duty. Buttoning up his jacket, he said, "This wind is chilly, don't you think?"

"Yeah, it is a bit cool. Ah, David, I just saw Chris Sorrel and two boys go over behind the air conditioner. Could you check them out?"

Obliging, Mr. Pence walked to a point where he could see behind the large metal box. The boys were leaning up against the wall. It was apparent that Chris was watching someone. Following his line of sight, Mr. Pence saw Arianna—who was walking alone toward the library. When she entered the covered library walkway with its brick lattice walls, Chris shoved the boys, hoodies pulled over their heads, toward her. When they hesitated, he balled up his fist and gestured aggressively. Reluctantly, they backed up, and then ran toward the defenseless girl.

Realizing that something was about to happen, Mr. Pence also began to run toward Arianna. He signaled to Miss Swallow to get moving, too. They saw one of the boys dart behind the concealing brick lattice, shouting some "dinging" nonsense.

The other boy slipped and fell, but jumped up and started waving his arms, hollering "Ding! Dong! Ding! Dong! Ding! Dong!"

When Mr. Pence and Miss Swallow converged at the walkway, they could see the two boys circling a paralyzed Arianna, yelling in her face. Caught by the alert teachers, the assailants abruptly choked off the dinging and donging. Now instead of one frightened student, there were three. Dumptruck and Tater Tot backed away from Arianna. Wide-eyed and saying nothing, they nodded timidly when Mr. Pence ordered them to get to the principal's office. Both Mr. Pence and the boys flashed a look toward Chris's hiding place, but he was gone. Dumptruck and Tater Tot were on their own.

Miss Swallow gently put her arm around Arianna and ushered her through the library door. Glancing over her shoulder, the stricken girl saw Mr. Pence leading the two culprits away. Like many children, Arianna's first thought was 'What did I do to them?' Miss Swallow took Arianna to a nearby table. Very softly, she said, "Just take a deep breath, sweetie. It's over."

Wiping away a tear with the back of her hand, Arianna said, "I don't understand, Miss Swallow. They were making fun of the sound my insulin pump makes. It was only a low battery. Why are they making such a big deal about it? It's because I have type 1 diabetes, isn't it?"

"No, Arianna. What just happened didn't have anything to do with your having type 1 diabetes. Thunder Rock has a lot of people with the type 2 kind of diabetes—even some very young people. We'll get to the bottom of it. In the meantime, I don't want you to worry."

"Do you think they were picking on me—for the same reason they tried to pick on Simon and Boomer?"

"They've done things to Simon and Boomer, too?

"Yes, Dumptruck threw a hamburger at Boomer. And they called Simon names."

"Maybe they are picking on you for the same reason. We'll just have to figure out what that reason is," the teacher said. "Are you sure you're going to be okay?"

"Sure, Miss Swallow," Arianna smiled. "I'm tough. Just write me a note to Miss Otter's class. I'm late."

Chapter 13

"I have a theory, Mr. Berry. But first, here is the list of newspaper staff I promised. I think there's only one name of interest."

Toads and Targets

Miss Swallow left Arianna in Miss Otter's good hands and headed directly to Mrs. Corn's class. She had heard the rumors about the posting on "Apple for the Teacher" and felt that Mrs. Corn should hear about the most recent bullying incident.

Miss Swallow knocked on the doorjamb of Mrs. Corn classroom. The language teacher was giving a test and motioned for her to come in. They went to a corner of the room and talked quietly. Miss Swallow described what had just happened in front of the library, and Mrs. Corn shared the information she had just discovered in her newspaper planner. Satisfied that they both had identified the master manipulator behind much of the bullying at the school, the two teachers agreed to share their conclusions with Mr. Berry.

After the bell rang and she dismissed her class, Mrs. Corn shoved her new evidence into a manila folder and dashed to the school office. It was her planning period. She had time to talk to Mr. Berry and run off the test copies she needed for her 5th period class. She passed by the usual number of mischief-makers that sat slumped in plastic office chairs, waiting for their turn with the principal. Mrs. Corn spotted Dumptruck and Tater Tot, the guilty party in the "ding-ding" attack. She wondered if Mr. Berry had talked to them yet.

Eager to find out, she leaned over the counter and asked Miss Shield, "Is Mr. Berry free?"

Without interrupting her typing, the secretary said, "Go right in, Mrs. Corn. Everybody else has."

Mrs. Corn poked her head into the principal's office. Mr. Berry, who was on the phone, waved her to a seat. She sat down quietly.

"Yes, I understand. Miss Swallow told me about the threat Chris made against Hummingbird."

Mrs. Corn eyes flew open. She scooted to the edge of her chair.

As he nodded and "uh-huhed," the principal noticed Mrs. Corn's agitation. He mouthed, "What is it?"

Mrs. Corn scribbled on a scratch pad and handed it to the principal. He quickly read the note. "Well, I appreciate your calling. In fact, I'm glad you did. We've…uh… had an incident at lunch today. It involved Arianna, but she's just fine." Putting his hand over the phone, Mr. Berry whispered, "She is okay, isn't she?"

Mrs. Corn nodded. "Yes, Miss Swallow handled it."

"Mrs. Corn is here now to fill me in. We think it was some kind of bullying." Mr. Berry paused. "I agree. There's something going on." Sweating, he wiped his forehead with a tissue. "Yes, we'll get to the bottom of it. We want parents and guardians fully involved. I'll keep in touch." After a few pleasantries and more reassurances, the principal rang off.

Mr. Berry gave the teacher a cheerless look. "So what did you find out?"

"I have a theory, Mr. Berry. But first, here is the list of newspaper staff I promised. I think there's only one name of interest."

Glancing at the list, the principal saw the name "Chris Sorrel" circled in red. Intrigued, he said softly, "Tell me about your theory, Mrs. Corn."

Mrs. Corn explained how she had pulled up her staff assignments for the first edition of the school newspaper. Chris Sorrel and Hank LaChaise had been assigned to distributing *The Thunderbird* in the lunchroom on the day in question. She remembered letting them into the newspaper room to pick up the stacks. That was when Boomer had showed up claiming that he had to round up the papers distributed off-campus. Concluding, Mrs. Corn said, "So, as you can see, Mr. Berry, Chris was only one of two students who could have heard Boomer say that the interview was a fake."

"But Mrs. Corn," the principal pointed out, "what if Chris or Hank told other students what Boomer said. Any one of them could have impersonated you on the 'Apple for the Teacher' website. I agree, however, that it is very suspicious."

"Be that as it may, Mr. Berry," she countered, "there are other reasons to suspect Chris. I don't think the phony blog was about me at all—just a way to get at Rain and Simon. Miss Swallow told me that Chris had harassed Hummingbird, and that Mr. Pence saw him instigating the incident against Arianna."

Mr. Berry was surprised. "Really? I didn't realize Chris was involved in that."

"Oh, yes." Mrs. Corn described what Mr. Pence saw and gave details about the "dinging" and Arianna's insulin pump.

"Well, then, I'd better talk to the two young men cooling their heels outside my office. I'll let you know what I find out."

Mr. Berry talked to Dumptruck and Tater Tot for almost fifteen minutes. Both boys were scared and clammed up almost immediately. The principal was a gentle man—never threatening. He could usually win a student's trust pretty quickly. But he wasn't successful this time. When asked if Chris had anything to do with their harassing Arianna, the boys just looked away and said, "No." They had no motivation and were clueless about the connection to the insulin pump. Mr. Berry believed everything they said, except their denial that Chris was involved. An astute judge of children's character and emotions, the principal recognized he wasn't talking to "bad guys," just scared ones. He gave them two days of detention and required each of them to write Arianna an apology.

Stepping out to Miss Shield's desk, he asked her to send a message to Miss Swallow and Mr. Pence to come by his office after school.

Mr. Berry glanced at the clock. It was after 3:30. Only twenty minutes, he thought, before the Tribal council meeting starts. He was busy stuffing papers into his briefcase when Miss Swallow and Mr. Pence showed up at his door.

"Come on and follow me out to my car," he said. "I've got a presentation to make."

As they walked across the parking lot, Mr. Berry said, "So…I've been hearing Chris Sorrel's name a lot lately. First, from you, Miss Swallow, about his bullying Hummingbird. Then, Mrs. Corn tells me she thinks he was the one pretending to be her on the teacher website. In fact, she thinks he has been targeting Rain, Simon, and Boomer—and now Arianna."

Miss Swallow said, "That's what I think, too. It makes sense. Arianna lives with Hummingbird's family. All this started with Hummingbird."

Stopping at his car, Mr. Berry said, "We may not have any proof that Chris is behind any of this. Despite what you saw, Mr. Pence, the boys making fun of Arianna today wouldn't admit that Chris made them do it." He looked at the two teachers, "Do we have any other evidence?"

"Well, he took a science test of Hummingbird's," Miss Swallow replied, "and wrote an insult on it— to make it look like she wrote it. She saw him take the test, but she didn't see him write on it."

Mr. Pence's face flushed a deep red. He looked at Miss Swallow. Did she know what was written on the test?

"What did it say—the insult?" Mr. Berry asked.

"Well, um," Miss Swallow stammered, "it's not very nice. Ah…"

Mr. Pence held up his hand to relieve her discomfort. "I'll tell him, Betty. It said 'Miss Swallow says Mr. Pence is a dork and a loser.'" He explained to the principal that one of his students, Mindy, had returned the test to him, thinking that a student had lost it.

"David, it was an awful trick!" Miss Swallow said indignantly. "Hummingbird was so upset because you thought *she* wrote it." Miss Swallow smiled sweetly at Mr. Pence. "And, just for the record, I don't think you are a dork or a loser at all."

"Oh, the trick was on you, too, Betty!" Mr. Pence protested. "I hope you weren't upset, either. I'm just glad Hummingbird didn't write it."

Embarrassed, Mr. Berry interrupted. "Well, ah, this is getting a bit complicated and I have to go." Eager to end the awkward conversation, he added, "Glad you two got that straightened out." The principal slid behind the steering wheel of his car and started the engine. Backing out of his reserved parking space, he poked his head out the car window and gave his teachers a hearty assurance that all would be well. "We'll work this out. We've got some great kids at Thunder Rock Middle School. Tomorrow's Science Fair awards will be proof of that!"

Chapter 14

Only the first place trophy remained on the table.

Wins and Losses

Coyote lowered the binoculars and grinned so big his mouth hurt. He had taken up his position on the hill overlooking the school, eager to observe the fun. The old yellow-eyed cuss hadn't been disappointed. He'd never enjoyed so much "sticky-sticky" in his entire tricking career. And tomorrow would be even better! Yipping in glee, he couldn't wait to tell Thistle. He loved boasting to the rabbit about how easy it was to make humans look incredibly silly. Thistle would get huffy trying to defend the people—which is why Coyote did it. He liked to get her riled up.

———————

The next morning, Mr. Berry pulled into the school an hour after Coyote and Thistle did. The principal parked his car and walked past the bushes in front of the auditorium, unaware that two animals were hiding inside the foliage. Coyote had insisted that they arrive before dawn, not because he feared discovery (or so he said), but because he wanted a good seat. Thistle tagged along to keep an eye on Coyote. After all the bragging he'd done the afternoon before, she had to see for herself what he was up to.

Coyote watched Mr. Berry hurrying across the parking lot. The trickster nudged Thistle and giggled: "'Berries are good for thickening a stew. Don't you agree, Rabbit?"

Thistle sighed, "Yeah, the stews you cook up are thick, all right."

———————

The principal rushed into the school office. He immediately detoured to the coffee machine. Miss Shield was waiting for him. She leaped up from her desk, blocking him before he could make another move. Gulping coffee, the principal stated the obvious: "Good morning, Miss Shield. I'm late."

The school secretary got right down to business. "You've got less than ten minutes before the assembly starts. Here's the agenda. Oh, and Mr. Berry, please remember to acknowledge the teachers from the high school. They were a bit upset last year when you forgot to thank them for judging the science fair."

"Thank you. I'll try to remember all that. Ahh, Miss Shield, what's on my schedule this morning…after the assembly?"

"You have a meeting with Hummingbird's parents."

"Oh, yes, of course, about the bullying."

"And this afternoon you have a teacher observation, payroll, and a bully prevention meeting with the teachers." With that final bit of information, Miss Shield reached for Mr. Berry's briefcase, handed him his assembly folder, and herded him to the door.

Offering a small measure of resistance to her secretarial efficiency, Mr. Berry hesitated at the door. He turned and handed his empty coffee cup to Miss Shield. "I think it's about time we bought a new 'Mr. Percolator.' That coffee was awfully *thick*."

The principal headed to the auditorium. He was in a good mood. The science fair had proved to be a real success in the past few years, getting coverage in the reservation newspaper and local radio. He was hoping this year for a spot on the Tribe's website.

He went through the side entrance to the auditorium and was greeted with the babbling din of 300 middle schoolers. All the homerooms were present. Running up the steps to the stage, he spotted the photographer from "Around the Rez." Mr.

Berry stepped to the edge of the stage and called him over. "Hi, Steve. Let's get a good picture of our first place winner. I want this Native Science fair to get some real attention."

After noting the photographer's thumbs-up, Mr. Berry moved to the podium. He held up his hand. The auditorium fell silent as the whole school stood up for the Pledge of Allegiance. At its conclusion, the school band played a squeaky, but acceptable version of the national anthem, followed by "Thunderbirds Forever," the school song. Mr. Berry always grew a bit misty when the kids sang the last refrain, "We will fly higher and higher, always together, always forever."

Following Miss Shield's instructions, Mr. Berry moved smoothly through the assembly program, only glancing once or twice at the agenda. He thanked, blessed, and praised all those who participated in the science fair so profusely that the students began to grow restless.

Taking note of the fidgeting, Mr. Berry got to the point. "Now I come to the part that we've all been waiting for. The awards for this year's science fair: 'Native Science: Yesterday, Today, and Tomorrow.'" As Mr. Berry called out their names, the "honorable mentions" began tromping up the aisles, accompanied by polite applause. But when the principal announced Little Deb's name, a shriek went up from her girlfriends. To the sound of wild clapping, Little Deb bashfully crossed the stage to receive her certificate of merit. Mr. Berry joked, "Wow, I didn't know that "Ash and Corn: Releasing the Nutrition" would be such a popular subject!"

"I didn't either," Little Deb gasped, and ran off the stage.

Mr. Berry reached for the third place plaque on the table beside the podium. It was time for the winning entries. He paused for dramatic effect and then proclaimed: "For 'The Inuit Kayak: From Hunting Boat to Modern Sport,' third place goes to Hank LaChaise!" After Hank had loped up to receive his award, Mr. Berry asked him if there was anything he particularly enjoyed about his project. Not one to talk very much, Hank said, "I liked learning about the boat design and how you could roll it back up if you flipped over in the water. That was cool."

Moving on after the applause for Hank, Mr. Berry became even more expansive. "Our second place prize goes to another outstanding student, Mindy Two Horses for her project, "Freeze-Dried Potatoes: The Inca Way!"

Chris's head jerked up. Mindy! Totally surprised, he whispered to Pooch, one of the boys on the 8th grade basketball team: "She entered the science fair?"

"Yeah, she's been working on it, forever. Man, don't you ever think about anything but your own stuff?" Chris stood up and clapped loudly, hoping to get Mindy's attention. But she never looked his way.

Mr. Berry was really getting into it. Smiling, he invited Mindy to tell the school about her project: "Well, people in the Andes Mountains developed potatoes from these little wild tubers about 4,000 years ago. They preserved potatoes by freezing them and then adding water to make them soft again. They call it 'choon-yo.' It would stay good for like ten years."

Thinking, I hope Steve is getting a picture of this, Mr. Berry asked, "How did you make the 'choon-yo,' Mindy?"

"I froze the potatoes in the freezer because it wasn't cold enough to freeze them outside, and then I stomped them until they were mashed to bits."

"You stomped them?" the principal prompted.

"Yeah, with my feet. But I washed them first."

"The potatoes?"

"No, my feet. Then I laid them out to dry in the sun. And then I did it all over again. It's just like the instant potatoes at the grocery store."

Mr. Berry laughed and said, "Well, I guess I have the Incas to thank for the potatoes we eat at my house. Thank you, Mindy."

The principal's attempt at humor created some charitable laughter that accompanied Mindy as she walked primly down the stage steps. Chris waved to get her attention, but she was too busy "high-fiving" her friends as she took her seat. What is wrong with her? he thought.

Only the first place trophy remained on the table. It was a clear glass oval with the word 'Science' etched onto its surface. On its base was a small gold plaque where the first place winner's name would later be inscribed by a local crafts shop. Mr. Berry picked up the award solemnly and composed his face for his predictable "inspirational speech."

Mr. Berry was a popular and admired principal, but his speeches, expected to motivate the student body and honor exemplary pupils, usually stimulated exactly the opposite. After five minutes of "applying ourselves…building character…good citizenship and community…the future is ours…and reaching for the stars," the entire assembly was in suspended animation on its way to an outer arm of the Milky Way.

Finally, Mr. Berry brought his oration to a merciful end. Opening his assembly folder, he continued: "I am pleased to announce that the winning exhibit is "The Invention and Manufacture of Rubber in Central Mexico." A small stir erupted. Some of the students and teachers knew who was responsible for that project. The uninformed students craned their necks to catch a first glimpse of the exalted one that would claim the trophy. Mr. Berry enjoyed the building excitement. Yes, he thought, this is how it should be. These kids were really pumped up about the science fair! A big smile on his face, he swept his eyes proudly across the assembly.

Suddenly, he noticed that a boy sitting in an aisle seat in the third row was beginning to rise. His smile froze. Slowly Mr. Berry's eyes drifted down to Miss Shield's agenda notes. Visually scrolling down the page, he had the most peculiar feeling that a big joke was being played. Perhaps Miss Shield had typed in "gotcha" or LOL? But no, no smiley face or other "funny" preceded the words: First Place Winner: CHRIS SORREL.

The principal looked up. Chris was standing in the aisle, waiting for him to read out his name. Did the boy know that he had won? Mr. Berry cleared his throat, making the awkward silence even more awkward. Forcing a strained grin, he choked out, "The first prize goes to Chris Sorrel."

Chris characteristically swept back his hair with his hands and bounded onto the stage. The applause was uneven.

The 8th grade basketball team was enthusiastic and the sixth graders were happy to clap for anyone. But Chris's girl groupies were sitting on their hands. When you added some missing toadies (who spent a lot of time in in-house suspension) and the teachers that were now wise to him, Chris's fan club had apparently shrunk.

Determined to be fair, Mr. Berry congratulated Chris and held out the trophy. Smiling brightly, the boy grasped the translucent award and pulled it forcefully from Mr. Berry's hand. Holding the prize close to his chest, Chris glanced up at Mr. Berry—his eyes betraying a terrible, terrible need for approval. The principal was surprised by the boy's vulnerability. This was the villain who had supposedly terrorized Hummingbird, maligned Miss Swallow, stolen Mrs. Corn's identity, spread lies about Rain, and instigated the attack on Arianna?

Feeling sorry for him, Mr. Berry asked Chris a few polite questions about his project. Unfortunately, the first prize winner provided more information about indigenous latex than anyone really wanted to know. Thanking Chris for his most interesting description of Maya rubber products, Mr. Berry signaled for Miss Swallow to bring the Big Foods manager on stage. Mr. Standing carried a big replica of a $1,000 check the grocery chain had donated to the school for science supplies. Making a brief speech, the store manager endorsed the benefits of investment in community schools, and reminded everyone that green peppers and cucumbers were on sale this week at the Big Foods Super.

Mr. Berry brought the assembly to a close by congratulating everyone and asking all the honorable mentions and place winners to stay behind for pictures. Standing in front of the big check, he stiffly reenacted the presentation of the first place trophy to Chris. Blinded by the flash of the photographer's camera, he didn't see the high school teachers leave in a huff. He had forgotten Miss Shield's last instruction.

Coyote and Thistle vacated their front row seats and slowly made their way around to the back of the auditorium—staying hidden behind the hedge that bordered the building. Thistle had enjoyed the assembly and had shared some chuckles with Coyote who had to muffle his 'yips' when Mr. Berry had announced Chris as the first place winner. But now she wasn't feeling very well. She had some discomfort in her back. As an experienced mother, she knew that her bunnies were about to be born.

Coyote noticed her slow hopping. "You getting old, Ms. Rabbit?" he teased.

"No older than you, Coyote. I just need to get back to my nest. The little ones will be here soon—but not right away. I have a little time."

"Ahh, well, then," said Coyote, understanding the situation.

The trickster and the cotton-tail retraced the path they had followed to the school. They didn't advertise themselves, traveling instead in the shadows of the abundant weeds and shrubs. Occasionally they stopped so that Thistle could rest. Before long, Coyote spotted the rabbit's brush heap. He also saw Sky Heart's shadow cross their path as they climbed the low hill to the nest.

"Looks like we made it, Thistle."

"Yes. And just in time, too." She wiggled into the security of her nest and turned around so that her head poked out of the weedy enclosure.

"I have to go. I hope all goes well," Coyote said. "Sky Heart is here," he added, jerking his nose skyward. "You won't be alone."

Now that she was safe in her home, Thistle wasn't quite ready for Coyote to leave so hastily. "I am curious. How did you manage to wangle the first place trophy for Chris?"

"I didn't. He won it fair and square." Coyote smiled wryly. "I don't meddle in *everything*."

"Well, you meddled enough to get Hummingbird kicked out of the competition."

Frowning, Coyote said, "Ahem, well, yes." He had forgotten about that. "But I had my reasons."

Thistle suspected that the "giant plan" had something to do with those reasons, but she said nothing. Instead, she protested, "Chris has done a lot of bad things lately."

"I know, but he has a good mind. His project was a good one." Coyote sighed. "But he only thinks of winning… and that's the twist an old trickster like me can appreciate—winning for Chris is really losing."

"Look at this, Arianna. This fertilizer is made of dried blood, and this one is seagull guano. Yuk! It sounds terrible."

Thinking Big

And so it seemed to Mr. Berry, too. Later that day, after his meeting with Hummingbird's mother and father, the principal called Chris's parents. Mr. Berry didn't expect that they would welcome the reason for his call, but he was taken aback by the stepfather's angry refusal to even discuss Chris's bullying. In reply to the principal's request for a meeting, Hoke Sorrel bellowed that Chris was "a star student and athlete, and no bunch of loser, jealous kids are gonna dump all over my son's winning the science fair!"

Offering some tactful comments to calm the situation, the principal quickly realized he was talking into dead air. Mr. Sorrel had hung up on him. Deeply dismayed, Mr. Berry hit the 'off' button on his phone. Frowning, he made a mental note to tell Ms. Shield to add another agenda item to tomorrow's staff meeting: how to engage parents of students who bully.

The angry words, however, had a very different effect on another listener. Having eavesdropped on the phone call, Chris was positively ecstatic! This was the first time the old man had ever shown any interest in him. Whether Hoke Sorrel really cared about his stepson's achievements didn't really matter to Chris. It was the attention that the boy craved. Even Melvin and Jesse were giving him "high fives!"

Over the next few days, Chris became convinced that life couldn't get any better. His family was backing him up against the teachers and kids like Hummingbird. And they were proud of his trophy, too. His mom, Althea, even put it on the shelf next to the plaque that recognized her mail-order business as "Tribal Enterprise of the Year" Not so strangely, the Sorrel family's refusal to recognize Chris's bad behavior actually resulted in a break for the tormented at Thunder Rock Middle School. Chris was just feeling too good to worry about being top dog. The bullying died down considerably, even though Chris and his cronies were by no means the only trouble-makers at the school.

In fact, the whole school took a breather. Without distractions, Mr. Berry and the teachers were able to complete the school's anti-bullying policy which they called "Being a Good Relative." Dumptruck and Tater Tot didn't get any new detentions; and the 6th graders were even leaving school with a few quarters in their pockets. As for the Veggie Crowd, Hummingbird's exile ended and Simon's heels were not trod upon. The "insulin pump incident" also receded, but Arianna made one request of Boomer—no more "dingfods" please. She'd been "dinged" enough. The only real moaning was from Rain and Boomer when they kept making mistakes at drum practice.

The health messages in Bird's science project got a hearing, too. Miss Swallow took Bird to present her science project to Dr. Bamsey's freshman biology class at Medicine Cave Tribal College. Tom, Darlene, Aunt Chick, Arianna, and Simon had front row seats. Even Mr. Pence attended. Dr. Bamsey said her project was very important to the Tribal Food Sovereignty Program; he would make sure that her findings about land stewardship were featured in the College's newsletter. It was a nice moment for Hummingbird and her father.

As for the "Giant Plan" Hummingbird was moving ahead. Her imagination was fired up! Hummingbird couldn't wait to get the garden going. Arianna was the first to notice that she was making plans.

"What are you reading?"

"One of Aunt Chick's garden catalogs. I didn't know there were so many varieties of giant veggies." Banging the three-inch tome shut, Hummingbird looked up—her eyes full of ambition. "Arianna, you've got to have nitrogen, potassium, and phosphorus to make the plants grow big and fast." Laughing at her own impatience, she said, "But it's way too early to be thinking about that. We have to turn a dirty old shed into our experimental laboratory!"

The girls started with their promised partners—Rain, Boomer and Simon. The boys helped them scrounge for all the goodies they needed—soap, mops and buckets, and a hose for cleaning; and all kinds of hardware and attic surplus that would make the shed fit for human use. Simon also brought a six-inch roll of bubble wrap. Where he got it and what it was for nobody knew—but the girls weren't turning down anything.

Recruiting other allies, Bird and Arianna discovered that electricity and mechanical items would not a problem, either. Boo volunteered his skills as an electrician as well as the vast contents of his junky garage. And Aunt Chick was a gold mine! She gave them all kinds of equipment and supplies: flower pots, potting soil, garden tools, seeds, and fertilizer. Even better, Tom offered to fix the fence and Gerald, Rain's dad, was bringing his tiller. There would be a winter garden!

Everybody assembled early Saturday. The kids took on most of the cleaning jobs while Boo, Tom, and Aunt Chick started the shed and fence repair. Soon their hammering and banging was accompanied by the steady chug of the tiller's old Briggs and Stratton motor. When it jumped out of gear going over a hard spot, Gerald would just twist a couple of bolts and fire it up again. Nobody stopped except to gulp down some water.

By lunchtime, the lights were on in the shed, the fence had new boards where there were none before, and dark furrows of newly-turned earth waited for spade and seed. The shed wasn't exactly sparkling, but it was swept and mopped, and Boo had repaired the collapsed shelving and replaced the broken window panes with plywood. A big old table from Aunt Chick's basement now sat under the overhead lamp. On it, the girls had assembled most of their garden products and Miss Swallow's contributions: a couple of alcohol lamps, a thermometer, an old scale, and an assortment of beakers that had seen better days.

Tired, but proud of their accomplishments, the "Giant Plan" work crew convened outside the shed to thank and congratulate each other on the morning's labor. Aunt Chick wanted to get the project off to a good start, and had asked Tom to offer a blessing. They waited for Boo who was still inside the shed; he was testing a space heater to make sure the electrical outlet was working safely. Not realizing he was holding things up, Boo apologized and hurried to stand respectfully with the others. Tom said:

"First, I want to express my thanks to our children, who have gathered us all together to help them do something good for the people. And I want to thank the Creator for the food gifts we are about to eat. Please watch over our children as they will be working hard to plant and grow food that will help our people to eat healthier and prevent type 2 diabetes. I ask our Mother Earth, and the seeds, sun and rain to work together, so that the vegetables for our people can grow in a good way. I ask these things on behalf of all our relations."

Everyone smiled. It was a very good day. Aunt Chick looked around proudly at her family and friends and announced, "Darlene's got lunch on the table. Let's eat!" After the morning's hard work, the grilled buffalo on wheat buns didn't last very long.

After lunch, Hummingbird and Arianna thanked everyone by promising them a dish from their first giant vegetable (even though they knew that would not be possible until next summer). Boo said he was looking forward to it—he couldn't wait to carve up that five-foot lima bean!

When everyone left, Hummingbird and Arianna went back to the shed. They wanted to "play" in their new lab. Their first job was to inventory their materials. Hummingbird was interested in the bags of fertilizer (most of which had already been opened). Reading the labels, she saw they were either composed of inorganic chemicals or organic material that came from living things. Bird thought the organic ingredients were cool. "Look at this, Arianna. This fertilizer is made of dried blood, and this one is seagull guano. And here's some feather meal and fish meal, and a sack of crushed oyster shells. Yuk! It sounds terrible!"

"What's guano?"

"I don't know. Look it up in Aunt Chick's garden book," Bird said, pointing to the table where Simon had piled the gardening books and a stack of Internet articles on giant vegetables. Excited by so many fast-grow ingredients, Bird couldn't contain herself any longer. "Hey, let's make some fertilizer for the winter vegetables!"

"I don't think you're supposed to plant seeds in a lot of fertilizer," Arianna said. "Simon read that it could burn the seedlings."

"I think you're right, but it wouldn't hurt to see what would happen if..." Hummingbird argued. She picked up a small unopened bag of inorganic fertilizer that said "5-10-5" —5% nitrogen, 10% phosphorus and 5% potassium. "That doesn't sound too strong. We don't have to use much. The directions say 'add one tablespoon per gallon of water.'"

Bird sorted through a 'grab box' of junk that Simon brought over, finding a bunch of plastic measuring spoons. Then, she filled a metal pail with water from the outside spigot, measured out a tablespoon of fertilizer, and dumped it in the water.

Arianna said, "Is that all there is to it?"

"Why don't we jazz it up a bit?" Bird giggled. Reaching for the organic fertilizers, she measured out a teaspoon of dried blood, feathers, fish, and shells—tossing each spoonful into the pail. Grabbing the sack of seagull guano, she turned to Arianna and asked, "What did the book say it was?"

"I haven't looked yet." Arianna opened the book at the index and turned the pages until she got to 'G.' Flipping to the referenced page, she read:

> The word "guano" originates from the Quechua language of the Andes and means "the droppings of sea birds." Indigenous peoples collected guano from the coast of Peru for use as a soil fertilizer. It is high in nitrogen and phosphorus. The Incas assigned great value to guano, restricting access to it and punishing any disturbance to the birds with death.

"Oh, cool! Indigenous fertilizer! We've got to have some of that!" Hummingbird chucked in a whole tablespoon of the guano for good measure.

Now that the fertilizer was mixed, Arianna pulled down a sack of fiber peat pots and some potting soil from their newly-built shelf, and Bird opened three seed packets—turnips, carrots, and cabbages.

"How many should we plant?" Arianna asked.

"Let's do twenty with fertilizer and twenty without. That way, if the fertilizer is too strong, we'll only lose half of them."

The girls filled the fiber pots with soil, planted the seeds, and added some water to each. Arianna arranged the seeded pots in two groups of twenty on the table, and Hummingbird squirted a dropper full of fertilizer into only one group. Then she set up the plant-grow light and plugged it in. A ghostly florescent glow filled the shed.

Arianna said, "Gee, it looks a little spooky."

"Spooky? It's not spooky! It's more like a night light," Bird said whimsically. "When the seeds sprout, they won't be afraid of the dark."

Satisfied with their first experiment, the girls cleaned up the spilled dirt and water splatters from their seed planting. They would come back on Monday afternoon to check out the seed's progress. Hummingbird closed the door behind them and slipped the latch in place. Unfortunately, she had forgotten the old combination lock that Dale, her brother, had given her.

"At last! Coyote griped, "I thought they'd never leave!" He'd been hanging out at Thistle's nest all day—waiting to throw his whammy.

Thistle had been out of her nest for most of the day and had now returned to nurse her new babies. She had given birth to a large litter—seven kits, all blind and naked. Tucking her brood around her, she gave Coyote an irritated look: "What do you care when they leave?"

"It's not like I don't have a schedule to keep, you know," he said pompously.

"Schedule? You've been lying up there sleeping all day."

"Not at all. I've been observing. Waiting for my moment. I have my own plans for the winter vegetables."

"Like what?"

"Like this," he said. Coyote stood up and shook himself vigorously. Then, he pranced back and forth a few times, warming up his magic. When his power was near, he reached for it quickly—transforming the girls' newly planted seeds with a little ditty:

> *Cabbage to Coyote,*
> *Carrot to Coyote,*
> *Turnip to Coyote.*
> *Jinx and stinks!*
> *Make them mine!*
> *Make them mine!*

Pleased with himself, he said, "Well, Miss Birdie, let's see how your garden grows now." He reared his head back for a big laugh, but stopped. Thistle was giving him a disapproving look.

"Can't you leave that poor girl alone?"

"The garden doesn't have to be *all* mine," Coyote joked. "Actually, Thistle, you didn't let me finish. I am a very generous fellow. I fully intended to "deed" one of the plants back over to Hummingbird. Now pay attention." He cleared his throat, "Ahem…

> *Scratch a burr in the fur,*
> *Then the burr sticks on her.*
> *Birdie's wish becomes a dish,*
> *Some say it smells like licorice.*

"That's it, Mr. Big? That's the magic?" the rabbit said not impressed.

Smiling confidently, Coyote replied, "You'll believe me when you see it. And you'll agree that I'm big—very big."

Waiting for the school bus the next morning, the girls were thinking and talking big, too. Googling "biggest vegetables" on Sunday afternoon, they had found a cabbage that was 129 pounds and a carrot nineteen feet long! Hummingbird boasted, "Just wait, Arianna. Next summer we'll have a crop like that."

Unfortunately, when the bus came, the girls suddenly had to "think small." It was packed with kids from another bus that had broken down. There were only two empty seats left.

Hummingbird squeezed over Little Deb to a window seat at the front; and Arianna moved toward an aisle seat at the back.

Arianna plopped down just as the bus lurched forward. Her eyes drifted to the window and soon she was not seeing the passing landscape. Instead, she was thinking about the shed and what was happening to the vegetable seeds they had planted. Although the girls didn't expect much progress, they planned to check out their little experiments that afternoon.

Despite the intensity of her thoughts, Arianna's eyes were attracted to the sweeping hand movements of her seat mate. Oh, she thought, he's drawing! Silently, she watched him penciling in the reflection of fir branches in a mountain pond. Arianna could see that the artist knew how to draw water.

Unable to keep quiet any longer, Arianna said, "That's really good. It almost looks real!"

The artist pushed back the cotton hood that had obscured his face and turned to Arianna. "Gee, thanks. I'm trying to get the light just right, but..." The rest of the sentence froze in his mouth. Recognizing Arianna, his jaw dropped like a stone.

Arianna was equally startled. All she could see was a fireworks display of red hair. She almost hollered, "Tater Tot!"

Recoiling from each other, they quickly broke eye contact and stared nervously ahead. They sat like two kids on ice for several miles—while the bus seemed to crawl slower and slower. Arianna looked on ahead and saw that they were behind a truck towing the broken down bus. Oh, this is just great, she thought, we'll be on this ride forever!

She decided to thaw a little. Glancing out the corner of his eye to gauge his reaction, Arianna said shyly, "Well, you don't have to stop your drawing."

Tater Tot couldn't stand the strain either. He murmured, "No, I guess not." He made some half-hearted pencil strokes, but just wasn't into it. Sighing, he shoved the colored pencils back into their box.

Hearing the sigh, Arianna couldn't help but respond. It just was in her nature. "Why did you stop? You're a good artist."

"Not everybody thinks so."

"Then they must be crazy."

"Tell that to Chris Sorrel."

Arianna didn't know what to say—so she asked another question. "Why don't you draw cartoons for the school newspaper?"

"Yeah, well, like I said, tell that to Chris."

"Well, I'm new here. I don't really know Chris." Trying to encourage the conversation, she continued, "Umm, my parents are moving here after Thanksgiving. But I'm living with Hummingbird's family right now. I came early so I could start school here at the beginning of the year."

Tater Tot didn't seem to mind being drawn out of his shell. "I'm new, too. I moved here last summer. My mom is a contractor for the Tribe. It's just for two projects, but I should be here at least this year." Quietly, he added, "Since my parents divorced, we move around a lot."

Feeling self-conscious, Tater Tot broke off the conversation and stared out the window. Several minutes went by while he struggled with his thoughts. Suddenly, he turned and faced Arianna. Biting his lip, he said, "Look, I'm sorry about hollering that 'ding' stuff at you. The principal said we had to write that apology, but I really meant it. I didn't know about the pump and all—not until Mr. Berry told us."

"You didn't know I have type 1 diabetes?"

He shook his head. "No, I was just yelling dumb stuff because…because somebody told me to."

"But why?"

Since he had started this, Tater Tot decided to plow on ahead even though he wasn't sure why he was confiding in Arianna. "See, I've been to a lot of schools. And getting pushed around all the time really gets old. I guess I never had time to make friends… or something. Anyway, when I got here I knew it would be hard to fit in. So I thought I'd join up with the guys who do the bullying."

"That wasn't very smart."

"No, I guess not. But it's better than getting beat up all the time."

"I wouldn't know about that. I just know it didn't feel very good having everybody gang up on me. I never did anything to you."

As the bus turned into the school driveway, Tater Tot realized he needed to hurry up and make his point. "No, you didn't. But, that's not me, Arianna. I'm not really like that."

The bus pulled into the curb and kids started bunching into the aisles, eager to escape the over-crowded seats. Arianna grabbed her jacket and picked up her backpack. Frowning a little, she fixed her eyes on the red-haired boy and asked very simply: "So who are you…really?"

Not expecting an answer to her odd question, Arianna turned around and joined the students spilling out the bus door. Tater Tot was right behind her. When they came down the bus steps, he saw Hummingbird waiting for her friend. Tater Tot hesitated when he saw the expression on Bird's face, but answered Arianna's question: "I'm really…Larry."

Arianna laughed a little: "Glad to meet you, Larry. I'm really Arianna."

Glancing at Hummingbird, Tater Tot muttered, "Well, I gotta go. I guess we're all pretty late."

Bird watched the embarrassed boy flee the bus stop. Wide-eyed, she turned to Arianna. "You were talking to him? What was that all about?"

"Tell you later, Bird. I don't want to be late either."

"Oh, come on, Arianna! Tell me now! I won't be at lunch today. I've got to…"

Smiling sweetly, Arianna said, "Then you'll just have to wait 'til after school!"

Chapter 16

Coyote had said "Make them mine" and, indeed, the embryos in the fertilized seeds had become his. By late morning the next day, the plants were 12 inches high.

Fast-Grow Formulas

Although Hummingbird was hard put to *wait* on anything, she was a model of patience compared to the seeds that were germinating in the shed. Whether it was Hummingbird's fast-grow formula or Coyote's whammy, the seeds would have been judged "whiz kids" by any measure. As soon as the water the girls had poured into their little pots had moistened the soil, their seed coats had swelled and split. Eagerly, they pushed their baby roots downward and their baby stems upward. As soon as the stem's green bumps emerged from the soil, two leaves unfurled and joyously greeted the energy from the plant-grow light above.

Coyote had said "Make them mine" and, indeed, the embryos in the fertilized seeds had become his. By late morning the next day, the plants were 12 inches high. Feeling tall enough, they redirected their energy toward their root system. Some roots soon forced their way through the bottom of the fiber pots and sent out scouts to capture (some might say "steal") more nutrients from the bag of fertilizer on the work table. Other roots encircled their neighboring pots, pulling them into a close community of green relatives. By afternoon, having worked hard for almost 48 hours, the plants were exhausted. Shutting down the phloem and xylem flow, they rested before starting their next growth spurt.

After school, the girls hurried to Aunt Chick's, eager to see what their vegetable seeds were doing. As they walked, Hummingbird listened avidly to Arianna describe her conversation with Tater Tot. They had almost arrived at the shed when Hummingbird asked Arianna the question that most intrigued her.

"So what did you say that made him apologize?"

"I didn't make him do anything. I just told him he was a good artist."

"Did he say Chris put him up to calling you Miss Ding-Ding?"

"No, he just kinda said that Chris didn't think he could draw," Arianna said. "Like he was standing in his way or something. I don't think he likes Chris."

"Well, I don't either!" Hummingbird laughed and playfully pushed Arianna through the shed door. Arianna stopped suddenly. Puzzled, she said, "What is that, Bird?" pointing to a dark mass under the cold blue light of the plant-grow bulb.

When Bird flipped on the switch to the overhead lamp, the answer to Arianna's question prompted the biggest "WOW! the girls ever hollered. The prim rows of little pots they had planted the evening before had disappeared. In their place was a stand of seedlings about 14 inches high. They had tall leggy stems that bushed out at the top into a crown of pointy little leaves.

Both girls jumped up and down, shrieking and laughing. "I can't believe it! Look! Look! They just didn't sprout—they grew! They're so tall! I didn't think anything could grow that fast."

Gasping, Arianna said, "The fast-grow formula worked! What do you think it was…the feathers or the oyster shells?"

"No, it was the blooood meal…," said Bird in her best Dracula voice.

Hummingbird and Arianna started dancing around the table. Finally, they collapsed into a couple of wobbly lawn chairs from Boo's garage. After catching her breath, Bird got up and examined the seedlings more carefully. "It must have been the fertilizer," she concluded. "The pots without it have hardly done anything at all. There's a couple with a little green nub poking up, but that's all."

"Look," Arianna said, "the roots burst out of the fiber pots. I guess we'll have to plant them in the garden. They're too big for the cold frames."

The girls found several cardboard boxes that they used to haul the plants outside. Then, Hummingbird got the shovel that Aunt Chick donated. She dug out four parallel rows in a far corner of the garden. As Bird dug, Arianna followed, inserting the plants at eighteen inch intervals and giving each a good drink of water. She had to pull apart the roots of some of the plants—they were so entangled. Arianna could have sworn the roots tightened up and actually resisted her tugging.

After they were finished, the girls stood back and admired their work. Realizing that they had forgotten something, Arianna picked up a pot that had torn away from one of the seedlings. Looking at it, she asked, "Which are the cabbages? And which are the carrots and turnips?"

"I don't know!" Hummingbird giggled. "I forgot to label the pots. I guess I'm not a very good scientist."

Hummingbird was right. She hadn't been thinking scientifically. And she wasn't thinking that way now. A good observer would have noticed that the leaves on the plants were identical. But it would have made no difference if Bird had put a billboard in each pot that read "cabbage," "turnip," or "carrot." They were all "coyotes" now.

At supper, Hummingbird and Arianna could talk of nothing but their precocious seedlings. Tom and Darlene were glad to see Hummingbird so happy; but Dale and Richard were especially relieved. She had been no fun at all since the 'elephant's toothpaste' episode.

Looking around the table at her family, Bird said, "I just knew we could grow giant vegetables!"

"I got to give it to you girls," Tom said, smiling. "It sounds like you've found the magic formula."

"Right, Dad! We don't need those old seeds of yours anymore. They'll never be able to produce as much food as my giant vegetables!"

Talking around a spoonful of carrots and celery, Dale said, "If they grow as fast as you say, you could grow a pumpkin and enter it in the contest at the Harvest Pow-Wow."

"Oh, my gosh, we could! A pumpkin! Arianna, wait 'til the guys hear about this!"

Reaching for another helping of Darlene's delicious chicken chili, Hummingbird's father smiled and said, "Well, if you don't mind, Birdie, I think I'll hold onto those old Native seeds for a little while longer. You don't know how nutritious your giant vegetables will be or even if they'll taste very good. Right now, I'd say just be proud of your science project. That's gonna help us work out the best way to improve the buffalo pasture."

But Hummingbird wasn't listening. She was just thinking about that big blue ribbon.

That night on the phone, before school the next day, between classes, and at lunch—all the boys heard about was the seedlings. After a whole day of Hummingbird's babbling, enough was enough. They wanted to see them.

Simon arranged to go home with Rain and help him with some chores he had to do for his mother. That way Rain could cut out faster and make it over to the garden before it got too dark. Boomer had no such obligations. He told the girls he was going to the garden as soon as he dumped his books.

As eager as Boomer was to see the plants, he was a slow-poke compared to Hummingbird. As soon as she hit the house, Bird was in a race to see how fast she could shuck off her school clothes and throw on some old jeans and a hand-me-down sweater better suited to dirt and shovels.

Arianna heard the back door bang shut before she could even take off her new jacket. She fumbled for some old clothes in her drawer, but then thought, Oh, forget it. Imitating Hummingbird's fast exit from the house, Arianna raced after her sister scientist.

"Wait up!" Arianna cried.

"I can't! I've got to see how big the plants have grown!"

Arianna didn't catch up with Hummingbird until she arrived at the garden gate. The two girls exchanged a look of anticipatory glee. Hummingbird flipped up the latch and pushed at the heavy slatted gate, which resisted her unbearable curiosity by digging deeper into the dry, weedy soil.

"What's wrong with this gate?" Hummingbird growled. "It's never stuck this bad before." When both girls put their shoulders to the gate, it surrendered, allowing a narrow passage. They squeezed through the splintery gap. The two girls stopped abruptly. Hummingbird gasped, but Arianna uttered no sound at all. She could only stare at a massive green blob lying in a nest of tendrils and floppy vines.

"Oh my gosh…what is it?" Arianna asked.

"Um…I don't know. The leaves look like squash."

"But we didn't plant any squash seeds."

"I know." Hummingbird reached down and placed her hands on each side of the huge green blob. It was as wide as a truck tire.

Arianna waded into the foliage that spread out from the four original rows where they had transplanted the seedlings. "Hummingbird, over here!" she squealed, "There's another one!"

"And one over there, too!" Hummingbird cried, pointing to a monster veggie that blocked part of the gravel pathway that encircled the garden.

"Do you think they're the seedlings?"

"What else could they be?"

"Maybe the fast-grow formula is too fast."

"Does anything look like cabbage, carrots, and turnips to you?"

The girls jumped when the gate tried to block another intruder. "Hey, Bird! Arianna! How do you get through this thing?"

"Just squeeze, Boomer!"

Boomer compressed himself and popped through the gate. He didn't expect to see a jungle on the other side. "Holy Moly! This is what you're growing?"

"Yes. Well, no. We didn't know they'd look like this... or grow this fast" Arianna explained.

"What are they?"

"The squash that ate Chicago?" Hummingbird half-joked.

"Well, they must be the 'body snatchers' 'cause that one over there is moving."

"Moving?" Bird choked.

A grin began to plump out Boomer's cheeks: "Yeah."

The three kids watched intently as the blob blocking the pathway began to rock back and forth. Boomer edged up on the oversized squash—very slowly. He stopped and cocked his head, listening intently. "Shhh, I can hear something," he whispered over his shoulder.

The girls went silent. They could hear a weird blend of licking, scratching, and smacking noises. Suddenly, the squash's fat bottom bulged outward and a large piece of the outer skin split. Then, the scratching grew louder as the occupant began to dig faster from its overgrown interior. A hole appeared. "Oh gross! Maybe it's a giant worm!" Arianna cried.

"Not unless worms have fur!" Boomer shouted. "Look!"

At that moment Coyote's head popped through the hole. He pushed his paws through the small opening and widened it, allowing passage for the rest of his body. As he emerged, the squash's skin collapsed into a shapeless green sack. Shocked, Hummingbird and Arianna stumbled backwards. But Boomer stood his ground.

Coyote staggered as he tried to stand up. Unable to sustain his weight, he flopped on his haunches—his belly swollen with squash flesh. Glancing with disinterest at the kids, he emitted a loud, contented belch.

.....shredded squash leaves and dirt drifted lazily down upon the scene. Coyote could barely make out the soles of three pairs of naked human feet. Obviously, he had burped the kids' shoes off.

The Big Burp-Off

Boomer laughed at the coyote's unashamed burp—one that was not followed by "excuse me." A free spirit, he didn't believe in apologies for natural bodily functions either. Then, spontaneously, just as he did when his brother, Sam, burped— Boomer swallowed some air and burped back.

Coyote's ears pricked up. Was the boy offering a game? Of course he was! The trickster loved burping contests. But which belches, he asked himself, would be appropriate for a match with a human? Thinking for a moment, he decided to start with The

Floater—a good choice, since his stomach was overstuffed and the burp didn't require much air. Talking a small gulp, Coyote constricted his throat and produced a buoyant, almost silky belch that drifted slowly toward Boomer and dispersed politely.

"I can't believe it," Boomer whispered. "He burped back at me." Admiringly, he said, "Wow, he's got control…"

Frightened, Arianna tugged at Bird's sleeve. "Come on, let's get out of here. He might bite!"

"Boomer," Hummingbird protested, "Arianna's freaking out…"

The boy turned and put his finger to his lips: "Shhhh…not now."

Boomer and Sam's burping battles usually involved only two performance features: length and loudness. He knew he couldn't match the coyote's technique, but he could demonstrate his longest burp. Sam had timed it at twenty seconds! Certain that the coyote would approve, Boomer downed a lungful of air and let rip a vibrating rumble that seemed to go on forever. Finally, to Hummingbird and Arianna's great relief, the burp crossed the twenty second finish line and stopped. Boomer smiled proudly.

Coyote was impressed. The burp had no finesse, but he liked the boy's stamina and determination. However, to show the abilities of a true professional, the trickster replied with an "eructation"—a belch of interrupted short blasts. Requiring superb diaphragm support, each individual discharge of air was perfectly bounded; there was no bleeding of one blast into another. (Burping judges term this skill "bracketing.")

Boomer was blown away. He couldn't wait to try that one on Sam! But, overcome as he was with excitement, he wasn't thinking about who would teach him the burp commonly known among non-amateurs as the "Choo-Choo." Realizing that the coyote was waiting for his response, he turned and warned the girls to put their hands over their ears. Then, breathing in deeply, he prepared for the burp that Sam called "The Howler." Opening his mouth as wide as possible, Boomer emitted a guttural roar that would have shamed the male monkey for whom it was named. The burp's only elegance was its very sharp and abrupt conclusion.

Coyote broke eye contact with Boomer. He turned his head to the side and considered the situation. Boomer had violated protocol by escalating the volume too quickly—but the trickster liked the boy's spunk. Nonetheless, the burping code of conduct required him to put Boomer in his place. Few people, if any, knew that Coyote was responsible for the loudest sound ever recorded in human history. He was the source of "The Bloop"—a low-frequency sound detected by scientists in 1997. The U. S. National Oceanic and Atmospheric Administration (NOAA) believed it originated in the Pacific Ocean west of the southern tip of South America. Most scientists believed The Bloop sounded more like an animal than an underwater volcano or earthquake, but they never offered any credible theories about its origin. In truth, it was the winning burp in Coyote's contest with a Blue Whale.

Glancing at Hummingbird and Arianna whose presence complicated things, Coyote weighed his options. Finally, he settled on a soundless belch called a "Grand Silence" or "GS" (pronounced "gas") that would administer discipline, but not punishment. A "Trickster GS" was measured on the Fugita Scale like a tornado. Although soundless, it registered a F0 level, the equivalent of a forty mile per hour wind.

As Coyote gulped air, the kids began to feel dizzy. He'd swallowed so much air that the garden's barometric pressure had suddenly dropped. Already feeling light-headed, Arianna totally panicked when the coyote stood up on his back legs. She shrieked, "Run! He's standing up!"

Stupidly, as if it would reassure her new friend, Hummingbird smiled and said, "It's okay. He does that."

Bird still had the silly smile on her face when they were struck by the gale force belch. There was no "It was like a train a-coming" warning—just a soundless wall of white wind that struck them flat on their backs. With their heads acting as plowshares, Hummingbird, Boomer and Arianna were shoved along the ground, scraping three straight furrows that halted just shy of the fence. The power of the tornadic gust unexpectedly did Aunt Chick a favor. It blasted the old paint off the fence— preparing it for a fresh coat.

Coyote peered through the shredded squash leaves and dirt that drifted lazily down upon the scene. He could barely make out the soles of three pairs of naked human feet. Obviously, he had burped the kids' shoes off. Concerned that he had used too much force, he trotted over to give them a sniff. First he checked out Hummingbird and Arianna. They were fine, just a little stunned. Then he turned to Boomer. With his muzzle poised over the boy's face, Coyote examined him carefully. Apparently there was no harm done. Pausing to reflect, Coyote realized there were several things he liked about Rain's oldest friend. Boomer was playful, receptive, and he managed his energy expertly. He thought the boy had a tendency to rush things, but understood that would change with maturity.

When Boomer opened his eyes, Coyote withdrew and returned to the squash plants. The boy blinked away the dirt and raised himself up on one arm. He reached over and pulled Arianna up to a sitting position. She brushed back her hair and mumbled, "What happened?"

Hummingbird, who was struggling to stand up, was clueless: "Whahhh, we fell down?"

Then, as the kids' heads began to clear, their eyes focused on the coyote. They jumped up and bunched together, staring nervously at the scruffy-furred creature. Coyote remained standing on four legs. No need to freak them out again, he thought, I'm through for today. He signaled his leave-taking with a short "Yip!" followed by a deep and very human chuckle. Then, the old mischief-maker sailed over the fence and was gone.

Dancing from foot to foot, Boomer jabbed his fist in the air, yelling "Yes!"

Arianna stumbled backwards from Boomer. "You're happy? He almost killed us!" Getting angrier, she pointed a finger at Bird. "And what did *you* mean, 'It's okay, he does that?' Does what? Huff and puff and blow your house down?"

Boomer corrected her gently. "Uh, that was a wolf that huffed and puffed—not a coyote, Arianna."

Arianna stared at Boomer like he was insane. Exasperated, she furiously started brushing the dirt off her jacket. That's when she saw the rip. Her new jacket was ruined. Counting to ten, Arianna closed her eyes. "I knew I should have changed clothes."

Hummingbird started to explain, but Arianna cut her off. "There's something going on here you haven't been telling me." Arianna gestured wildly around the garden. "Coyotes jumping out of giant green things! Bur…bur…burping and…" Arianna took a deep breath and stopped stammering. Glaring at her friends, she added quietly, "And they don't walk around on two legs, either."

With all the dignity she could muster, Arianna found her shoes and stomped off. She hollered over her shoulder, "I'm going to find out what going on and I know who's going to tell me! Rain that Dances!"

Boomer and Hummingbird followed her—at a distance. When they rounded a slight bend in the road, they saw Arianna, hands on hips, standing in front of two very startled young men.

Puzzled, Simon said, "Hi, Arianna, we were just coming over to the garden."

"Well, someone already beat you to it. Like a coyote that stands up like a man? Sound familiar?"

Rain glanced at Simon. "A coyote, huh?"

"Do you want to tell me about it?"

Rain nodded. "Sure, Arianna. We should have told you before." When Boomer and Hummingbird caught up, he added, "Come on. Let's sit down. It's kind of a long story."

Rain told Arianna about the day the eagle showed up at an old tree stump near Salt Lick Creek. "I was fishing that afternoon. I looked over at the old tree stump and there he was. He looked kinda bummed out. I thought there was something wrong—so I went over and looked at him up close. That's when he started talking to me. He said lots of things had changed on our rez—like people were just sitting around and kids were playing indoors too much and eating junk food. All that inactivity can make people unhealthy—maybe even get sick with type 2 diabetes. He said we needed to go back to our traditions—eating the food our ancestors ate and working and playing the way they did. Then, he said he had to go, but he would be back the next day to tell me more stuff. That's when I brought Boomer with me."

"Oh, man," Boomer said, "I remember it like it was yesterday. His wings were so huge! He started right off telling us to get moving—so we were running around and leaping and jumping all over the place! Remember that, RD?"

Rain laughed. "Oh, yeah. We went totally bonkers."

"But it made him really happy," Boomer went on. "Then he taught us a song about moving our bodies and played a game with us."

"Didn't you think a talking eagle was a little strange?" Arianna said.

"Not really," Rain answered. "Maybe because we were little, it just seemed normal."

"The next day," Hummingbird said, "Rain brought Simon and me to meet the eagle. He invited this rabbit to talk to us. She was really cute with these big floppy ears. Mostly, she gave us the low-down on healthy fruits and vegetables." Looking at Boomer, she teased, "She had a hard time with Boomer, but she finally convinced him."

"Vegetables weren't always my favorites," Boomer admitted.

"The last day the eagle came," Rain continued, "he brought the rabbit and this coyote, too."

"Was it the same coyote that we saw today?" Arianna asked. Hummingbird and Boomer nodded.

"The coyote tried to trick us into eating some cookies he'd stolen," Simon said. "I think he was trying to teach us about "tricky" snacks. Like somebody says they're good, but they really aren't." Simon smiled at Hummingbird. "He was warning us in a funny way, but Bird told him off anyhow."

"Yeah," Bird remembered, "he said he wouldn't trick us again."

Figuring that everyone had had their say, Rain said, "After that, we didn't see the animals again—not until the beginning of this school year."

No longer angry, Arianna asked, "Rain, have you ever told anybody else about the eagle, rabbit, and coyote?"

"When we talked about the animals, our parents just thought we were pretending or playing. Then later as we got older, we realized that we had been honored by something very special. That's when we stopped talking. So, yes, you're the first person we've told."

"Are you afraid to tell other people?"

"No. It's not that, Arianna. And, um, it's not like we're the only ones who have this knowledge. For sure, we're not afraid to tell people what the eagle told us." Looking for support from the others, Rain said, "I think we kept it to ourselves because the eagle chose us for some important purpose."

"Yeah, he picked us," Bird said, "but we're not really sure why."

Remembering the coyote's spying on Hummingbird, Simon gave Rain and Boomer a guarded look. "What was the coyote doing at the garden?"

Boomer couldn't wait to tell. "Man, I wish you guys could have seen him! He'd been eating one of these big squashes. Oh, yeah, you gotta see these things. Bird made the mother of all fertilizers! They're huge! Anyway, he did this big burp, so I burped back. We were burping back and forth…and then he just blew us away. It was the coolest trick in the world! Way better than the 'elephant's toothpaste!'"

Bird's antennae went up. She turned on Boomer. "What do you mean *better* than the 'elephant's toothpaste?'"

Realizing he'd spilled the beans, Boomer hemmed and hawed.

Hummingbird was instantly suspicious. "Did the coyote cause the explosion? Was he tricking me into doing that stupid stuff?"

Rain spoke up. "The coyote was in the picture that Sammie took with her cell phone. He was watching you from the hill behind the school. He had a pair of binoculars. We would have told you before, but, um, we thought it just might make things worse."

"It's been him all along!" Hummingbird wailed. "He's been tricking me…"

"He's not always up to something bad," Rain said, trying to reassure her. "He helped us before. He helped Granma. I know he did. He tricked the fossil poacher."

Hummingbird went silent, contemplating her fate as the butt of coyote jokes. Obviously, she thought, the coyote's promise not to trick them was limited to preventing diabetes. He felt just fine about other kinds of tricks.

Keeping an eye on Bird, Rain turned back to Arianna. "Anyway, now you know it all."

"Wow, no wonder you guys know everything about type 2 diabetes."

"And now because of you," Simon said, "we know about type 1 diabetes, too." Unable to contain his curiosity any longer, he pointed toward the garden, "Ah, do you mind if we take a look at the plants now? I'd like to see these 'jolly green giants.'"

Chapter 18

Thistle stopped her twirling. She fixed her eye on Chris and spoke in a low, menacing growl:
"I wouldn't do that if I were you."

Guarding Gardens

That night, Hummingbird and Arianna talked late into the night. Bird was totally whacked out about the coyote. She suspected that the trickster had something to do with the squashes growing so fast, but she wasn't sure. The girls decided that the best thing to do was to check it out with Miss Swallow.

The next morning, Hummingbird stopped off at the science teacher's classroom and described the miraculous growth of the "jolly green giants" (as Simon was now calling them). Miss

Swallow said she'd never heard of seeds sprouting and producing fruit so quickly. She invited Bird to join her at her computer. They went web surfing.

"Well, Hummingbird. This site says giant pumpkins can gain thirty pounds in one day."

"But, Miss Swallow, they were just sprouts the day before. Besides, the plants weren't even from the seeds we planted. I don't know what they were. The leaves looked like a squash"

Miss Swallow frowned and shook her head. She was stumped. "Bird, I'd like to visit your garden. I want to see these plants for myself." Hummingbird and Miss Swallow agreed to take a trip out to Aunt Chick's on Thursday afternoon. Miss Swallow wanted to photograph the plants and gather samples.

A thorough scientist, she would try to gather as much information as she could before the visit—which is what prompted her to call Alfred Badger to her desk during first period. Miss Swallow knew that Alfred's father had experimented with various fertilizers, trying to speed up the growth of sunflowers and other produce that he grew commercially. "Alfred, has your dad ever used any fertilizer that could cause cucumbers or squashes to double or triple their size in just a few hours?"

Looking surprised, Alfred said, "I don't think so, Miss Swallow. That sounds pretty impossible. But if there's anything you want to know about manure and compost, Dad can fill you in."

Miss Swallow laughed. The growth inducing properties of manure really wasn't her thing. Turning on the overhead projector for today's lesson, she said casually, "Actually, I'm asking because Hummingbird has been trying to grow some super-sized vegetables. She's had some interesting effects from the fertilizer she's using."

Chris Sorrel, who was also in the first period science class, saw Alfred talking to Miss Swallow. When he returned to his seat, Chris leaned across the aisle and asked what the teacher wanted. Alfred laughed. For years he had heard his father griping about the Sorrels always winning the blue ribbon for the biggest pumpkin at the Harvest Pow-Wow. Seizing the opportunity to give Chris a jab, he said, "Hey, Chris, tell your dad he's got competition. Hummingbird's growing some giant pumpkins or something. You just might get beat this year." Alfred smiled when he saw Chris's face darken. His punch had landed.

"So, where's she growing these pumpkins?"

Alfred decided to draw out the fun. "She and her pals have been hanging out at her Aunt Chick's. They're probably growing 'em on her place somewhere." Smirking, he added, "That's across from our place, you know."

Chris ignored Alfred. He would deal with him later. He also ignored Miss Swallow and the class's preparation for their seed classification lab. All he could think about was Hummingbird. What was she up to now? She was like a whack-a-mole game. You bang her head down in one hole and she pops up through another!

When the bell rang, Chris rushed out into the hallway and headed for Tater Tot's locker. He had a plan. He would round up Tater Tot and Dumptruck and they would do a little scouting at Aunt Chick's after school. They'd find out what Hummingbird and the "Greenies" were growing.

Chris was almost at Tater Tot's locker when he saw that his toadie had a visitor. Was that Arianna? Hummingbird's friend? Chris drew back against the hallway wall and waited for the girl to leave. Then he slid up silently behind Tater.

"What are you doing with little Miss Ding-Ding?"

Tater Tot didn't look at Chris. He finished arranging the stuff in his locker. Then he pulled out his lunch bag and slammed the door shut. Looking up he said in a quiet voice, "She's wants to show some of my drawings to Mrs. Corn. They're looking for somebody to do cartoons for the *Thunderbird*."

"I got something for us to do this afternoon. And it's not any of your cruddy drawing. You better be there."

"Sorry. My mom's coming to get me. I won't be around."

"Don't be running out on me again, Tater," Chris threatened. "Not like you did before."

Chris turned away and tramped to the lunchroom looking for Dumptruck. He wasn't there. For once, his frequent in-house suspension was not a bad thing. Chris would have to do his dirty work on this own.

That afternoon, Chris got off the school bus two stops early. He turned down Old Agency Road and headed toward Alfred's house. He passed by a few horses and cows he guessed belonged to Aunt Chick. Their pasture showed no evidence of giant pumpkins. Nor did the yellowing fields of dried corn stalks reveal any garden patches. Puzzled, Chris stopped and looked around, waving off swarms of gnats that flitted about in the late day sun. Where was Hummingbird hiding the pumpkins? That's when he spied the red fence behind Aunt Chick's old ranch house. He headed in that direction.

Sky Heart had been curiously watching Chris from a nearby power pole. Being suspicious of the boy, the eagle flapped into the still air and flew toward the fence. Circling above, he looked down into the garden. Were those big blobs what Chris had come to see? Maybe Thistle knew something about them. He banked away and flew the short distance to Thistle's nest. Landing in front of her brushy house, the eagle rustled his wings, announcing his presence.

Thistle called out to him from inside her enclosure. "Give me a moment, Sky Heart."

"Thistle, please hurry. It's the boy, Chris. He's headed toward Hummingbird's garden. I thought you ought to know."

Thistle's head popped out from the nest. "You mean Coyote's garden, don't you? Did you see the big green fruits?" When Sky Heart nodded, she went on. "They're coyote squash. He grew them for his own eating. Ohh, he's up to tricks. You should have seen him having fun with Hummingbird and her friends yesterday."

"Something tells me Chris is up to no good."

"Gardens are my territory, Sky Heart. I'll go down there and see what's going on. Watch the bunnies—they shouldn't be much trouble. They're sleeping. Oh, and back me up if I need it."

By the time Thistle had hopped down the hill, Chris was peering in the windows of the shed. Because the small building couldn't be seen from Aunt Chick's house, Chris had no fear of discovery. He pushed open the door and glanced inside. The work table immediately drew his attention. He made a quick inventory of the equipment and plant nutrients. However, it was the stack of articles on growing giant vegetables that told the tale. Chris rummaged through the photocopies quickly. So, he thought, she's not just interested in pumpkins—she's trying to grow *everything* big!

Chris stomped out of the shed. This wasn't turning out the way he'd planned. When he put people down, they stayed down! Foul as his mood was, it wasn't as bad as a disgusting smell that seemed to be coming from the area enclosed by the red fence. Pinching his nostrils, Chris headed for the garden. Tiring quickly of the gate's tug-of war, he kicked it open. At first, all he could see was "green." Then the stink hit him. Chris gagged. The plants reeked like a locker room of stinky socks and sewage.

Despite the tangle of pointy triangular leaves that would have discouraged most intruders, Chris pushed his way into the dense growth. In the 24 hours since "the big burp-off," the plants had taken over the garden. Chris discovered the gravel path around the vegetable patch and followed it. He came upon some crushed leaves that looked like an animal's bed and the empty skin of the squash Coyote had eaten. Beside it, another huge green-striped globe had taken its place. Chris squatted down to examine it. It reminded him of a gourd, but its size was awesome! But, true to his nature, Chris's sense of fascination and wonder was soon overcome by envy and resentment. The gourd (or whatever it was) was twice as big as anything his family had grown. Hummingbird, that stupid *girl*, had discovered a way to win every giant pumpkin contest in the world!

His heart thumping, Chris crashed about in the jungle growth, looking for something that he could use to smash the monster fruit/veg. He found an old ax handle leaning up against the fence. He picked it up and slapped it against his open palm. This would work fine. He would pulverize her giants!

A sudden movement in the undergrowth alerted Chris that he wasn't alone. Watchfully, he made his way back to his intended target. He was very surprised, to say the least, to discover a rabbit sitting on top of it. Waving his arms, Chris yelled, "Shoo!" But Thistle didn't budge. She just stared at him.

Somewhat unsettled by this unusual behavior, Chris hesitated. Chiding himself, he thought, So, you're afraid of rabbit now? Chris sniggered, "Okay, bunny-wabbit. Stay where you are and get whacked!" He raised the ax handle.

Thistle stood up on her hind legs and waved her paws over her head. Then she began to turn in a circle. The old girl hadn't pulled a trick in many a year. She was rusty, but she still had the memory. She just needed a minute to get her trickster "groove on."

Chris's mouth fell open. Was she dancing?

Thistle stopped her twirling. She fixed her eye on Chris and spoke in a low, menacing growl: "I wouldn't do that if I were you." Scared silly, Chris staggered backwards and fell into a dank nest of leaves. Dropping the ax handle, he clutched at a mass of tendrils and stems, trying to pull himself up. The hairs on the stem's rough surface chafed against his face and arms, already damp with sweat. He began to itch madly.

Gaining his feet, Chris bolted for the gate. Once he had escaped the garden, he tugged off his shirt and slapped it wildly at his arms, trying to remove the prickly hairs. But they only burrowed deeper into his skin. Hollering gibberish, Chris ran like a crazy man toward the road, wriggling and pawing at his face.

Thistle hopped over to the fence post where Sky Heart had perched, observing the whole performance. Looking up, she said, "Is he gone?"

Sky Heart nodded. "Running like a turkey. Sorry, I left the nest. I thought he might hurt you."

"Oh, Sky Heart," Thistle said, "you know I have a few tricks up my sleeve."

Still watching Chris, the eagle observed Thistle in his side vision. He smiled. "So, you used your power, Thistle. It's been a long time."

"Yes, I didn't want him to destroy the squashes. But, all I could manage was a scary voice." "And," she giggled, "an itchy rash."

"A bad rash?"

"No, it'll be gone in an hour. My power is weak, Sky Heart. Chris ran away, but the effect won't last. He'll be back."

Pointing to her left ear, Sky Heart said, "Your power may be stronger than you think."

Thistle reached up and felt her ear. It was standing up straight. Laughing, she said, "Ahh, the old power. I'm a *wild rabbit* now..."

Chapter 19

Yellow flesh, seeds, and liquid sprayed from the gigantic wounds that Chris inflicted on the young behemoth.

Pulp and Seeds

The next morning at school Chris stood staring at his reflection in a mirror in the boy's restroom. He squeezed a small dollop of cortisone cream on his finger and dabbed it on the reddened skin under each eye. Thankfully, the itching had gone away after a shower, but his eyes looked like he'd been crying. Chris tried out several tough-guy faces in the mirror. He'd dare anybody to say anything about his weepy eyes.

When Thistle's little whammy had worn off the night before, Chris's bravado had returned. He convinced himself that the talking rabbit was the result of a bad bologna sandwich he'd eaten for lunch. Determined to smash Hummingbird's garden, he recruited his brother, Melvin, who was only too glad to lend a hand. Now he just needed some help from his toadies.

Tater Tot was nowhere to be found, but Chris managed to rope in the unlucky Dumptruck. His other recruit was Freddie, a sometimes toad that was scared to death of Melvin and Jesse. Chris had originally tapped Lester, but he had the misfortune to ask "Who died?"—pointing to a tear rolling down Chris's face.

Immediately after school, Melvin picked up the "demolition" crew and they drove out to Aunt Chick's property. Chris wanted to get there first before Hummingbird or any of her friends. Melvin parked his truck behind a stand of cottonwoods, and gave each boy a baseball bat. The trespassers approached the garden along a little rise behind it, rather than from the road. They actually passed within ten feet of Thistle's nest. Chris didn't bother to tell Dump and Freddie why they were destroying the plants—only that he wanted them gone. As they drew nearer to the garden, Freddie said, "Do you smell something funky?"

Dumptruck laughed and whispered, "I thought it was Melvin."

Freddie started to laugh, but stifled it. Keeping an eye on Chris and his brother, he whispered back, "Hey, Big D, I wonder what we're gonna do with these bats. Do you think we could get in trouble?"

"Yeah, maybe."

The two reluctant vandals saw Chris up ahead, standing beside the garden gate. He waited for them to catch up. "Okay, there's a bunch of super-stinky plants in there. Some kind of really big squash or gourd. We're going to find every one and beat 'em to a pulp. Got it?"

Freddie stood up on his toes, trying to see over the fence. "Yeah, I guess. What's Melvin doing at that shed?"

Chris laughed, "Don't ask." Just then, the boys heard the sound of shattering glass and banging metal.

Freddie asked anyway, "That must be Melvin, huh?" Chris ignored him. He was squirting a tube of white cream on his face.

"What are you doing that for?" Dumptruck wanted to know.

Rolling down his sleeves, Chris smirked. "Don't worry about it. Come on."

The boys followed Chris into the garden. It wasn't hard to spot the squashes. Overnight they had continued to grow. Each one must have weighed 300 pounds. Chris began pounding on one that was growing near the gate. Its shell was immature and still tender. Yellow flesh, seeds, and liquid sprayed from the gigantic wounds that Chris inflicted on the young behemoth.

Dumptruck and Freddie followed Chris's example. Over the next thirty minutes, they battered, hammered, and crushed. Occasionally they heard loud thumping and what sounded like splintering wood coming from the shed.

When they had finished liquefying the squashes, Melvin joined them to complete the job. Holding up an ax he found in the shed, he said, "Okay, who wants to chop up the vines?"

Chris pointed at Dumptruck, "He does."

Panting and wiping sweat off his forehead, Dumptruck reached for the ax. "Okay, give it to me."

"Say, please," Melvin grinned.

Dumptruck gritted his teeth. "Please."

The bigger boy shoved the ax at him. Dumptruck glanced away and started chopping at the vines with a vengeance. He didn't want Melvin to see the tears of humiliation in his eyes. Then, Chris, Melvin and Freddie provided the final insult by stomping the leaves into the ground. An appalling stench rose from the crushed greenery. It grabbed the back of the throat like something dead.

Dumptruck was still hacking at a couple of vines when he realized that the others had stopped. He looked up. "Are we done?"

Melvin laughed. "Yeah, we're done. Hummingbird's squashes won't be winning any ribbons this year!" The brothers gave each other a fist bump. It was a great day for bullies.

The boys rounded up their baseball bats and headed back to Melvin's truck. Dumptruck tramped along with his head down. He said nothing, but his mind and spirit were anything but quiet. Riding in the back of Melvin's pick-up, he realized that something important had happened back there in the garden. A metamorphosis had begun. He didn't really understand how he had become a toadie, but he was sure of one thing. He didn't want to be one anymore.

Yesterday, Hummingbird and Arianna had raced to get to the garden. But today they weren't exactly eager —not since running into the coyote. However, Bird reminded Arianna they should check out the plants since Miss Swallow would be making a visit tomorrow.

Leaving the house, Arianna teased Hummingbird. "Yeah, Bird, 'how does your garden grow?' Did you hear any 'silver bells' or see some 'cockle shells?'"

"No, just some burps and blobs!"

Arianna laughed, but got serious. "Will Miss Swallow be able to tell if the fertilizer had anything to do with them getting so big?"

"Maybe," Hummingbird said. "But none of our unfertilized seeds sprouted overnight. That makes me think it's all the coyote's work."

Caught up in their chatter, the girls had not noticed the paper that was blowing about in Aunt Chick's pasture—not until a sheet blew up against Arianna's foot. She picked it up. "Look, Bird, this is a page from that article on growing giant carrots."

"That's weird. How did it get out here?" Alarmed, the girls ran the rest of the way to the shed. The door was standing open. Hummingbird glanced at Arianna: "I thought we shut the door."

They peeked fearfully in the doorway. The destruction was almost complete. Windows were broken, the worktable was turned over, and bags of soil and fertilizer covered everything in white and brown dust. Even Boo's new shelves were hacked off the wall. What really hurt was the pile of debris on the floor that had once been the equipment that Miss Swallow donated and the pots of unfertilized seeds. There was nothing left of their laboratory.

Arianna was crushed. "Who could have done this?" She crept cautiously into the shed, being careful not to step on any broken glass or nails.

Hummingbird didn't follow; she was already running toward the garden. Arianna was tip-toeing out of the shed, when she heard Bird crying: "Arianna! Arianna!" She dashed to her friend, but staggered to a sudden stop. The sight before her eyes was like nothing she'd ever seen before. Nothing was recognizable. The mysterious and miraculous squashes were no more. The garden looked like a salad that had been through a blender. A rotten salad that stunk to high heaven.

Arianna pulled on Hummingbird's arm. But she didn't move. "Come on, Bird. Let's get out of here! Whoever did this might still be around. Something bad has happened."

Finally, Hummingbird backed out of the garden. She mumbled, "We better tell Aunt Chick." The girls hurried to the ranch house, but no one was home. Obviously, Chick hadn't been around to notice any trespassers.

The girls slowly walked home, totally depressed. At one point, Hummingbird started crying—which made Arianna start crying, too. When they got to the house, Bird told her mother and father what had happened. Tom immediately phoned the Tribal police to report the vandalism. When he hung up, Arianna called Rain, Boomer and Simon. She told them that the laboratory and the squashes were history.

Sky Heart, of course, saw the attack and had flown immediately to alert Coyote.

The eagle searched for him in his usual hangouts, but he wasn't anywhere to be found. Sky Heart abandoned the hills and began looking closer to town. He finally found the trickster mouse-hunting near a dumpster in back of the Tribal college.

"Thanks, Sky Heart, that wing-flapping scared off my snack."

"Sorry, but I thought you would want to know. Melvin and Chris just wiped out your big squashes."

Without even a "What?" the joking rodent hunter suddenly transformed before Sky Heart's eyes. Furious that his squashes had been so insulted, he bristled into a spikey hair ball. (For a moment, the eagle thought that Coyote had turned into a porcupine.) Then, ears flattened and eyes burning, he reached for his power and disappeared in a blinding streak of light...

Following a furry bullet isn't that simple. Sky Heart had to gain some altitude before he could make out the trickster's path. In places, it actually smoked! However, when the eagle arrived at the garden, he found Coyote quietly squatting in the middle of the green chaos.

Watching the eagle find a perch, Coyote laughed. "What took you so long?"

"I didn't think I'd find you laughing, Trickster."

"I don't like humans interfering with my business. But when they do mess with me, I find that I do my best work." Very slowly, he added: "That makes me very happy." Coyote sniffed the air. "Somebody has played a little joke here, and it wasn't me." He looked at Sky Heart quizzically.

"You mean the stink?" the eagle asked.

"Stink? You offend me, Eagle. I invented that perfume. It's why the plant bears my name. I prefer coyote squash, but you may have heard it called coyote gourd—or maybe even stinking buffalo gourd. It's all the same. I wanted something that would draw flies, but repel grasshoppers." He sniffed again. "But I'm getting off the point. No, I was talking about a trickster joke."

"Oh, that was Thistle. She tried to drive off Chris yesterday when he tried to smash a squash. It worked—but only for a short time. He came back with his brother and two other boys."

"I'll stop by and thank her before I leave. Now I must begin. Good thing I didn't eat that mouse."

Sky Heart didn't know what Coyote meant—not until he waded into the lagoon of what looked like baby food spinach, and began his meal. The trickster stuck his nose into the glop that had once been his beautiful garden and began to eat the squash roots still anchored in the ground. He also snuffled around for any seeds he could find. He didn't want to miss any of those.

Sky Heart watched him slurping along for several minutes. But Coyote's lip-smacking and burps (and other noises we won't mention) proved to be too revolting for the bird. He soon retreated to Thistle's nest.

Before long, Sky Heart and Thistle heard a sloshing, gurgling rumble that sounded like a waterbed in an earthquake. It was Coyote dragging his swollen body up the hill. Even though the noise he made was disgusting, it was his appearance that made their eyes pop. He looked like a big undulating *tick*.

"Need any help?" Sky Heart offered.

"No, I got it," Coyote panted. "I just need to lie down a bit. So I can digest." Flopping down with a groan, he turned over on his back, breathing laboriously. Thistle hopped over to assist. "Here, sit up, Coyote." He raised himself up and she patted him on the back until he rewarded her with two mega-burps.

Lying back down, he thanked her. "Ahh, that was a serious burp—not recreational. I feel much better." Breathing more easily, he said proudly, "I got it all: roots, vines, pulp and seeds."

"What are you going to do with it?" Thistle wanted to know.

Holding his gut, he grinned and said, "Make a mountain for Hummingbird. I'll plant the seeds with my own fertilizer."

Thistle screwed up her nose. "Eewww, that's gross."

Sky Heart jumped in. "No, it isn't Thistle. My bird relatives, the seed-eaters, do it all the time. Some plants depend on us to spread their seeds that way."

Coyote's gut suddenly emitted a high-pitched whine that caused them all to stop talking. Looking down at his stomach with satisfaction, the trickster said, "We do what we have to." Then he added, "Besides, Thistle, rabbits re-cycle nutrients from their pellets all the time. You shouldn't be criticizing...."

Thistle cut him off sharply. "Let's not go there, please! That's private rabbit business."

Coyote started to get irritated, but Sky Heart intervened. "She's just prissy sometimes, Coyote. Forget it."

The trickster's annoyance passed and he said. "Thank you, Thistle, for trying to protect the garden. Teasing a bit, he added, "I noticed that you used your power."

"Well, it wasn't much," she said, blushing under her fur. Then recovering herself, she said loudly, "I don't know what your game is, Coyote, but I know you do things for a reason. Those boys had no right to mess with that squash!"

"I agree. Chris and Melvin made a *big* mistake," Coyote smiled toothily.

Noticing that the sun was going down, Sky Heart said, "You better get going if you are going to do any planting this evening."

Coyote said, "So true, my friend." He hiccupped and burped one more time; then whispered, "Later!" and was gone. A bit wobbly at first, he soon found his legs. He swung into an awkward, but steady gait that put him at the foothills to Shell Ridge in no time. He headed to an area he knew had tree cover and water. It wasn't difficult to find a concealed spot that provided at least six hours of sunshine every day.

Coyote began to scratch up the ground cover. He loosened the soil to at least four inches and then began to make his deposits. He pooped out the seeds at one foot intervals, making sure they would not crowd each other. Satisfied with the precision of his scat, Coyote raked dirt over the fertilized seeds with his paw. Remembering his promise to share with Hummingbird, he scratched "a burr from his fur" and planted it with one of the seeds. Now, it would sprout as "Hummingbird's Squash."

He sat down next to the neat rows of freshly mounded soil. Now that his gut was empty, Coyote felt revitalized. In fact, he felt like singing. He warmed up with a few yips and howls. Finding his voice, he sang and sang coyote songs long into the night. Growing tired, he stopped and took a short snooze. Waking refreshed, he started singing again and was still singing when the sun came up the next morning.

The seeds heard him.

"Need any help?" Sky Heart offered. "No, I got it," Coyote panted. "I just need
to lie down a bit. So I can digest."

Chapter 20

Coyote had become a buzzing cloud in which it was impossible to predict where or when he was. From inside the swirling uncertainty came the sound of wild cackling and the trickster's conjure, "put everything back the way it was."

Back the Way it Was

Wednesday started out weird and it kept getting weirder as the day went on. Not long after the first bell, an unusual morning storm rolled through Thunder Rock that shorted out the school's electrical system. The sky grew so black that the hallways were almost completely dark. For safety's sake, the teachers were told to keep the kids in homeroom until the storm passed.

Dumptruck sat in his desk, only half conscious of the downpour hammering the roof. He vaguely noticed that Mr. Braun was lowering the blinds, but paid no mind until he heard hailstones crashing against the windows. Now, the gray light that edged the blinds barely illuminated the classroom. Gee, he thought, it's really dark in here. Taking advantage of the extra time in homeroom, Dumptruck slipped over to an empty desk beside Tater Tot. As usual, the red-headed boy was drawing—even in the dark.

"Hey, Tater. Where ya been?"

"Around. Staying out of Chris's way mostly."

"Yeah, I figured. I heard he gave you a hard time 'bout talking to that Arianna girl."

"Word gets around."

"Look, ah, I've been thinking. About this stuff we've been doing for Chris." He looked around and lowered his voice. "I wanna get out of it."

Tater Tot stopped his doodling. Dumptruck had got his attention. "How?"

"I don't know yet. But something tells me you don't like it either...I thought maybe we could work on it together. You know, two heads better than one?"

Tater Tot nodded. He was interested.

"Um, so what is Arianna like? I mean, after you apologized and all?"

Tater Tot was puzzled by Dumptruck's questions, but he answered anyway. "I just talked to her a couple of times. She's was pretty nice to me. She lives with Hummingbird."

At the mention of Hummingbird's name, Dumptruck looked away. "You know, Chris has really got it in for Bird…and Simon. But, I don't think he'll tangle with RD and Boomer. So, I'm thinking tha…"

A crack of lighting and thunder boomed right over the school. Mr. Braun looked up nervously at the rattling ceiling tiles. He directed the kids sitting near the windows to move to the other side of the room.

Tater Tot didn't have to be convinced. "Man, that lightning was close." He followed Dumptruck back to his desk and took the empty seat next to him.

Dumptruck lowered his voice even further. "So, like I was saying, I'm thinking maybe we should team up with RD and his friends."

"But, man, we've been messin' with those guys. They don't want anything to do with us."

"Tater, I know everybody thinks I'm dumb. But I'm gettin' smarter all the time. Look, who do we know that didn't bow down to Chris…and lived?"

Tater Tot didn't have to think about it. He replied immediately, "RD, Boomer, and Simon."

"Right. They kept their cool. Acted like he was being funny. It made Chris nervous, didn't it? They didn't run either. And no matter how much we dog Simon, he doesn't freak out." Leaning in closer to Tater Tot, Dumptruck added, "Besides, they're best friends with Hummingbird."

"So?"

"So like..." Dumptruck took in a deep breath and blew it forcibly out his nose— like he was purging a bad thought from his head. "I've done something really bad to Bird. If I can square things with her—then maybe we can make friends with the guys. She might even help us."

Tater frowned. "Like what? What have you done?"

Dumptruck confessed his part in the attack on the garden. He gave Tater Tot the lowdown on Melvin breaking up the shed and Chris getting him and Freddie to help him destroy the giant squashes. Finishing his tale, Big D said, "Man, you never seen a bigger mess...or smelled anything so bad!"

Tater Tot had listened avidly, his eyes getting bigger as the story went on. He even made Dumptruck tell him about the giant squashes again—they were cool. But the story made him uneasy. What if somebody called the police? Knowing that Chris had been looking for him the day before, Tater panicked, "Oh man, if this gets out, I hope nobody thinks I did it!"

Trying to assure his friend, Dumptruck said, "Don't worry, Tater, I'd tell'em you're innocent."

Suddenly the lights came back on. The class whistled and clapped their hands. Kids started stirring about, gathering up their things. Dumptruck hurried to get his point across to Tater Tot before the bell rang. "Tater, we got to change sides on this thing. I want it to be the way it used to be—before we were doing all this bully stuff. I got to make this up to Bird... somehow. So, you think Arianna could help me?"

"What do you want *her* to do? Besides, you did that "ding-ding" thing on her."

"Well, you did it, too! Anyway...I want her to get Hummingbird to talk to me."

Tater's mouth fell open. "You're not gonna tell Bird what you did, are you?"

"Yeah, I am. I know it's crazy."

Tater Tot thought about it, but only for a second. "Well, okay. I guess we're both crazy. I don't wanna take orders from Chris anymore, either. I'll find Arianna."

Dumptruck pointed to the window. "Hey, look, Tater. The sun's out."

It Tater Tot had gone looking for Arianna when the storm hit, he would have found her in Miss Swallow's room—with Hummingbird. When the lights went out, Miss Swallow told everyone to just sit tight. Going on with business as usual, she called the roll and filled out the absentee slips. Writing in the dark wasn't easy, but she was reasonably sure she hadn't botched it too badly. Certain that Hummingbird and Arianna had come to give her an update on their plants, Miss Swallow made her way toward them in the darkened room. "So, tell me about your fast growing veggies, girls...how big are they now?"

When there was no reply, Miss Swallow strained her eyes toward the dim outline of the two girls. "Bird, did you hear me? Is there something wrong?"

A small voice answered: "Everything's wrong, Miss Swallow. Somebody smashed them. The garden is ruined."

"Yeah, and they tore up the shed, too," Arianna added. "We'd set up the lab already. They broke everything—even the stuff you gave us."

Miss Swallow's attempt to ask more questions was lost in a crash of thunder and the continuous rumbling that followed. Whether it was because of the darkness or her inability to get more information (if only temporarily), Miss Swallow felt totally frustrated, even disoriented, by what she'd heard. Thinking about the bully attack on Arianna, she felt certain that the girls were being targeted again.

When the lights came back on, Miss Swallow tried to offer a more positive face to the girls. "Bird, I was hoping that I could get some photos of your squashes, but now that they're gone, let's see what we can re-grow from what's left. There must be some roots or seeds. We'll go to the garden tomorrow and see what we can find."

Miss Swallow's words, however, offered no comfort to Hummingbird. She was ready to hang it up. That afternoon, when she and Arianna returned to the scene of the crime, Hummingbird started chucking everything in the shed into a big pile. She refused to consider anything that could be salvaged. Although Arianna agreed that they should clean up the mess, she didn't agree that they should abandon the project.

"Please, Bird, at least wait until Miss Swallow checks it out. You shouldn't throw away stuff that's still good. She said there might be some roots or seeds that could be saved."

Handing Arianna a dust mask like the one she was wearing, Hummingbird said, "Look, Arianna, this was probably all some big trick of the coyote's. He's probably laughing his tail off right now. This was all a big mistake."

Arianna slipped the mask over her face. Now both girls sounded like they were talking from the bottom of a paper sack. "But Rain said that the coyote doesn't always pull bad tricks. Sometimes he helps."

"Like he helped me blow up Mr. Pence, get suspended, and kicked out of the science fair? He wasn't staring at me through those binoculars for nothing, you know!"

"But, Bird, that's when you thought of the giant vegetables. You might not have ever thought of growing them if he hadn't…"

Hummingbird interrupted. "Sure, he made me do that, too! Just so he could eat them. For Pete's sake, Arianna, the coyote probably tore up the big squashes himself!"

"If he wanted to eat the squashes," Arianna said logically, "why would he destroy them?"

Hummingbird shrugged. "Well…I guess you're right. That doesn't make sense."

Suddenly, Arianna made a discovery. "Look over here, Bird, under Simon's bubble wrap. It's some of the pots you didn't fertilize. They've sprouted! See their little leaves. Come on, Bird. Let's plant them in the cold frames!"

Hummingbird paused to think. Maybe Arianna was right. They shouldn't *totally* abandon the seedlings or the idea of the giant vegetables. Giving in a little bit, she said, "Sure. We might as well give the seedlings a chance. But I'm not starting any more giant vegetables—not this season anyway." To make her point, she emptied the remains of her fast-grow formula behind the shed. "If there are some seeds left, fine. Miss Swallow can collect them. Right now, let's just clean up and put everything *back the way it was.*"

Arianna rescued eight seedlings that had managed to survive Melvin's wreckage. A couple of the little plants had spilled out onto the floor, but she tenderly pressed them back into their fiber pots. While Hummingbird continued her sweeping, Arianna transplanted the little cabbages, turnips, and carrots into the cold frames. When she returned to the shed, Hummingbird had bagged most of the rubble. The place looked better, but not good.

Hummingbird switched off the light (at least something still worked) and the girls went outside to wash their hands. They didn't know that the spigot was one of Coyote's watering holes. He had been drinking from the hose when they had arrived at the shed. Coyote had heard everything they said.

The trickster watched the girls wash up and brush off each other's clothes. When they left, he waited impatiently as their silhouettes disappeared across the pasture. The sun was going down and twilight was fast approaching. The trickster trotted over to the cold frames and lifted the lid from one of them. Although he had excellent night vision, he was glad there was still some remaining light in the day. He wanted to make his selection carefully. After examining the characteristics of each seedling in detail, he chose a turnip. He pulled the seedling from its fiber pot and carried it into the shed. There he found one of the half-filled bags of dirt that Arianna saved from the garbage pile. Nestling the seedling into it, Coyote shaped the plastic bagging around it like a pot. Then, he placed it on the work table.

Coyote sat down on his haunches and considered what the girls had said. So, he thought, Hummingbird knows I had something to do with the 'elephant's toothpaste' explosion. Hmmm, *someone* is clever. He scowled. It annoyed him when humans figured out what he was doing.

However, his irritation passed when he reflected on what Thistle had said. Maybe he was being too tough on Hummingbird. Too many "tricks" and not enough "treats?" Well, he would give her a treat (a tricky treat, of course). Yes, a great understanding that would put her ambitions and the giant vegetables in perfect perspective. And he would use her own words to do it.

Coyote got up and trotted to the work table. He stared at the little turnip. Although its origins were far from this land, it would do fine for his purposes. Coyote's powers were great.

He took a deep breath and began to walk slowly backwards around the table. After four rounds, he picked up the pace—and the walk became a run. After sixteen rounds, the run had become a blur. After that, there was no counting. Coyote had become a buzzing cloud in which it was impossible to predict where or *when* he was. From inside the swirling uncertainty came the sound of wild cackling and the trickster's conjure, "put everything back the way it was."

Chapter 21

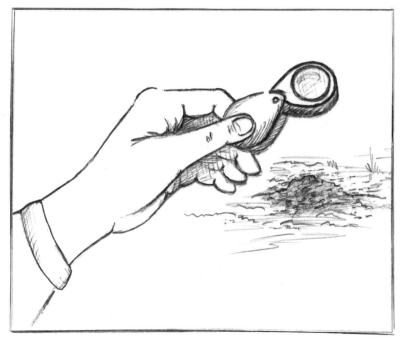

Scooping up a small amount of soil, she examined it carefully, looking for evidence of animal or plant life. Strangely, she didn't see any fungus filaments, insect debris, or even the casting of an earthworm.

Green Ancestors

Ms. Swallow came running up the hall. "Sorry, girls. I hope you haven't been waiting long."

The science teacher unlocked the door to her classroom. "Come on in. I'll be just a minute." The last hour of the school day was Miss Swallow's planning period. As chair of the new Anti-Bullying Committee, she had set up some time with Mr. Berry to discuss the training for teachers scheduled next week.

They had gotten into the details about teacher responsibilities and lost track of time.

Miss Swallow disappeared into the lab storeroom; when she emerged she had a botany field kit tucked under her arm. Grabbing her sweater and purse, she announced, "Okay, let's go see what kind of plants you were growing…and collect some seeds."

On the way over to Aunt Chick's in her old station wagon, Miss Swallow quizzed the girls about who might have vandalized the garden. Naturally, Hummingbird thought of Chris, but she didn't say anything. How could she prove it? Turning up the road to the old ranch house, they saw Aunt Chick pulling some sheets off the clothesline in the backyard.

Miss Swallow pulled the car over and leaned her head out the driver's window. "Hi, Chick! We're going to take a look at what's left of the garden."

Hummingbird's aunt stuffed the sheets in a laundry basket, and walked over to the car. She leaned down and greeted Miss Swallow and the girls. "Go on up and check it out. I haven't been to the garden myself, but I did see the shed. I can't believe somebody would do that." Looking at Hummingbird, she said, "An officer from the Neighborhood Watch came out. He said your dad called. I think he took some pictures." Turning back to Miss Swallow, she said, "Come by and visit when you're done."

Miss Swallow parked the car in back of the house and they walked the quarter mile to the garden. As they drew near the red fence, Arianna warned Miss Swallow about the smell: "The whole place stinks really bad—like somebody who never takes a bath."

Miss Swallow took out her notebook and wrote a note about the odor. "Sounds like a stinking buffalo gourd." Looking over at Hummingbird, she asked, "You didn't plant any gourd seeds, did you?"

"No, just turnips, carrots, and cabbage."

Sniffing the air, she said, "Well, I don't smell anything now."

"Don't worry. You will!"

The girls dramatically pulled open the gate as if to say, 'Okay! Get Ready!' Miss Swallow stepped inside. What she saw produced no gasp of dismay or even a minor "Yuk." Her reaction was a flat "I don't understand."

The girls stepped around Miss Swallow. Bewilderment couldn't describe their expressions. Arianna mumbled, "Where's the green stuff?" The garden looked like a parking lot on the moon. The dirt was so smooth it must have been vacuumed—or better yet, buffed with a floor sander. Surely, nothing had grown here in a hundred years.

Hummingbird recovered first. She raised her eyebrows and silently mouthed one word at Arianna: coyote.

Miss Swallow turned and asked, "Did somebody clean up the garden?"

Hummingbird said, "We didn't hear about it if they did."

"I'm sorry, girls. It will be really hard to prove that this garden was vandalized...or that anything grew here at all. Let me see what I can find." Miss Swallow walked slowly toward the center of the garden, carefully scanning the surface for any remnants of crushed leaves, stems, roots, or seeds. She saw nothing. Next, she took her field kit off her shoulder and squatted down. She removed a small leather case from the kit and pulled out a loupe. Scooping up a small amount of soil, she examined it carefully, looking for evidence of animal or plant life. Strangely, she didn't see any fungus filaments, insect debris, or even the casting of an earthworm. Miss Swallow stood up and called the girls over. Shaking her head, she said, "I've never seen anything like this. This soil looks completely dead."

"It sure wasn't dead day before yesterday," Arianna said.

Baffled, Miss Swallow sighed, "Sorry, I don't have any answers to this. Why don't you show me the shed?"

Hummingbird nodded and led the way. As they walked the short distance to the little building, Miss Swallow began to speculate about the destruction of the garden. "Girls, my biggest question is *why* anybody would be interested in destroying the giant squashes. I'm just disappointed I didn't get to see them. I'm going to call the Neighborhood Watch and ask that officer to email me his photos."

Miss Swallow chattered on, talking about possible ways soil can be sterilized. But Hummingbird wasn't listening. She knew of only one person who would be mean enough to destroy the giant squashes—Chris. But Chris couldn't have turned the garden into a desert. Only the coyote could have pulled off that stunt. Lost in these thoughts, Bird led the little party to the shed door and started to push it open. But she suddenly stopped.

Miss Swallow said, "Bird? Is something wrong?"

"Yes…well, no, not wrong. It's just…" Turning to look at the teacher, Hummingbird said, "Miss Swallow, it's just that every time we open this door or go through the garden gate, it's like there's something on the other side that's jumping out at us. Like a jack-in-the-box."

Understanding how the vandalism had shocked the girls, Miss Swallow said, "Do you want me to go in first?"

Both Hummingbird and Arianna said, "Yes."

Confidently pushing open the door, Miss Swallow continued her absorbed discussion. "What did you use in your fertilizer, Bird? I'm curious about your formula. We need to get a sample of that."

But Hummingbird never had a chance to tell Miss Swallow that she had poured out the fertilizer. The beautiful science teacher, usually so smart, self-possessed and cool, was making an odd gasping sound. Oh, no! Bird thought, glancing at Arianna. What has the coyote done now?

Hummingbird reached in and flipped on the light switch. An oddly-shaped tree about five feet tall was standing in the middle of the work table. The tin lamp above it directed its rays of light downward like a star in the heavens. In the darkness of the shed, only the tree benefited from the light.

Wide-eyed, but making no sound, the girls stared at the strange plant. Their "surprise buttons" had been hit one too many times. But Miss Swallow was another story. She continued to make funny little noises as she pointed to the pineapple that was "blooming" from the top of the tree. Finally, finding her voice, Miss Swallow whispered, "Have you seen this…before?"

Arianna shook her head and Hummingbird said, "No."

Miss Swallow walked slowly toward the work table. She started to say something about pineapples, but stopped when she saw a vanilla bean and a pawpaw on two nearby twigs. She quickly realized that she was in uncharted territory. She didn't know what she was looking at. Circling the table, she began to count the different vegetables, fruits, nuts, pods, and flowers that dangled or blossomed from the tree.

Miss Swallow was having a hard time figuring out something else. Were the different plants attached like ornaments or did they grow from the tree? She leaned over the table and parted several limbs which bushed out into shaggy grasses, clumps of differently lobed leaves, and tangles of vines.

Hmmm, she thought, they look like they're growing from a funny-looking stalk. A stalk? That's not very tree-like! Then, running her eyes downward, Miss Swallow saw why. The tree was emerging from what appeared to be a large white turnip root. She laughed uneasily. In a low voice, she asked, "Do you know anyone that does grafting?"

"No," Hummingbird replied. "What's grafting?"

Miss Swallow didn't answer. "Do you know anyone that keeps very, very old varieties of native seeds?"

"My dad has some. He's always talking about them getting contami…"

Miss Swallow gasped. She put her hands on the table and leaned in to look at a spray of bumpy spikes growing from a long-leaved grass on a lower limb of the tree.

"Oh my…I don't believe it!"

"What is it, Miss Swallow?" Arianna asked.

"Come over here, girls. You've got to see this. First, she pointed to a grass clump with a spray of little feathery cobs with only one row of kernels. "That's teosinte. See how each of its kernels is inside a husk? It's the ancestor of corn that still grows in the wild today." Then, pointing to the spray that drew her attention, she said, "Now look at this one. The little cobs have four rows of kernels. I think this is a very early stage of maize domestication—what corn looked like 4,000 years ago when our ancestors were first growing it."

Miss Swallow had seen photos of these tiny cobs before. Several had been found in Mexican caves. But no one to Miss Swallow's knowledge had ever seen a living, growing specimen.

Not until now, that is.

Miss Swallow...leaned in to look at a spray of bumpy spikes
growing from a long-leaved grass on a lower limb of the tree. "Oh
my...I don't believe it!"

Chapter 22

By 1:00 a.m. Miss Swallow was staring at a pile of papers that documented the history of horticulture in the Americas.

The Miraculous Tree

Regaining some composure, Miss Swallow said, "I'd like to look at this plant more carefully. We'll have to carry it to the car." Hummingbird emptied a cardboard box where she and Arianna had stored some of the undamaged garden tools. Then, the three of them carefully picked up the miraculous tree and placed it in the box. With Hummingbird on one side and Miss Swallow on the other, they carried it down the hill to the car.

"Where are you going to take it?" Arianna asked.

"To my classroom. I want to examine it there." To herself, she mumbled, "I wonder if Dr. Bamsey is around tonight."

Miss Swallow opened the back hatch and lowered the backseats, making room for the tree which they laid gently on its side. Passing up Aunt Chick's invitation to stop in, Miss Swallow drove the girls home. She told them to meet her in the lab before homeroom the next morning. Her intention had been to stop at Hummingbird's and talk to her parents about the vandalism. But vandals and bullies had suddenly taken a back seat to the mystery that was *on* her backseat.

As she drove to the school, Miss Swallow called and left a message for Dr. Bamsey. Unfortunately, her call went into his voice mail. He was out of town. She left a message, asking him to come by the school in the morning.

Realizing that she was in for a long night, Miss Swallow stopped off at Boo's. She told him she had a lot of work ahead of her and needed some big-time energy. Boo knew just what to do. He dispensed a large cup of coffee and wrapped up some fresh bean bread. He also insisted that she take the rest of a plastic container of thick vegetable soup his mom had brought by for his supper. Despite her protests, he added in a thermos of coffee and some extra cups and napkins.

With Boo's admonition not to work too hard still in her ears, Miss Swallow drove to the back of the school. She parked as close as possible to the side entrance near her classroom. Luckily, this was the door Floyd usually left unlocked until he was ready to leave. She could hear his vacuum cleaner in a nearby hallway. She followed the sound and asked the janitor for the key to the utility room. She wanted to borrow the hand truck.

As usual Floyd was accommodating. He got the hand truck for her and wheeled it out to her car. Helping Miss Swallow load the tree on the truck, he tried to be extra careful. The teacher seemed mighty skittish about the funny-looking bush. Carefully secured, Floyd pushed the precious cargo to the lab. As the teacher nervously watched, he gently picked up the tree and placed it on the lab table she indicated. Curious, he asked, "This one of your experiments, Miss Swallow?"

"No, not one of mine," she said, with a smile. "Thanks for helping me. I'm going to be here late tonight. So, don't worry if you see the lights on in here when you lock up."

Pushing the hand truck to the door, the janitor said, "Don't work too hard now."

Betty Swallow had no intention of listening to Boo or Floyd. She got to work right away. First, she shot photos of the tree and each of its edible products. Satisfied that she had made a good visual record, she rewarded herself by popping off the lid of the still-steaming cup of coffee. One swig and she was wired! Powering up her laptop, she logged onto her accounts with several online science journals.

Over the next few hours she managed to identify a good number of the specimens. Her list of plants included the wild and domesticated teosinte, knotweed, goosefoot, sumpweed, maypop or passion flower, pawpaw, sunflower, wild potato, wild bean, wild rice, wild barley, primitive squashes and tomatoes, pumpkins, gourds, hickory nuts, cacao, and vanilla. After stretching her legs and getting a drink from the water fountain in the hall, she was able to add amaranth, chili peppers, cayenne peppers, jicama, manioc, papayas, peanuts, pecans, quinoa, persimmon, sweet potatoes, and, of course, the pineapple. There was only one fruit on the tree that did not appear to be a food. It was the coyote gourd or stinking buffalo gourd she had mentioned to the girls earlier.

She thought some of the tree products were possibly ancestors of today's domesticated species. These were usually the small, hard, or bitter fruits and tubers like primitive squashes, beans, tomatoes, and potatoes; and seeds from primitive sunflowers or grasses like teosinte. Others were on their way to becoming domesticated (like the primitive maize), and still others appeared to have been formerly domesticated species that had reverted to their wild state (like knotweed and sumpweed). Those she immediately recognized looked very similar to foods and spices grown today like cacao beans (chocolate) and vanilla beans.

Miss Swallow printed off as much information as she could find on the various foods and their origins. By 1:00 a.m. she was staring at a pile of papers that documented the history of horticulture in the Americas. There was no way she could plow through all the archeological sites, theories, and migrations of plant foods in one night. But she had a good start.

Flipping through the journal articles, she found the one that would help her classify the foods into their areas of origin: the Andes, the Amazon, the lowlands of Mexico, and the Eastern United States. Although the coffee was gone, there was a cup of soup left. Maybe she could squeeze in another hour of work before hanging it up.

Miss Swallow, however, worked longer than she meant to. At 4:00 a.m., she laid her head down on the lab table just to rest her eyes for a few minutes. When she woke up, the glare from the bright overhead lights was almost painful. She wiped her eyes with the backs of her hands. Ohhh, she thought, I must have dozed off. Sitting up, her shoulder muscles were so stiff she could hardly move her head. Rubbing the back of her neck, she murmured, "What time is it?" She glanced at the schoolroom clock. Six-thirty!

Jumping up, Miss Swallow thought, I've got to get this place cleaned up! She grabbed the food wrappers, napkins, and empty coffee cups from last night's marathon and chucked them in the garbage. Then, she raked her research papers and notes together into an untidy pile. She would have to organize them later. It was the tree that presented the real problem. Dismissing the idea of putting a trash bag over it, she decided, instead, to lock it in the supply closet. She dragged the tree across the classroom and into the small room where hazardous chemicals and breakable glassware were stored. Before locking the door, she gave the tree one last look. Only then did she ask herself the questions that she had been too excited (or reluctant) to ask before: Who did this? Where did the tree come from?

With her head spinning, the science teacher grabbed her purse, cell phone, and laptop. She exited the lab and headed for her car. Maybe after a shower and a change of clothes she would be able to think more clearly. Please, Dr. Bamsey, she thought, be back in town today!

Coyote turned over and snuggled into the pointy leaves of his namesake. Ahh, I'm comfortable—too comfortable, he thought. Why is that? Feeling the delicious warmth on his back, he murmured in recognition, "The sun." He yawned and sat up. He made a quick perusal of his garden. Because of his excellent guardianship, there were no grazers about—no big ones, that is. However, he knew the little nibblers would be busy. No aphids, beetles, slugs, or grubs would make breakfast of his beauties. Rather, they would be his breakfast.

Coyote began grooming the squash fruits that were in all stages of development. He picked, plucked, and licked up all the pests that would dare to eat the green-striped globes. He paid special attention to the young giant-to-be that he had named Hummingbird's Squash.

His belly full, Coyote lay back down. Noting the time of morning, he thought, well, it must have happened by now. Closing his eyes, he imagined himself spinning again in the wormhole that had turned back time. He smiled. Yes, the backward spiral could be slowed for a while, but once started, it couldn't be stopped. Miss Betty Swallow was about to find that out.

The kids arrived at the lab only seconds before Miss Swallow did. She was walking at a fast clip down the hall, talking on her cell phone. Arriving at the door, she said good-bye to Dr. Bamsey and rang off. Looking at Hummingbird, she said breathlessly, "Dr. Bamsey is coming over at noon." Noticing the boys, she seemed surprised. "Oh, we have a crowd. I guess you told them about the tree?"

While she was rummaging in her bag for the room key, Hummingbird explained. "Yes, Miss Swallow, they helped Arianna and me set up the shed and the garden. And they saw the giant squashes—before they were destroyed. I thought you might want to talk to them, too."

Miss Swallow stopped fumbling for the key. "Oh, of course. Sorry, boys, I'm just a little frazzled this morning" It wasn't like the kids hadn't noticed. Miss Swallow had big dark circles under her eyes; and her hair, which was still wet from a shower, had been hastily pulled back into a lop-sided pony tail. Nervously, she kept pushing down her shirt collar which stuck up on the side of her neck.

"It's just that last night was the most momentous of my entire life. I researched all night long. I didn't leave the school until after 6:30 this morning. It was just as I expected, but had to prove to myself. That tree holds the whole evolutionary history of plant domestication in the Americas! The sweat and intellect of Native people over thousands of years!" She laughed giddily, "It's like someone created it for our Science Fair!"

Miss Swallow leaned up against the classroom door and closed her eyes. "Maize, beans, sunflowers, squashes, pumpkins, peppers, chocolate. I can see the grandmothers and grandfathers, generation after generation—selecting, growing, tending, trading..." Suddenly blinking open her eyes, she grabbed Boomer's shoulder (because he was standing nearest to her) and cried, "Oh my gosh, kids! What gifts our ancestors left to us! Gifts that now feed the whole world!"

As if coming out of a dream, Miss Swallow released Boomer's shoulder. Getting hold of herself, she said more rationally, "We better hurry if you want to see the tree. Homeroom will be starting soon." She found her key chain, unlocked the door, and led the little group to the supply closet.

While Miss Swallow shakily shuffled through her keys again, the kids became aware of dozens of photos of flowers, fruits, and seeds scattered across one of the lab tables (Miss Swallow had overlooked those in her attempt to tidy up). They also couldn't help but notice the stacks of Googled articles and handwritten notes that were piled up everywhere. Simon turned and looked at a bunch of hastily scribbled charts and diagrams that were taped haphazardly on the blackboard. Under his breath, he said, "Boy, she's been busy."

Stepping over a splatter of coffee on the floor, Rain whispered back, "Maybe that's why she's so whacked out..."

"Yeah," Boomer agreed too loudly, "she's acts like she gonna faint or somethin'."

"Keep it down, man," Simon warned. "She'll hear you."

However, Boomer's usual overstatement proved to be an understatement. When Miss Swallow opened the supply room door and turned on the light, she almost *did* faint. Her eyes grew wide and her mouth fell open. She stopped breathing. If she'd had anything in her stomach, it would have come back up. Trying to steady herself, she dropped her purse and clutched at the edge of a storage cabinet. Suddenly, she went down on a plastic box of chemistry equipment. Apparently, her legs had failed, too.

The boys, in back of Hummingbird and Arianna, immediately knew something was wrong. "What's going on? What happened?"

Miss Swallow stammered, "My purse. Quick! My phone . . . photos. . ."

Hummingbird picked up the purse and put it in her lap. Miss Swallow snatched it open and pulled out the phone. Fumbling frantically, she retrieved her photo album and scrolled down to the folder where she had stored almost thirty photos of the tree. It was empty...

When Simon demanded again to know what was happening, Arianna answered, "I don't know, I think Miss Swallow is sick." But, Hummingbird looking around the supply closet began to understand. "Where's the tree?" she cried.

"Over there!" Arianna said. "Isn't that the sack it was in?"

The plastic sack was sitting on a piece of newspaper at the back of the closet. Rain, craning his neck over Boomer's shoulder, said, "There's something in it."

Consumed by curiosity, the kids edged respectfully around Miss Swallow and approached the sack. A spindly stalk lay crumpled over its folded plastic rim—like a dead white worm. The worm was sprinkled by copious amounts of a powdery black dust that radiated outward in a star shape.

Looking at the others, Boomer asked, "What's that black stuff?"

Simon turned to Miss Swallow. "Um, Miss Swallow, do you know what it might be?"

When she didn't answer, Arianna said, "Maybe we ought to get somebody."

"I'll go get Mr. Pence," Rain volunteered, "and tell him she's not feeling very well." As he was leaving, he whispered to the stricken teacher, "I'm really sorry about the tree, Miss Swallow."

Simon heard voices in the classroom. "Pssst. Hey, some kids are starting to come in."

"You guys go on to homeroom," Hummingbird said. "I'll stay until Mr. Pence gets here."

Arianna pulled the door to, leaving it cracked. Noticing some more papers lying about on the classroom floor, she picked them up and put them on the lab bench. She thought they must be important because there were scrawls of hand-written notes with big exclamation points in the margins. She really felt sorry for poor Miss Swallow.

Hummingbird did, too. She was also feeling a little guilty because if it were not for her, Miss Swallow wouldn't have been pulled into the coyote's tricks. She scooted over an old lab stool and sat down next to her favorite teacher. They sat in silence for a while. Finally, Miss Swallow stirred. She looked as if she was waking from a long sleep. Relieved, Hummingbird asked, "Miss Swallow, are you feeling better?"

Miss Swallow turned her head slowly toward Hummingbird. Smiling, she reached out and took the young girl's hand. Very quietly, she said, "One day you and I are going to have a long talk, aren't we?

Hummingbird sighed and said quietly, "Yes, m'am, I'm afraid we are."

Chapter 23

With Joe's help, Miss Swallow realized that the tree was a metaphor for the wonderful story of the people and their remarkable use of gifts from the natural world.

Lessons and Confessions

After Miss Swallow went home that morning, Mr. Pence called Dr. Bamsey and told him that she'd had a shock and needed a couple of days off. He asked the biology professor to come by the school the next day. A substitute was called in to take over the 8th grade science classes and everything went on as if nothing had happened.

But something *had* happened. After getting a few hours of sleep, Miss Swallow went to see Joe Red Crane. They sat together on the bleachers at the school's baseball field and talked for a long time. Miss Swallow knew better than try to explain her experience with the tree rationally, but she would try to understand it. With Joe's help, she realized that the tree was a metaphor for the wonderful story of the people and their remarkable use of gifts from the natural world. There was no uncertainty about that. The true mystery was the identity of the storyteller. Miss Swallow told Joe that she believed Hummingbird had the answer to that mystery. Looking kindly at Miss Swallow, Joe gave her his simple advice. "Hummingbird will tell you about it when the time is right—if ever. Until then, Betty, just appreciate what the story has taught you and share it with others."

The next day Mr. Pence met Dr. Bamsey during his planning period and took him to the see the black dust in the supply closet. Unlocking the door, he lowered his voice so the students in the lab couldn't hear: "I've never seen her like that, Dr. Bamsey. You know, Betty. She doesn't get rattled easily."

Mr. Pence stood aside, shivering as usual. Dr. Bamsey went in to take a good look at the bag of soil and the fine powdery substance on the floor. Even though he was on the hefty side, he tiptoed delicately around the tree's remains, careful not to create any movement of air (the dust was very fine).

"This looks like carbon to me," the professor said. "But not like the burned ash from wood. It's more elemental like a mixture of coal and graphite." Coyote would have agreed with Dr. Bamsey. Indeed, the tree (except for the turnip) had disassociated into molecules of carbon and a dozen other trace minerals—just as they had existed on the primitive earth millions of years ago. Turning back time, it seemed, just may have been the *oldest* trick Coyote had ever played!

Continuing his observations, Dr. Bamsey said, "Betty asked me if I knew of any research about reverting plants back to their ancestral forms. I don't know of anything like that around here, but I'll check it out." Squatting down so he could get a better look at the wilted stalk, Dr. Bamsey added, "She said it looked like someone had grafted some ancient species onto a turnip." He shook his head and chuckled. "*That* looks like a turnip root to me..."

Hearing the bell, Mr. Pence said, "The class is leaving for lunch. Let me show you some of Betty's work from the other night." Mr. Pence had gathered all of Miss Swallow's work and carefully arranged it in a set of folders. He spread them out for Dr. Bamsey's to examine. Almost immediately, the biologist recognized that most of the papers referred to domesticated plants native to North, Central and South America. He was most interested in one of the drawings (Luckily, Miss Swallow had made a sketch of a few of the fruits and vegetables). "Hmm, this looks like an intermediary stage between a wild and a domesticated tomato. I don't recall seeing that before." (Coyote would have laughed. Dr. Bamsey had never seen it because it had disappeared thousands of years ago.) The professor took off his glasses and started polishing them with a handkerchief. Squinting at Mr. Pence, he asked, "Did anybody else see this tree?"

"Yes, two of our students helped her bring it to the school."

One of those students was staring at her uneaten lunch. Poking at her salad, Hummingbird sighed. "I should never have started the giant vegetable thing. The coyote's made that pretty clear. It was all right there…like Miss Swallow said 'the gifts our ancestors gave us.' But I wanted to change everything—I wasn't satisfied with those gifts."

Rain didn't agree. "There's nothing wrong with experimenting—trying to make something better. We wouldn't have those gifts if the people hadn't experimented."

"Rain's right," Simon said. "They never quit trying to grow different kinds of corn. Blue corn, red corn, yellow corn—corn that grows where it's cold."

"I wish you guys had seen that tiny corncob Miss Swallow showed us," Arianna said. "It was like a baby step toward making big corn. I kept thinking about the first people who grew it—the people who took those baby steps."

"Yeah," Boomer said, getting into it. "Who grew the first popcorn? Who grew the first chili beans?"

"No," Hummingbird said, shaking her head. "RD was right the first time. I was just trying to impress Miss Swallow and Mr. Pence."

"Maybe that's how it started out," Arianna said, "but we all thought it was a good thing. Didn't we?"

But, not to be consoled, Hummingbird let out a long "Ohhhh" and slumped in her chair.

"What now?" Arianna cried. Boy! she thought, Bird sure is a drama queen sometimes.

"You should have heard the way I talked to my dad! He was trying to tell me about his Native seeds…but, noooo, I didn't have time for *that*. That was too slow—I had to do it all my way."

Simon laughed. "Come on, Bird. Your dad will get over it. You can apologize."

Rain looked around the table at his friends. "I know the coyote jerks us around sometimes. And he's been playing lots of tricks on you, Bird. But how else would you—we—really get it? The point is—there aren't any short-cuts, no miracle pills. It's simple: we honor the foods that feed us and keep us healthy. We do that by growing and eating them." Glancing at Arianna, he said wistfully, and not without a little envy, "I just wish I'd seen that tree."

"The tree is one thing," Simon said, "but what happened to the garden? That had to be the coyote too."

"Sure, it was. It was *his* garden," Boomer said. "Sorry, Bird, but I don't think your fast-grow formula did the trick. The coyote did the trick. I think he was really mad that somebody tore up the squashes and left that big mess. So he cleaned it up." Boomer wadded up a napkin and expertly tossed it into the trash bag Arianna held open. "I just know I wouldn't want to be one of the guys that did it."

Dumptruck stood at the cash register buying an extra milk. He was watching Arianna head to the garbage bin next to the window where students dropped off their dirty trays. He nudged Tater Tot who was in line behind him. "There she is, Tater. She's alone."

When Tater Tot hesitated, Dumptruck said, "Go on! Talk to her."

The red-headed boy saw Arianna dump some trash and then hurry toward the courtyard exit. He changed direction and fast-walked toward her, catching her just before she went out the door. Not too loudly, he called her name. "Arianna!" She turned. "Could I talk to you for a minute?"

"Yeah, I guess so."

Tater Tot led Arianna outside. "Look. Um, I know you've only talked to me a couple of times. But I have a favor to ask. You know Dumptruck—the guy that threw the hamburger at Boomer? Well, he wants to talk to Hummingbird. Would she go to the library right now? That's where he is. It's important...*real* important. Please?"

The "please" got to Arianna. "Well, okay. But I can't promise she'll come."

"I'll tell him you'll try." While Tater Tot ran off to get Dumptruck, Arianna looked around for Hummingbird. She was sitting alone on the bench by the gym.

Crossing the courtyard, Arianna tried to think of what she would say. Chris's toadies want to have a little chat with you? Yeah, that sounded convincing! By the time she was standing in front of Hummingbird (who was still stuck in "I'm so bad" mode), Arianna had just decided to spit it out: "Dumptruck wants to talk to you in the library."

Hummingbird rolled her eyes and gave Arianna the biggest "Oh, please" look ever. Quietly and rationally, she started counting on her fingers: "After the 'elephant's toothpaste,' it was the giant squashes, and *then* the garden and *then* the tree. And yesterday it was the black dust." Looking up at Arianna, she yelled, "Every time we turn around, our eyeballs are bugging out of our heads and we're hollering 'What! What?!'" Folding her arms on her chest (Hummingbird's favorite grumpy-mood gesture), she said, "And now the biggest surprise of all; Dumptruck wants me to help him check out a library book!"

"I didn't make it up," Arianna giggled. "Maybe it's another coyote trick."

"I'm sure *it* is! What does he want?"

"I don't know. It seemed awfully important."

Hummingbird gave in. "Well, come on. The day couldn't get any worse."

Dumptruck and Tater Tot were sitting at the same table where Rain had told Hummingbird about his dream of the eagle. The boys had wanted a private place to talk. They were lucky. The library was almost deserted.

Tater Tot waved. Hummingbird glanced at Arianna and whispered, "This is so weird." She half-expected the boys to start flailing their arms and yelling, "Ding-Ding!"

Arianna smiled and waved back. "Come on, Bird. Be nice."

Hummingbird hated to admit it, but she was curious. Why would the boy they called "Big D" want to talk to her? Arianna walked on ahead and sat down. Bird followed reluctantly. Trying to "be nice," she arranged a more pleasant look on her face. Apparently, it didn't work. Dumptruck looked petrified.

Hummingbird stood awkwardly. Finally, Tater Tot said, "Why don't you sit down?" He nudged his friend. "Dumptruck has something to say. Don't ya, Big D?"

Hummingbird perched on the side of a chair and waited.

Dumptruck said, "Hum…," then broke down before he'd even begun his apology. After several false starts, he revved up his nerve and finally succeeded. "Hummingbird, I…I'm sorry." Trusting a girl he hardly knew, Dumptruck blurted it out: "I tore up your garden!"

Once he'd started, the rest of it rolled out like a flood: "And I'm sorry about throwing the hamburger at Boomer, and trying to trip Simon, and yelling 'ding-ding.'" He looked at Arianna. "I feel really bad about that. And…" Dumptruck didn't finish his "ands"—there were some other things he decided not to bring up.

Tater Tot filled in. "I'm sorry, too. I was doing that stuff with him."

Dumptruck looked at the two girls sitting across from him. "Honest. I just want to stop before my mom finds out. She's got enough to worry about."

Hummingbird wasn't interested in Dumptruck's other offenses—only the squashes. "You didn't tear up the garden by yourself, did you?"

"No. It was Chris's idea. Him and his brother. He's pushed us into doing other stuff, too."

Hummingbird muttered to Arianna, "I knew it was Chris."

"We just want Chris off our backs," Tater Tot said earnestly. "That's the real reason we're telling you all this."

Dumptruck nodded, "Yeah, before we get in real trouble."

"What do you want me to do?"

Dumptruck took a deep breath. "Talk to your friends—Rain, Simon, and Boomer. See if they'll help us."

Chapter 24

Simon started snorting. "Man! What a great trick! They jump out of a hat like a rabbit—right in front of the captain of the basketball team!"

Rabbits in a Hat

That afternoon, Hummingbird and Arianna waited for the boys at the bus pickup. The girls told them briefly about their meeting with Dumptruck and Tater Tot. Hummingbird informed everyone that they needed a "tree stump meeting." They all agreed to meet in the meadow, before doing homework or anything else. This was top priority.

Later that afternoon, Rain and Boomer were the first to arrive at the tree stump. They sat down in the grass, now crinkly and brown. It was early October and the days were growing shorter. Rain laid back, staring at the autumn sky, and began thinking about Miss Swallow and the coyote's tree. But it was too complicated. He moved on to a less difficult subject. Glancing at Boomer, he said, "I can't wait for the Harvest Pow-Wow."

"Me neither." Boomer started beating on the ground, singing a Round Dance song under his breath. Rain joined him.

"I know that one!" a voice shouted. "It's a Two Step song!" It was Simon. He was running across the meadow; Hummingbird and Arianna were close behind.

Rain and Boomer stood up and waited for the others to take their places around the old tree stump where the eagle had given them his healthy wisdom. Arianna positioned herself next to Hummingbird. This was her first meeting. Hummingbird told Arianna that they always took a few moments to think about the eagle's messages before talking. Arianna thought about what the eagle meant to her. Because she had type 1 diabetes, he would want her to work hard at preventing damage to her body caused by imbalances in her blood sugar levels. She thought about her responsibility to eat healthy and be active every single day. Arianna knew that what she did today determined her health in the future. She felt sure that the eagle would want people with type 2 diabetes and other diseases to think this way, too. Yes, the great bird made her feel strong—strong enough to keep doing whatever she had to do to keep her body well.

Boomer voice broke into her thoughts. "Okay, what exactly did Dumptruck and Tater Tot say?"

Hummingbird cut to the chase. "They're asking us for help—especially you guys."

"From us?" the boys cried. "To do what?"

"To get Chris Sorrel off their backs." Explaining, Hummingbird repeated most of the library conversation point for point—with the highlight being Dumptruck's admission that he'd had helped Chris destroy the garden.

"You mean he actually *told* on himself?" Simon asked skeptically.

"Yeah," Arianna said. "He apologized for messing with you guys and making fun of me, too. Tater told me that they didn't know "ding-ding" was about my insulin pump."

Simon wasn't convinced. "How do you know they weren't jerking you around?"

"Yeah," Boomer said, "They could be playing us for chumps."

Hummingbird said, "I don't think so. I'm sure they're afraid of Chris—I think it's because of his brothers."

Arianna backed up Hummingbird. "Bird's right. Chris bosses them around all the time, and puts them down. Tater told me as much."

Rain had been quiet for most of the meeting. Finally, he spoke. "So what are we gonna do? Turn in Dumptruck for vandalism?"

Hummingbird was shocked. "Huh? Turn him in? You mean like to Mr. Berry or to the police?" It was obvious that Bird didn't want to do that.

"Mr. Berry's says to tell our parents or report it to a teacher if a bully is bothering us. Well, that was some bad bullying

Dumptruck did—smashing the squashes. Didn't your dad call the Neighborhood Watch to report vandalism? Didn't a policeman come out and take pictures?"

"I bet his photos disappeared like Miss Swallow's did." Hummingbird grumbled.

"You know it. The coyote doesn't like to leave evidence of his tricks," said Boomer—now the big expert on coyotes.

Rain was persistent. "Pictures don't matter. Dumptruck said he did it."

Starting to get upset, Arianna cried, "But then *we* would get him in trouble when he's trying to do what's right."

Hummingbird shook her head. "This is complicated. What should we do?"

Rain was ready with the answer. "Think like the eagle and the coyote."

"How's that, RD?" Simon asked.

"Actually, I don't want to get 'em in trouble, either. I say let's help the guys. Remember what the eagle said about keeping our traditions? Everybody working together, playing together. Dumptruck is a member of our Tribe. We should remember that. Tater's not a member, but he goes to our school. That's good enough for me. Besides, we shouldn't push away anybody wanting to be friends with us."

Everybody nodded. Boomer said, "I think the eagle would go for it."

"So, how are we going to help them?" Simon asked again.

Rain smiled devilishly. "That's where the coyote part comes in."

Hummingbird laughed, "So you got it all worked out, Mr. Smarty-Pants?"

"Maybe not everything, but here's my idea. Coach Brown is holding tryouts next month for two positions on the 8th grade boys' basketball team. What if they get on the team? We could get Boo to coach them, and Boomer and I can show 'em what we know. Even if they don't make the team, they'll get in good shape and be a lot healthier. That should pump up their confidence."

Arianna brightened. 'Yes! That's what Tater needs—confidence! Like with his drawing. He just needs a chance."

"They're not exactly buffed up," Boomer said. "They'll really have to train."

"Don't forget the food," Arianna said. "They'll have to eat healthy food."

Rain agreed it would be a lot of work. Then, he grinned. "But, here's the kicker. We keep it all under wraps. Chris doesn't know anything about it until the tryouts!"

Simon started snorting. "Man! "What a great trick! They jump out of a hat like a rabbit—right in front of the captain of the basketball team!"

"Chris will have a cow!" Hummingbird giggled.

Simon choked back a snort. "I just thought of something. We might be keeping too many secrets. We're keeping it a secret that Dumptruck tore up the garden *and* we're not telling anybody that Chris was behind it. Should we do that? Remember how you guys promised not to tell anybody that Vernon Smeed was after Jimmy? That didn't turn out too great, did it?"

Rain sighed, "Simon's right about that."

"But RD!" Hummingbird said. "The coyote fixed it so it looks like there never was a garden! How do we say Chris destroyed something that was never there?" Hummingbird was just beginning to appreciate how tricky the coyote really was. He sure made it hard figuring out the right thing to do.

Boomer, boy of a thousand defenses and brilliant appeals (usually made to his mother) put on his best lawyer face. Hands behind his back, he began to walk back and forth, pretending to be in deep thought. (Boom watched lots of old Perry Mason reruns on TV Land and Judge Judy, too.) He halted dramatically. "Let's forget Chris—for now. So, Mr. Berry says bullying should be reported. And it has been. Dumptruck reported his bullying *to us*. End of story. Besides, we accept his apology for all the crummy things he did, don't we?"

A chorus of "yeses" answered his question.

Simon wasn't giving up. "I still think Dumptruck should do more than just say he's sorry."

Turning to the girls, Boomer said, "You planted the garden. And he did the 'ding-ding' thing on you, Arianna. So, how does he make it up to you?"

Hummingbird didn't hesitate. "That's easy. Just stop bullying."

"And be real friends—if that's what they want to be." Arianna added.

Boomer shrugged at Simon: "I rest my case."

Chapter 25

He could see that his work was cut out for him. These guys had never seen a potato chip they didn't like.

Healthy Secrets

Sky Heart watched the kids at the tree stump. He was always happy to see them continue the tradition of remembering his messages about diabetes prevention. Arianna was there, too. The eagle noticed how respectfully she stood with her friends. Thistle would want to know that their little posse had officially added another member. As he flew toward her nest, Sky Heart saw Thistle trying to round up her bunnies. Several had broken away from their mother's supervision and had scattered down the hill.

"Need some help?" he called out.

Thistle looked up, "Yes, could you herd those two down there toward me? And I'll grab this one." Sky Heart landed and flapped the two escapees toward their mother. She safely stuffed them back into safety of their brushy home.

Out of breath, Thistle gasped. "Thanks? What brings you this way, Sky Heart?"

"Rain and his friends were meeting at the tree stump today. They included the girl, Arianna."

"Oh, I'm not surprised. Coyote showed his power in front of her." She laughed. "The burps, you know. I thought my eardrums would burst." Nibbling on a bit of grass, she said, "They probably had to tell her about us. I'm glad. She teaches them about the other kind of diabetes."

"So what is Coyote up to? Have you seen him?"

"He's come by several times. All he talks about is his garden. Have you seen what he's growing?"

"I've spotted his work. His squashes are getting big—very big. I don't suppose he's said what he's going to do with them, has he?"

"No, nothing about the squashes. He was just going on about that thunderstorm earlier this week. Said he summoned it. He started yipping and yapping—you know how he does—about Rain that Dances being the hail and Boomer, the thunder. Something about lightning shaking things up. I just couldn't follow him—he's so crazy sometimes." Thistle closed her eyes. She suddenly looked very tired.

"Do you think the storm had anything to do with Hummingbird? Is he still playing tricks on her?"

Thistle opened her eyes. "I don't think he's through playing tricks on anybody." Turning to go into her nest, she said wearily, "I'm just too busy with my babies right now to worry about Coyote. But I'd say he's planning more tricks. This game isn't just about Hummingbird."

Thistle could usually read Coyote pretty well. His storm had blown the kids right where he wanted them—playing a joke or two that would teach plenty of lessons and bringing new players into his fun and games.

One of those new players was Boo. Dumptruck and Tater Tot were already at Boo's Gas 'n Grocery the next afternoon when Rain and Boomer got there. They were pretty excited about the basketball idea. They almost couldn't believe that Rain, Boomer, and Simon had agreed to help them unload Chris.

The boys huddled together to make sure that everybody understood the plan. Boomer laid out the details. "You guys wait out here while RD and I talk to Boo. If he says he'll coach you, come on in and talk to him yourselves. Okay?" Dumptruck and Tater Tot looked a little nervous, but they nodded.

Rain and Boomer casually walked into the store and went to the counter. They asked Boo if they could talk to him after he was through with his customers. Then, they drifted over to the comics and pretended to be looking at the new arrivals. They had bought this month's *Mammoth Boy*, their favorite comic, last week; nothing else of interest was on the shelf. Keeping an eye out, Boomer saw Boo coming over and nudged Rain. "Here he comes."

Boo was smiling. He was always happy to see the kids who had given him the idea to sell healthy Native foods in his store. "What's up, guys?"

Rain took a stab at it first. "Um, well, we know you're a really good basketball player and um…well, have you ever thought about coaching, Boo?"

"Coach basketball? Noooo. I play on the men's team at the rec center, but that's all."

Boomer decided to pour it on a bit. "Well, everybody knows you're really good, and uh, were like a big star in high school."

Uh-oh, Boo thought. I'm getting the Boomer treatment. His radar went up. "I thought you fellas got enough coaching at the school."

"Yeah, we do. Boomer and I are on the 7th grade team," Rain said, "but there's these guys we know that would like to try out for the 8th grade team. They don't exactly play a lot. Not right now, that is."

Boo asked, "Can't Coach Brown help out?"

"Well, not really," Boomer explained. "Because, see, it's a secret that they want to tryout."

"A secret? Who exactly are these guys?"

"They're outside in the parking lot." Rain answered.

Boo walked over to the front window and peered over the top of the "everyday snack" shelves. Two boys were standing by the gas pumps. Hands in their pockets, they kept glancing anxiously in the direction of the store. Boo recognized Dumptruck, but didn't know the red-headed boy.

"He's new," Rain said. "His mother's doing some contract work for the Tribe."

Boo frowned. "They don't look very athletic."

Thinking Boo was going to say "no," Boomer panicked and went for the "big beg" too early. "Boo, you *gotta* help them learn to play basketball! Please!?"

"When are the tryouts?"

Rain smiled sheepishly. "Um, in six weeks?"

"Six weeks! Give me a break, guys! I'm not a miracle worker!" The crushed look of disappointment on the boy's faces told Boo that there was more to their pleas than just basketball.

"Okay, hold on. I'll talk to them. But, you've got to fill me in on this big secret before we go any further. Deal?"

"Deal, Boo!" Rain cried. "I'll get 'em."

Rain charged to the front door and waved excitedly for the boys to come in. Dumptruck gave Tater Tot's arm a playful punch. "He's gonna help us!" The two would-be athletes skirted around a car pulling in to pump gas and hurried to meet their new coach.

Boo watched as the boys followed Rain to the counter. He could see his work was cut out for him. These guys had never seen a potato chip they didn't like. Trying to put them at ease, he smiled and said, "Come on in, fellas. I hear you want to be basketball players."

Dumptruck was eager to convince Boo they were serious. "We don't expect anything for free. We promise to work real hard!"

Boo got right to the point. "RD says you want to keep it a secret. Why is that?"

Dumptruck tried to explain. "Well, ah, see there's this guy, Chris Sorrel, that's been makin' us back him up when he's bullying people. ...and we don't wanna do it anymore. He's captain of the basketball team. He'd give us a lot of grief if he thought we were trying out. He likes to call the shots on everything."

Tater Tot chimed in. "Chris says we're a couple of losers. But I don't think Dumptruck and I are losers. We just want to do something right for a change—like play basketball."

"Yeah, kids on the same team don't think about who's popular or who's different. But, mostly, we need to get some new friends," Dumptruck added.

Boo said he knew who Chris Sorrel was and asked the boys to go on. Tater Tot swallowed uneasily and went first. "I'm new here and thought that if I joined up with the bullies, they'd leave me alone. But I was wrong. I know that good basketball players get respect around here. I'm not saying I want to be a big hot-shot or anything. We just thought Chris would back off if..." Tater had been doing pretty well up to this point, but now he stumbled. "You know, if we were..." He stopped, at a loss for words. Looking desperately at Boo, he suddenly burst out. "I just don't want to be 'Tater Tot' anymore!"

Boo looked confused. "Tater Tot?"

"That's the name Chris gave me when my mom and I moved here last year. He says I look like an overblown french fry! I hate it! Everybody calls me that!" Rain, Boomer, and Dumptruck were surprised at Tater's outburst. They didn't realize how much he disliked the nickname.

Dumptruck jumped in. "Yeah, he calls me Dumptruck because he says I'm a 'big load.' I don't mind the 'truck' part. That sounds kinda cool. But 'Dump' really stinks."

The boys burst out laughing. Boomer roared, "That's a good one, man!"

Boo walked around from behind the counter. He put a hand on each of the boy's shoulders. "All right, 'Dumptruck' is out from now on, Walter. And 'Tater Tot' is gone, too. I'm sorry, son, what's your real name?"

Self-consciously, the former "french fry" said, "I'm Larry."

Boo could understand why Rain and Boomer wanted to help these guys. They were in a tight spot. Boo sighed—he was a hooked fish. Looking at the boys, he said, "So how are we gonna keep this big secret?"

Rain and Boomer smiled at each other. Boo was in.

Chapter 26

Boo got the boys comfortable on the court—skipping, running backwards, hopping and landing, and moving laterally.

De-Bullification

Over the next few weeks, Boo supervised the transformation of 'Dumptruck' and 'Tater Tot' into Walter and Larry. Everybody had a role. Simon volunteered to help Boo with strategies for physical conditioning and the girls took over the "training table"—nutrition was critical. Rain and Boomer's job was on the court.

As coach, Boo took his job seriously. He arranged for his buddies to take Walter and Larry out every morning before school for a half mile of running. After that, they'd do push-ups, sit-ups, and jump rope. He was working them up to running a seven-minute mile.

For two hours every afternoon, Boo turned over the store to his sister, Kitty. Then he'd pick up the kids and they'd go over to the old school building used to house canned goods and produce for the Tribe's food distribution program. The gym still had a pretty serviceable basketball court and middle schoolers never hung out there. It was the perfect hideout.

Boo got the boys comfortable on the court—skipping, running backwards, hopping and landing, and moving laterally. Only after they showed him they could move, did he advance to the basketball basics: shooting, dribbling, jumping, and passing. Boo pulled everybody into running drills with the boys. Interestingly, Simon, Hummingbird, and Arianna proved to have a real talent for agility drills.

Some days Boo ran the boys up and down the court doing layups until they were ready to drop. His favorite exercise was "the weave." Later, when they had built some power into their action, he taught them some strategy fundamentals and how to improve essential skills like dunks and good jump shots. He knew they couldn't possibly be expert at any "smooth moves" in just six weeks, but he wanted them to be familiar with a few of his favorite "fakes." Mostly, he just wanted them to start thinking like basketball players.

Watching the boys play two-on-two against Rain and Boomer, Boo could see that the hard work was starting to pay off. However, physical training was only half the story. It took a lot of coordination to get the boys eating right in such a short time. The boys' moms were thrilled that their sons had become so motivated to get healthy (although they were in the dark about their reasons). However, they weren't sure about the nutrition the boys needed. After doing some Internet research at reliable websites, Hummingbird and Arianna learned that young athletes engaged in high levels of activity needed lots of protein and complex carbohydrates to sustain their energy. Because she was a community health representative for the Tribe, Roberta was able to offer some excellent advice about nutritional requirements. With her help, the girls carefully planned Walter and Larry's meals and snacks. Then they copied out the recipes and shopping lists and gave them to the boys to take home.

Leona, Walter's mother, was especially appreciative. She had been diagnosed with pre-diabetes; the glucose in her blood was higher than normal but not high enough to be diagnosed as diabetes. Worried that she might develop type 2 diabetes, Leona was happy to get information that would help her stay healthy, too. To show Walter that she was serious, she'd even taken the advice of the Tribe's diabetes health educator and enrolled in the "Stop Smoking" program. As for Marge, Larry's mom, the fresh vegetables from Aunt Chick's garden were helping her to keep down the grocery bills. But mostly, she was just glad that her son was making friends.

Soon, Walter and Larry were talking a new language. No one could remember who started calling a breakfast of whole grain cereals, fruits, and low-fat milk the "the starting lineup," but it stuck. However, Boomer claimed he was the first to think of "MVP: Most Valuable Players" for lean meat, fish, poultry, eggs, beans, peas, nuts, and seeds (proteins for building muscle, of course); and Simon made up "dribbling," to mean drinking enough water. Hummingbird and Arianna's snack motto was "bench the empty calories." Walter and Larry really took that one to heart. They had dropped sodas, chips, and candy from their snack list. Hummingbird and Arianna also advised the boys to make whole grains half of all the grains they ate. The complex carbohydrates in the whole grain foods burned slowly and gave them energy for a long time. Now their favorite snack was whole wheat waffles with peanut butter. To keep the message going strong, Hummingbird and Arianna made a sign that they hung on the gym wall: *Complex carbs rule!*

Because the boys were frequently invited to eat at Rain's house, supper began to look like an NBA training table. Before long, the program began to pay off. It was Rain that noticed first.

"See, what'd I tell ya? You guys are looking good."

Walter and Larry stood in front of the full-length mirror that hung on the door of Roberta's closet. Lying across his parent's bed, Rain pointed out one of Walter's more noticeable achievements. "Your stomach's not sticking out, Walter." (The kids no longer forgot and called the boys Dumptruck and Tater Tot. The nicknames had become ancient history.)

The big eighth grader pulled up his T-shirt. "Hey, yeah. It doesn't look like a doughnut anymore."

Larry was sucking in his breath and turning from side to side admiring his abdomen. "That's because we're not *eating* doughnuts, man." Feeling happy about his healthy lifestyle, he added, "Good thing we didn't start smoking like Chris wanted us to."

"Aw, man," Walter said, "Chris wasn't smoking. He was just showing off with those cigarettes. He thought it made him look tough."

Impressed by his emerging physique, Larry started flexing his biceps, too. He'd never had muscles before. Taking a cue from Larry, Walter inflated himself into a quivering crab pose like the "Hulk." Rain laughed and jumped off the bed. "Hey, let's do the *Incredible Hulk!*" The three boys were in various stages of transforming themselves into the green muscle-bound humanoid, when Roberta rapped on the door.

"Sorry to interrupt, guys, but supper is in ten minutes. We're having Granma's venison and corn stew." Doing a double take at Larry who had taken off his shirt, she cried, "Wow! You're getting ripped!" Larry's blush, the color of strawberries, set off his red hair rather nicely. He mumbled, "Thanks," and smiled.

When Roberta left to round up Margie and the twins, Rain said, "Seriously, guys, people are going to start noticing. You were just lucky you had health class instead of P.E. this quarter. It's time to cover up if you don't want Chris to figure out you're up to something."

Walter replied, "I got some loose jeans and a real baggy hoodie I can wear. But I don't think we can fool him much longer. We're avoiding him and he wants us to do stuff. He'll figure out something's going down."

Suddenly, Larry announced. "One of my aunts gave me this dorky fleece sweater for Christmas." Quickly trying to erase the "huh?" look on Rain's face, he explained, "Uh, you know, under a jacket it would puff me out—cover up the bod?"

Politely, Rain said, "Sure, Larry, that'd work." But Rain was now curious about how the guys were avoiding Chris. "So, Walter, what does he think you're doing every afternoon?"

"I've told him I've got detention and stuff, and uh, I told one of his stuck-up friends that my mom said I gotta look after my little brother after school. I figured it would get back to him."

Larry had laid some false trails, too. "I spread it around that we signed up for tutoring. But who would believe we'd do that?"

Turning to his best friend, Walter objected proudly, "We don't need tutoring. My grades have come up since we've been doing homework with these guys. Yours, too, Larry."

Larry smiled. (He was smiling a lot these days.) "Yeah, just *doing* the homework kinda helps."

Rain heard the scraping of chairs being pulled back from the kitchen table. "Come on, guys, they're gonna start without us."

Granma was sitting at the table ready to give her blessing when the boys sat down. Larry took a seat beside Granma and Walter sat next to Rain. As Roberta put the big pot of stew on the table, Granma leaned over to Larry. "Rain tells me you participate when Joe teaches Native language."

"Yes, ma'am," Larry replied. "Not everybody gets a chance to learn the stuff Joe teaches. Anybody can take French or Spanish at school. But a Tribal language is special. When we move away, it's a way I'll be able to remember everybody here."

Suddenly, Larry realized that the whole table was listening—including Walter, who had a troubled look on his face. "What do you mean 'when you move away?'" he asked.

"You know, when my mom gets a job somewhere else." Looking back at Granma, Larry said sheepishly, "I like trying to learn the language, but I have trouble pronouncing the words."

Granma smiled at her great-grandson. "Rain, these are some fine young men you've brought home." To Larry, she said: "After we eat, you come with me. I'm going to teach you to say the prayer I say every night before we eat. You might not pronounce all the words just right. But you'll remember it for a long time— and know what it means—that's even more important."

Chapter 27

Arrogantly ignoring the coach's warning, Chris dug an elbow into Larry's ribs.

Drills and Thrills

Larry must have said Granma's prayer a hundred times over the next two weeks—especially the part she'd added about asking for strength because he and Walter were trying so hard to become good relatives. He now understood what it meant to have friends that were really like your family. Larry wanted to make them proud. Finally, the fateful day of the tryouts arrived. Everybody was jumpy. The boys' plan was to get to the locker room early that afternoon and dress out before anyone else. They wanted no premature run-ins with Chris and his buddies.

They ate a high-protein lunch of grilled chicken sandwiches at lunch, and then went over to the music room where they met up with their new friends. Instead of best wishes, they got some of Boomer's best jokes and teacher imitations. Walter and Larry (who had never seen his Mrs. Biddy) were rolling on the floor. The kids blew out the jitters like bad exhaust. Before going back to class, Hummingbird, still giggling, slipped them a whole grain snack bar to eat thirty minutes before the tryout.

The rest of the school day was no problem. They had a quiz in health class, the last period of the day. It was a snap—true or false questions about "The Food Pyramid." They'd been living it for six weeks.

As soon as the dismissal bell rang, they headed to the locker room. The boys were surprised when Rain, Boomer, and Simon showed up a few minutes later. They said they wouldn't be able to watch the tryouts. Coach Brown had closed the gym to spectators; only teachers were allowed. The guys wished them luck and said they would be waiting outside the gym with Hummingbird and Arianna.

It was time to dress out. Walter changed into a new LeBron James T-shirt and baggies his mom bought him. Larry took off his shirt to reveal a "shooter shirt" that he'd borrowed from Boo. The boys ate their snack and put back on their hoodies. Then they gave each other a wordless fist bump, and strolled slowly down the hall to the big double doors that opened into the gym. The gymnasium never looked so big. Walter swallowed hard and glanced at Larry. He saw a flicker of nerves pass over his friend's face. Walter did a Mrs. Biddy "squawk" and gave Larry his usual punch on the arm. They laughed nervously at each other and stood up a little straighter.

Several basketball players from the high school were laying out markers for the drill stations. They would be assisting the coaches today. One of the bigger guys saw them and hollered, "If you're trying out, sit over there!"—indicating the bleacher seats where the team candidates would assemble. Pulling their hoods down over their heads, Walter and Larry sat down and waited.

The eighth grade Thunderbirds team soon began to drift in. Chris and his friends Pooch and Cruiser sauntered into the gym last, laughing over a private joke. Following them was a clump of seven boys who huddled together like a small bevy of quail. A high school assistant pointed to Walter and Larry and they quickly scurried to join the other members of their flock.

A door banged open on the other side of the gym. All heads turned to see Coach Brown and his assistant, Coach Horn, striding across the court. Both men were in their middle thirties, tall, and broad-shouldered. They looked impressive in their dark blue Thunderbirds jackets.

Halting in front of the assembled students, Coach Brown waved the current 8th grade team members to the bleacher seats behind the boys who were trying out. He smiled kindly and thanked the boys who were coming out for the team. He said he was sorry that there wasn't a spot on the team for everyone, but he knew he could count on their good sportsmanship. Then he got down to business. Addressing himself to the team hopefuls, he said, "Okay, listen up. When I call out your names, come up and get a number from Coach Horn." Reading from his clipboard, the coach quickly ran down the roster. When he called the last two names, Walter and Larry took off their hoodies and jogged over to the assistant coach.

The gym went silent. Coach Horn pinned on the boy's numbers and glanced over at Coach Brown. The head coach was staring point blank at Walter and Larry's miraculous transformation. A small buzz started to waft down from the upper bleachers where a group of teachers had gathered to watch the tryouts.

Chris slowly stood up. The expression on his face was a strange mixture of stunned surprise, sideshow gawking, and fury. Finally, a voice that came from one of the Thunderbirds asked the obvious. "Who *are* those guys?"

"Dumptruck and Tater Tot." Chris's reply, whispered quietly between clenched teeth, was more like a conviction for high treason than an answer. He sat down heavily.

Pooch leaned over and said, "So, now you know what they've been up to." Cruiser laughed and shook his head. No way would he want to be in Dump and Tater's shoes right now.

When the boys returned to their seats, the coach finished up by explaining the tryout routine and how they would be judged. Smiling, he wished everyone good luck and promised not to keep them guessing too long. "The names of the three players chosen for the two team positions and one alternate will be posted by noon tomorrow."

The tryout started with drills. The coaches and their high school assistants took the candidates through dribbling, shooting, passing, and layups. There were also two agility drills laid out on the court—the Box and the Zigzag. Walter and Larry were the first ones lined up for agility. Larry turned around and gave Walter a confident thumbs-up. They had done these drills with Simon and the girls a hundred times. When it came their turn, the boys sprinted, sidestepped, and shuffled backwards with ease. Walter even showed a certain grace that didn't go unnoticed. Coach Brown wrote "Excellent" beside both boys' names on his checklist.

Several Thunderbird players murmured their approval. "Dumptruck's okay." "Yeah, he moves pretty good." Chris whipped around to see who was talking, but his teammates had gone silent. His scowl elicited a couple of snickers, but nobody had much to say after that. They were too busy watching the performance on the court.

The two coaches scribbled away on their clipboards as the boys dribbled around cone obstacles, passed at targets on the wall, demonstrated layups with the left and right hand, and did their best to land a ball in the basket. When the coach called up two Thunderbirds, Robbie and Cruiser, to throw passes to the contenders, Chris snarled, "Make'em look bad." They followed orders once it was Walter's and Larry's turn—making sure to mix in balls that were too short, too high, or off to one side. The harassment only put a spotlight on the abilities of the newly trained athletes as they dove, leaped, and did everything but somersault for the ball.

Chris stood with his arms folded across his chest, glowering at Robbie and Cruiser as they ran off the court. Plopping down next to Pooch (who thought it was pretty funny), Robbie took a swig of water and shrugged. "Man, they were just too…" Chris cut him off with a short and snappy message, "Shut up or I'll bust your nose."

Coach Brown blew his whistle and waved everyone off to the sidelines. Joining him at midcourt, Coach Horn said, "You ready to watch'em play some B-ball?" The head coach nodded. "Yep. I think we know who's strong, but let's go three-on-three, 10 minutes each. We should be done in a half hour."

Coach Horn randomly called out three sets of numbers assigned to the nine boys. By chance, Larry and Walter were two of the three selected for the first scrimmage. Dexter, a tall, thin boy was the third man. Coach Brown called out the numbers of the Thunderbirds who would play their opposition. Chris was ecstatic when the numbers for himself, Cruiser and Pooch were called. As he led his players onto the court, Chris whispered to Pooch, "This is gonna be sweet."

Coach Brown motioned to Chris and then to Walter to join him at center court for the jump ball. Tasting revenge, Chris whispered, "You're history, Dumptruck." Walter ignored him. His concentration paid off. When Coach Brown tossed the ball into the air, Walter was a little quicker. He tipped the ball toward Larry and the game was on. Larry dribbled toward the basket, trying to get around Cruiser who was a good defender. When Cruiser proved to be too good, he passed the ball to Walter.

Chris moved aggressively to block Walter, forcing him to pass off the ball to Dexter. Then Walter turned quickly to screen out Pooch who was guarding Dexter. The screen would have freed Dexter to pass to Larry. He was in a good position for a shot. But instead of initiating the pass, the tall boy crumpled forward on his skinny knees and crashed to the boards.

"Phweeeeeet!" Coach Brown stared at Chris, his whistle hanging in his mouth. Did he see what he thought he saw? Ready to chew nails, he marched angrily over to the captain of his 8th grade team.

"Chris? Do you mind telling me what that was about?"

Turning on his biggest "suck up" smile, Chris said, "Ahh, sorry, Coach. I guess I'm just too pumped or something. I didn't mean to hit him."

Coach Brown looked around for his assistant coach. "Coach Horn!"

"Right here. Behind you."

The coach spun around. "Oh, there you are…did you see that?"

"Who didn't?" Coach Horn and everybody else in the gym had seen Chris violently shove his left shoulder into the back of Dexter's right shoulder blade. The assistant coach couldn't believe it. Surely, there was some explanation.

Turning back to Chris, Coach Brown said, "I'm calling that a flagrant foul, Mr. Sorrel. What do you think this is? An NBA final?"

Widening his eyes innocently, Chris protested in his most ingratiating voice: "No sir. Really it was just a mistake."

In his firmest voice, the coach said, "I'm watching you Chris." Turning away from Chris, he called out, "Where's Dexter!?"

The injured party said, "Over here, Coach."

"You okay?" When Dexter nodded, Coach Brown signaled to resume the scrimmage. Coach Horn announced the penalty. "Two free throws and the tryout team keeps possession of the ball." Holding the basketball out from his body like it was a bomb, Dexter walked slowly to the penalty free-throw line.

Walter gave him an encouraging smile and Larry murmured, "Just relax, man."

Dexter could feel every eye in the gym on him. He shrugged and said, "Well, here goes." He shot two air balls.

The ball went back into play. Chris and Pooch traded a triumphant grin as they moved in aggressively to box out the tryout team. In the confusion of the hustle, Chris saw an opportunity for a sneak hit. Arrogantly ignoring the coach's warning, he dug an elbow into Larry's ribs. When Larry dropped the ball, Chris hissed gleefully, "Can't ya take it, Tater?" Dexter saw the foul and glanced toward the coaches, but they hadn't seen it. They were watching Pooch who had possession and was passing the ball to Cruiser. Walter, Larry, and Dexter chased Cruiser down the court. They were unable to head him off. The Thunderbirds scored on an easy dunk. The points were rewarded by a few whistles and isolated claps from the Thunderbirds, but one look from Coach Brown quickly squelched the poor sportsmanship.

Back at their goal, the tryout boys scrambled for a shot at the basket. Pressured by Cruiser and Pooch, Larry threw a quick pass to Dexter who surprised everybody by scoring two points. The Thunderbirds were so overfocused on Walter and Larry that they made a common error. Don't ignore any player on the court. Heading to the opposition goal, Walter jogged by Larry and puffed, "You okay?"

Larry rubbed his side and gasped, "Yeah. I'll live."

Grinning, Walter streaked by his buddy, mouthing silently, "Fake Layup."

Larry slipped back for the break the way Boo had taught them. He wondered how Walter was so sure he could get possession of the ball. But as promised, the big boy got a rebound. He hurled the ball to where Larry was waiting. Larry took off, but not so fast that Walter couldn't catch up with him as he headed for the basket. That slight slowing put the Thunderbirds, all fast runners, right on his heels.

At the net, Larry launched his jump and pretended to go for a layup on the right. Chris and his teammates rushed in to pick off the shot. They were so fooled they didn't see Walter move in on the left. Larry knew this was his moment! He pulled back the fake and sailed the ball to Walter who snatched it and rammed it through the hoop. Coach Brown jotted something on his clipboard. Keeping an eye on the players, he walked slowly over to Coach Horn. "Calvin, that play look familiar?"

The assistant coach shook his head and laughed. "Yeah, it's got Boo all over it."

The coach blew his whistle to stop the play. "That's fine, boys. Okay, next group!"

Dexter headed back to the locker room, but Walter and Larry ran for the hallway where their friends would be waiting to hear the news. They shoved open the gym doors, momentarily making their fan club visible before the tension on the door closer cut off any further observation. But Chris and Pooch had glimpsed just enough to see Rain and Simon pumping their fists in the air. Pooch hooted, "Looks like the jokes on us, man…and the Veggie Crowd thinks that's just fine."

Chris stopped and glared at Pooch. "Nobody jumps my 'team' and gets away with it!"

The intensity of his fury took Pooch by surprise, although he was used to Chris's moods. "Oh, come on, man. Let it go… "

But Chris spun on his heels and stomped after the coach. "Hey! You stopped the game. That's not fair. We didn't get to…."

Coach Brown looked up from his clipboard. Was this kid yelling at him? In a commanding voice, over-enunciated but perfectly under control, the coach said, "You better check it, Chris."

"No!" Chris grabbed at the coach's jacket. "You played favorites! You didn't give us a chance to score again! No fair!"

Coach Brown shook the boy off. "That's enough. Get dressed and wait for me in my office. Now!"

Chapter 28

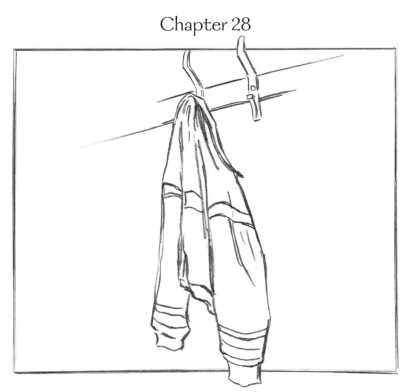

Not understanding, the boy stood up and slipped off his school jacket. The coach took it and hung it up on a coat rack in the narrow hallway.

Harvest Time

Chris sat slumped on a couch outside the coach's office. He was enjoying himself. He'd come up with some great schemes for getting even with Dumptruck and Tater Tot. Chewing at a nail, he smiled when he thought about what Melvin and Jesse had in store for them. Confident that his stepbrothers were the ultimate weapon, Chris boasted to himself, "They're gonna wish they'd never been born." When he heard Coach Brown coming down the hall, he straightened up. Chris had rehearsed several "lines" that he'd used on teachers before. He had no reason to think they wouldn't work on the coach, too.

Coach Brown walked by Chris, ignoring him. He shut his door and called Chris's mother. The conversation was short, but his mom understood that this was very serious. She told the coach she was worried about her son. She promised that the family wouldn't shrug off the school the way they did the last time. The coach's next call was to Mr. Berry. He gave a short summary of the situation and said he would come by the office shortly.

Coach Brown stepped outside his office. To Chris he said quietly, "Chris, give me your school jacket, please."

Not understanding, the boy stood up and slipped off his jacket. The coach took it and hung it up on a coat rack in the narrow hallway.

Chris eagerly opened his mouth, ready to let fly with a variety pack of prepared excuses and scams: "Nobody understands me, but I can trust you, Coach Brown;" "I'm just studying so hard that I'm tired and strung out;" and a new one he thought was brilliant, "I think I'm going through puberty."

The coach just walked past him. "Go home, Chris."

———

Coach Brown walked unhurriedly to Mr. Berry's office. When he got there, a group of sixth graders and their parents were just filing out of the office. Mr. Berry opened his door and ushered out two sixth-grade teachers. To the teachers he said, "I think this shows just how important bystanders are in preventing bullying. I'm proud of you. You handled it just right."

The principal saw the coach and asked him to come in and sit down.

As he passed by Miss Shield's desk, she looked up and said in her world-weary way, "Welcome to the Fun House, Mr. Brown."

The coach parked himself in one of the armless guest chairs opposite the principal's desk. Mr. Berry looked over his glasses at his athletic director. "So, you think he should be dismissed from the basketball team?"

"Yes, I do."

The principal rummaged in his desk drawer for an aspirin, but only found an empty bottle. Closing the drawer, he sighed, "It seems Chris is a very busy boy."

"What do you mean 'busy boy?'"

"Our anti-bullying policy is paying off, Coach. We've got kids reporting that older boys are threatening sixth graders and stealing their lunch money. Several children in Mrs. Davis's and Mrs. Freneau's class confirmed it. They pointed a finger at Freddie. But he said Chris Sorrel made him do it. Chris threatened him—saying his brothers would beat him up if he didn't deliver."

Not completely surprised (not after Chris's behavior today), the coach asked, "What are you going to do?"

"Suspension. Counseling, I suppose. It's sad because he's intelligent. Chris is smart and finds ways to get other kids to do his bullying for him. We thought he might be behind several incidents, but it was hard to prove. His father flat-out refused to hear anything about it. I'll recommend family counseling. I hope the parents cooperate."

"Chris's mother listened to what I had to say. She seemed very concerned. Anybody else involved?"

The principal frowned. "Yes. You know Walter and Larry—the guys they call Dumptruck and Tater Tot?"

The coach suddenly felt the floor drop. "Yeah? What about them?"

"Well, Freddie said Walter and Larry had been doing the shakedown for Chris. He got roped in because they just weren't around the last few weeks to do the collecting."

The coach stood up. "You're kidding! They tried out for the team. Walter and Larry were my top choices. They outperformed everybody else on the court. It was like the Pillsbury Dough boys turned into the *Transformers*!"

Suddenly things were getting very unpredictable. The coach thought, the captain of the basketball team is a mugger and the "good guys" he saw today are his goons? (Gee, can anybody say Coyote?) He sat back down. "How can I kick Chris *off* the team and put them *on* the team?" He looked up at the principal. "Miss Shield is right. It's like a Fun House around here."

"You don't know the half of it." Mr. Berry thought about telling the coach that a scientist from the state university was coming to the school. Supposedly, he was going to investigate some strange black stuff that Mr. Pence claimed had been a tree until it collapsed into a heap of dust. But he decided not to. No reason to start rumors. Maybe the seventh-grade science teacher just needed to go to Florida at Christmas and get warm.

The coach stood up and pulled on his jacket. "I'm gonna go see somebody."

"Who?"

"Boo."

———————————

Coach Brown decided that he would walk over to Boo's Gas 'n Grocery. He needed a few minutes to think. Smiling to himself, the coach was remembering that game Sky Bluff High had played against Thunder Rock back in February 1992. He was playing point guard for Sky Bluff when Boo had pulled that fake layup and Thunder Rock won 45–43. Boy! The rivalry between the schools was crazy after that game!

Pushing open the double doors to the store, Coach Brown looked around for Boo. Kitty was at the register. "Your brother around?" She pointed to the back of the store.

Down on one knee, Boo was stocking the lower shelf of baby foods and diapers. He looked up to see Coach Brown, hands in pockets, standing at the end of the aisle.

"What are you grinning at?"

"Got time for a cup of coffee?"

Boo stood up. "Sure. That's about it for the strained prunes."

Boo went over to his big Roastmaster coffee urn and pulled down the lever for two cups. Coach Brown added a squirt of milk and asked Boo the burning question: "So what do you know about Walter and Larry?"

Now Boo was grinning. "You figured it out?"

Taking a sip from his steaming cup, the coach smiled, "The fake layup. It was perfect."

Boo laughed. "I've never seen kids work so hard."

Then the coach dropped the bomb. "I hear they hang out with Chris Sorrel."

Boo stopped smiling. "Not anymore." He told the coach about Rain and his friends coming to him about the boys. "Walter and Larry want to get away from Chris. I think they can handle it if he comes after them again."

"I hope they can. But, we still have a problem. I was going to put them on the team, Boo. But I can't now. They stole money from sixth graders for Chris."

"I know," Boo said casually. "But that shouldn't keep them off the team."

The coach's eyebrows shot up. "What? Why not?"

"Because they paid it back. All $65 of it. They did odd jobs for me—when I wasn't running their butts off."

Coach Brown was back in the Fun House. He went sliding and twirling across a spinning floor. Wheeee! "You know, Boo, this is gonna be all right!" Swigging down the last drops in his cup, he smacked his lips and said, "Thanks. That's the best coffee I ever tasted!"

The coach charged back across the road to the school. Mr. Berry was still in his office. They struck a deal. Walter and Larry would do community service as part of the school's contribution to the Harvest Pow-Wow. That should set everything square.

The weekend before Thanksgiving was the start of the Harvest Pow-Wow and Fair on the Medicine Cave Indian Reservation. Planning a pow-wow was no small job. The whole community was involved. The pow-wow committee had been working for months raising prize money, inviting drums, choosing head men and women dancers, screening traders and vendors, organizing the dance competitions, and debating the selection of a carnival company for the midway. In the week before opening day, the biggest challenge was organizing the volunteers who would set up and manage the pow-wow grounds.

Coach Brown made sure Walter and Larry got in their basketball practice and had time to make signs, deliver trash barrels, and help set up the kitchen and tent where dancers would be fed. The boys would have been lying to say they were happy about being "kitchen helpers" and "trash pick-uppers" on the opening weekend, but "working the gates" and "parking/traffic" sounded like fun.

All the kids were incredibly busy. But, unlike the basketball tryouts, nobody was suffering from butterflies. Although they would be entering drum and dance competitions, this wasn't about winning—just fun. Rain and Boomer went into high gear with drum practice and everyone (except Simon) was trying to get down their dance moves.

Today the boys were practicing for the grass dance competition in their age category. Rain liked to wear the deeply fringed apron that was part of his regalia. He said that he needed the swirling yarn and ribbons to give him the right feel of the "grass" swaying in the wind. As the grass dance song was ending, he repeated his last dance step on the right side of his body, and then tried to bring both feet down simultaneously on the ground.

Frowning, Rain looked over at Simon who was holding an MP3 player. "You better replay that, Simon."

Protesting, Boomer cried, "Why? We've done it five times. I'm thirsty!"

"'Cause we're ragged on the stop. You gotta stop right on the beat, man."

"I thought I did."

"No, you didn't, Boomer," Hummingbird said. "Good thing today is a teacher planning day. Without it, you guys wouldn't be ready." She was sitting in one of the lawn chairs the kids had set up in her backyard. In between playing "judge" for the boy's rehearsal, she was repairing some loose threads on her pink dance shawl.

Simon started up the MP3 player again. Nodding his head up and down and bending his knees in a deep whirl to the left, Rain hollered, "Simon, you watching? You're gonna enter next year!"

"Yeah, I guess," Simon said without much enthusiasm.

Hummingbird looked up. "Come on, Simon. At least come with us on Grand Entry. Arianna is."

"She is?" he said brightly. Then he thought about the teasing. "Oh…nah, I'll look like a goof."

"You gotta get over your cousins!" Hummingbird cried. "They'll never stop making fun if you don't get out there and show 'em you don't care what they say."

A soft metallic thrumming/tinkling sound distracted Simon before he could think of a reply. It sounded like millions of little raindrops coming. Bird turned around, a big smile on her face. Arianna was running across the yard followed by Darlene and Aunt Chick.

"Bird! Bird! Look!"

"Oh! Arianna!" Hummingbird cried. "I knew it would fit!"

Arianna twirled and jumped up and down, the hundreds of small tin cones on the jingle dress beating out a unified percussion. "Listen! I'm an instrument!" In the middle of her impromptu dance, she puffed: "Your mom told me the story about how the first jingle dress healed someone who was sick!" Finally coming to a stop, she looked down at the rows of jingles on the yellow satin dress: "It makes me feel good just wearing it. Maybe I shouldn't say this, but I'm glad you outgrew it!"

"I just told Simon you'd be in the Grand Entry with us," Hummingbird said. "You're going to look just beautiful."

Arianna sneaked a glance at Aunt Chick. "You will, too, Bird."

Darlene said, "Honey, Aunt Chick has a present for you."

Aunt Chick held out a small paper shopping bag to her niece. "Keeping this secret wasn't easy, Miss Birdie."

Bird accepted the bag and peeked inside. She gasped. She reached in and lifted out the most beautiful pair of beaded leggings she had ever seen. She ran her fingers over the smooth background of pink seed beads, so expertly applied that no glimpse of buckskin backing was visible. Blue stars edged the tops and bottoms, and fluttering down the leggings, Aunt Chick had sewn rows of lavender, blue, and deep purple triangles. They looked just like butterfly wings. Hummingbird could imagine the hours of labor and love that had been put into each stitch. Tears clouded her eyes. Hugging her aunt, she whispered, "Oh, Aunt Chick, you're just the best."

Arianna ran jingling over to Simon. "You'll be in the Grand Entry, too, won't you, Simon?

Looking for an excuse to bow out, Simon said, "But I don't have any regalia."

"Come on. At least a friendship dance, for Pete's sake!" Boomer shouted.

Simon smiled. "Okay, okay. But only if Arianna dances next to me."

Sky Heart perched in a tall pine and watched the dancing. He had been observing the intense physical training that had been going on in recent weeks and was glad to see the kids just having a good time. When Simon started up the drum music again, the bird bobbed his head in time with the steady beat of the song.

"Hey! You sleeping on the job up there?"

Sky Heart looked down. Coyote was sitting at the base of the tree. "I haven't seen you in a while, Trickster."

"I've been busy."

"So I've heard."

"You've been talking to Thistle," Coyote said matter-of-factly. He shifted to a spot where he could see Sky Heart better. "I need you, Eagle. Bring the young humans to my garden. I have a gift for Hummingbird. A little coyote—a coyote *squash*, that is." Batting his eyes at the bird, he pretended a pitiful plea: "Pleeeese?"

"And just how am I going to get Rain, Hummingbird and their friends to your garden? It's a long way from here."

Coyote ignored the question. His attention had already gone elsewhere. "I feel like a little dumpster-diving tonight. Care to join me?"

The eagle looked away. "Stale hamburger buns? No thanks."

Coyote yipped at the eagle's disdain for his appetites. "You eat *carrion*, Sky Heart. Give me a break!"

"Maybe so. But it's not pizza garbage!" Sky Heart was rarely irritated, but Coyote had dumped a real problem on him. He was the messenger, but how did he become responsible for this part of Coyote's plan? Would it backfire on him like most of the trickster's crazy schemes?

Coyote trotted off. "I'll be at the Trading Post Diner," he sniffed. "You don't know what you're missing."

Sky Heart looked at the sun. It was time for his midday flight around the reservation anyway. He took off and flew toward the foothills to chart the shortest distance to the garden by road. As he soared above he saw a truck climbing steadily toward the area where Coyote had planted his seeds. A truck! Of course, the bird thought, why didn't I think of Boo before?

Chapter 29

Boomer started running toward the clearing and disappeared into the trees.
Within seconds, the shockwave hit. "Hey! You're not going to believe this!!"

Coyote's Garden

The next afternoon, Sky Heart was waiting on a nearby telephone pole at Boo's Gas 'n Grocery. With great relief he saw Rain, Boomer and Simon dashing over to Boo's before their bus came. Launching his plan, the eagle fluttered down and landed on the roof of Boo's big wide-bodied truck. Lowering his head so he could see thorough the store's glass double doors, Sky Heart spied the boys at the comic books. Boo, he saw, was filling the coffee urns.

When the two customers in the store left, the eagle went into his act. He flew to a pile of sticks he had deposited behind Boo's garage the night before. He swooped low and picked up a big stick with the talons of his left foot. Then flapping above the truck, he dropped it on the cab! Bang! Before the noise had stopped echoing, he did it again—only with a bigger stick. BANG!

By the time Boo got to the window, Sky Heart was dropping a *bundle* of sticks. Some of them hit the cab roof and others clinked and clanged in the bed of the truck. Boo hollered, "Hey, guys. Get over here!"

The boys hustled to see what was going on. Boo said, "Look." Sky Heart was perched on the rim of the truck bed—an extended foot firmly grasping another stick.

Rain yelled, "It's him!"

Simon and Boomer simultaneously gasped, "The eagle!"

The boys flung open the glass doors and ran outside. Rain stopped suddenly, causing the other boys to skid to a halt. Rain whispered, "We should show respect." They walked slowly and quietly toward the eagle. The three boys were standing before the great bird when Boo came up behind them. Astounded, he watched as the eagle let Boomer gently take the stick from his talons.

"You remember me, don't you, Mr. Eagle? I'm Thunder Cloud. You don't need this stick anymore. We're here."

Boo knew he was witnessing something extraordinary. Unsure that he should even be there, he started slowly to back away. Rain and Simon heard him and turned around. Rain smiled. "Mr. Eagle, that's our friend, Boo."

Sky Heart shifted his gaze to the man. Ahh, yes, the eagle thought, the one who will take us. Boo locked eyes with the Great Messenger. For a moment he felt like he couldn't breathe. Finally, he managed to draw in a raggedy mouthful of air. At the sound of Boo's gasp, Sky Heart emitted a shrill whistle: "Eeeeeeeee!"

Everybody jumped. The boys had never been this close to the eagle when he called out. Rain knew that the eagle wanted something from the man—right now. "Boo, we've got to go somewhere. The eagle will show us the way."

Boo cleared his head and nodded. "Get in the truck. I'll lock up." Reaching into his pocket for his keys, he thought, Just follow the kids on this one. Just follow RD. As he was turning the door sign from "Open" to "Closed," he saw the boy looking out the window of the truck. He whispered to himself, "Déjà vu. Just like Granma and Shell Ridge. Here we go again…" Boo climbed in the truck and said, "Where to?"

It was Simon who replied. "I think this is about Hummingbird. We should pick her up at school—and Arianna, too. Their bus hasn't come yet."

Rain added: "Even if it isn't about her—she'd really be upset if we went off and left her."

"Is she in trouble?" Boo asked.

"No, Boo. Nothing like that."

Trying to understand, Boo said, "But the eagle is trying to help her?"

"Yeah, kind of," Rain answered. He had never talked to an adult about the eagle before. He was afraid to say too much.

Boo pulled the truck in front of the school gym and Boomer hopped out to get the girls. They were sitting on a bench in the courtyard. Boo watched Boomer pull up Hummingbird by her arm and gesture toward the truck. She took off running.

Simon opened the cab door and Hummingbird jumped in, followed by Boomer and Arianna. Out of breath, she gasped, "Where is he?"

Rain pointed to the eagle. He was perched on the roof of the gym. When Boo pulled out onto Old Schoolhouse Road, Sky Heart flew out in front of the truck and set a course for the foothills.

Sitting in the front seat next to the window, Rain acted as the spotter, keeping them on the right path behind the eagle. As they drove out of Thunder Rock, Boo reminded everybody to call home on his cell phone and to keep buckled up. He was always super safety conscious when he was driving the kids.

When he reached the state highway, Rain directed Boo to go left. Then, they drove fifteen miles before the eagle took them onto a two lane road that meandered up into a line of evergreen trees that bordered the northern foothills of Shell Ridge. Boo cut his speed. As the trees got denser, Rain was having a hard time keeping the eagle in view. When he completely lost sight of the bird, Boo pulled over.

Nobody had spoken for a while. Boo looked back at Hummingbird and said, "Hummingbird, the boys thought you might have some idea what this is about."

She shook her head. "I don't know where he's taking us, Boo."

Rain interrupted. "There he is! He's come back for us."

Sky Heart was circling over the truck. Boo started up the engine and continued up the road. Then, Rain saw the eagle perched in a tree next to a fire road that led into denser tree cover. As directed, Boo bumped off onto the unpaved gravel road and drove slowly. Rain couldn't see the eagle now, but everybody could hear him calling. They kept driving. Suddenly, Boo jammed on the brakes. The eagle was standing in the middle of the road.

Everybody got out of the truck. The bird flapped over to a tree about 20 yards to their left. The trees seemed to be thinner in that direction. Arianna walked to the side of the road and peered through the undergrowth. "I think there's a clearing over there."

Boomer started running toward the clearing and disappeared into the trees. Within seconds, the shockwave hit. "HEY! YOU'RE NOT GOING TO BELIEVE THIS!!"

Boo and the kids took off. When they caught up with Boomer he was pointing toward a huge mass of tangled triangular leaves that entirely filled the highland clearing. "It's just like the garden at Aunt Chick's, but bigger than…I can see this big…maybe it's a…giant, uh…" He didn't need to point— everyone could see it! "It" was the top of a golden dome that seemed to be floating on the surrounding greenery. Reflecting rays of late afternoon sun, the perfectly round object glowed against a background of cascading leaves, waving tendrils, and ornate curlicues of yellow tubular flowers that drooped dreamily into the green lushness. It was exotic and beautiful!

Boomer yelled, "Come on!" and invaded the choking growth that surrounded the mysterious orb. Rain and Simon followed, helping him pull aside handfuls of leaves and vines. Here and there they discovered some green-striped squashes like those that had grown in Aunt Chick's garden—and the remains of those the coyote had eaten. Finally, tugging aside a very dense cluster of obstructing vegetation, the boys saw daylight. The small party stepped through the opening into a sunny arena.

Neither man nor child said anything. Lying there on its side, still connected to its umbilical stem was a vegetal wonder as formidable and bold as any geological formation. Unlike the green and white stripes of its juvenile stage, the fruit in its maturity had turned a deep golden yellow. But it was the size that was beyond words! King-sized, titan, behemoth, colossal, mammoth, or even gargantuan did not begin to describe it. Coyote had, indeed, grown a food *mountain*.

After a few moments, Rain broke the silence. "Where's the eagle?"

Boomer yelled, "Up there!" Everyone looked up to see Sky Heart circling in the clouds far above. He called out to them once and then flew away to the south.

Simon said, "I guess this (nodding toward the plant) is why he brought us here."

Hummingbird looked jubilantly at Arianna. "Obviously."

Arianna asked, "How big is the squash?"

Rain walked around the massive yellow fruit. "I'd say nine feet. And about the same across."

Boo was flabbergasted at the level-headedness of Arianna's question and Rain's response. Strangely, the kids seemed to be getting over their shock rather quickly. Frowning, Boo asked, "How do you know it's a squash?"

Bird replied instantly. "It's a coyote squash." Remembering Miss Swallow's identification, she added, "But some call it a coyote gourd or buffalo gourd."

Boo glanced at Bird. These kids knew a lot about this thing. "Well," Boo said, "someone's been sleeping here. See? There's the impression of a body."

Boomer stooped over where Boo was pointing and picked up a clump of dead grass and crumpled leaves. A gray fuzzy wad was stuck on it. Boo said, "Let me see that—it looks like hair." Boomer stretched up his arm and handed him the clump. Suddenly, Boo recoiled, almost gagging. "Good grief, Boom, don't you use deodorant?"

"It's not me! Honest! I took a shower this morning."

Simon started laugh-snorting.

"No, no, Boo. It's the squash leaves," Hummingbird explained. "When you step on them, they smell like (giggling) armpits!"

"You got that right!" Teasing some hairs from the fur wad, Boo said, "This looks like dog or maybe coyote." He sniffed it. "*Boy,* that's bad." Flicking the fur bits off his fingers, he added, "You ought to call it stinking coyote squash."

"Actually, I think that is one of its names," Bird admitted.

Suddenly, Boo's face lit up. "Hey! Do you know what this could be? Global warming!"

Hummingbird decided to come clean—at least a little bit. "Actually, this squash probably grew from some seeds I started in my Aunt Chick's garden. I'm not exactly sure how a seedling got up here or how it got so big...but I did use a lot of fertilizer."

Suspicious, Boo said, "You've seen one of these before?" The kids said that they had not seen a yellow squash, but they were familiar with the smaller green ones. Hands on hips, Boo turned around and looked at the squash. "Fertilizer. Hmm, so that's what this is..."

Rain added some details. "Bird had the idea to grow some giant vegetables so everybody on the rez could have fresh food. Arianna was helping her. We were thinking of entering one in the pumpkin growing contest at the pow-wow."

Boo laughed. "Well, I'd say Hummingbird's squash would win hands down!"

Rain looked at Bird. "Boo's right! We could enter it in the competition!"

Everybody began to talk at once. "Where would we take it?" "When does it have to get there?" "Can we move it?"

Boo walked over to the squash and started rapping on it with his fist. The reflected sound was dull and heavy. "It feels pretty solid to me. I think we could move it."

"How?" The kids cried.

"You know your friend, Jimmy? Well, his Uncle Luther runs a small moving business. Maybe he'd know where to get a truck with a crane."

Arianna asked, "How much can a crane lift?"

"Depends on the weight," Boo said. "How much do you think this thing weighs?"

Hummingbird smiled, "Ask Simon."

Simon always loved it when his friends said "ask Simon." Thinking for a few seconds, he said, "Boo, do you have a rope or some cord in your truck?" Boo nodded. "Okay, somebody find me a stick about a foot long. I'll be right back."

Boo was impressed. "Wow. Simon can really think on his feet."

Rain laughed. "Simon's a smart guy. When we teach him how to grass dance, you're gonna *really* see some fancy footwork!"

Neither man nor child said anything. Lying there on its side, still connected to its umbilical stem was a vegetal wonder as formidable and bold as any geological formation.

Chapter 30

Somebody says a truck down there is hauling the biggest pumpkin you ever saw. They're gonna enter it in the contest.

Moving Mountains

Simon hurried to the truck and found a big coil of rope and a metal tape measure in Boo's toolbox. When he returned, he tied the rope onto a stick that Arianna found. Then he gave the stick to Rain and told him to put it on the widest part of the squash—about 4.5 feet from the bottom. Simon ran around the giant with the rope until he reached the stick, measuring its circumference. He marked his end of the rope. Laying out the rope on the ground, he used the metal tape measure to measure the distance from the stick to the mark.

Looking up, Simon announced the result. "It's a little more than 28 feet around." Then he explained his thinking. "When we were looking up stuff on the Internet about growing giant vegetables, there were lots of sites about giant pumpkins. We saw a picture of one that was about 15 feet around, and it weighed between 1,700 and 1,800 pounds. You remember that one, Arianna?"

"Yeah, it was like the biggest one ever grown."

"So we're looking at something double that weight?" Boo said.

Simon turned around and looked at the giant squash. "Maybe. Pumpkins are mostly water. I don't know how much water is in a coyote squash."

Boo dropped off the kids and drove back to his store. He had Luther's phone number somewhere in his an old customer list. He reached him on his cell. Jimmy's uncle listened patiently to Boo's problem. When he started to explain that he was moving the big squash for Rain, Hummingbird and their friends, Luther interrupted. "Why didn't you say so? I'd do anything for those kids! RD saved Jimmy from Vernon Smeed—that fossil poacher!"

Uncle Luther offered to bring his flatbed truck or something better. He'd figure out the best way to move it. "We don't want to drop the sucker," he said. He suggested they meet at Boo's Gas 'n Grocery no later than 8:00 a.m. They'd need an early start.

The next morning all the kids were at the store except for Simon. He had planned to bring his dad, Henry, to help since he knew all about hauling heavy loads. Unfortunately, Henry got a late assignment to drive an oil tanker to California. So, Simon went on ahead with Hummingbird's father, Tom, and her two brothers to show them where the giant squash was located. They would be clearing a path into the clearing for Uncle Luther's truck.

Hummingbird was so excited she couldn't stand it. She and Arianna started jumping up and down when they saw a truck pulling a funny-looking trailer into the store parking lot. It was big enough to haul a small house. Uncle Ralph leaned out the cab window. "Everybody ready to do some movin'?"

The girls shouted, "We are!"

Looking down the road, Rain asked, "Where's Dad?"

"Right behind me." Just then, Gerald came into sight, pulling a trailer with a loader on it.

Boo appeared in the open door of his garage. "Wow, man. Look at that elevating platform trailer. You must have some friends!"

"Well, if the equipment they use to lift the pumpkins for weighing isn't strong enough, we can use this trailer."

Boomer came out of the garage wiping his hands on a rag. "Anything else, Boo?"

"Nope. We're ready." Rummaging through his garage, Boo had drug out every conceivable tool that might be useful in transporting a giant coyote squash. The only thing missing was the food—but it wasn't missing for long. Nadine, Boomer's mom, drove up with her backseat and trunk loaded with high nutrition snacks, coffee for the adults, and lots of water.

Going over the last details, Hummingbird announced to everybody that the squash had to be delivered to the farm pavilion at the fairgrounds no later than noon. Her mom, Darlene, had already filled out the entry papers. She would take them to the judge's tent by 10:00 a.m, the deadline for registration.

With that, everybody was ready to go. Boo revved up his truck and led out the convoy. As drivers passed the tight group of vehicles heading out of Thunder Rock, several waved. Others looked in their rearview mirrors, probably curious about where that bunch was going. They'd find out soon enough if they were going to the pow-wow.

The procession made good time on the highway, but slowed down considerably on the roads leading into the foothills. When they reached the fire road, Boo pulled in beside Tom's truck, which was parked on the shoulder. With some help from Boo, Uncle Ralph expertly turned the platform trailer onto the gravel road. He didn't do much damage except for some smashed undergrowth and a couple of unfortunate saplings. Gerald followed easily.

They drove very slowly to the clearing. Ralph stopped when he saw Simon and Tom signaling to him from an opening in the trees. Tom yelled that the ground was firm—the vehicles wouldn't bog down. Then, walking on ahead, Bird's dad guided the trailers to the giant coyote squash.

Dale and Richard had stopped cutting back the squash plants when they'd heard the roar of the truck engines. Standing aside, they watched the trucks pull up as close as possible to the "Big Stinker" (that's what Hummingbird's brothers started calling the squash after they'd chopped a few of its vines and leaves). Shutting down their engines, the two men got out of their vehicles for a good look at the nine foot tall yellow ball they were supposed to move. All Uncle Luther could say was, "Well, Gerry, paint me purple! I've seen it all now..."

Everybody gathered around and strategized how to move the squash onto the trailer. Their solution was to lower the trailer to ground level, push the squash with the loader up the trailer's ramp, fit blocks around it once it was centered on the trailer, and then tie it down. Because it was perfectly round and tended to roll, they secured it with a chain, pulled a cargo net over it, and strapped it to six tie-downs. As an extra measure, Uncle Ralph attached the trailer's cargo winch line onto the chain.

With the squash lashed down securely (and some fortitude provided by a snack break), everybody pulled out of the clearing and headed back to the two-lane road. Once Uncle Luther was on the highway he accelerated somewhat, but was afraid to go too fast. Soon drivers started noticing the truck's big yellow cargo; some were honking their horns. The more curious turned around and started following. It was 11:00.

By the time that the trailer arrived at Jim Thorpe Road, Uncle Luther was leading a parade—which made the congested traffic near the fair grounds even worse. Old Mr. Curley, who lived in a house next to the industrial park, had been sitting on his front porch waving at the creeping cars. But when he saw the approaching trailer, he hollered to his granddaughter: "Suze, come out here! What's that thing?"

Suzanne opened the screen door and looked up the road. Standing on tip-toe, she was barely able to make out the top of the yellow squash. "It's, uh, one those parade balloons. I think its Bart Simpson, Granddad."

As the mysterious yellow ball got closer to the pow-wow gate, people began to tag along beside the truck. "Say, what is that? Where'd it come from" "Where you taking it?" Uncle Luther leaned out the cab window and pointed to Nadine's car: "Belongs to a kid named Hummingbird. It's a squash. Gonna enter it in the big pumpkin competition."

The word began to spread along the road. Melvin and Jesse, Chris's brothers, had been hanging out at the gas station across from the fair grounds when they heard the hubbub. Mildly curious, Melvin moseyed over to a bunch of rubber-neckers. "What's going on?"

"Somebody says a truck down there is hauling the biggest pumpkin you ever saw. They're gonna enter it in the contest."

Melvin didn't believe it. No way. Dad's pumpkin last year weighed in at 1,500 pounds. Nobody could grow pumpkins bigger than Dad! He started jogging toward the truck. As he came up on the giant squash, he started laughing. People are so stupid! No pumpkin's *that* big. It was probably a plastic container of corn oil or something. Melvin stopped and let the truck catch up with him. Walking alongside the cab, Melvin sneered, "Hey, that ain't no pumpkin you're hauling, Mister."

Uncle Luther wasn't easy to rile. "Little girl back there says it's a coyote squash. Some kinda gourd."

The cocky went out of Melvin. "What little girl?"

"Name's Hummingbird. Says she started the squash down here in her aunt's garden." Melvin didn't bother to say 'goodbye.' He started running to the farm pavilion where the Sorrel Family had just unloaded their pumpkin.

Finally, the parade made it to the gate entrance. Walter was taking tickets. He had been watching for Hummingbird all morning. She'd called the night before and told him they had an entry for the pumpkin competition. Chris hadn't destroyed all the giant squashes after all! But now Walter was on pins and needles. The deadline was 12:00 p.m. and the clock was ticking.

When he saw Hummingbird's head sticking out the back window of Nadine's car, he hollered frantically, "You better hurry! You only got 30 minutes!" At that moment, however, Uncle Luther wasn't as concerned about time as he was about the *turn.* He was going to have to back up and make a sharp left to get inside the gate. He signaled to the four vehicles in their party that they would have to back up. Tom yelled back, "We can't! There's too many cars behind us!"

Watching from the parking area, Larry could also see that the big yellow thing wasn't going anywhere. He figured it had to be the squash. When Larry saw that it was Gerald towing the loader, he temporarily abandoned his community service. Running across parking lots A and B, and jumping a roadside ditch, he landed next to Gerald's truck. Frustrated, Rain hopped out on the passenger side. "Man, where did all these people come from?"

"Yeah, there must be a billion of 'em. I gotta get back in a minute. I'm parking cars." Gesturing up ahead, Larry said, "Man, that pumpkin's awesome!"

Gerald checked his watch and slumped further down in his seat. "Well, it doesn't matter how wonderful it is if we don't find a traffic cop."

Larry nudged Rain. "Hey! I know where the police chief is. I saw him writing a traffic ticket."

Rain perked up. "Don't worry, Dad, we'll get Willard."

Willard Fox Chief was cousin to Rain's mother, Roberta. He'd come to Rain's aid at Shell Ridge when Vernon Smeed had kidnapped Granma. Dodging cars, pow-wow dancers, and tourists, the boys found the police chief making assignments to a group of volunteers working "security." Safety and moving cars efficiently were the chief's top priority. When Willard saw the anxious look on Rain's face, he asked, "What's wrong, RD?" Rain wasted no time summarizing the situation. The chief told the boys to jump in his squad car. "Sounds like we got a traffic problem."

By the time they got back to the gate, the watching crowd had doubled in size. Jingling bells, waving plumes, and the flashing colors of brilliant pow-wow regalia created a riotous reception for the giant squash. Coyote would have been very pleased.

Hummingbird, Arianna, Boomer and Simon had become tired of sitting in Nadine's car and had joined Walter at the gatehouse. Miss Swallow was with them. Sammie and Star were there, too. They had grabbed Miss Swallow from the dance arena to come see "Hummingbird's Squash"—the tag that was quickly replacing "the big yellow thing" among the chattering on-lookers. Hummingbird and Arianna were beaming. Now Miss Swallow would know that the big squashes had been real!

When the squad car pulled up, the science teacher leaned down to the girls. "Don't you worry. Willard will get it through." And she was right. With whistle blasts, well-aimed pointing, and a commanding palm, Willard pushed back the cars to allow the trailer's passage through the gate. Unfortunately, Miss Swallow was only half right. When Uncle Luther started his turn, the trailer's left back wheel bumped into a pothole. Suddenly, the truck lurched and jolted the blocks loose. Hummingbird's Squash tilted backwards, the cargo net split, and the big ball began to roll. Someone yelled, "It's going in the ditch!"

With horror, everyone watched as the weight of the squash unbalanced the trailer, lifting its front wheels off the ground. Only the chain and straps held the squash on the trailer. Then, one by one the straps began to pop as the weight of Coyote's child strained them beyond their capacity. Hummingbird and Arianna screamed, and a loud "Ohhhh" went up from the crowd.

Clinching his teeth, Uncle Luther growled, "Hold onnn..." He reached for the power switch to the cargo winch—the last trick up his sleeve. He prayed the winch would hold the chain. He knew he would have to reel in the line tight enough to support the remaining straps. The crowd watched anxiously as the winch whirred and then abruptly stopped. The straps held. The pull on the chain even rolled the squash slightly back toward the center of the trailer. The front wheels returned to earth.

Willard gave the signal and Uncle Luther drove the truck slowly forward, unblocking the gate entrance. The crowd erupted into cheers, high-pitched trilling, and booms of approval from a drum group that had been stranded on the road.

Tom and Boo jumped up on the trailer and replaced the blocks. Hopping down, they returned to their vehicles and followed Uncle Luther. When they pulled in front of the farm pavilion it was one minute before noon.

Chapter 31

A northern traditional dancer, Betty Swallow was nothing less than stunning in her white buckskin dress, its heavily beaded yoke seeming to fall weightlessly from her shoulders.

A Grand Entry

The squash convoy drove to a large open area that doubled as a parking lot and site for various contests and other events. It was big enough for the Tribe to host a tractor pull, horseshoe and archery tournaments, a kite flying contest, and a little kid's parade. Bordered by the open-sided farm pavilion and the home arts building, it attracted a large number of visitors who came to see the livestock judging and crafts displays. Uncle Luther's destination was a large tent, commonly called the "judge's tent," that served as the headquarters for all the fair and pow-wow operations.

Uncle Luther parked the trailer and everybody jumped out of the cars. A tall, sandy-haired man came running from the entrance to the judge's tent. It was Les Johnson, director of the local county extension service and a popular official at the annual fair. He called out, "Boy, you guys cut it close!" He shook hands with all the adults, greeting Tom and Gerald by name. They had served with Les on various agricultural business committees over the years. Turning to the kids, he asked, "Which one of you girls is Hummingbird?"

Bird smiled and held up her hand. "That's me."

"You're famous, honey! The radio station's got a reporter out here that's been talking about nothing but 'Hummingbird's Squash' for the last hour." Looking around at the rest of the group, he said, "Don't be surprised if he wants an interview."

"Well," Darlene cut in, "he'll have to wait until after Grand Entry. These kids have got to get dressed and over to the arena by 1:00."

Les's cell phone rang. He excused himself and answered. "Johnson. Yeah? A protest?" After a long pause, he said, "Okay. I'll bring 'em over." Frowning, he re-pocketed his phone and said, "That was one of the pumpkin judges. He said that somebody's filed a complaint against your entry. They say it shouldn't be allowed in the competition."

Simon spoke up quickly. "Wait! That's not right! It's okay to enter a squash in a pumpkin contest. I read it on the Internet!" All the kids began to protest loudly.

Tom motioned for everyone to pipe down. "Look, the judges will have to decide what's fair. We'll find out what the rules are. There must be some rules. Right, Les?"

"Yep, we generally follow the policies set up by the International Pumpkin Federation."

A car horn interrupted any further discussion of pumpkin policy. Roberta was pulling in next to Nadine's car. She'd been delayed waiting at the gate for a golf cart to take Granma over to the Senior Center booth. Leaning out the car window, she called, "Come on, kids! We're going over to Joe's camper to change clothes."

Rain ran up to the car. "Mom, you won't believe it. We might get kicked out of the pumpkin contest!"

"Well, you guys won't be in the Grand Entry either, if you don't get a move on."

Boomer grabbed a suit bag from his mom's car and laid it on top of the other regalia that filled Roberta's trunk. Jumping in the back seat next to Simon and Rain, he wasn't surprised to hear Simon worry-warting. "Guys, I've *got* to do something to keep Bird from being disqualified!" Rain and Boomer just looked at him... what could he possibly do?

Following Darlene to her car, Hummingbird was still making a big noise, too. "It's gotta be Chris, Mom! That's why he destroyed the squash at Aunt Chick's. He wanted to keep us out of the contest!"

Darlene turned around and gave her daughter a funny look. "What are you talking about, Bird?"

Realizing she'd said too much, Hummingbird said, "Oh, nothing, Mom." Getting in the car, she glanced at Arianna and whispered, "Me and my big mouth." Arianna warned, "Yeah, you're gonna get Walter in trouble."

Darlene lowered her head down to the car window. "Girls, I've packed everything in the trunk." Handing the car keys to Dale, she said, "Just follow Roberta, we'll meet you at the arena." Before Hummingbird could protest again, she smiled sweetly: "Calm down, Bird. Just remember, whether you stay in the contest or not—you and Arianna got that giant vegetable you wanted…"

As the cars pulled out with their disgruntled passengers, Darlene and Nadine headed over to the judge's tent. Entering its dim interior, they saw that only a few people were about. Tom and Gerald were standing in front of a table talking quietly to Mrs. Elva Eddy, one of the judges. Apparently more interested in farm machinery than pumpkins, Uncle Luther had wandered away to check out a poster display of John Deere tractors.

Suddenly, a man's angry voice broke the silence. "Rules are rules! This is a *pumpkin*—not a squash contest!" Hoke Sorrel was shaking a paper in the faces of two pow-wow officials who didn't seem to be very moved by his outburst. Putting an exclamation point on his anger, he turned abruptly and stormed out the back entrance of the big tent.

Darlene sighed, and said "Oh, dear. Bird was right. It *is* the Sorrels…"

Tom and Gerald came over and described the situation. "We're supposed to come back at 3:00," Tom said. "The judges are giving us an opportunity to argue against the protest. Hoke Sorrel says that squashes are excluded according to this..." He handed Darlene the same photocopy that Hoke had been waving around.

Gerald explained, "It's the official rules of the International Pumpkin Federation." Checking his watch, he said, "We better get going. I'd like to get some pictures."

Darlene read the judging guidelines out loud as they made their way to the pow-wow arena. When she got to the part about the color requirements, Uncle Luther (who wasn't a gardener) broke in. "Boy, some people really take this stuff seriously!"

Darlene said, "If you think that's serious, listen to this." She was about to recite the rules about skin quality when they heard the host drum launch the song for the Grand Entry. Quickly stuffing the rules in her tote bag, she said, "The rest of this can wait." Hurrying to join the huge crowd of spectators, they could see above the heads of the onlookers, the crook of the furred eagle staff begin its forward movement into the arena.

Tom and Darlene broke off, looking for a pathway through the crowd. Uncle Luther, Gerald, and Nadine did the same. Finally, Tom found an opening behind a row of lawn chairs occupied by members of the Senior Center—just in time to see the men fancy dancers and grass dancers twirling past. He and Darlene watched as the traditional women dancers followed, their long fringed shawls, draped over their arms, swinging gracefully in time with the drum. Darlene nudged Tom, "Look, there's Miss Swallow." A northern traditional dancer, Betty Swallow was nothing less than stunning in her white buckskin dress, its heavily beaded yoke seeming to fall weightlessly from her shoulders. She looked like a willow in the wind.

After the women came the boys. Tom and Darlene saw Rain and Boomer go by with the junior grass dancers. Knowing that Hummingbird and Arianna couldn't be far behind, Darlene craned her neck, looking for the girls. Spotting a pink and yellow pattern emerging from the churning colors of the Grand Entry, she cried, "Here they come, Tom!" Tom raised his cell phone and snapped pictures as Hummingbird's pink shawl spun past. Arianna was right behind her. Although a beginner, she side-stepped and zigzagged just as Aunt Chick had taught her—flashing a smile that was almost brighter than the jingles on her yellow dress.

Being pressed by the people behind them, Tom and Darlene decided to make an escape—they needed air. Fortunately, they spotted Uncle Luther on the outer fringes of the crowd and joined him. They stood respectfully until the Grand Entry concluded with the invocation and closing song. After the spectators broke up, it didn't take long for the kids to find them.

Hummingbird called out, "Mom! Dad! Did you see us?"

"We sure did. And Daddy got pictures."

Boomer's tongue was hanging out. "Mom, if I don't get something to drink, I'm gonna pass out."

Nadine said, "These kids need water. Let's go back to my car and get out the cooler."

"Good idea," Tom said. "We have to get back to the judge's tent by 3:00 anyway. It's almost 2:00 now." Turning to Hummingbird, he said, "We're going to have to defend your squash's entry in the contest, Bird. Your mom's got the official rules."

Arianna looked around, "Simon! Where's Simon? He just disappeared before we lined up for the Grand Entry."

"He's right over here!" Roberta answered. Everybody turned to see Roberta, Simon, and Miss Swallow hurrying around the periphery of the pow-wow arena. Simon was looking pretty sharp in a ribbon shirt that Darlene's boys had outgrown.

"Where did you go?" Rain asked.

"Your mom took me back to your house," Simon said. Smiling proudly, he said, "I printed off the websites of pumpkin contests where a squash was allowed into the competition." Looking up at the science teacher, he continued. "Then we went to find Miss Swallow. She knows all about coyote squash."

Miss Swallow explained. "Simon remembered some information about coyote squash that I had…uh…thumb-tacked on my bulletin board. I'm sure that Hummingbird's Squash is a stinking buffalo gourd. It's sometimes called a coyote squash."

"Well, its leaves sure do stink!" Uncle Luther said.

"Whew, yeah, that stuff is ripe. I can still smell it," Tom laughed.

Darlene fished in her tote for the copy of the rules. Handing the paper to Miss Swallow, she said, "These are the judging guidelines they gave us."

Miss Swallow glanced at the paper. A little smile passed over her face. "If somebody will drive me to the school, I'll get my research folder."

"I'll drive," Nadine volunteered. "I'd like to hear more about this stinking gourd." As they were leaving, Nadine turned and laughed, "Will somebody feed and water Boomer, please?"

"Yeah, Mom," Rain cried, "the food smells are driving us crazy! Can we eat?"

Roberta said, "Let's go over to Food Alley. Boo's selling his Native snacks and the county extension service is serving up grilled corn in the husk, baked potatoes, turkey legs, and chicken and bison kebabs. Oh, and just wait until you see the Tribal health department's booth! You'll love it! It's called 'On a Stick.' We've got veggie dogs—roasted potatoes on a stick, peanut butter on a stick—that's peanut butter balls between grapes, turkey medallions on a stick, salad on a stick, frozen fruit on a…"

"What about water on a stick…?" Boomer gasped.

Gerald grabbed Boomer around the shoulders and pushed him playfully toward the vendor booths. "Come on. Let's go find this boy some ice cubes."

Chapter 32

Pointing to a family tree chart on the easel, she explained, "The pumpkins and squashes all belong to the gourd family and to a tribe of gourds called the Cucurbiteae."

Pumpkin Arguments

Hummingbird ran on ahead. It was just before 3:00. She slowed when she saw the crowd milling about in front of the entrance. Suddenly, a man with a microphone came running toward her. It was MC (Medicine Cave) Charlie, the DJ from KHOT—"The Home of the Thunderbirds"—the reservation radio station. He was doubling as the roving reporter at the pow-wow today.

The rest of the group caught up to Hummingbird, just as she was wondering what it would be like to be on the radio. Biting off a wedge of potato from his veggie dog, Rain said, "Looks like he's gonna ask you some questions."

Tom wiped his mouth with a napkin and said, "Why don't the rest of you go on in? Bird and I will talk to Charlie." Still munching, the little troop of "squash supporters" headed for the big tent, smiling at the DJ as they passed. Tom shook hands with Charlie, who announced into the microphone, "Well, folks, we've finally found the famous Hummingbird and her dad here at the judge's tent. Let's see what she can tell us about her 9-foot squash. How did you grow it so big?"

"I don't really know. Um, I put some fertilizer on the seeds and then it got transplanted and it just grew...kind of on its own."

"Uh huh. Well, everybody's waiting for the judges to make the decision whether it's eligible for the monster pumpkin weigh-off. What are you going to say to convince them, Hummingbird?"

"Well, Miss Swallow is going to speak for us. Ah, I guess she'll talk about its scientific classification—you know how it's related to pumpkins?"

"Sure, of course, its, uh, classification. I know our listeners will be really interested in that. Best of luck!" Looking for a more exciting interview, MC Charlie had quickly moved on to a small crowd gathered around a table advertising "Guess the Giant Squash's Weight." Granma Hettie was selling guesses for a dollar. The prize was a lap quilt pieced by the ladies at the Senior Center.

Tom laughed and said, "We've got some enterprising elders around here." Father and daughter ducked into the tent. Simon stopped them before they got past the entrance. He was handing out copies of his web searches about the eligibility of squash in pumpkin contests. Apparently, Granma wasn't the only one being enterprising that morning. Giving a copy to Tom, Simon explained excitedly, "Maybe it'll help us if we can get the crowd on our side!" Tom thought, this boy will be running for Tribal Council before he's out of high school.

Walter and Larry rushed past them, hauling in extra chairs to seat the still-growing audience. They stopped long enough to tell Bird they were pulling for her. Walter said, "Mr. Johnson's letting us off parking lot duty so we can stay and see how it turns out!"

Larry pointed to the portable bleachers that had been hastily assembled by some pow-wow volunteers. "Look, Bird, everybody's here!"

Mr. Berry, Coach Brown, and a small cluster of teachers had commandeered a whole row of the bleachers. Mr. Pence wasn't with them—he was seated on a portable camp stool he had set up behind the judge's table. "Thunder Rockers" from the middle school were sitting on some butcher paper they had spread out on the sawdust floor. Who needed chairs?

Little Deb, Star, and Sammie jumped up from the group and ran over to congratulate Hummingbird. Sammie was gushing as usual. "This is so much better than the science fair, Bird!" Hummingbird bumped fists with her "gal pals" and said thanks. She was really glad they were there.

Not to pass up a little enterprise himself, Boo was setting out bottles of water on the judges table, complements of "Boo's Gas 'n Grocery." He handed a bottle to Miss Swallow, who was already back from the school. She was busy moving the easel holding the John Deere tractor display to one side of the judges table. When she saw Bird, she called out, "Bird, will you help me put up these pictures of the coyote squash?"

"Sure, Miss Swallow!" Bird went to the easel and took down the tractor advertisements. Pinning up the photocopies, she said, "Just think. If the coyote squash hadn't been on the tree we found in the shed, you wouldn't have printed off these pictures."

Miss Swallow reflected on Hummingbird's comment. "You're right, Bird. If it wasn't for the tree, I wouldn't know much about coyote squash." She glanced at her stack of notes. "Maybe nothing at all." Hearing a little stir in the crowd, she turned and looked toward the tent entrance. The Sorrel family had come in and was looking around for seats. A volunteer indicated three metal chairs at the front. Hoke, Melvin, and Jesse headed toward those seats, while Althea and Chris climbed to the top row of the bleachers and found an empty space on one end.

Since his 10-day suspension began, Chris had been spending most of his time at home. He had focused on his school assignments and had attended a counseling session his mother set up with the Tribe's Youth and Family Counseling Program. Chris had made only brief replies to counselor's questions, but had opened up to his mother when they returned home. For the first time, she really listened to his complaints about Melvin and Jesse. In the days since then, things had been more relaxed between Chris and his mother. She had even stood up to his stepdad when Melvin started hassling him for getting kicked out of school. *That* was a first.

Chris watched Hummingbird helping Miss Swallow. He wasn't very interested in what his self-perceived rival was doing. Even when the judges entered the tent, he merely glanced at them with indifference. He already knew how this debate was going to turn out.

Les Johnson, the contest coordinator, made his way to the judge's table. He laid out a set of folders at each judge's place containing the registration forms for the contest entries, the Sorrel's complaint, and a copy of the International Pumpkin Federation (IPF) manual. He checked the microphones on the table, and then pulled out a chair for the senior judge, Elva Eddy. She was a well-known gardener on the reservation. Dave Corn (Mrs. Corn's husband), famous for his prize-winning pie pumpkins, seated himself next to Elva. The last judge was Mike Good Face, a respected referee in the junior division at local Golden Gloves bouts. Mike had a reputation for being a fair man; everybody trusted his rulings.

Looking around the tent, Hummingbird saw that it had just about reached capacity. The police chief, Willard Fox Chief, was one of the last people to squeeze in. He was escorting Rain's great-grandmother (who was also Willard's great-aunt) to some lawn chairs that had been set up for elders. Granma Hettie sat down and waved at Bird, mouthing, "Good luck." Hummingbird waved back and quickly finished tacking up a hand-drawn chart Miss Swallow gave her. Then, passing on the "good luck" wish to her favorite teacher, she hurried to join her family and friends.

Les opened the hearing by welcoming everyone and thanking the volunteers for setting up the seating so quickly. He reminded the attendees of the no smoking sign, and quickly reviewed the issue to be debated, explaining that Miss Swallow would answer the judges' questions for Hummingbird. The judge's questions, he added, would give the audience a good idea of the criteria for a qualified entry.

Elva led off with a statement that would not have surprised anyone who had correctly read the rules of the International Pumpkin Federation. "Mr. Hoke Sorrel has protested that the fruit entered by Hummingbird is not a pumpkin and is, therefore, not allowed. We disagree with Mr. Sorrel. The IPF allows squashes to enter a giant pumpkin competition. The winner is the heaviest pumpkin *or* squash."

Someone in the audience impatiently called out, "Who cares *what* it is—how come it's so big?"

Elva nodded. "I know, I know. Like everybody here, I want to know how Hummingbird's entry grew so large. But our job right now is to determine what it is, not how it got to be 9 feet tall. So, Betty, can you tell us what that big yellow thing is—a pumpkin or a squash?"

Miss Swallow stood up. "No, Elva, I can't."

Hummingbird's yelp was lost in the crowd's surprised reaction. Boomer protested—loudly, "That's not what she's supposed to say!" Nadine shushed her son but, like everyone, she didn't know what Miss Swallow was up to. Rain and Simon didn't miss the celebration in the front row. Hoke was clapping and Melvin and Jesse were "high-fiving" each other.

When the audience settled down, Mike Good Face leaned forward and asked, "Then what is it, Miss Swallow?"

"It's the fruit of a plant whose scientific name is *Cucurbita foetidissima*. It's a gourd—most often called the stinking gourd or stinking buffalo gourd. But sometimes called a coyote squash."

Miss Swallow continued, "I would like to request that this gourd be allowed in the contest. I have several photos of the plant here. As you can see, its fruit is normally about the size of a tennis ball." Pointing to two photos, she said, "The stinking gourd has green and white stripes like a squash when it is young, and it's yellow like a pumpkin when it is mature. Therefore, it meets the IPF's color requirements for a squash *and* a pumpkin."

"Which is it most related to—a pumpkin or a squash?" Dave Corn asked.

"Actually, a pumpkin *is* a squash—a winter squash. Sorry, I know this is very confusing. These plants are so closely related that it is hard to classify them as different." Pointing to a family tree chart on the easel, she explained, "The pumpkins and squashes all belong to the gourd family and to a tribe of the gourds called the Cucurbiteae. One of the groups in that tribe is called the "cucurbits." They are the edible gourds—like squashes and pumpkins. The stinking gourd is a cucurbit—but the fruit is poisonous. It is not edible."

Trying to smash Hummingbird's Squash one more time, Melvin suddenly yelled, "Yeah, nobody *would* want to eat it. It stinks like a rotten sewer! Step on it and you'll have to throw away your shoes!"

Miss Swallow turned and stared at Melvin. How did he know what a stinking buffalo gourd smelled like? Of course, she thought, he *would* know if he had crushed its leaves...like in Aunt Chick's garden. Willard was thinking similar thoughts. He had stepped out from behind Granma Hettie to see who was talking. Those were the same words that the Neighborhood Watch officer had used to describe that vandalism case. Willard made a mental note to ask Melvin a few questions.

They both refocused their attention on the judges when Elva Eddy responded to Melvin. Playing on Miss Swallow's reference to the "cucurbit tribe," she joked, "Because a Tribal member stinks, young man, you wouldn't take away his enrollment, would you? Maybe he just needs a bath!" Laughter rippled across the crowd.

Elva held up her hand for quiet. Getting serious again, she said, "Betty, you just said that squashes and pumpkins are 'edible gourds.' Can we eat any part of the stinking gourd? Or," she smiled, "is it really just a big weed?"

Miss Swallow smiled, too. "No, it's much more than a weed. Our ancestors roasted the seeds or ground them into flour. They're really high in protein and healthy fats. Traditionally, the fruit has been used as soap and for medicines, and to control insects. I think we should take into account that animals benefit from the gourd, too—porcupines and coyotes eat the seeds. There are even new uses being discovered for the stinking gourd. The root can weigh as much as 220 pounds and can burn like wood. There's some research showing it can be used for fuel in countries that have few natural resources."

The judges jotted down a few notes. Then they looked at Les and nodded. They had no more questions. Les turned to the Sorrels. "Is there anything you would like to say, Mr. Sorrel?"

Hoke just folded his arms and stated forcefully, "A pumpkin is a pumpkin!"

The judges got up and conferred with Les. He pulled a microphone toward him and announced that they were retiring to make their decision. People immediately began to stand up and chat with their neighbors, but nobody left. They weren't giving up their seats. This show was too good.

Elva, Dave, and Mike picked up their folding chairs and exited the tent. They placed them in a circle under a nearby awning set up for picnickers. Putting their heads together, they quickly arrived at the most important questions to be discussed.

Mike went first. "What about the fact that it's poisonous and can't be eaten?"

"We don't eat giant pumpkins either—they're just ornamentals. That shouldn't be a reason to exclude Hummingbird's entry," Dave replied.

"Okay, that settles that," said Elva. "What about Miss Swallow's request that we broaden the rules to allow gourds?" Not waiting for an answer from her fellow judges, she went on. "I don't like the idea of excluding any plant in the gourd family. I think we should allow it as a gourd."

"But should we be creating our own rules?" Dave asked.

"Why not? It's *our* contest." Elva was a big supporter for Tribal sovereignty. She had been an activist in her day and always took a stand for self-determination. "We should follow our own values. Why do we need the IPF? I say family comes before rules!"

"But think about it, Elva," Dave countered. "Can you imagine how much that thing out there weighs? The IPF would recognize our Tribe as growing the biggest "cucurbit" in the world! If we don't go by the rules—the weight won't count. Hummingbird's Squash could put us on the agricultural map!"

Elva considered this and backed off a little. Then she said, "But we all agree that it is in the same *tribe* as the squashes and pumpkins?" Both men nodded 'yes.' "Then we can safely classify it as a squash. That doesn't violate any rules—even the ones about the color requirements. I think we're done."

"We're making the right decision," Mike said, "but I'd like to offer a suggestion. Why don't we have two divisions—one for pumpkins and one for squash. The winner of each division goes on to compete for the title of biggest squash *or* pumpkin. Hoke won't win the overall title, but he can still claim he grew the biggest pumpkin—which will probably be true. Then, we write to the IPF and suggest that they include gourds in the competition. I'm with you, Elva, on the 'family' thing. We just need to change the rules, not break them."

Elva and Dave smiled at Mike. "You're a wise man, Mr. Good Face," Elva said. Apparently the crowd that had been waiting for their decision agreed. The cheer that went up could be heard across the fairgrounds.

Chapter 33

Chris bought three throws and aimed a fast pitch at the two bottom bottles. The bottles went flying and he won a small teddy bear.

Holes and Soft Spots

The tent emptied quickly. Roberta and Nadine herded the kids back to Joe's camper where they changed clothes. The moms wanted their regalia to be in good shape the next day when the junior dance and drum competitions were scheduled. The rest of the day they could run the midway.

The plaintiffs in the great pumpkin/squash debate went their separate ways, too. Hoke Sorrel found his wife and admitted that, although he was disappointed, the judgment was fair. He would settle for the title of biggest pumpkin at the weigh-off. Melvin and Jesse's sullen expressions said it all—they thought he'd been robbed. They slunk off without saying anything. Chris listened a while longer to his stepdad prattle on about keeping his pumpkin title, but he was sick of the whole subject. He told his mom he was going to play some carnival games—he would win her a teddy bear.

Chris headed toward the midway but he didn't get very far. Jesse was waiting outside the tent. He grabbed Chris's arm from behind and spun him around. Sticking his nose in Chris's face, he snarled, "If you had busted up that garden like you said, this wouldn't be happening. You can't even knock out some crummy squash. Now everybody's laughing at us! Loser!"

Chris immediately flared up, "Melvin was there, too. Why not blame him?"

"Cause he's my brother...and you're not!"

"Who would want to be your brother, Jesse? Huh? You and Melvin think the answer to everything is beating up people and being stupid. You're the losers!"

Melvin suddenly appeared behind Jesse. Backing up his brother, he said, "You better watch it, Chris."

Chris laughed. "If you could read, Melvin, you'd know that the rules allowed a squash in the contest. All that Hummingbird and that pile of green stuff she calls her friends had to do was *prove* that it was! Didn't you see that stuff Simon was passing out? Miss Swallow had all the evidence. Dad made a fool of himself! I didn't make people laugh at you—you did!

"Yeah, well," Melvin said smugly, "if you're so smart—how'd the big science fair winner get suspended from school?"

"Ha!" Chris snapped. "That's nothing, Mr. Genius, compared to what's going to happen to you. You just confessed to everybody with half a brain, like Willard Fox Chief, that you vandalized that garden!" Giggling like a little girl, Chris mocked, "'*Oooh, stepping on the leaves got stinky stuff all over my wittle shoes!*'"

A look of uneasiness passed over Melvin's face. "No way, man. Busting up that garden was your idea. You just better keep you mouth shut." Melvin turned away, glancing nervously at his brother. "Come on, Jesse. This guy's crazy."

Still laughing, Chris shouted after them, "You're so stupid you don't even know Dad could still win!"

Chris didn't move for several seconds. He just stared at the backs of the stepbrothers that made his life so miserable—until they disappeared into the crowd. Then, head down, he started walking toward the midway. He trudged about aimlessly for a while before turning into Arcade Alley. The "Lucky Duck" shooting gallery caught his eye and he bought a ticket. But Chris couldn't concentrate. He popped off several rounds with the toy rifle and hit nothing. Next, he tried the "Test Your Strength" game. He banged away with the mallet at the base of a tall scale that rose like a giant thermometer. But he came nowhere ringing the bell. His swing was too wild.

Discouraged, Chris wandered around watching other people play the carnival games. He lingered at the Ring Toss and Dime Pitch, but they were boring. Finally, he focused on the

Milk Bottle Topple. He watched player after player throw a ball at three milk bottles stacked in a pyramid—and lose their money trying to knock them over. Chris noticed that the three bottles toppled only when the ball was thrown with enough force at the ones on the bottom. He bought three throws and calmly aimed a fast pitch at the two bottom bottles. The bottles went flying and he won a small teddy bear. He did the same on the next two throws—trading his prizes up to a big teddy bear. Chris bought more throws…and more throws.

Finally, the carnival worker running the game took him aside. "Say, kid, why you don't move on. I gotta keep my job." Chris smiled agreeably. No reason to be greedy, he thought. Mom will like the stuffed monkey, tiger doll, and gum ball pillow—but she'll really love the giant teddy. The clown wig and "I'm with Stupid" T-shirt he would save for Melvin and Jesse. Chris's bad mood seemed to have passed, but as Coyote said, winning always had a bad effect on him.

Unlike Chris, Hummingbird, Arianna, and the boys had passed up the games—they were more interested in the rides. The girls started off slowly on the family rides. They rode the Spinning Sombreros and the Ballerina Twirl before moving up to scarier fare. They were standing in line with Rain and Simon at the Flying Octopus when Boomer challenged them all to the Loopy Anti-Gravity ride. He firmly believed that stomach-churning terror was the only way to have fun at a fair. They wisely decided to stick with the Octopus. Boomer later wished he had. He found out that gravity has a funny way of re-exerting its powers—especially on your lunch when you are strapped into a gondola car that's upside down and thirty feet off the ground.

After Boomer recovered, everybody headed back to the pow-wow arena. They were supposed to meet up with their families at 5:30. Social dances were scheduled about that time and everybody wanted to join in. Two very special visitors were already at the arena, hidden behind the stage where the well-amplified Master of Ceremonies was announcing the upcoming contests and which drums were singing. They had spent the afternoon watching the dancing competition and were now indulging in some chow provided by that well-known gourmet—Coyote.

Thistle exclaimed, "Fruit salad! Where did you find it?"

Coyote nudged the plastic container toward the rabbit. "Never mind, there's more where that came from." Sticking his head into his other prize, a large white paper sack, he dragged out half of a chicken sandwich. Coyote wolfed down his treat quickly, but Thistle wasn't as hungry as she thought she was.

"Thanks for finding this fruit for me, Coyote. But I'm suddenly feeling a little down…" Her chin started to tremble. "It's just that it's hard when my babies start foraging for themselves. I'm going to miss them so much."

Coyote stopped licking the mayonnaise off the sandwich wrapping. "Thistle, eat a pineapple chunk. You'll feel better. Besides, your babies haven't run off yet." Cocking his head to the side like coyotes will do, he asked, "Were there any rabbits like you in this litter, Thistle?"

"No, not this time. But over the many years, there have been some like me." Thinking about this, she frowned and asked, "How old are we, Coyote?"

"Well, let me see. We were born in that winter when the first story was told. That was long, long ago when it was cold most of the time."

"So, what does it mean when one of our children is like us?"

Coyote thought carefully. He wanted to express himself in the right way. Finally, he said, "When one like us is born, it means that the stories the people tell about us are changing. If they only told the new stories, we would only live through our children. But, it seems they still like and remember the old ones, too. We are still here." Then his mouth stretched into his big toothy grin. "The old tricks are the best! And I love to play them. They'll be telling stories about me forever!"

Thistle began to eat her fruit. Swallowing a grape, she said, "Coyote, you are so bad and so good, so wise and so crazy... You've lifted my heart today."

Suddenly the drumming and singing stopped and all the dancers came to a halt. "What's happening?" Thistle asked.

"Somebody's dropped an eagle feather."

"Ohhh. Yes, of course. Everyone is standing. Sky Heart must be very happy when the people honor him."

"He deserves the honor," Coyote said quietly.

The animals watched as a ceremony was performed and the feather was returned to its owner. Then, the young men's fancy dance competition resumed. After it concluded and the dancers got a drum roll, the MC announced a Rabbit Dance. "This is a social dance. Everybody come into the arena—men and women, all tribes, all visitors!"

"Did you hear, Coyote? A Rabbit Dance!"

"Maybe they are honoring you now, Thistle," Coyote teased.

"Look! There's Rain and Hummingbird and their families, and Boomer and his mom." Naming off the couples, she went on, "Walter asked Miss Swallow…oh, how funny—Larry is dancing with Margie. And Simon and Arianna—they're holding hands! That's so sweet!" Thistle squealed.

When the social dance ended, everyone clapped and laughed as they exited the arena. "It looks like the kids are leaving. They're headed toward the parking lots," Thistle said. "It's probably been a long day." Her eyes gleaming, she hopped to the coyote. "When am I going to see Hummingbird's Squash?"

"Soon. Everybody's going on supper break. Wait 'til it's almost dark. Then we'll leave before the people come back for Grand Entry tonight."

While Thistle continued to gawk at the comings and goings she found so fascinating, Coyote kept an eye on the sinking sun. When there was only the slightest tinge of pink on the horizon, he said, "Come on. Let's go."

The two animals made a dash for the scrub on the periphery of the pow-wow grounds. Once concealed, Coyote leisurely guided the rabbit around to the farm pavilion. They squatted in some weeds behind an electrical transformer box that supplied power to the nearby buildings, tents, and booths. Coyote said, "Look over there." Thistle peeked around the edge of the metal box toward the deserted area where the tractor pull would be held the next day. And there it was! The giant squash rested on the platform trailer—proud and regal. It glowed like dull gold in the dim light of the light towers that had winked on as the sun faded.

Coyote said, "So, what do you think?"

The sight of the squash—so pumpkin-like—over-stimulated the rabbit's herbivore brain. She was enthralled. "Oh, it's magnificent. Your masterpiece!"

"Yes, it is," he said proudly. "I want you to enjoy it." Rubbing his stomach, the trickster said, "That half sandwich wasn't enough for me. I'll find dinner. What do you want?"

Still gazing at the squash, Thistle drooled. "How about black bean soup, a southwestern Caesar salad, and a pumpkin smoothie for dessert."

"What? I'm not running a restaurant, Thistle."

"Oh, sorry! Never mind," she said embarrassed. "I can pick off the lettuce and tomatoes from whatever you find."

After Coyote left, she settled in to "enjoy" the squash. She thought about the hours of tender care that he must have devoted to the needs of his plants. These pleasant thoughts made the little garden-raider very happy. Her spirits rose even higher as she listened to the muted roar of the midway that floated across the fairgrounds. Against the whirr and grind of the carnival rides, she could hear the booming of a drum warming up for tonight's dance competition. Focusing her ears forward, she could even make out the exhilarated screams of rollercoaster riders, rising and falling with each plummet and loop of the track. But sight was as thrilling as sound. When she looked up, it was to thousands of twinkles and the beauty of the Ferris wheel's neon-bright lights rotating against the night sky. Thistle was dazzled by the splendor of it all.

She was turning her interest back to Hummingbird's Squash when she detected some movement. Straining her eyes she tried to see what had attracted her attention. Suddenly, the Harvest Fair and Pow-Wow receded far away. She was looking at Chris Sorrel.

Chris was walking swiftly and confidently toward the giant squash, sitting alone and vulnerable on the platform trailer (the other entries were inside the farm pavilion). He had waited until dark to make his move—patiently waiting for the extension service volunteers to close up the judge's tent for the night. He carried a 5-foot tent stake he had found propped against an equipment van near the midway. Grasping the stake firmly, he whispered over and over under his breath, "Holes and soft spots—holes and soft spots." He would show Melvin and Jesse how to win! Indeed, Chris had read the International Pumpkin Federation rules. He knew that soft bruised areas and holes that went through to the inner cavity of a pumpkin/squash would disqualify it. A winner had to be perfect.

In a panic, Thistle watched Chris mount the back steps of the trailer and then circle the squash, examining it carefully. Suddenly, he went behind the squash and did not reappear. What was he doing? Then, Thistle's sharp hearing picked up the sound of dull thuds. What she couldn't see was Chris plunging his pocket knife over and over into a thin spot in the squash's hard skin.

Thistle looked around wildly. Where was Coyote? Although it was against all her instincts, she hopped out into the open area that offered little protective cover. She bounded quickly behind a sign pointing to the horseshoe tournament. At least it would give her some protection and a view of the squash's other half. Thistle wasn't prepared for what she saw. Chris had plunged the stake through a deep puncture he had made with the knife and was scissoring it back and forth—tunneling through to the heart of the beautiful squash. Appalled at the violation of Coyote's creation, she watched him pull out the stake and push his arm into the opening.

Behind her, Thistle heard a low growl. She gasped and spun around. Teeth bared and haunches quivering, Coyote was crouched, ready to spring. He howled and reared back, his power so near and angry that even Thistle's hair stood up. The rabbit knew she had to do something—fast. Just as Coyote launched himself forward, Thistle somersaulted into the air, knocking the trickster aside. She reached for her power—as hard as she could ever remember—and hurled her judgment at Chris. Deflected, Coyote's power shot toward the home building and shattered a window.

Catching her breath, Thistle leaped toward the trailer, shouting over her shoulder, "Don't, Coyote! Stop! Pull back your anger!"

She jumped onto the platform. The rabbit was relieved when she heard Chris grumbling and yelling. "This is all I need. No bars on my cell phone! I hate this squash! My arm is...I can't get out! Help!" She had feared that her power, dormant so long, was too wild and may have hurt him. Anxiously, she followed the curve of the squash until she spotted one of Chris's hands braced against the floor of the trailer. She thrust her head out far enough to see him kneeling on one knee and kicking at the squash with his left foot. He tugged at his right arm, which was trapped in the squash up to the elbow.

Furious, Chris shouted, "Let me go! You dumb, stupid piece of…" Suddenly, he caught sight of the nose blinking cottontail. He abruptly stopped his rant and stared, open-mouthed, as the rabbit hopped into full view. He jerked his head around, following her with his eyes as she hopped to his other side.

Thistle was checking him out. Apparently, Chris was in no pain. Her whammy had done what she intended. He was trapped in his own wrongdoing—and would not be released by the squash until a kind human pulled him free.

Chris stammered, "It's you. That…that rabbit at the garden. But you're not real!" Thistle turned her head and stared at Chris. Her eye reflected no light. Not being "real," she was unknowable to him—which was really a shame.

Thistle broke eye contact when Coyote began to yip, calling her to come away. Desperate, Chris pleaded, "No, don't leave me. Help me get out. I was only trying to get the seeds!"

His tail sagging, Coyote trotted to the trailer and looked up at Thistle. She hopped down and approached him. Quietly, she said, "I had to do something, Coyote. You would have hurt him. Are you calm now?"

"Yes, my rage is gone. I'm grateful to you, Thistle," he replied huskily. Suddenly, his face broke into a big smile. "Your ears! They're up straight!" Admiringly, he said, "Your power is greater than I thought, little rabbit."

Climbing on Coyote's back, she said, "Yeah, so you better watch it, you old rascal. Now take me home the way you brought me." She leaned forward, spraddled across the top of the trickster's backbone. Clutching his fur, she said, "Tell Sky Heart to come in the morning. He will take pity on the boy." She glanced up at Chris, who was slumped against the squash—watching them with a stupefied expression. In Coyote's ear, she teased, "He only wanted some of your seeds, Coyote."

Coyote yipped at the joke. "Ha! My dearee…there are no seeds. Hummingbird's Squash is an only child!"

Chris saw a gray streak zap across his line of vision—and the rabbit and coyote were gone. Completely whacked out, he jerked uselessly at his arm and started crying. Wiping his nose on the sleeve of his free arm, he looked up at the giant yellow fruit that had become his jailer. Kicking at it again, he whined, "I've gone craaaazy…and it's all your fault!"

After a few minutes Chris got control of himself. Surely someone would see him. Maybe Melvin and Jesse would come looking. That's when he remembered that he'd told his mom he was going to spend the night at Cruiser's house. That was his cover for the night. He'd wanted plenty of time to disqualify Hummingbird's Squash. But his plan was too good. Now his family wouldn't miss him.

Chris got into the most comfortable position he could find and waited. He passed the first hour singing some songs under his breath and playing a mental game of tic-tac-toe. But time was dragging and he got cold. Intelligently, he used the stake to drag over the cargo netting that had covered the squash. He pulled it over his head. As the clock approached 11:00, the pow-wow arena closed down for the night. Shortly thereafter, someone shut off the light towers.

Chris was left alone in the dark—with only his thoughts and *Cucurbita foetidissima* to keep him company.

Thistle leaned forward, spraddled across the top of the trickster's backbone.
Clutching his fur, she said, "Tell Sky Heart to come in the morning. He will take
pity on the boy."

Chapter 34

It was not clear to Sky Heart why Chris had chosen such an odd place to sleep. …he angled his wings to create a little air drag and settled gently on top of the home building.

All In It Together

The gray light of morning found Sky Heart flying across the Medicine Cave Indian Reservation. Coyote had awakened him in that darkest hour before dawn to tell him that a boy needed him. The trickster's only instruction was "go to Hummingbird's Squash." Approaching the pow-wow grounds, the eagle veered toward the farm pavilion where he had seen the giant squash the previous day. Circling above, he spotted it easily. The boy pressed up against its massive body was also easy to identify. It was not clear to Sky Heart, however, why Chris had chosen such an odd place to sleep. To better assess the situation, he angled his wings to create a little air drag and settled gently on top of the home building.

Before long, Sky Heart saw Chris turn his head and restlessly pull off a wad of cargo netting that covered his shoulders and legs. He was on his knees with his cheek resting on the top of his right shoulder. Strangely, his right forearm seemed to disappear into the squash. Chris moved again, shifting his body around the unmoving arm, trying to find a more comfortable position. It became obvious to the eagle that he was trapped.

Sky Heart took pity on the boy just as Thistle said he would. Looking for help, he gazed across the pow-wow grounds. Surely, some humans would be arriving soon. Luckily, he was right. He spotted a truck and a car turning in at the main gate. He launched himself into the air and followed the vehicles to Food Alley. He watched as the truck and car pulled up behind a vendor booth. Sky Heart circled over the booth, waiting for his moment. The driver of the truck got out and walked over to the car. Sky Heart recognized him! It was Boo!

The eagle suddenly swooped downward, and skimmed just above Boo's head. Les Johnson, the driver of the car, hollered, "Look out, Boo!"

Boo had instinctively crouched when he felt the swoosh over his head. When he looked up, he saw an eagle landing on top of a shuttered food van. Les opened the car door and leaned out for a better look. "I've never seen anything like that! Have you?"

Boo sprinted around to the passenger side of Les's car and got in. "Les, I'm afraid you're gonna have to wait for that cup of coffee. That eagle is gonna take us somewhere."

"Take us somewhere?"

"Yeah, trust me." Les gave Boo a "you gotta be crazy" look, but he dutifully followed the eagle when he took to the air again. Keeping the bird in view, Les drove toward the road that led to the farm pavilion. As he turned into the parking lot, Boo said, "There he is—on top of Hummingbird's Squash." Les drove directly across the lot, ignoring the areas roped off for the contests, and pulled up in front to the trailer. Boo jumped out of the car.

Sky Heart raised his wings and called out a series of high-pitched whistles. His job was done. In amazement, Boo watched the bird fly away. Then, he focused his attention back on the squash. What was he supposed to see?

Les leaned out the car window and said, "What do we do now?"

Boo held up his hand for Les to be quiet. He'd heard something. In the silence, the men heard a small voice wailing, "Help me!" Without hesitation, Boo bounded up onto the trailer. He followed the cries to the back of the squash. Startled, he found Chris crumpled up on the trailer floor. Not understanding what was wrong, he squatted down and asked, "Are you hurt?"

"My arm's stuck," Chris said weakly.

"Hey, Les!" Boo yelled, "get up here. Looks like the squash rolled over on Hoke Sorrel's son." He reached down to give Chris some support, but as soon as he touched him, the squash released the boy with a soft slurp. Les got there in time to see Chris sink back against Boo's leg.

"Is he okay?" Les asked.

"I don't know. We better get him checked out." Boo helped Chris to his feet. "Can you walk?"

"Yeah, but my feet feel numb."

Les reached over to help steady the boy, but it was the squash that suddenly commanded his attention. "For the love of.... what is this?" He stepped back, shocked at the gaping slashes and clusters of ugly stabs that now spoiled the squash's once pristine beauty. Looking down he saw a large hole, surrounded by pulpy bruises where Chris had kicked his feet, trying to free himself. That's when he spotted the tent stake and the pocket knife that lay next to it.

Les picked up the stake. Then he knelt down and inserted it into the opening where Chris's arm had been. The entire 5 feet of the metal bar disappeared into the squash. Les looked over at Chris. "The damage goes all the way through to the interior." Sighing, he said, "You know what that means don't you, Chris? You did this, didn't you?"

Chris glanced away and said nothing. His expression was hard to read.

Boo said, "So, what does that mean?"

"The squash is disqualified. Out of the contest." Mindful of the boy's physical condition, Les added, "Let's get somebody over here from First Aid to take a look at him. He needs to move—we can walk him around in the judge's tent. What's your phone number, Chris?"

Luckily, Althea picked up Les's call right away. He described briefly what had happened and assured her that her son did not seem to be badly hurt. She said she and her husband would come immediately. The early arriving volunteers at the First Aid station were just as responsive.

Chris was complaining of thirst when Simon's brother Billy showed up from First Aid. A well-qualified EMT, he gave Chris some water and checked out his arm for bruising, broken bones, and compression injury. Thankfully, no damage was done. Chris could feel and move everything; he had no pain. Boo also brought Chris a breakfast sandwich, figuring that he needed some energy after his ordeal. Chris was eating at the judge's table when his mom arrived. She hurried over and sat down beside him.

"Is your arm all right?"

Chris put down the sandwich and wiggled his fingers. "It's fine, I guess."

"Do you want to tell me about it?"

Chris had had plenty of time during the long night to figure out what he wanted to say to his mother. Gradually, his growing exhaustion had forced all the excuses and lies out of his head. They took too much energy to think up. Instead, his explanation was short, matter-of-fact—and very truthful. "I damaged Hummingbird's Squash so it couldn't be in the contest. And I wanted the seeds so we could grow one even bigger. Something happened and I got my arm stuck in it. I was here all night. I lied about going to Cruiser's." In the same emotionless voice, he continued, "I tried once before to make sure she didn't get in the pumpkin contest. I got Melvin to help me tear up her garden. He smashed their garden shed, too." Chris laughed a little. "Melvin's real good at smashing."

Dumbfounded, Althea asked, "But why, Chris?"

Chris met his mother's eyes directly. "I wanted Dad to win. That's all. I thought I could make him care about me. I thought he might make Melvin and Jesse leave me alone. They hate me and I hate them..."

Stunned by the bleakness of his motive, Althea put her arm around her son's shoulder and hugged him. "We'll work this out, Chris," she said quietly. "Is there anything else you want to tell me?"

Chris looked at his mother, desperately wanting to tell her about the rabbit and coyote. But he was afraid. If he told his mother he saw a rabbit riding on a coyote's back, she might think he was seeing things. Would that mean he was crazy? The only other explanation was that the animals were real. What did that mean? Chris was stuck. He shook his head: "No, mom, there's nothing else."

Althea smiled and said, "Finish your sandwich. I'll be back."

Althea found Les Johnson and asked to see the damage. He took her to the squash. Appalled by the violence of the attack, Althea was deeply affected by the desperation that it revealed. She murmured, "I should have seen this coming a long time ago."

"There's probably going to be a police report," Les warned her gently. "I'm just letting you know. Um, sorry, but I've got to go. We have to set up the scale for the weigh-off this morning."

Althea nodded. She was about to follow Les when she saw Hoke approaching the trailer. "What's he done, Althea?" he angrily demanded.

"He dug holes in Hummingbird's Squash. It's going to be disqualified."

Hoke looked at the judge's tent. "Is he in there?"

"Wait! Stop, Hoke. Come up here. I want you to see this."

Almost reluctantly, Hoke stepped up on the platform. His eyes went to where Althea was looking. "He did this for you, Hoke. To help you win. To make you care about him. We have not been calling out Melvin, Jesse, and Chris when they've done wrong. We've been using the excuse that boys will be boys, and we have let it get out of hand. This isn't just about Chris. It's about all of us. We have all got to make some changes."

Hoke stared at what Chris had done to make him "care." He was shaken. Troubled, he said, "He did this for me?" Hoke had never spent much time thinking about family relationships. But, seeing this, he understood that Chris had been trying to reach out to him—in a confused and twisted way that was not really his fault. Hoke looked at his wife and said, "Let me talk to him. By myself, Althea."

Hoke walked over to the judge's tent. Chris was sitting where Althea had left him. Hoke sat down. They talked. Chris told him the same thing he told Althea. Feeling scared, he asked his stepdad what was going to happen to him. Hoke said not to worry; they would work it out—together. Focused so intently on Chris, Hoke didn't notice Willard Fox Chief standing at the end of the table.

"Morning, Hoke. Can I talk to you?"

Chris glanced up nervously. Hoke gave his stepson a clumsy, but fairly reassuring smile. He replied, "Sure," and followed Willard outside where they could talk privately. When they were alone, Willard said, "About this squash thing. It's vandalism, Hoke."

"Yeah, I know," Hoke admitted. "I'm worried. We've got some real problems with Chris. Ahh, are you going to talk to him?"

"Not right now. But stick around for a while." Willard didn't know Hoke all that well, but he offered him some advice. "Look, Hoke, there is somebody that can help you. Her name's Bertha Lapin." He took out a slip of paper and wrote a phone number on it. "She consults for Tribal Social Services. She's helped families with a lot worse problems than you have. Sometimes folks worry that if they go to Tribal services, everybody on the rez is going to know their business. Bertha's not like that; she zips it up."

Taking the phone number, Hoke said, "Thanks, Willard. I appreciate this. I'll give her a call on Monday." Awkwardly, he said, "Um, I see somebody I need to talk to. Thanks again." Hoke had seen Tom, Luther, Hummingbird, and Arianna walking toward the farm pavilion. The weigh-off was scheduled in one hour. He didn't know if they knew about the squash. Hummingbird's father stopped when he saw Hoke coming toward them. The expression on his face said that he did.

Chapter 35

People screamed and scattered as the squash zoomed past them, on its way to…somewhere.

The Offering

Hoke was out of practice when it came to offering apologies, but he made a humdinger that day. "Tom, before you say anything, I want you to know I'm pulling my pumpkin out of the competition. That's only fair." Taking a breath, Hoke continued. "And Hummingbird, I'm sorry for what's happened. Chris won't be hassling you anymore. I should have paid attention to those calls from Mr. Berry. I know about the garden and the shed, too. Melvin and Chris will make good on that. They'll fix what needs to be fixed and pay you for the damages."

"It would be nice if they could put the shelves back up," Hummingbird said brightly.

"Yeah, and buy some more bags of that organic fertilizer!" Arianna added.

Hoke had expected a bit more drama. But Hummingbird and Arianna had already discussed the coyote's role in the squash's fate. The girls just accepted that the trickster would do with it what he wanted.

Tom was still a little steamed. "I just say it's a darned shame, Hoke."

He got a bit more upset when Les came running over. "Tom, you're gonna have to move the squash. We've got the tournaments and the kite flying going on this afternoon. I'm afraid it will get in the way."

Tom was startled. "You mean, we're not gonna get a chance to weigh it?"

Hoke looked surprised, too. "Yeah, everybody—including me—would like to know how much it weighs!"

"Well," Les said, "why don't we find out right now? The digital scale is set up. It's got a 5-ton capacity. And the weigh-off's not for another hour. We can weigh Hummingbird's Squash and your pumpkin, too, Hoke." He added, "All unofficial, of course."

"Just give me a few minutes to hook up my truck," Uncle Luther said. After securing the heavy-duty trailer hitch, he drove the squash to a small stage that had been set up in front of the main entrance to the farm pavilion. A large banner attached to the judge's podium flapped in the wind proclaiming "The

Annual Harvest Fair and Pow-Wow Monster Pumpkin Weigh-Off." Hummingbird and Arianna were watching Uncle Luther line up the trailer when Roberta's car pulled in. The boys jumped out and ran over to see the scale, a square metal platform that rested on a piece of outdoor carpet in front of the stage.

"Hey, Bird! We thought the weigh-off wasn't until 10:00!" Rain shouted.

"It isn't," Hummingbird replied. "This is the unofficial pre-weigh off." She explained how Chris had made sure the squash would be a no-show at the official weigh-off. The boys jumped up on the trailer to get a good look for themselves. Although they were disappointed, they knew the coyote was directing this show. Boomer tried to lighten the mood. He leaned down to Arianna and whispered loudly, "Chris didn't do anything. It was really attacked by a giant squash bug." Rain and Simon laughed.

Arianna climbed up on the platform to see for herself. "Well, it must have been a hungry bug! Don't you want to see, Bird?"

"No. I'd rather not. I'll just remember it the way it was."

Tom asked the kids to get down. The men needed to figure out how they were going to get the squash on the scale. They decided that it would be easier to move the scale than the squash. There was plenty of room for it on the trailer. With a little help from the boys, the scale was easy to lift. Since the squash was perfectly round, a slight push would roll it onto the scale. For safety, Tom and Les tied several straps around the squash and held on. When Luther removed the blocks, Les gave the "Big Stinker" a gentle push. Cooperating, it slowly rolled a few inches and stopped. Tom smiled. "I think we got this under control."

"Okay, push again, Les." Les repeated his low-energy nudge. But the effect was different this time. Suddenly, the straps started zizzing through Tom and Luther's hands! Uncle Luther yelled, "Owww!" and the squash took off! It jetted across the scale's shiny metal surface—and shot off the end of the trailer, sailing 10 feet before hitting the ground. People screamed and scattered as the squash zoomed past them, on its way to…somewhere.

This section of the fairgrounds sloped slightly toward Jim Thorpe Road—a feature that the squash took full advantage of. It began to roll faster and faster—spinning end over end through a gauntlet of trucks and cars before escaping into a flat sandy lot. The lot was bordered by a low concrete parking barrier 200 feet further down the slope. By the time the squash hit the barrier, its momentum was so great—it launched into the air like a great flying sun, spun out of control and wobbled crazily toward the back of the fairground's road sign. It hit the sign with a great thump and split right down the center!

Everyone that had seen the runaway squash ran after it. The news of its escape spread quickly to the farm pavilion and the home arts building. They began to empty. Folks that had arrived for the children's parade soon were hurrying to see what was going on.

Les stayed behind to pick up the scale's digital monitor that had crashed to the ground. He glanced to see if there was a weight reading—but the power cord was disconnected. Luckily, the monitor wasn't damaged. Then, he ran to catch up with the crowd. Worried that someone may have been hit,

Les was relieved to find that there were no casualties. Looking toward the road, he could see that Hummingbird, Arianna, and the boys had already reached the squash wreck. One half of it leaned vertically against the fairgrounds sign and the other half lay face down. The kids were standing in front of the vertical half, examining it closely.

"Look," Simon exclaimed, "there aren't any seeds!"

"Nobody's gonna grow another one of these, for sure," Arianna said.

Peering into the large cavity at the center of the squash, Rain said, "It's got a lot of empty space inside. Maybe it wouldn't have weighed as much as we thought."

Boomer hollered, "Hey, I thought it would stink!"

Hummingbird dismissed Boomer. "Oh, Boom, you know only the leaves smell bad." However, she was slowly becoming aware that "not stinking" would hardly describe the squash's smell. She sniffed and then sniffed again. "Does something smell awfully *good* to you guys?"

And, indeed, it did. A heavenly scent was beginning to waft from Hummingbird's Squash. It hovered momentarily over the curious crowd that had begun to gather, and then drifted on the wind toward the fairgrounds. The onlookers couldn't decide what it smelled like. Some said it smelled like roasted hickory nuts; others swore it had an aroma like spring flower honey. One man moved forward to say they were all wrong: it was sweet-smelling—like a newly picked ear of corn.

Boomer reached into the squash and dislodged a loose piece; he held it up to his nose. The fragrance prompted him to pull out his pocket knife and slice off a big chunk. He popped it into his mouth. Closing his eyes, he sighed, "Hmm…. it tastes like my mom's corn casserole with those little green chilies she puts in it."

A voice called out, "Boomer! Stop! It could be poisonous!" It was Miss Swallow. "Excuse me. Let me through, please!" She rushed to Boomer, expecting him to be retching up stinking buffalo gourd. Instead, he offered her a piece of his "casserole." Miss Swallow took the fruit and examined its delicate orange color and velvety texture. Puzzled, she said, "Maybe the giant form isn't bitter or poisonous."

"And it's seedless, Miss Swallow!" Rain pointed out.

"Of course, that explains it. It's more like a domesticated fruit."

"Yeah, and we know who domesticated it," Hummingbird whispered to Arianna.

"What are you going to do with it, Hummingbird?" someone in the crowd yelled.

Looking up the hill, Hummingbird could see more people coming, including her father who had gone to fetch her mom, her brothers, Aunt Chick, and Gerald and Roberta. Joe Red Crane was with them, too. "Well, I wouldn't want it to go to waste. We always wanted to grow a giant vegetable that could feed everybody. It just turned out to be a fruit, instead."

A large woman suddenly burst out of the throng that was beginning to look like the whole Tribe. It was Elva Eddy. "Here, let me taste it," the head pumpkin judge demanded. Boomer reached into the squash and cut off a nice-sized lump. Elva placed it in her mouth and rolled it around, savoring the flavor. She announced her verdict. "Just like the dried meat soup with Indian turnips my granny used to make!"

A honking car horn interrupted Elva's decision-making. People made way for the pow-wow's Arena Director, a big burly man who appeared to be in a very big hurry. It was Frank Big Weasel, owner of the local Jif Mart, and Boo's biggest competitor. "What's going on here, Elva? Nobody's at the pow-wow arena and Grand Entry is in less than an hour! The schedule's gonna be off!"

"Well, there's a reason we've got Indian Time, Mr. Frank Big Weasel! It's so we can shove schedules around—instead of them shoving us! Right now, I think these folks would say the schedule is to feed everybody—right here, right now. Just like Hummingbird said."

Before Big Weasel could say another word, Boomer handed him a squash chunk. Elva nodded, "Go on, Frank. Eat it." Obliging, he bit into the golden morsel and started to chew.

"So, what does it taste like?" Elva prompted.

Big Weasel got a faraway look on his face. He just smiled and licked his lips. Then he said, "It tastes like the blackberry pudding my wife makes, but it smells like some tobacco my dad used for a blessing once—he said it was flavored with licorice." (Readers may wonder if Coyote had Big Weasel in mind when he threw the whammy on the seed that would become Hummingbird's Squash. There is no way of knowing. The whammy could have been directed at a specific person or it may merely have sought out someone with a licorice memory).

A cheer went up and everybody started pitching in. Guys grabbed axes, hand saws, and tarpaulins from the back of pick-up trucks. Women brought scissors and rolls of white paper that had been used to cover display tables at the crafts and homemaking exhibits. Even the little kids, who were signed up for the kite flying contest, offered their string. Naturally, Boo showed up with his rebuilt, 8.4 hp chain saw. Boy, could that baby roar! Built for "extreme logging," it diced the big gourd like a Veg-O-Matic. In lickety-split, Hummingbird's Squash was carved, wrapped, and tied.

Elva organized the distribution, helped by the kids and their family members and friends. She declared, "This is going to be like old times. Old folks first. If you're gettin' some for grandma or granddad or somebody that can't get it for themselves—you come up, too. Then families with kids. And young adults last."

Elva lined up her distributors in a "bucket line" for maximum efficiency. Dave Corn and Mike Good Face were her deputies, making sure everyone got a fair share. Hummingbird stood between Rain and Arianna, tossing the wrapped packages forward to Miss Swallow and Mr. Pence who handed them out to eager hands.

Rain had never been happier in his life. "Bird, this is exactly what the eagle wanted us to do. The giant plan was the best idea you ever had."

"I might have had the idea, RD, but I sure didn't grow the squash. I'm not even sure anymore if the idea really *was* mine."

"Well, I know one thing's for sure," said Arianna who was watching Mr. Pence snack on squash bits. "You'll never be banned from science class again!"

Boomer tossed a package to Rain over the girls' heads. "Hey, where are Walter and Larry? I guess they gotta work, huh?"

"They might be working the parking lots," Rain yelled back. "We'll find 'em."

An hour later, the giveaway was over. Hummingbird's Squash had become "groceries." Bird made up a couple of snack plates for Walter and Larry—fancily arranging the squash cubes in concentric circles. She made a plate for Rain's Granma Hettie, too. Bird was really curious how Granma's taste buds would interpret the squash. The other kids stayed behind to help clean up. The leftovers made a huge mess. The scraps of the squash's tough skin alone must have weighed over a thousand pounds.

Roberta phoned the Senior Center booth. They said Hettie was at the judge's tent. She'd decided to enter her pickle recipe in one of the preserved foods competitions. Rain and Bird headed there first. Entering the shadowy tent, it took a few minutes for their eyes to adjust. They didn't see Granma and turned to leave—and ran directly into Chris. Hoke and Althea were right behind him. They had just come from talking to Willard.

Hoke nodded and said, "Hummingbird, please tell your folks thanks for not filing a complaint. We appreciate it."

"Oh, sure," she replied like she knew all about it. Actually, Hummingbird didn't have a clue, so she didn't say too much.

"We heard that everybody's got some of your squash to take home," Althea said. "They say it's delicious."

"Would you like to try a piece?" Hummingbird uncovered the plate and held it out to Chris's mom.

Rain tried to be polite, too. He said, "Mrs. Eddy's got extra packages of it if you want some."

Althea tasted the squash and smiled. "It reminds me of when I was a little girl—but I can't quite put my finger on it."

Hummingbird looked at Chris, but he avoided her eyes. For some reason (she didn't know why), Bird decided to set out across a shaky bridge to a place where she might not be welcomed. Holding out the plate, she asked, "Do you want some, Chris?"

Chris hesitated and looked at his mother. She nodded, encouraging him. He picked up a piece of Hummingbird's Squash and took a small bite. The expression on his face did not change. He said "thanks" and swallowed it quickly. At first he thought the squash tasted like medicine, but he decided it was more like grapefruit—extremely sour, with a hint of sweetness. Chris was not yet welcoming those who would reach out to him. He had a long way to go. But his ability to taste something friendly was a hopeful sign. Rain nudged Hummingbird. "We've got to get back. It's getting late. Our dance contests are coming up."

"Yeah, we've got to go." Offering the paper plates to Hoke, she said, "Would you like to taste the squash or share it with someone else?"

Hoke smiled and took the plates. Althea said, "Thanks, sweetie."

———

As they walked away, Rain said, "Boy, Chris looked pretty miserable."

"I guess you would, too, if you were in a squash trap all night. Did you notice how he didn't seem to like the squash that much?"

"Yeah, everybody else thought it was great." Rain stopped suddenly. "Hold on, Bird. Something just hit me. Most of the people that tasted it got this big smile on their face or said it reminded them of a food our ancestors grew...or maybe it was something a relative or elder made for them."

"Yeah, funny, isn't it, that the squash tastes like *all* our traditional fruits and vegetables? Even stuff that we can gather like honey and nuts." She laughed. "Gee, does it remind you of the miraculous tree...?"

"Yeah, it does. And it's exactly what the eagle wanted," Rain marveled. "To remind us about our own healthy traditions. The coyote promised you he'd never trick us about type 2 diabetes again. And he didn't!"

"Rain, do something for me, please. Go to the tree stump and offer some of the squash to the eagle and coyote. And to the rabbit, too. It's what she wanted us to do—taste everything. We should honor them. They've done so much for us."

Frank Big Weasel had stayed behind to supervise the clean-up. The big dump truck pulling out onto the main road was hauling off the leftovers to the reservation's newly built compost piles. All the odds and ends would feed the community gardens planned for next year's growing season. (Indeed, Coyote wouldn't have appreciated the squash rind being thrown away as garbage.) He thanked the "sanitation crew"—Walter, Larry, Boomer, Simon, and Arianna—for helping out. Now he had to get back to the pow-wow arena. There was lots of event juggling to do. Anxious to find out what his most pressing problem would be, he opened his car door on the passenger side to get his event scheduler. A paper bag from Jolly Ed's Corndog Heaven was lying on top of his papers. Puzzled, he picked it up and looked inside. It was his lost binoculars!

Big Weasel was trying to figure out how they got there when he heard his name being called. Looking up, he saw two young men running toward him. One had a video camera on his shoulder.

"Excuse me, Mr. Big Weasel! Could I talk to you? One of the kids over there"—he pointed at Boomer—"said you could tell us about the big squash."

"Ah, yeah. What do you want to know?"

"I'm Brad Sommers. This is Todd...we're from the NBC affiliate in the state capitol. We heard about your 9-foot squash. This could be a big story, Mr. Big Weasel. Big enough to make the nightly news. Yes, sir, I mean the *national* news!"

"Uh-huh." Big Weasel wasn't much interested in the national news. He was still thinking about the binoculars.

Looking around, Brad said, "So, um, where is it?"

"The squash? Oh, it *was* over there," Big Weasel said, pointing to a big wet patch on the ground in front of the fairgrounds sign.

"Was? What did you do with it? Did you move it?"

"No, we ate it," he replied casually.

Disbelieving, Brad slowly repeated Big Weasel's words. "We ate it. You mean you *ate* the only 9-foot tall squash in the whole world?"

"Well, we cut it up—so we *could* eat it."

Brad Sommers' shoulders slumped in disappointment. Glumly, he kissed his big New York newsfeed good-bye. He told Todd to stow his camera (No, he didn't want a shot of the wet patch!) and not to mention this to anybody back at the station. All he could say—over and over—as they drove the 150 miles back to the state capitol was "They ate it."

And indeed they did. Over the coming days, the people ate the squash fresh, frozen and pickled. But mostly they dried it and bagged it—just like in old times. Hummingbird's Squash fed hundreds of people. It was baked, boiled, broiled, grilled, fricasseed, and bar-b-qued. It found its way into casseroles, pies, puddings, breads, salads, soups, and even a healthy recipe for sugar-free brownies. The shelves in a drug store couldn't have held all the vitamins served up by the giant squash.

But those were meals to come. At the end of *this* day, Rain that Dances sat at his kitchen table preparing a simple late-night snack. The young Indian boy enjoyed these quiet times when everyone else was in bed. As he cut an apple into slices, Rain thought about the drum competition held that afternoon. Boy, that had been fun! As much as he liked dancing, Rain had to admit that he liked drumming and singing most. He thought the guys should start practicing earlier next year. The 7th grade boy's drum *might* place third in this year's pow-wow—if they were lucky. But Joe had been proud of them. That's what was important.

But all that could wait. Tonight he had a promise to keep. Rain ate the last apple slice and put his knife and plate in the sink. Then, he went to the counter and got one of the packages of squash his mom had brought home. He unwrapped it and cut off several generous portions, placing them on three pieces of newspaper. These he rolled up and put in a paper bag.

Grabbing his jacket and the bag, he slipped out the back door. The moon wasn't quite full on this chilly night, but there was plenty of light for him to see. He walked purposefully down the driveway and across the road. Soon he was in high grass making his way across the meadow toward the creek. Long shadows from the cottonwoods that grew along the banks fell across his path. They made beautiful spindly shapes in the gray-silver light. He angled away from the creek when he spotted his destination—the old tree stump.

Rain kneeled down next to the long-time gathering place and opened the bag. He took out the three packages, opened them carefully, and arranged the pieces of newspaper around the tree stump—one for the eagle, one for the rabbit, and one for the coyote. On each was an offering of thanks from the ripest part of the squash. These gifts were a small way to say we know you try to teach us, especially those of us who are troubled, and we love and respect you. This is what was in Hummingbird's heart. These were the messages Rain promised to bring.

In the pink of pre-dawn, the "Animals of Stories" came. Coyote and Thistle's hearts were glad when Sky Heart told them that an offering was waiting. In a reverent manner, they positioned themselves around the tree stump. When they were ready, each animal ate a piece of the squash, accepting it as a sign of respect and affection. Once this ritual acceptance was done, they ate the rest of the offering as a meal. Coyote, however, did not eat all of his squash. He nosed out an especially tender piece and brought it to Thistle, laying it in front of her. Very simply, he said, "For the next generation." Thistle understood and looked to Sky Heart. The Great Messenger picked up the squash in his beak and flew to her nest. Then Thistle climbed on Coyote's back and held on fast. In a flash, she was home.

Once there, the eagle and the coyote waited with the rabbit for her young ones to come. As the sun broke over the red fence at Aunt Chick's, the young rabbits began to appear. Nose blinking, they quickly discovered the succulent gift that Sky Heart had placed on the ground in front of the rabbit hole. Gathering round, they nibbled until all that was left was the juice that moistened their chins. Then, they presented themselves to their mother, and she groomed them, giving them her blessing for the last time.

Then, one by one they bounded down the hill toward the rising sun—eager to explore their world and to find their place in it. But they would always remember their mother's lessons and the stories she told. And when a taste of goodness filled their mouths, they would think of her and hold in their hearts the memory of Hummingbird's Squash.

Cast of Characters

(In Order of Appearance)

The Animals

Coyote: The Trickster. Coyote entertains himself by entangling the human characters in games and tricks that teach life lessons and lead them to deeper understanding of themselves and their culture. Fond of challenges and tests, he takes Hummingbird down a road that ultimately allows her to see her own limitations and reorients her direction to the extraordinary gifts and wisdom of her ancestors.

Thistle: The Rabbit. Thistle keeps a close eye on Coyote's antics and the magical garden he grows for Hummingbird. She states her disapproval when he gets too wild, but she understands his motives. Occasionally, Thistle uses her own trickster nature to control the fiercer aspects of Coyote's power—especially when bullies cross his path.

Sky Heart: The Eagle. Flying over the town of Thunder Rock, Sky Heart sees all. As the Great Messenger he watches over our young friends, as well as those whose behaviors trouble him. He gives warnings that protect them, guides them to good health, and accepts their love and respect when they recognize the healing power that he and the other "animals of stories" provide.

The Kids

Hummingbird: (Bird). Rain's best friend (of the girl variety). Like Rain, Hummingbird is totally committed to helping the community become healthy. Smart and popular, she is unprepared for the results of a Coyote trick that makes her vulnerable to school gossip and a bully. Undaunted by setbacks (and as bossy as ever), she launches a "giant plan" to grow oversized vegetables to feed reservation families—a plan that is soon under Coyote's control.

Chris Sorrel: A school bully. Captain of the 8th grade basketball team, president of school clubs, and winner of science fairs, he is known among the teachers as an outstanding student. Unfortunately, his "smarts" serve as a screen behind which he bullies younger and less popular students, and tries to bully others that present a challenge to his "rule of the school."

Arianna: Hummingbird's new "sister." Arianna is temporarily living with Hummingbird's family. She is from a Hispanic family that will soon be moving to the community. Arianna has type 1 diabetes and teaches her new friends about this form of diabetes. A soft-hearted girl, she plays an important role as the person who brings students together to work out their differences. (The character of Arianna is based on a real girl by the same name. Like the character in the book, she is very active and loves sports.)

Rain: (Rain that Dances; also called Rain or "RD" by his friends). The boy chosen by the eagle. Every day, Rain tries to spread Sky Heart's messages about eating healthy and being active. At school, the kids call him "Veggie-Man," but Rain doesn't mind, because preventing type 2 diabetes is all-important. When Hummingbird devises her "giant plan" to solve the scarcity of plentiful fruits and vegetables in Thunder Rock, Rain signs up right away. He also comes to the aid of Hummingbird and others who suffer the plots of bullies.

Boomer: (Thunder Cloud). Rain's best pal. Friendly and loud, Boomer is the joker always ready for excitement and a game of basketball. When everybody gets stressed out, Boomer snaps them out of it with his good humor. Although he often speaks before he thinks, Boomer is very resourceful when the kids get in a tough spot—especially when bullies are around.

Simon: The "nerdy" kid. Simon's family has recently returned to the reservation after spending several years in the big city. Because he is small for his age and unsure how he fits in with other kids who have grown up in Thunder Rock, he is an easy target for bullies. However, Simon's quick wit and intelligence help him work his way out of most confrontations. A wiz on the Internet, the "Veggie Crowd" depends on him as their "answer man."

Walter aka Dumptruck: A member of the "Invisible Club." A student "nobody," Walter wants to be accepted by other students and becomes one of Chris's toadies. When he is forced to do something that shames him, he confesses what he has done and seeks help from Arianna and Hummingbird.

Larry aka Tater Tot: A new boy at the school. Having been bullied at other schools, Larry tries to get on Chris's good side by becoming one of his toadies, too. He soon regrets this decision and joins Walter in seeking a way to escape Chris's control.

Rain's Family

Gerald: Rain's father. Gerald works long hours as the business developer for the Tribe. He is sometimes puzzled by Rain's obsession with healthy foods and physical activity, but he always helps his son and his friends with their projects, including their plan to enter a giant pumpkin contest.

Roberta: Rain's mother. Roberta works as a community health representative for the Tribe. She is proud of Rain and always tries to support his (and his friends') interest in diabetes prevention. Roberta and Rain are very close and enjoy doing things together.

Granma: Rain's great-grandmother. "Granma" is Roberta's grandmother and the heart of the family. She gives good advice to Rain, Boomer, and Simon about how to respond to bullies and teaches all the kids about being "good relatives."

Hummingbird's Family

Darlene: Hummingbird's mother. Darlene understands her daughter's ambition to improve the health of her community. However, she also tries hard to help Hummingbird keep her energies and emotions in balance with her hopes and dreams.

Aunt Chick: Hummingbird's aunt. Aunt Chick offers a shed, garden plot, and tools to Hummingbird after her niece asks for her advice about growing giant vegetables.

Tom: Hummingbird's father. Tom manages the Tribe's Bison Co-op and supports his daughter's interests in Native science, particularly protecting the bison's grazing grounds and raising healthy foods.

Dale and Richard: Hummingbird's older brothers. The boys suffer Hummingbird's bad moods, but they support her "giant plan."

Chris Sorrel's Family

Jesse and Melvin: Chris's stepbrothers. Jesse and Melvin are well-known bullies at the high school. Their poor example and mistreatment of Chris has helped to create the situation that fuels his anger and bullying of other children.

Hoke: Chris's stepfather. Hoke is a distant father who allows his sons to torment Chris with no fear of correction. He puts Chris at risk by ignoring reports from the school that Chris is harassing other students.

Althea: Chris's mother. Although successful at her mail-order business, Althea's relationship with her son is poor. Almost too late, she understands that the whole family must change if Chris is to be helped.

The Teachers

Mr. Pence: The 7th grade science teacher. Mr. Pence recognizes Hummingbird's gifts in science, but her reckless behavior in lab experiments forces him to discipline her. It is his well-known admiration for Miss Swallow that allows Chris to initiate a scheme that makes the shy teacher believe that Hummingbird disrespects him—a possible factor in the in-house suspension that initiates her dreams of the vegetable giants.

Ms. Betty Swallow: The eighth-grade science teacher. Miss Swallow is the first teacher that Hummingbird and Arianna go to when they need questions answered about the habits of fast-growing plants and bullies. She joins them in investigating the mysterious destruction of Aunt Chick's garden and becomes the target of one of Coyote's more miraculous tricks.

Joe Red Crane: A Tribal elder. Joe teaches Native heritage classes, which include language and drumming. He not only gives wise counsel to the kids about bullying, but also to Miss Swallow about events that cannot be explained by science.

Mrs. Corn: The seventh-grade language teacher. Mrs. Corn becomes the target of a cyber bullying attack that discredits her as well as Rain and Simon. Angered by the ugly rumors that spread across the school, Mrs. Corn helps the school principal track down the identity of the attacker.

Mr. Berry: The school principal. Mr. Berry, much-admired for his leadership and understanding of children, leads the teachers, parents, and students in adoption of a "stop bullying" policy at Thunder Rock Middle School.

Coach Brown: The head coach. Coach Brown punishes Chris for poor sportsmanship and disrespectful behavior, and gives Walter and Larry a chance to prove that they can make the school and their friends proud of them.

Dr. Bamsey: A biology professor. A friend of Miss Swallow, Dr. Bamsey examines one of Coyote's astounding creations. He cannot explain its existence, but he knows that it is testimony to the amazing advances in horticultural science made by the Native peoples of the Americas.

Other Characters

Boo: Owner of Boo's Gas and Grocery. Boo remembers how Rain and his friends helped him boost sales at his store by encouraging him to promote healthy foods. In appreciation, he always comes to their aid. In this story he leads the kids in training Walter and Larry to achieve their athletic dreams, and helps them discover a very strange garden in the foothills of Shell Ridge.

Uncle Luther: Owner of a small trucking business. To show how much he appreciated the kids helping his nephew, Jimmy, when he was in trouble, Luther uses all his driving skills to transport a big yellow ball called the "Big Stinker" to the Harvest Fair. True to his word, he gets it there just in time to enter a very big contest.

Willard Fox Chief: The chief of police. Willard is the well-respected head of "law and order" on the reservation. He steps forward, not to administer punishment, but to help the Sorrel family find a counselor who can help them make changes that will heal the whole family.

Frank Big Weasel: Owner of Big Weasel's Jif Mart. Serving as the pow-wow arena director at this year's Harvest Fair, Big Weasel helps to get the pow-wow schedule back on track when an unplanned opportunity for healthy food distribution suddenly arises.

Glossary

A

Abandoned (to abandon): to leave without intending to return.

Abashed: uncomfortable; embarrassed.

Absentee: a person who is absent; not present.

Accelerated (to accelerate): to increase speed.

Accommodating: ready and willing to help.

Adjustment: a correction or setting something right.

Admission: an acknowledgment; confessing a mistake or wrongdoing.

Admonition: a criticism or warning.

Adoringly: in a loving, admiring, or devoted way.

Adversaries: those who oppose or resist another person.

Advertising (to advertise): to publicize; promote; market.

Afghan: a blanket or shawl made of knitted or crocheted colored wool.

Agenda: a list of items to be considered as at a meeting.

Aggressively: in a forceful or hostile way.

Agility: ability to move quickly and easily.

Aimlessly: acting without a goal or purpose.

Air raid siren: a sound to warn of attackers from the air.

Ambition: a desire to achieve a particular goal.

Amiably: in a friendly and pleasant manner.

Amid: during; in or throughout the course of something.

Amplified (to amplify): to make bigger or louder.

Annoyance: the act of disturbing or irritating, especially by repeated acts.

Antennae: a pair of slender movable organs of sensation on the head of an arthropod (like an insect or a crab).

Anticipating (to anticipate): to expect ahead of time.

Antics: attention-drawing acts that are playful or funny.

Aphids: small soft-bodied insects that suck the juices of plants.

Appeal: a plea or request.

Aquarium: a container in which living water animals or plants are kept.

Arcade Alley: a section of a carnival or fair where games are played.

Arced: (to arc) to move along a curved path.

Archeological: science pertaining to ancient human remains and culture.

Arctic: very cold.

Assailants: those who attack violently with blows or words.

Assumption: the belief that something is true.

Astounded (to astound): to fill with puzzled wonder.

Astute: having understanding and the skill to make good choices or decisions.

Athletic: active; strong; muscular.

Atmosphere: general feeling of a place or environment.

Atomic: relating to atoms, atomic bombs, or nuclear energy.

Auditorium: a room, hall, or building used for public gatherings.

Avalanche: a sudden overwhelming rush of a substance like snow.

Avidly: eagerly; greedily.

Awesome: breathtaking or remarkable.

B

Babbling (to babble): to talk foolishly, unclearly; or to talk too much.

Baffled (to baffle): to confuse; to puzzle.

Balmier: warmer; gently soothing.

Banner: a long sign made of cloth or paper; a flag.

Barometric pressure: the measure of the weight of the atmosphere above us.

Beaker: a deep glass with a wide mouth and a lip for pouring.

Beaming (to beam): to be full of joy.

Bed head: a hair fashion in which the hair is untidy; hair that is messed up after sleeping.

Behemoth: something of monstrous size, power, or appearance.

Belch: to expel air suddenly from the stomach; a burp.

Bevy: a group of animals and especially quails.

Billow: a rolling mass (as of flame or smoke) that resembles a high wave.

Bin: a box or barrel used for storage or to hold something (like garbage).

Binoculars: an optical device, such as a pair of field glasses to see distant objects.

Bizarre: odd; out of the ordinary.

Bleachers: a stand of benches arranged like steps.

Bleakness: lack of life, warmth, or kindliness.

Bleated (to bleat): to make a sound like a sheep.

Blind: an object behind which one can hide.

Blissfully: in an extremely happy manner.

Blood glucose meter: an electronic device to measure the blood glucose level.

Blossoming (to blossom): to make an appearance; become evident; come forth.

Blurted (to blurt): to say something suddenly and without thinking.

Boasted (to boast): to speak with excessive pride.

Bogus: not genuine; counterfeit or fake.

Bonkers: crazy; mad.

Botany field kit: equipment used to explore plant life.

Botched (to botch): to make or perform clumsily.

Bounded (to bound): to leap forward.

Braced (to brace): to support against something.

Bravado: false expression of bravery.

Breather: a break in activity for rest and relief.

Bristled (to bristle): to stand stiffly on end; to stick up like a bristle (a stiff hair).

Broke ranks (to break rank): to desert a position; distance oneself from a belief held by others.

Brood: a litter or group of offspring.

Buck up: to pull oneself together; to rise to a challenge.

Bucket line: a line of people who are passing objects (like buckets) from one to the other.

Buckthorn: an ornamental shrub.

Buffed: having excellent physical appearance; to be muscular as a result of bodybuilding.

Bustle: to move with energy.

C

Cackling (to cackle): to laugh or chatter noisily.

Camouflage: to hide or disguise by appearing to blend in with one's surroundings.

Candidate: one who seeks to be chosen or elected.

Carbohydrate: a compound (usually represented by sugars, fiber, and starches) that supplies energy to the body. Carbohydrates are found in dairy products, fruits and vegetables, and grains.

Career: a long-term job or way of making a living.

Cargo winch: a motor-driven hoisting machine having a drum around which a chain or rope winds as a load is lifted.

Carrion: carcass of a dead animal.

Cascading (to cascade): to pour in; to spill or tumble down.

Casting: the fecal matter of an earthworm composed of dirt and plant matter.

Casually: in an informal way; relaxed.

Casualties: persons who are hurt as a result of violence or an accident.

Catalyst: something that causes a rapid change or action.

Catastrophe: a sudden and widespread disaster.

Catcalls: yells meant to mock or express disapproval.

Ceremoniously: formally polite.

Ceremony: a formal observance that celebrates a traditional or religious activity.

Challenged: demanding; difficult.

Characteristically: being normal or expected.

Charge: to accuse; to blame.

Charitable: generous.

Chattering (to chatter): to talk idly, continually, or rapidly.

Chemical equation: a symbolic representation of what happens when chemicals come in contact with one another.

Chemical reaction: a process in which one or more substances are chemically changed into one or more new substances.

Chimed in (to chime in): to break into a conversation or discussion especially to express an opinion.

Chitchat: small talk.

Choke-cherries: Wild cherries growing in North America that are eaten dried and used in jams and syrups.

Chorus girls: women who accompany a performance by singing or dancing together.

Chug: a dull explosive sound that repeats. Usually made by a machine.

Chump: a slang expression for a foolish person.

Churning (to churn): to stir up; to shake.

Clamor: any loud and continued noise.

Classification: a group or class to which things belong.

Clip: to move swiftly.

Clumped (to clump): to cluster or group together.

Clumsy: lacking physical coordination, skill, or grace.

Clutched (to clutch): to hold with the hands strongly and suddenly.

Cocky: to act in a bold or arrogant way.

Cold frames: an unheated outdoor structure consisting of a wooden or concrete frame and a top of glass or clear plastic. Used to grow plants in the winter.

Collapsed (to collapse): to fall or shrink abruptly and completely.

Collections: collecting a sum of money (in this case, stealing money).

Combination lock: a lock that opens when dialed through a sequence of numbers.

Commercially: done with the intent to make money or profit.

Commotion: noisy disturbance.

Competition: a contest between individuals or groups.

Complemented (to complement): to balance or harmonize with.

Complex carbohydrates: carbohydrates that the body breaks down slowly. This slow digestion creates a constant release of energy. Complex carbohydrates are found in foods like whole grains, beans, oatmeal, brown rice, and vegetables like broccoli and spinach. The less healthy simple carbohydrates like table sugar, honey, candy, sodas, and some fruit juices enter the blood stream immediately, causing blood sugar levels to rise and fall rapidly.

Complicated (to complicate): to make difficult or complex.

Compliment: an expression of respect, affection, or admiration.

Compressed (to compress): to press into a small space.

Conceited: having an excessively favorable opinion of one's abilities or appearance.

Conclusions: what is assumed to be true after evidence has been examined.

Conferring (to confer): to award; to give.

Confessed (to confess): to admit.

Confidently: having a sense of being sure of oneself.

Congratulated (to congratulate): to express pleasure to a person, as on a happy occasion.

Conscious: aware of one's own existence, sensations, thoughts, and surroundings.

Consoled (to console): to give comfort; lessen disappointment.

Contemplating (to contemplate): to consider thoroughly; think fully or deeply about.

Conveniently: suited to a person's needs; usually referring to a suitable time.

Converged (to converge): to come together and unite in a common interest.

Coordinates: a set of numbers that show an exact position or location on a map.

Coordination: the smooth working together of parts.

Cortisone: a hormone used to reduce inflammation; often applied as a cream.

Cosmetics: powders or creams used to beautify the face, skin, and hair.

Counsel: advice.

Countered (to counter): to go against.

Crags: steep, rugged rocks or cliffs.

Crinkly: wrinkled.

Cronies: friends of someone who can bestow favors on them.

Crouched (to crouch): to stoop or bend low with the arms and legs close to the body.

Crown vetch: a perennial European herb in the pea family that spreads as a weed.

Crumpled (to crumple): to press, bend, or crush out of shape.

Cucurbiteae: is a tribe of the family of plants that includes the cucumber, melon, squash, and pumpkin.

Curiosity: a desire to know or learn.

Curlicues: fancifully curved or spiral-shaped figures.

Custodian: one who takes care of something; a janitor.

D

Dazzled (to dazzle): to impress greatly or confuse with brilliance.

Debris: rubbish; messy remains.

Decided: firm or certain as in "a decided bounce in his step."

Deed: to give; to make a legal arrangement that grants possession of something to an individual.

Deemed (to deem): to believe or have an opinion.

Degrade: to lower in value.

Dejectedly: being low in spirits.

Delicious: very pleasing to the taste.

Demolition: destruction often by means of explosives.

Demonstration: a presentation used by a teacher to show a process.

Deodorant: a liquid or cream that destroys or masks unpleasant odors.

Deposits: piles of something (as in Coyote's droppings that contain seeds that germinate).

Depressed: sad; discouraged.

Descended (to descend): to move from a higher to a lower place.

Desperation: extreme anxiety or hopelessness.

Destination: the goal of a journey; a place to which something is sent.

Detention: a place where one is detained or held as punishment.

Determination: strength of mind; fortitude; or resolve.

Detour: to go another way.

Devious: sneaky and deceptive.

Diagram: a chart; an illustration that shows the relationships between elements of a plan.

Diaphragm: a sheet of muscle separating the chest and abdomen that helps one to breathe.

Digital scale: an electronic measuring device.

Dilemma: a difficult choice.

Din: a loud confused mixture of noises.

Dino-geek: a slang expression for someone who is crazy about learning everything there is to know about dinosaurs.

Disappointment: a setback; failure; or feeling of dissatisfaction or frustration.

Disassociated (to disassociate): to remove the connection between things; not related.

Disgruntled: in a bad mood.

Dismissive: treating someone in a rude or curt manner; ignoring someone's presence or opinion.

Disoriented: loss of one's sense of direction in space; confused or mixed up.

Dispensed (to dispense): to distribute or give out.

Dispersed (to disperse): to give out or send off in various directions.

Displacement activity: a behavior not relevant to a situation that makes a person or animal feel less stressed, such as a dog licking himself when being threatened by another dog.

Disqualify: to make or declare unfit; to judge not eligible as in a competition.

Dissolved (to dissolve): to melt; to collapse.

Distraught: disturbed with doubt or painful feelings.

Dome: a large rounded roof or ceiling shaped like half of a ball.

Domestication: the act of adapting to living with human beings or serving their purposes.

Doodling (to doodle): to scribble or sketch while thinking of something.

Dorky: a slang expression for being like a "dork"—someone who looks silly or is socially clumsy.

Dormant: not active but capable of becoming active.

Dramatically: doing something in an exciting or emotional way.

Dribbled (to dribble): to move forward by tapping, bouncing, or kicking.

Drills: a physical or mental exercise that is regularly practiced.

Dutifully: to do something without protest; respectfully.

Dweeb: a slang term for a person that is socially foolish.

E

Earnestly: serious in intention, purpose, or effort.

Eavesdrop: to listen in on another's discussion.

Economic: based on the production, distribution, and consumption of goods and services.

Edible: suitable for eating.

Efficiency: done without waste.

Elated: feeling or state of great pride and joy.

Electricity: any presence and flow of electrical charges such as lightning and static electricity, the flow of current in an electrical wire.

Elegance: having a graceful appearance or style.

Elemental: relating to the most fundamental nature of an object, force, or issue.

Elicited (to elicit): to draw out by skillful questioning or discussion.

Emit: to throw or give off.

Empowered: possessing a feeling of control or ability.

EMT: emergency medical technician; healthcare provider who treats emergencies.

Enchilada: a tortilla stuffed with meat or cheese and served with a chili spiced sauce.

Energetically: doing something in a lively or vigorous manner.

Entangled (to entangle): to be entwined; twisted together.

Enthralled (to enthrall): to hold by or as if by a spell; charm.

Enthusiasm: strong excitement and active interest.

Enunciated (to enunciate): to speak very clearly.

Enveloped (to envelope): to surround; to be enclosed by something.

Eructation: the process of belching.

Eruption: a sudden, often violent outburst.

Escalated (to escalate): to increase, enlarge, or intensify.

Escapees: persons or things that run away.

Exasperated (to exasperate): to frustrate; to annoy.

Exchange: a conversation between two or more people.

Exhaust: the gas emission from an engine.

Exhaustion: a feeling of fatigue; drained of energy.

Exhilarated: overjoyed; very cheerful.

Exited (to exit): to go out.

Exothermic: characterized by giving off heat.

Exotic: very different or unusual.

Expansive: being in a good or talkative mood.

Expired (to expire): to come to an end.

Explosion: a violent expansion or bursting with noise, as of gunpowder.

Expounded (to expound): to explain; interpret.

Extra measure: something that is added to be more generous or effective.

Extraordinary: remarkable.

F

Faltering (to falter): to move unsteadily.

Fantasized (to fantasize): to imagine in the mind.

Fascination: a state of having appeal or interest; great attraction.

Fashionable: very stylish; up-to-date in what one is wearing.

Fatalism: belief or attitude that events are caused by powers beyond one's control.

Feathery cobs: referring to the appearance of the small cobs on the teosinte plant.

Festooned (to festoon): to decorate with.

Fidgeting (to fidget): to move about restlessly.

Flabbergasted: astonished; totally surprised.

Flagrant: so bad as to be impossible to overlook.

Flattery: praise that is excessive or not sincere.

Flickered (to flicker): to move irregularly or unsteadily.

Fluorescent: glowing brightly.

Fluttering (to flutter): to move with quick flapping motions.

Foliage: a mass of plants or leaves; plant life in general.

Food sovereignty: a policy adopted by a population to widen their control of the foods they eat.

Foraging (to forage): to make a search, especially for food or supplies.

Formidable: very impressive or strong.

Formula: the required elements of a method or approach; the kinds of atoms and their quantities found in a compound or molecule.

Fossil poacher: a thief who steals fossils.

Fossil: a bone, body, or print of a dead plant or animal preserved in rock, earth, or tree resin.

Fragrance: a pleasant smell.

Frazzled: to be exhausted physically or emotionally.

Fretting (to fret): to be nervous; upset.

Fugita scale: the scale used to rate the intensity of a tornado by examining the damage caused by the tornado after it has passed over a man-made structure. An F0 tornado causes the least damage and an F5 the greatest damage.

Fungus: any of a kingdom of living things (as molds, rusts, mildews, smuts, and mushrooms) that lack chlorophyll.

Funky: having a strange or bad smell.

Furtively: done in a sneaky or sly manner.

G

Gargantuan: gigantic; of immense size.

Gauntlet: a line of people standing opposite each other through which a person must run. The people strike or yell at the running person. To "run a gauntlet" is an expression that means to endure a difficult situation in which one is talked about or criticized.

Gawking (to gawk): to stare; to look at someone rudely.

Generation: the length of time between the birth of parents and their offspring.

Geological: referring to the physical environment.

Gesturing (to gesture): to make a movement of the body that expresses an idea or a feeling.

Gibberish: nonsense talk.

Giggled (to giggle): to laugh with repeated short high sounds.

Gingerly: cautiously or carefully.

Giveaway: an event in which gifts or other objects of value are shared freely with others.

Glimpsed (to glimpse): to take a quick look; see a little bit of something.

Glistening (to glisten): to be shiny or glimmering.

Global warming: the heating up of the earth's atmosphere and oceans that can be attributed to natural forces or pollution by humans.

Glucose: blood sugar that provides energy to the body's cells.

Glum: gloomy and sad.

Goggles: a pair of tight-fitting eyeglasses worn to protect the eyes from hazards.

Gondola: a small enclosed car on an amusement ride.

Goons: a person hired to beat up opponents.

Graduated cylinder: a tall narrow container used for measuring liquids.

Grafting (to graft): to join a plant onto another plant.

Great Removal: the removal of Native American tribes from the eastern and southeastern states to the West by the U.S. government in the 1830s.

Grist: the grain that is ground in a mill. It is sometimes used to mean the rumors that are being passed around in a "rumor mill."

Groove-on: a slang expression that means to be doing something with expertise or confidence.

Grouchiness: an irritable and complaining condition.

Groupies: a slang expression for fans who usually follow a rock group or rock star on a concert tour.

Grubs: the wormlike larva of beetles and other insects.

Guardianship: a relationship in which one person has legal responsibility for the care of another person or their property.

Guiltily: having an uncomfortable feeling of having done something wrong.

Gushed (to gush): to flatter; to admire too much.

Guttural: characteristic of sounds made deep in the throat that are harsh or rough.

H

Habitat: where a plant or animal naturally or normally lives or grows.

Half-hearted: lacking spirit or interest.

Haphazardly: done randomly or messily without a plan.

Harassment: annoyance; pestering; or persecution.

Harmony: a state in which everything works together in balance or in agreement.

Harried: worried; stressed.

Harrumphed (to harrumph): to comment disapprovingly.

Hatchback: a car that has a rear door.

Hawed (to haw): to hesitate in speaking as in the expression "to hem and haw."

Hazardous: dangerous; risky.

Heckling (to heckle): to interrupt with the intention of being annoying.

Hefty: quite heavy.

Herbivore: a plant-eating animal.

Hiccupped (to hiccup): to make a loud sound caused by a spasm of the diaphragm that pushes air through the vocal cords.

Hindenburg: a German dirigible or airship (similar in appearance to a large blimp) that was kept aloft by hydrogen, a gas that is lighter than air. It exploded at Lakehurst, New Jersey in 1937 as it was trying to land during a lightning storm. When the hydrogen, which is highly flammable, ignited, the airship crashed in flames.

Honorable mentions: awards that are given for work that is very good, but not the quality of a first, second, or third prize winner.

Horticulture: the practice of growing fruits, vegetables, flowers, or ornamental plants.

Hub: the central part of a circular object (as a wheel); a center of activity.

Huddled (to huddle): to crowd, push, or pile together.

Humanoid: having human form or characteristics.

Humdinger: a striking or extraordinary person or thing.

Humiliation: loss of pride or self-respect.

Humongous: extremely large.

Hustle: energetic movement in which persons can be shoved or jostled.

Hydrogen: a colorless and odorless gas that is highly flammable; the simplest of all elements.

Hydrogen peroxide: an unstable compound composed of two atoms of hydrogen and two atoms of oxygen (H_2O_2). It is used as an antiseptic, a propellant, and as a bleaching agent.

I

Illuminated (to illuminate): to shine a light upon.

Imitation: the act of pretending to sound or behave like someone else.

Impression: an imprint or dent left on a substance, like the imprint of a foot left in clay.

Indigenous: referring to peoples who are native to a particular part of the world (as the Incas are native to Peru).

Indignant: offended; resentful.

Inner sanctum: a private place where only certain powerful people are allowed to enter—in this case, the principal's office.

Inorganic: composed of matter that does not come from living things.

Inspirational: in a motivating or encouraging manner.

Instincts: behaviors that are based on automatic actions.

Insulin: a hormone, produced by the pancreas, which helps the body use carbohydrates and fats for the energy it needs. It helps the cells in the liver, muscle, and fat tissue to take up glucose (blood sugar) from the blood and store it as energy.

Intellect: brain power.

Interfering (to interfere): to get involved in a situation without approval; to meddle.

Intertwined: twisted together.

Intimidated (to intimidate): to frighten people into doing one's will by threatening them.

Intrigued: being curious or very interested by something.

Intrusion: wrongfully or inappropriately breaking into a conversation, a property, or the privacy of another person.

Inventory (to inventory): to make a count of supplies or goods.

Invocation: the part of a pow-wow when the master of ceremonies calls on the Creator and the spirit world to help the people and make the pow-wow a good experience.

Involuntary: done without choice.

Irrational: unreasonable; foolish.

Irresponsible: reckless; careless.

Irritated (to irritate): to annoy or aggravate.

J

Jitters: a feeling of extreme nervousness.

Jubilantly: expressing great joy.

Juvenile: a young person, animal, or plant.

K

Kernel: the inner softer part of a seed, fruit stone, or nut.

Kits: the young of rabbits, badgers, beavers, ferrets, foxes, minks, polecats, raccoons, skunks & squirrels.

L

Lab bench: a workbench in a laboratory.

Laboriously: working in a hard manner; taking a long time to do something.

Land stewardship: the responsible planning, management, and restoration of resources that are found on the land such as soil, plants, and minerals.

Latex: the substance that is tapped from rubber trees; also a mixture of water and fine particles of rubber.

Lattice: a framework of brick or wood that has open spaces.

Launching (to launch): to take off with force.

Leisurely: unhurried; at ease.

Liberate: to free or release.

Lobbed (to lob): to throw something (as a ball) in a high arc.

Lobed: describing a curved or rounded part of an object like a leaf.

Loosestrife: an herb related to primroses that has invaded farmland; a weed.

Lop-sided: leaning to one side.

Loupe: a hand lens used to magnify small objects so they can be seen.

Low carb: not high in carbohydrates.

Low-down: a slang expression that refers to information that everyone doesn't know.

Lurched (to lurch): to roll or tip suddenly.

M

Magnificent: superb; glorious; grand.

Majestic: imposing; splendid.

Mammoth: enormous; massive.

Maneuvered (to maneuver): to move or manage skillfully.

Manila: the off-white color of envelopes and folders.

Manipulator: a person who acts with the intent to get their way or to deceive.

Marathon: a very lengthy activity like a long-distance run.

Marine: relating to the sea.

Marveled (to marvel): to fill with surprise or astonishment.

Masquerade: pretending to be someone else; being in disguise.

Matter-of-factly: speaking in a simple and concise way.

Mayonnaise: a dressing consisting chiefly of egg yolk, vegetable oil, and vinegar or lemon juice.

Meandered (to meander): to wander without a goal or purpose.

Measly: so small or unimportant as to deserve scorn.

Menacingly: in a threatening or sinister way.

Metamorphosis: an extraordinary change in appearance, character, or circumstances.

Meteorite: a meteor that reaches the surface of the earth.

Metaphor: a symbol; a figure of speech in which a word or phrase is used in place of another to mean the same thing.

Miffed: to be offended; displeased.

Milky Way: the galaxy of which the solar system is a part.

Minerals: solids that have specific chemical compositions and physical properties. They appear as rocks, metals, or crystals.

Mocking (to mock): to tease; to make fun of.

Molecule: the smallest particle of a substance having all the characteristics of the substance. It is always composed of two or more atoms of different elements. For instance, a water molecule is composed of two hydrogen atoms and one oxygen atom.

Momentarily: in a short period of time.

Momentous: very important; considerable.

Moseying (to mosey): to move in a leisurely or aimless manner.

Motto: a saying or phrase that represents the values of a person or organization (as in "Our motto is 'The customer is always right.'").

Muffled: hushed; barely heard.

Munchkin: a small person (derives from a population of very small people in the book, "The Wizard of Oz").

Murmur: to speak in a voice too low to be heard clearly.

Mustering (to muster): to stir up or bring to action.

Mutant: a malformed or altered individual, which arises from exposure to a process or event that causes them to change.

Mystified (to mystify): to thoroughly confuse; to be puzzled.

N

Nano-second: one billionth of a second.

Natural resources: materials from nature that have various uses, such as timber, fresh water, or mineral deposits.

Neighborhood Watch: group of residents who work with local law enforcement to keep their communities safe.

Nestled (to nestle): to lie close and snug.

Nibbler: a person or animal that eats small amounts of food bit by bit.

Nose blinking: the term for a rabbit's wiggling its nose up and down.

Notoriety: bad reputation.

Nudged (to nudge): to touch or push gently.

Nutrients: sources of nourishment; healthy ingredient in a food.

Nutrition: healthy diet.

Nutritious: characterizes wholesome and nourishing foods.

O

Objectives: aims or goals.

Obliging (to oblige): pleased to help; glad to do a service for someone.

Obscure: unclear; little known; hidden from view.

Observations: spoken or written notes about something seen or heard.

Occupant: a person or animal that is living in a certain place.

Olmecs: the Olmecs were the first major civilization of Mexico, living in the modern-day states of Veracruz and Tobasco. They flourished during the period from 1500 BCE (Before the Current Era) to about 400 BCE. They laid the cultural foundations for the later civilizations of the Maya and Aztecs.

Optical: using properties of light to aid vision.

Optimistic: hopeful; confident; expecting everything to come out all right.

Orb: something in the shape of a ball.

Organic: describing a substance made from living things (a plant or animal product).

Ornament: a decoration.

Ornamental: a plant used for decoration, not for food.

Over-enunciated: pronouncing every word so precisely that one speaks very slowly.

Overstatement: a statement that is exaggerated or made too much of.

P

PA system: a public address system.

Papier-mâché: a material made of paper pulp held together with glue.

Parallel: objects in rows that are located next to each other, move in the same direction, and are always the same distance apart.

Paralyzed: to make powerless or unable to act, function, or move.

Patooties: an exclamation of frustration.

Patrolling (to patrol): the act of observing or guarding an area.

Pawpaw: a fruit tree native to the eastern woodlands of the United States. Its edible fruit has the appearance of a mango.

Payload: the capacity of an aircraft to carry its cargo and everything loaded on it.

Peel away: to leave or fall away.

Peered (to peer): to look at closely.

Pellets: a small, round mass of a substance, like tiny balls; can refer to the dung of a small animal.

Perceived (to perceive): to comprehend; understand.

Perusal (to peruse): to read carefully or thoroughly.

Phloem: the living tissue in a plant that carries nutrients (primarily a sugar called sucrose) to all parts of the plant.

Photocopied (to photocopy): to make an image of printed material.

Pixels: small elements that make up an image, as on a computer or television screen.

Plant grow light: an electric light, usually a fluorescent bulb, that promotes plant growth indoors.

Plaque: a flat plate or tablet that can be hung on the wall. It usually is awarded to someone to acknowledge a special achievement or event.

Plummet: to fall straight down.

Podium: a raised platform from which a speaker addresses an audience.

Poised: getting ready to do something.

Poison arrow: an expression that refers to a harmful message.

Poisoned apple: a gift that appears harmless, but is actually dangerous. In the story, Chris's posting to the blog "An Apple for the Teacher" may appear to be harmless, but its intent is to cause trouble.

Poisonous: containing a substance that is harmful or destructive.

Pondered (to ponder): to think or consider quietly, soberly, and deeply.

Posse: a group that has a common interest.

Postponed (to postpone): to delay.

Pow-wow: a gathering of North America's Native peoples where they meet to dance, sing, socialize, and honor indigenous cultures.

Pranced (to prance): to walk or move about in a lively and proud manner.

Prattle: to speak in a silly or childish manner.

Precise: exact; accurate; specific.

Precocious: showing mature qualities at an unusually early age.

Prediabetes: a condition in which a person's blood glucose levels are higher than normal but not high enough to be type 2 diabetes. People with prediabetes are more likely to develop type 2 diabetes. However, type 2 diabetes may be prevented or delayed in persons with prediabetes if they adopt a healthy diet, lose weight, and increase physical activity.

Prematurely: happening before the proper or usual time.

Prey: animals that are food for other animals.

Prime: to prepare; to get something ready.

Pristine: being unmarked; fresh and clean; perfect.

Privet: a shrub that is used for hedges.

Professional: persons educated or trained to do a specific job.

Protocol: a set of rules or way of doing something.

Psyching out: a slang expression that means to get someone distracted or upset so that they become confused or unfocused.

Puberty: period when the body matures; a time of great change.

Pulverize: to beat or grind into a powder or dust.

Puncture: a hole or wound made by piercing.

Purging (to purge): to rid; make free of something unwanted.

Pushed the envelope: an expression meaning exceeding the existing limits; to go beyond what is usually accepted.

Pyramid: a structure that has a square base and four triangular sides meeting at a point.

Quavering (to quaver): to tremble as in a shaky way of speaking.

Quivering (to quiver): to shake or move with a slight trembling motion.

Quizzically: curiously.

R

Radar: a device that sends out radio waves for detecting the position of an object.

Radiated (to radiate): to spread out from a center point.

Raggedy: having a rough or uneven edge or outline.

Rationally: in a reasonable or realistic way.

Reception: an event at which people are greeted or the arrival of something is acknowledged.

Receptive: open to new ideas; willing to listen.

Recliner: a chair with an adjustable back and footrest.

Recoiled (to recoil): to shrink back, flinch, or retreat.

Recruit: to seek persons to join an activity.

Reeked (to reek): to smell of a strong or disagreeable odor.

Referenced: describes something being cited regarding its location or origin.

Refrain: the part of a song that is repeated.

Refuge: a hiding place; a safe place.

Regal: of remarkable excellence or magnificence.

Regalia: highly decorative dance outfits worn in the arena during pow-wows that have very personal meanings to the dancers.

Register: in music, a register is the range of a note. To sing in a higher register, for instance, is to sing in a higher pitch.

Rehearsed (to rehearse): to prepare; to repeat an activity until it is perfectly done.

Relief: a sense of being released from worry or anxiety.

Relish: enjoyment or delight.

Relocated (to relocate): to move to a new location.

Reluctantly: acting in an unwilling or half-hearted manner.

Remnants: something that remains or is left over.

Replica: a copy exact in all details; duplicate.

Reprimand: a formal warning or scolding.

Research: to investigate, study, or explore.

Resentment: a feeling of anger in response to a wrong or injury.

Resolved (to resolve): to reach a decision or settle a problem.

Retail: describes a business that sells things to the public.

Retching: trying to vomit.

Retreated (to retreat): to return to a safe place or pull back from a difficult situation.

Riled up: in an upset or angry state.

Riotous: unrestrained so as to be festive and wild.

Ripped: a slang expression that means having a fine muscular build.

Ripple: to move like flowing water.

Ritual: an act that is always performed in the same way to signify its serious or sacred nature.

Rubberized: coated with rubber.

Rumbling (to rumble): making a low heavy sound that seems to roll on and on.

Rummaged (to rummage): to search quickly through the contents of a place or container.

Rumor mill: the source of rumors that are repeated deliberately.

Rumors: a statement or story that has not been proved to be true.

Rustle (to rustle): to make a crackling or crunching sound.

S

Salvaged (to salvage): to rescue or save part of something ruined or left after a disaster.

Sanitation: an act or policy that promotes cleanliness.

Sapling: a small young tree.

Sauntered (to saunter): to walk without hurry; to stroll.

Savor: to take pleasure in; appreciate.

Scanning (to scan): to look over quickly; to look across a wide view.

Scientifically: relating to the methods or rules of science.

Scored (to score): to make points in a competitive game.

Scoundrel: a rascal or crook; someone up to mischief.

Scrawls: writings or drawings done hastily or carelessly.

Screen: the word "screen" has many meanings that are used in the book. Noun: a monitor for a TV or computer; a partition or guard; a basketball move in which a player tries to keep an opposing player from scoring. Verb: to hide; to select using a set of criteria.

Scribbled (to scribble): to write quickly or carelessly without regard to clarity or form.

Scrimmage: a minor competition or battle.

Scrounge: to search about and turn up something needed from various sources.

Scrunched (to scrunch): to draw or squeeze together tightly.

Scurry: to move quickly.

Securing (to secure): to make safe; guard.

Self-consciously: unsure of oneself; somewhat embarrassed.

Self-possessed: in control of one's emotions or reactions especially when under stress.

Serviceable: still useful; lasting or wearing well in use.

Shake-down: a slang expression meaning to steal money from a victim.

Shattering (to shatter): to break or fall into pieces.

Sheepishly: done or said with feelings of embarrassment.

Shockwave: a rapidly moving energy wave (like a sound wave) that travels through the air and is heard as a loud crack.

Shoveled (to shovel): to dig or clean out.

Shrugged (to shrug): to hunch up the shoulders to express hesitation or uncertainty.

Shuck: to remove an outer layer of something like corn, a nut, or an article of clothing.

Shuddering (to shudder): to tremble or shake.

Shy: to be short of a certain distance; almost there, but not quite.

Silhouette: the outline of a person or an object seen against the light.

Simmering (to simmer): to stew gently in a liquid.

Simultaneously: done at the same time.

Sing-song: characteristic of speaking in a monotonous repeating way.

Skirted (to skirt): to go around; to avoid.

Skittish: marked by extreme caution; easily frightened.

Sly: in a manner intended to avoid notice.

Smirked (to smirk): to smile or say in an insincere manner.

Snare: a trap; something that gets one entangled in problems.

Snicker (to snicker): to give a small and often nasty or sly laugh.

Snoozing (to snooze): to take a nap.

Snout: a long nose that sticks out.

Snowed (to snow): to deceive, persuade, or charm with insincere or flattering talk.

Snuffled (to snuffle): to breathe loudly through a blocked nose.

Snuggled (to snuggle): to pull in close especially for comfort or in affection.

Sobs: crying; tears.

Solo: to do something alone; a performance by one person.

Solution: a liquid in which something has been dissolved.

Somersault: to leap or roll head over heels.

Sparkling (to sparkle): to give off small flashes of light.

Species: a group of animals or plants so closely related that they can interbreed and produce fertile offspring. They have great similarity in DNA, body organization, and ecological niche.

Specimen: a sample of something used for testing or examination.

Spectator: an onlooker; a watcher; someone not involved in a situation.

Speculating (to speculate): to think or wonder about a subject.

Spewed (to spew): to gush out.

Spikey: characterized by spikes (pointy).

Spindly: being tall or long and thin in appearance; suggests weakness.

Spirals: shapes that twist or coil in circles.

Splatters: small amounts of a spilled liquid.

Splint: a thin, flat piece of wood that is used to light or ignite various substances.

Splintery: having little slivers or pieces of wood sticking out.

Sportsmanship: fair play, respect for opponents, and gracious behavior in winning or losing.

Spraddled (to spraddle): to ride, sit, or walk with the legs apart

Sprinted (to sprint): to run at top speed especially for a short distance.

Spunk: liveliness; spirit; courage.

Spurt: to burst forth; erupt.

Squatted (to squat): to crouch; sit on one's heels.

Squelched (to squelch): to hush up; to smother an intent or stop an action.

Squinting (to squint): to strain to see with narrowed eyes.

Stamina: endurance; ability to withstand hardship or stress.

Stammered (to stammer): to speak in a halting manner.

Status: position or rank in relation to others.

Steeled (to steel): to fill with courage and determination.

Stench: a very disagreeable smell.

Stern: firm and not changeable.

Stifled (to stifle): to choke back; suppress.

Stooped (to stoop): to bend over.

Stow: to put away.

Strategy: a plan; an approach.

Strode (past tense of "to stride"): took a very long step.

Strut: to walk in a stiff proud way.

Stubbly: having a bumpy or rough surface.

Stupefied (to stupefy): to make stupid, groggy, or numb.

Sturdy: firm; stable.

Subconscious: the part of the mind in which thoughts occur of which we are not fully aware.

Succulent: moist and tasty.

Suit (as in the expression "to follow suit"): to be or act in agreement.

Sullen: gloomy or resentfully silent; not sociable.

Surged (to surge): to move forward as in waves.

Surrendered (to surrender): to give oneself over to something.

Suspended animation: a temporary loss of consciousness and breathing in which one continues to live.

Suspension: a temporary removal (as in a suspension from school).

Suspicioned (to be suspicious): to feel doubt and mistrust.

Swagger: to walk or conduct oneself with an arrogant way; strut.

Sweetly: done with gentle kindness.

Swig: an amount drunk at one time.

Sympathetically: being done in a kindly, sensitive, or caring manner.

T

Talons: claws of an animal, especially of a bird of prey.

Tarpaulin: a canvas covering.

Teasing: to make fun of; to kid or joke with.

Temporarily: lasting for a short term; not permanent.

Terminating (to terminate): to bring to an end.

Thermos: a container used to keep liquids hot or cold.

Thermostat: a device that automatically controls temperature.

Throng: a large number of people gathered together.

Thumbs up: a sign of approval or congratulation.

Toadies: people who flatter another, hoping to receive favors.

Toddled (to toddle): to walk with short unsteady steps like a young child.

Toddler: a young child just learning to walk.

Tousle: to rumple or mess up in a playful way.

Traditional: describing a long-established way of doing or believing; related to culture and custom.

Transformation: a change in outward appearance.

Transplanted (to transplant): to remove from one place and introduce elsewhere.

Trespassers: people who enter unlawfully upon the land of another.

Tribal sovereignty: refers to the inherent authority of indigenous tribes in the United States to govern themselves as "domestic sovereigns," as opposed to the full independent sovereignty of the United States.

Triumphant: having won a victory and being proud of it.

Trophy: an award given to celebrate a victory or other winning achievement.

Truck farming: growing vegetables for the market.

Trudged (to trudge): to walk with much effort.

Tubular: having the form of a tube.

Tucked in (to tuck in): an expression meaning to eat.

Tuning fork: a metal instrument that vibrates at a specific constant pitch when struck. It emits a pure musical tone that is used to tune musical instruments.

U

Unapologetic: not being sorry for a wrong committed.

Uncertainty: not being sure; doubt about something.

Uncharacteristically: not showing normal or expected behavior.

Uncharted: unknown; not located on a map, chart, or plan.

Under wraps: a slang expression meaning to keep a secret or to hide.

Underbrush: shrubs or small bushes growing beneath larger trees.

Understatement: a statement that is expressed mildly; not exaggerated.

Undulating (to undulate): to roll from side to side; or to heave up and down.

Unenthusiastically: not excited.

Unfurled: to open or spread.

Unrestricted: without limitations; freedom.

Ushered (to usher): to lead to a place; cause to enter.

Utility pole: wooden pole used to mount an electric source.

V

Vacated (to vacate): to leave or quit.

Vacuumed (to vacuum): to clean by sucking up dirt with an electrical appliance.

Valiantly: acting with bravery.

Vandalism: intentional destruction or damage to a property.

Vandals: persons who destroy or damage property on purpose.

Velvety: soft and smooth.

Vengeance: punishment given in return for an injury or offense.

Ventriloquist: a person who can speak so that his/her voice seems to come from somewhere else.

Vibrate: to move side to side or back and forth rapidly.

Vigilant: alert to signs of danger.

Vivacious: full of life and good spirits.

Volunteer: a person who does a job without pay.

Voracious: having a huge appetite.

Vulnerability: being defenseless or weak; capable of being physically or emotionally wounded.

W

Warble: to sing or speak in a high voice as if one were singing.

The Weave: a basketball maneuver that involves players moving down the court in a "weaving" pattern.

Were-dog: a play on the term "were-wolf" meaning a person who turns into a wolf. In this case, the term is jokingly applied to Simon who barks like a dog when he coughs. He is, therefore, a "were-dog."

Wail: to cry out in a sad way.

Whammy: a spell or charm.

Wheezed (to wheeze): to breathe with difficulty especially with a whistling sound.

Whine: to make a shrill troubled cry or a similar sound.

Wily: full of deceit; tricky.

Witnessed (to witness): to observe; to be able to tell others what was seen.

World-weary: being tired or fed-up with a situation.

Wormhole: a tunnel connecting points that are widely separated in space and time.

Wreckage: the remains from something that has been destroyed.

X

Xylem: tubes in plants that transport water.

Y

Yelped (to yelp): to cry out suddenly in a high voice.

Yielded (to yield): to give in to the wishes of another.

Z

Zoomed (to zoom): to rush or move quickly; to focus on an object with a computer, microscope or camera with the intent of enlarging or minimizing it in size (as in "zoom out" or "zoom in").

About the Native Diabetes Wellness Program

The mission of the Native Diabetes Wellness Program is to work with a growing circle of partners to address the health inequities so starkly revealed by type 2 diabetes in Indian Country. With social justice and respect for Native and Western science as grounding principles, we strive to support community efforts to promote health and prevent diabetes.

To request free copies of the *Eagle Books* series, or for more information about the program, please contact the CDC. Phone: toll free 1-877-CDC-DIAB (877-232-3422). E-mail: diabetes@cdc.gov

About the Author

Dr. Terry Lofton is a senior study director at Westat. She has been Westat's project director for the *Eagle Books* project since 2002 and has worked in public health for almost thirty years. A former middle school science teacher, Dr. Lofton often drew on the lessons of Native science in her classroom activities. She says that the collaboration with the illustrators of *Coyote and the Turtle's Dream* and the *Eagle Books* project's many friends in Indian Country has been the highlight of her career.

About the Illustrator

Patrick Rolo, Bad River Band of Ojibwe, draws from his rich Native American heritage to illustrate the *Eagle Books*. Mr. Rolo's career includes newspaper, magazine, comic book, and courtroom illustrations. Also a painter, his works in oil hang in galleries in Minnesota and Washington.

Praise for *Hummingbird's Squash*

"I absolutely love this book. Especially with the way it refers back to the stories from the *Eagle Book* Series about eating healthy and exercising, and to *Coyote and the Turtles Dream* about the fossils and restoring harmony back on the reservation. My favorite character in this book is the coyote. Once again, Coyote keeps the reader in suspense with his games and tricks. At the same time he sends messages about respect, harmony, and sharing. I can relate to the situations Rain and his friends experience at school. I would like to see a movie made out of this book. I can't wait to read more fascinating books like this."

—Derrick Chavarillo
San Felipe Pueblo, NM

"Hummingbird and Arianna & her friends try to help the community by growing really big vegetables. The coyote ends up doing a spell on them and he makes the elephant's toothpaste explode on Hummingbird. The story fits all together with the coyote being the trickster, and the Veggie Crowd always being close to each other and stopping the bullies picking on them. It was pretty cool."

—Caitlin and Lydia
Santee Sioux Tribe, Santee, South Dakota

"I liked the trickster coyote. He does all these tricks and he's funny. But in the end, he helps everyone out. I liked Granma, too. She taught the boys her prayer in her language. She didn't care if they didn't say the words right, just so long as they knew what it means. And Chris's mom, I admired her when she stood up for her son in the end. I liked the science experiments, too. I'd like us to have a science fair at my school like in the book."

—Tony, Jr.
Winnebago Tribe of Nebraska, Sioux City, Iowa

"*Hummingbird's Squash* is a great book to read about type 2 diabetes. We can relate to the book with our life here on the Navajo reservation. Our family grows corn, squash and all kinds of melons, and Mr. Eagle and the Rabbit do watch over our garden fields. We thank you for the education provided to everybody who reads this book. This book makes us think of what we put into our mouths that may not be healthy for our bodies."

—Reniah & Jacob Manygoats
Navajo Nation

"I have had a great time helping with *Hummingbird's Squash*. I am so proud to be involved with the book because it provides valuable insight into the issues faced by those of us who have type 1 diabetes. I have had type 1 diabetes for quite some time now, and I know how difficult the daily challenges can be. I really enjoyed all the characters, too, and thought that the messages—about food choices, the importance of exercise, taking responsibility, and bullying—are helpful to everyone. Bullying is an issue that people often do not like to discuss, but it really needs to be addressed."

—Arianna Baros
(The real Arianna)
Albuquerque, NM

To request free copies of the *Eagle Books* series, or for more information about the program, please contact the CDC. Phone: toll free 1-877-CDC-DIAB (877-232-3422). E-mail: diabetes@cdc.gov
http://www.cdc.gov/diabetes/pubs/eagle/index.html